# THE LAWLESS LAND

BOYD MORRISON is the #1 *New York Times* bestselling author of twelve thrillers, including six collaborations with Clive Cussler. His first novel, *The Ark*, was an Indie Next Notable pick and has been translated into over a dozen languages. He has a PhD in industrial engineering from Virginia Tech.

Twitter: @BoydMorrison
Facebook: BoydMorrisonWriter
Instagram: @BoydMorrisonWriter

BETH MORRISON is Senior Curator of Manuscripts at the J. Paul Getty Museum. She has curated several major exhibitions, including 'Imagining the Past in France, 1250-1500,' & 'Book of Beasts: The Bestiary in the Medieval World.' She has a PhD in the History of Art from Cornell University.

Twitter: @BethMorrisonPhD
Facebook: BethMorrisonWriter
Instagram: @BethMorrisonWriter

First published in 2022 by Head of Zeus Ltd,
part of Bloomsbury Publishing Plc

9 7 5 3 4 6 8

A catalogue record for this book is available from
the British Library.

ISBN (HB): 9781801108638
ISBN (XTPB): 9781801108645
ISBN (E): 9781801108669

Typeset by Divaddict Publishing Solutions Ltd

Printed and bound in Great Britain by
CPI Group (UK) Ltd, Croydon CR0 4YY

Head of Zeus Ltd
First Floor East
5–8 Hardwick Street
London EC1R 4RG

WWW.HEADOFZEUS.COM

# THE
# LAWLESS LAND

## BOYD ✝ BETH
## MORRISON

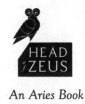

HEAD
of ZEUS

*An Aries Book*

# Europe 1351

N

London
Dover
Calais
Amiens
Honfleur
Rouen
Saint-Malo
Paris
Reims
Orléans
Limoges
Clermont-Ferrand
Bordeaux
Lyon
Turin
Avignon
Genoa
Marseille

| 0 | 50 | 100 | 150 miles |
| 0 | 100 | 200 | 300 km |

# CANTERBURY

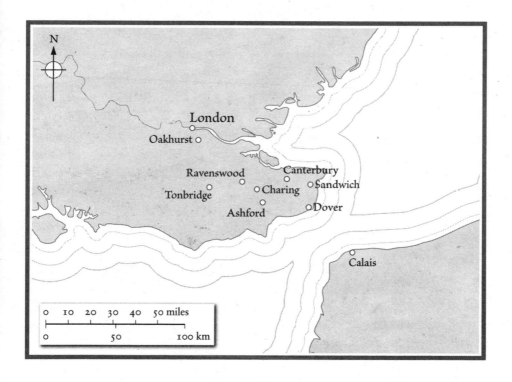

## July, 1351

### England

Gerard Fox's horse heard the approaching danger first. During his ride on the lonely forested road through Kent, Fox had been singing a selection of French drinking ballads to keep himself company. He was in the middle of a bawdy tune about a lecherous pirate and a clever tavern wench when Zephyr's ears pricked up. Fox went silent, and he heard the sound, too. It was the ominous rumble of pounding hooves sprinting toward them.

Fox's travels had trained him to be wary. Marauders roamed the highways preying on pilgrims and haggard families escaping from villages ravaged by the Pestilence, which had killed great swaths of people across Europe over the past four years. Most bandits were so poor that they couldn't afford horses and relied on rough knives for their robberies. During his encounters with them, Fox had discovered that the robbers usually left him alone when they saw a large man armed with a sword astride a warhorse, unless they thought they had the numbers to overpower him. In those few cases, they quickly learned that they should have listened to their instincts to leave him be.

He'd never encountered mounted bandits, but he couldn't be sure of anything these days. It sounded like a quartet of horses, enough to be trouble. Fox couldn't see them around the bend in the road, and he thought it sensible to be cautious.

He steered Zephyr into the woods, concealing himself behind a huge blackberry bush so that only his head peeked above the brambles. As a precaution, he strung his bow, a short recurved design from the Holy Land created specifically for use by horsemen.

"*Tace*, Zephyr," he said, patting the horse's neck. *Quiet*. He always spoke in Latin to Zephyr, a rare mottled silver Arabian courser with a black mane and tail and a distinctive white swirl on his forehead. The animal went still.

The sprinting horses were almost in view. Now the sound of their galloping was joined by the clatter of rolling wheels, creaking wood, and rattling chains.

Fox lowered the hood of his tan chaperon. His long brown hair would blend in with the trees, though he didn't know if the rest of his face would. He hadn't seen his reflection in still water for weeks, so he didn't know what he currently looked like. His beard was cropped close with a sharp dagger and he scrubbed himself clean in streams as often as he could. Though sun-weathered, his face might still stand out, so he slouched to keep just his eyes over the shrubbery.

What could be causing such a din and who would be speeding so recklessly over rough terrain?

His imagination didn't come close to the reality.

Hurtling around the corner was a lavish carriage pulled by four white horses foaming at the mouth from the strain. He'd occasionally seen nobility parading in such coaches around the great cities of the continent pulled by a team of horses in single file. This carriage had an arched roof painted in red with white trim, and black silk curtains covered the window openings. The rear door was swinging wide, slamming back and forth with each bump in the road.

But it wasn't the carriage itself that astonished Fox as he watched it hurtle in his direction. It was the driver.

A woman.

An elegant lady lashed the reins from atop the saddle of the lead horse where the coachman would normally sit. She wore a bright blue silk surcoat that must have cost a fortune. The kirtle and fine linen chemise underneath were both torn at the shoulder, revealing unblemished alabaster skin. Her blonde curls had escaped from their plaits and streamed wildly behind her in the wind. Her delicate face showed both determination and fear.

The coachman had fallen from his horse. He was dead, dragged along the ground by a foot caught in the stirrup. A crossbow bolt jutted from his chest. Another bolt was lodged in the coach.

The carriage wasn't out of control—that much was clear. The woman was actively driving the team, desperately trying to outrace someone following her. She whipped her head around to look behind.

Her pursuers had to be the same men who had killed the coachman. Not bandits. Bandits didn't use crossbows.

Fox heard the sound of additional hooves approaching. He guessed at least four more horses.

His curiosity had gotten the better of him. He craned his neck for a better view over the blackberry bush. A mistake. The woman saw his face.

They locked eyes for a moment. She wasn't afraid of him. Her look was pleading.

*Help.*

She didn't know who Fox was, but apparently she thought he couldn't be worse than whoever was after her.

The carriage flashed by and she disappeared from view. At the same time, her pursuers rounded the bend at full charge.

They weren't marauders, but men-at-arms, soldiers in service to a nobleman. Five, not four. Although they carried shields, none of them wore mail armor, and their tabards matched the colors painted on the coach. The coat of arms on their shoulder badges and shields bore the symbol of longswords arranged in the sign of the cross against a background of crimson and white. Two of them had crossbows at the ready and the others wielded broadswords. Their faces were contorted in vicious fury. It was clear that when they caught the woman, they would show no mercy.

She might have stolen the coach, but the sheer terror on her face implied that she had good reason to flee with it. The woman was no common thief, not the way she was dressed.

The soldiers were so intent on their quarry that they never even glanced in Fox's direction as they raced past.

Nobody else would ever know if Fox did nothing to save her. Five against one was not a fair fight.

*Just let it go,* he thought to himself.

But his instinct was urging him to go after her, that she didn't deserve the horrible fate that would befall her if she were captured. He knew his brother James would have quoted the Bible, as he often did from Proverbs.

*Do not withhold good from those to whom it is due, when it is in your power to act.*

Fox sighed. He had the power to act.

The images of the woman's obvious terror and the soldiers' cruel savagery flashed in his mind. If he did nothing to help her, *he* would know, and *she* would know, and that was enough. At least he would have a death befitting a knight.

With his bow in hand, Fox kicked his legs.

"*Oppugna,* Zephyr!"

*Attack.*

Without hesitation, Zephyr reared up and launched himself into a gallop. He knew it was time to go into battle.

 2

Facing martyrdom by fighting five men-at-arms at the same time would indeed be noble, but Fox had no interest in the rules of chivalry at the moment. He was going to pick them off one by one.

As Zephyr raced onto the road, Fox's hood and mantle flapped behind him. He steered by using his legs and made the sign of the cross in the way he'd been taught to remember it: *helmet, bollocks, shield, and sword.* Despite his lapsed faith, the gesture remained his ritual before combat.

The soldiers had a head start on him—perhaps twenty lengths—but their horses were slower than Zephyr. He would be able to catch up with them. The question was whether he could do it before they caught the carriage.

They still hadn't noticed him. Surprise was his only advantage.

The crossbowmen were his biggest concern. The weapons were easy to use while riding, but they were impossible to reload on horseback without a cranequin to crank the bowstring backward. There were no cranequins visible, so the crossbowmen would get only one shot each.

Fox loosened the drawstring on his arrow bag and pulled three shafts from the leather spacers, with each arrow held in the gaps between the fingers of his draw hand.

When he was within seven horse lengths, the soldiers were right behind the carriage. Fox knew it wouldn't be much longer until they heard him in pursuit, even with the clamor they were producing. He put the first arrow against his bowstring while holding the other two between his fingers and used his thumb to draw, a practice his ancestors had brought back from their crusades in the Holy Land. The technique allowed for much faster shooting.

He steadied himself in the stirrups, took aim at the rearmost rider, and let loose.

The arrow flew true and struck the soldier in the back. The crossbow dropped from his hand, but he stayed upright on the horse for a few more strides. He started to fall at the same time Fox nocked the next arrow and shot.

The rider beside the dead man noticed him hit the ground. He looked back, his body twisting so that the second arrow went into his shoulder instead of through his chest. He screamed in pain, causing the others to turn and see Fox behind them.

The advantage of surprise was gone.

Fox uttered a blasphemous curse that any good Christian would have to confess later. The injured soldier slowed and steered his horse off the road into the woods. Fox shot the third arrow at him as he went by, hitting him in the leg. The wounds might not be mortal, but they would be agonizing and put him out of the battle. Fox knew that from firsthand experience.

Three men-at-arms left. It was a fairer fight now.

While Fox reached for another arrow, the man-at-arms with the remaining crossbow slowed to turn so that he could face Fox and level his weapon, shooting his bolt as soon as his horse was sideways on the road. Fox nudged Zephyr to the side, and the bolt whizzed by his arm, drilling a hole through his mantle. He should have been elated that he wasn't impaled, but he was more annoyed that he'd now have to find a way to mend his favorite piece of clothing.

Fox loosed the arrow at the crossbowman before he could draw his sword. It went straight through his eye, dropping him like a sack of grain.

Fox was now less than five lengths behind the last two men. One of the soldiers was beside the carriage and racing forward to try to stop the team of horses pulling it. The other kept pace with the rear of the coach and had slung his shield across his back to protect him from further attack by Fox's arrows.

Fox placed the bow at his side and drew his sword. Stability was no longer important, so he squeezed his legs to tell Zephyr to speed up.

The woman driving the carriage screamed. Fox could see her wrestling with the soldier trying to take the reins from her. Failing to steal them away, the man leaped upon her, and they both went flying into a muddy creek next to the road.

The carriage, with no semblance of steerage, veered to the side of the road and its wheels dropped into the creek. The coach tipped over and smashed into a tree. The team of horses dragged it a little further before stopping.

The man-at-arms between Fox and the overturned carriage wheeled around, his sword held in his right hand, just as Fox's was.

"Surrender or run," Fox said, bringing Zephyr to a halt. "I will give no quarter."

"You are a coward who attacks from the rear without warning," the soldier sneered.

"I'm facing you now, and you've been warned, fool."

Fox's taunt had the intended effect. The soldier went into a rage, kicked his horse, and raced toward Fox, his sword prepared to strike.

At a press of Fox's heels, Zephyr charged forward. Each of them would have a single swing as they passed each other. The soldier, who wore a silver-edged badge on his shoulder designating him as the captain of the group, was likely the most skilled swordsman among them. To fell the man in one swing, Fox would need a lucky blow.

He liked to make his own luck.

At the last moment, he prodded Zephyr to the right so that he would pass on the opposite side. At the same time, he tossed his sword into his left hand.

The surprised man-at-arms had no time to maneuver away or retrieve the shield on his back, and his sword was now on the wrong side of his body for an effective parry. Fox slashed him across the neck as he rode by. He looked back over his shoulder to make sure the blow had the desired result. The captain tottered for a moment while he clawed at the blood spilling from his throat, then keeled over and fell to the ground dead.

Fox galloped toward the site of the wreck. The woman and final soldier had survived the crash and were struggling in the creek, both coughing up water they'd inhaled. The woman tried to get to her feet, but the soldier grabbed her ankle from behind, dragging her to him face down.

"Come back here, *Lady Isabel*," he snarled. "I'm not done with you."

His sword was nowhere in sight, likely lying on the creek bottom. Despite her kicks and screams, the man-at-arms was able to pull her to him as he drew a dagger from its scabbard. The wicked blade glinted in the sun.

Fox reached the edge of the stream, jumped into the water from Zephyr's back, and waded toward them.

The woman turned over with a stick she had snatched from the creek bed and cried, "Get away from me!" as she jabbed her attacker in the face. He howled and put a hand to his wounded cheek.

"You'll die for that!" he screamed. He reared back, ready to plunge the knife into her chest, unaware that Fox had closed the distance. With one slice of Fox's sword, the soldier's head was separated from his neck, and the body collapsed onto the woman, forcing her head below the surface.

Fox hauled the corpse aside and lifted the woman out of the water. She gasped for air and punched him several times in another attempt to get away. Fox admired her ferocious effort to fight back.

"It's all right," he said, pulling her close to him to arrest her blows. "I'm not going to hurt you. You're safe now."

She shook the drenched hair out of her eyes and finally saw the target of her punches. She stopped struggling and pushed Fox away, looking him up and down, breathing hard, her expression stunned and wary.

"You're the man in the woods."

"And you're the woman racing through the forest."

"Who are you?"

"Gerard Fox. And whom do I have the pleasure of rescuing?"

She hesitated, then said, "Lady Isabel of Kentworth." She attempted to smooth out her once-luxurious gown, but it was a hopeless, soggy mess. The kirtle's bodice was ripped and smeared with the soldier's blood, and the skirt was covered with muck from the stream.

"Lady?" He nodded to the destroyed carriage lying on its side. "Now why would a lady steal this coach?"

"How dare you! I didn't steal it. It was given to me."

"My sincere apologies, Lady Isabel of Kentworth. One doesn't often see a noblewoman driving a carriage while she's fleeing men-at-arms who are wearing the same colors as her declared property."

She looked as if she were about to launch into a long tale before simply saying, "It's complicated."

"The intention of these men didn't seem complicated," Fox replied. "They clearly wanted either to capture or kill you. Do you know who would put them up to such a task?"

She nodded. The shock of her ordeal had finally set in. Her stare was glassy and distant, and her lips trembled.

"It was my betrothed. We were to be married tomorrow."

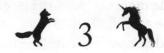

3

Fox searched the forest for the lone injured soldier, but the horse tracks he found showed that the man had fled. Fox retrieved his valuable projectiles from the two other men he'd shot and wiped off the arrow points with their tabards. He led the riderless horses back to the overturned carriage.

He found Lady Isabel inside sitting next to another body. It was a woman, almost as beautiful as Isabel, with a similar pert nose and high cheekbones, but having a squarer jaw and a small dimple in her chin. She had thick blonde hair elaborately plaited and was wearing a brown kirtle now stained with dried blood. A crossbow bolt had gone through a window and pierced her heart.

Isabel was gently caressing the woman's hair. She looked up at Fox and wiped away the tears streaming down her face.

"This is Willa, my maid," she said, her voice breaking as she was choked by sobs. "She… she was always so kind to me. Such a faithful… servant."

"A terrible price to pay for your escape," Fox said.

Isabel nodded, kissed her forehead, and pulled a covering over her face. She gathered herself, climbed down, and tugged at the handle of a trunk, struggling to take it from the coach.

"Would you like some help?"

She appraised Fox before saying, "That would be most kind."

He hauled the trunk out, careful not to disturb the body. "These warhorses are too large for you. Would you like me to unstrap the coach horses before I depart? The lead is a little smaller than usual, almost the size of a palfrey, and you wouldn't look out of place riding it."

"Depart?"

"I plan to continue on to my destination. You may join me if you'd like."

"Join you? It would be highly improper for a lady to accompany a gentleman on a journey alone."

Fox looked at her with bemusement. Her hair was caked with mud, her hands were scratched, and her clothes were torn and soiled, yet she was still concerned with appearances.

"Then I suppose you can ride onward by yourself," he said. "Or you can wait here until a larger party arrives."

She frowned at him. "Perhaps we can right the carriage."

Fox pointed to a shattered wheel. "Not unless you can fix this."

"Can't *you?*"

He laughed. "I'm not a wheelwright."

"You can't leave me here. It wouldn't be chivalrous. You *are* a knight, aren't you?"

Despite his common attire and his failure to introduce himself with a title, Fox's fine horse and weapons betrayed his noble status.

"I *am* a knight," he said. "And I have more than fulfilled my daily requirement for chivalrous acts. I killed four soldiers who were set to do you harm and grievously injured a fifth. Isn't that enough for my lady?"

Her face changed to an expression of horror. "You mean one of them got away?"

"He must have ridden off with the two arrows I put in him. He was in no condition to continue the fight."

"Then he'll warn Lord Tonbridge that we escaped."

Fox stared at her in utter astonishment. "Your betrothed is named Tonbridge?"

She nodded, her face as white as bleached linen. "Sir Conrad Harrington, Earl of Tonbridge."

Tonbridge Castle was Fox's destination, and Lord Tonbridge was the person he'd been planning to call on. The visit was supposed to bring an end to a years-long quest for justice, a chance to redeem his family name and reclaim the ancestral lands stolen from him. Now he realized he had ruined that opportunity in the span of moments by killing four of the earl's soldiers.

Tonbridge's betrothed seemed too concerned about her own troubles to note Fox's stunned expression. He quickly composed himself.

"What quarrel does he have with you, if I may ask, Lady Isabel?"

She flung open the trunk and drew out a clean kirtle and a traveling cloak.

"Lord Tonbridge is a dishonorable man. I was to be his second wife. His first wife and three children died in the Pestilence, as did my parents. My guardian arranged for me to marry him so I could bear him a new heir. It wasn't until the past fortnight that I realized how ruthless and vicious he truly is."

"And so you fled."

"If I return now, he'll certainly cut me down the moment he sees me."

"Murder his bride-to-be? I think not."

"You don't know him, and I hope you never have that misfortune."

Her words burned him. He wouldn't be able to meet with the earl now that one of his soldiers was riding back to report on Fox's attack. He had simply been on the wrong road at the wrong time.

If he returned Tonbridge's betrothed, the earl might give him an audience despite his assault, but he could just as easily execute Fox on the spot for murder. Since it didn't sound like Lord Tonbridge was the forgiving sort, Fox wasn't going to take a chance on trying to make amends. He'd made his impulsive choice, and now he had to live with it no matter the consequences.

Isabel plucked a large waterskin from the coach. "Now if you don't mind, I would like to wash out my hair and change from these wet clothes."

"Certainly." Fox eyed the unwieldy bladder in her hands. "Rinsing your hair on your own might be difficult."

Isabel ignored him and walked over to the creek. She emptied the ale from the waterskin and filled it with clear water. She dumped it over her head, but managed to spill most of it on her face. She coughed and spat out the water.

Despite the frustration with his situation, Fox had to stifle a laugh. "Would you like some assistance?"

She hesitated. He could tell that the idea of a strange man doing such a thing seemed shockingly inappropriate to her. But she had no other choice at the moment. Isabel handed the waterskin to him.

She leaned her head back and closed her eyes. Without comment, he poured the water and ran his fingers through her silken hair to comb out the bits of dirt and leaves. It took several minutes to finish the job, and he squeezed the excess water from her hair when he was done.

She took the bladder back and gave him an embarrassed "Thank you."

"My pleasure."

With a practiced hand, Isabel bound her hair into two plaits and nimbly bound the braids at the sides to frame her face. Fox studied her intricate weaving process.

She noticed him watching her and said, "I must have some privacy."

Isabel rounded the side of the carriage and changed into her clean clothes out of his sight. When she returned, Fox was astounded anew by her fresh-faced beauty. No wonder the earl was so eager to get her back.

"So will you join me or will you go your own way?" he asked. He could no longer head directly to Tonbridge Castle, but perhaps if he went to London for a few fortnights, he could try calling on Tonbridge once his injured soldier's memory wasn't fresh enough to identify Fox's face.

"Neither," Isabel said. "I would like to hire your services, my lord."

"My services?"

"You are obviously a capable man-at-arms. I would like you to help me reach my destination."

"And where would that be?"

"The estate of my cousin Claire in Paris."

He let out a huge belly laugh.

"You want to cross the Dover Narrows and ride all the way to Paris during England's war with France?"

"There are ways to make the journey, if one has money. I can pay."

Going back to the Continent was not in Fox's plans. "I can get you as far as the next town. Then I'm going on to London."

"I cannot stay at some traveler's inn by myself without so much as a maid."

"The nearest manor then?" He had often stayed at another lord's when traveling, as was customary for the nobility.

Isabel shook her head. "Lord Tonbridge has many friends in this area. I wouldn't know whom to trust."

"Then I would suggest a monastic guesthouse."

She scowled. "How much for you to take me to one?"

Fox considered her request. He'd already interrupted his quest to assist her once. But work as a man-at-arms had been scarce recently, so he could use the money. He knew of the right place for her to hide out.

"Canterbury has several monasteries and is along the road to the port at Dover where you can cross the Narrows. Canterbury is two days' ride. We would arrive in time for the Feast of the Translation of Saint Thomas Becket, and there will be many pilgrims in the city. You'll be able to find traveling companions for the rest of your journey. I would say ten shillings should pay for two days' escort."

"Ten shillings?" she cried. "That's outrageous! Knights are paid two shillings a day for service!"

He whistled, and Zephyr trotted to his side. "Then I'll wish you a pleasant journey, Lady Isabel." He climbed on.

"Wait!" she yelled. "You're not much better than a highway robber, but I'll agree to your terms."

"Half now and half when we arrive."

She grimaced at him, then retrieved a purse from the coach and counted out the coins.

He took them and said, "A pleasure to be of service." He didn't bother pointing out that a true highway robber would take all her money and kill her without a second thought.

He dismounted and liberated the horses from the carriage, so they could roam freely until they were eventually found. He removed the tack from all of them except the lead riding horse, which he left saddled. He also unsaddled the warhorses, which took the opportunity to graze in a nearby clearing.

When he was finished, he saw that Isabel had packed some extra clothes in a linen bag since the large trunk wouldn't fit on her horse. She also insisted on bringing a smaller box, a finely crafted wooden messenger's *coffret* big enough to hold two loaves of bread. On its lid was a carving of a rampant unicorn guarding a seated lady. Fox tried to dissuade her from carrying such a bulky object, but she threatened to cancel the bargain if she couldn't bring it along.

"What's inside?" Fox asked while tying it to the saddle. It had an ornate lock on its latch and strong iron clasps sealing it shut.

"That is none of your concern," Isabel replied testily.

"So it's valuable?"

"To me, it is."

Though Fox was curious, he let it go.

"What about Willa and the coachman?" Isabel asked.

"What about them?" Fox replied.

"We can't just leave them here unburied."

"If we bring them to a town with these wounds, the local sheriff will surely have questions that neither of us would like to answer, don't you agree?"

Isabel was aghast. "You mean we bury them here in unsanctified ground?"

"Unless you have a spade in the carriage, we can't bury them at all."

"That is unacceptable," Isabel said with crossed arms. "We must at least bury them properly, with a priest."

Fox admired her loyalty to her servants, but chafed at her stubbornness.

"Lady Isabel, I don't think you appreciate the gravity of our situation. The Earl of Tonbridge won't like what either of us have done here this morning, and I'm not going to risk taking the bodies to a priest. Now, do you have another suggestion, or shall I leave all three of you here to ponder your choices as I continue on to London?"

"There must be somewhere we can bury them."

She obviously wasn't going to budge on her decision, and Fox had already promised to take her to safety, an agreement he intended to honor. He may have had a price, but he was also a man of his word.

"There is one place where we can bury them without being seen," Fox said. "We can be there by this evening. A town called Ravenswood."

Her eyes went wide at his suggestion. "Ravenswood?"

"You know it?"

"It is well known in these parts for being haunted by spirits."

Fox shrugged. "No spirits appeared to me when I slept there last night. And as it happens, there were several unused graves already dug in the church cemetery."

Isabel was silent as she contemplated seeing the ghostly town in person.

"There would not be a priest," Fox continued, "but at least your servants would be buried in sanctified ground. If that suggestion doesn't suit you, I'll leave now."

Finally, Isabel nodded. "I agree to your terms. We will stop at Ravenswood."

As Fox cloaked the bodies of the maid and the coachman with the carriage's silk curtains and put them on one of the remaining coach horses, he mused about the degree of desperation that would make a woman voluntarily travel to a village emptied by the Pestilence.

## 4

TONBRIDGE, ENGLAND

Lord Tonbridge paced the battlements above Tonbridge Castle's noble gate, his scarlet robe trimmed with gold thread swirling around him with every turn. He glanced out at the road leading toward the front gate, but it was still as empty as the previous fifty times he'd looked. The men-at-arms he'd sent to retrieve his betrothed should have returned long ago. Now dusk was coming soon and there was as yet no sign of them.

Outside the walls of the fortress, peasants tilled the farms growing wheat, cabbage, onions, and carrots. Inside the castle grounds—which included stables, storage buildings, barracks for Tonbridge's soldiers and guards, and a chapel—horses grazed in the small pasture while men and women continued preparing for the upcoming nuptials with Isabel.

He was furious she had put that grand celebration and his legacy in jeopardy.

A man twenty years his junior leaned against a crenellation, lazily honing his sword on a whetstone and smirking every time Tonbridge passed. He wore a rich blue cotehardie and was broad-shouldered and fair-haired, with a strong jaw, Gallic nose, and large blue eyes that the ladies of Tonbridge's estate seemed to find irresistible since his arrival this morning.

It wasn't that Tonbridge felt envy for his guest. He couldn't compete with Basquin's looks, nor did he want or need to. With a squat torso, a pug nose, and graying hair, Tonbridge's birthright as an earl was his most important asset. Though Basquin was younger, more handsome, and better with a sword, he was not even knighted, so his misplaced self-confidence was irksome. Worse, he was illegitimately born.

"Where are they?" Basquin asked in French, not because it was the language of the royal court, but rather because he wouldn't soil his mouth with the English language if he didn't have to.

Tonbridge fumed at the bastard's impertinence. He should have addressed Tonbridge as "Your Lordship" or "Lord Tonbridge" as an earl deserved from a commoner. Nevertheless, Tonbridge had to bite his tongue at the slight.

"My men are capable," Tonbridge responded in French. "I trust they will return Isabel to me."

He couldn't understand her betrayal. He had promised to protect her and showered her with gifts. Someday he would have made her a queen. And all he had asked in return was her full devotion, the same fidelity that he had received from his first wife and children before they were struck down by the Pestilence. Their deaths had meant the destruction of all his carefully made plans for the advancement of his family. His need to start over had led him to the betrothal arranged with Isabel.

But he could see now that she was deceptive and had no plan to honor her vows to him. That he could not forgive.

"You might have told me earlier that she fled," Basquin said. "I would have chased her down by now."

"I didn't want to concern you with such a trivial matter."

"Nonsense," Basquin said with a sly smile. "You were embarrassed by her clever escape."

"I should have locked her away until the wedding," Tonbridge grumbled.

"That is one point on which we agree."

A shout from the watchtower stopped Tonbridge's pacing.

"Rider approaching!"

Tonbridge dashed to the edge of the battlement and peered at the wooded road. A lone rider emerged from the forest. Tonbridge recognized the colors of his coat of arms on the man's tabard. He strained to see the rest of his men, but none followed.

As the soldier drew closer, Tonbridge could see arrows jutting from his shoulder and leg. His clothes were drenched in blood.

"Raise the portcullis!" Tonbridge yelled. He ran for the steps down to the central courtyard, and Basquin followed. Chains rattled as the iron gate rose.

The horse plodded through the entrance, spent from the long trek. The soldier looked worse than his horse.

His face was ashen, and only his feet in the stirrups were keeping him upright. As soon as he crossed into the courtyard, he loosened a foot and toppled to the ground. He let out a cry of agony that dwindled into a mewling whimper. He looked as if he were about to pass out.

One of the guards kneeled beside him with a bladder of ale and tried to get him to drink.

When he was slow to rouse, Tonbridge said, "We don't have time to waste. Splash him with the ale." The guard upended the waterskin over the soldier's face.

The man sputtered and opened his eyes. When he saw Tonbridge hovering over him, he went whiter still.

"Your Lordship," he said.

"What happened?" Tonbridge asked in English. "Where are Isabel and the rest of my men?"

The soldier was silent, his eyes searching for an acceptable answer.

Tonbridge was furious, not with the soldier, but with Isabel for her treachery and with the people who had shot these arrows. An attack on his men-at-arms was equivalent to an attack on him personally.

Tonbridge leaned down, tempering the anger in his voice. "Tell me who did this to us."

"On the road to Canterbury, we found the carriage and killed her driver and maid as you ordered, Your Lordship, but Lady Isabel fled. We nearly had her until a bandit came out of nowhere. He must have been following us. He killed the rest of the men."

"One man? A single bandit defeated five of you?"

Basquin chuckled. "And here I thought you had capable soldiers." He bent down and ran his fingers over the arrow fletches.

"Do you recognize those?"

Basquin stood. "I'm simply admiring them. It's fine work. This lone man must know his weaponry."

"And the package I ordered you to recover?" Tonbridge asked. The box wasn't on the horse's saddle. "What of it?"

The soldier shook his head as he grimaced in pain.

Tonbridge glowered at the soldier. "Tell me about this ranger."

"I did not see him well, but I might recognize him if I saw him again. I'm sorry, Your Lordship. Once I am able, I will lead another squad myself to retrieve them."

That was unlikely. The soldier's grievous wounds would soon rot. With half his men dead from the Pestilence, Tonbridge couldn't afford to lose any more, and now five of his best soldiers were gone in one ride.

"You've done a great service returning to me with this information," Tonbridge said. He stood and turned to one of the guards. "Take him away and tend to his wounds."

The soldier was carted off. Despite Tonbridge's gesture, he didn't think the man would survive the night.

"The cardinal will not be pleased if you have to renege on your agreement," Basquin said.

Tonbridge blanched at that thought. If he didn't deliver what he'd promised, Cardinal Molyneux wouldn't hesitate to invent an excuse to excommunicate him and seize his lands, a tactic the powerful cleric had used many times in the past.

"I will do whatever it takes to get her back," Tonbridge said. He looked to the sky and saw gathering clouds. Traveling in a storm at night would be impossible. "I will assemble my remaining men and depart at first light."

"And I will accompany you."

"There is no need—"

"I must protect my patron's interests. Or would you rather I return to him in Paris immediately and share what has occurred here?"

Tonbridge could not decline his offer to join in the search, no matter his distaste for Basquin's disrespectful behavior.

"Of course, I would welcome your help in this matter."

"She will have a day's lead," Basquin said, "and there are many roads she could have taken."

"Isabel is too used to a comfortable life. She would never stay in common accommodations. We will not return until we have checked every noble manor and guesthouse between here and the Dover Narrows."

## 5

### Near Ravenswood, England

Fox and Isabel rode side by side through untended fields, the twilight sun turning the tall wheat golden. Heavy clouds to the west foretold of a rainy night. The horse carrying the bodies of her maid and the coachman trailed behind. They'd passed only two groups of commoners who were on foot, and neither had done anything more than glance curiously at them.

Isabel was a competent horsewoman, and the coach horse made a suitable palfrey for her. They hadn't stopped since leaving the scene of the battle, but she had not complained about the pace Fox had set. In fact, she hadn't spoken a word in that time. Although Fox had grown accustomed to traveling by himself, the companionship suited him.

At last, she said, "Do you know Lord Tonbridge?"

Fox was taken aback by the abruptness of her question. "Why do you ask?"

"When I mentioned his name, I noted a sign of recognition on your face."

So she *had* been paying attention.

"I've never met him," Fox said, which was the truth.

"But it was no coincidence you were on the same road as I, was it?"

Fox took a breath. He supposed there was no need to hide his intent to call on the earl.

"I was on my way to see him, yes."

"May I inquire as to the reason?"

"It has to do with my mother, Lady Emmeline. I thought she was killed during her travels when I was a child. It wasn't until a few years ago that I learned instead that she was secretly abducted."

"Held for ransom?"

Fox shook his head, but he wasn't ready to go into the details with a stranger. "For other reasons. Even my father didn't know of her fate until the same moment I learned of it. In my investigations since then, I discovered that Lord Tonbridge may have been a witness to the affair. I was hoping he could testify on my behalf."

"To what purpose?"

"Justice for my family."

The consequences of his actions suddenly dawned on her. Isabel turned to Fox with a look of regret. "Coming to my aid means you can't meet Lord Tonbridge and confirm whether he knows the truth about your mother."

"That does seem unlikely now."

"Based on my knowledge of Lord Tonbridge, I doubt you would have found the relief you sought anyway. He is corrupt."

"Then I will have to pursue my goal some other way."

"I'm sorry."

Fox shrugged. "Given the behavior of Tonbridge's soldiers, it seems as if you saved me some trouble."

"If you hadn't been there, I would not still be alive. I haven't thanked you yet for saving my life."

"None is needed. Zephyr and I are at your service."

"Zephyr?"

"My horse."

"Why did you name your horse Zephyr?" Isabel asked with an air of amusement.

"Why shouldn't I?"

"I didn't mean to offend. I've just never heard that name before."

"It's from the Greek word *zephyros*, the god of the west wind."

She raised an eyebrow at him. "So you're an educated man."

"I like to read. Does that make me strange?"

"Perhaps not strange. But unusual. I don't know many knights who enjoy reading. Who taught you?"

Fox had never met such a curious woman, but it was a bracing change from the men-at-arms he spent most of his time with. They cared only about womanizing, fighting, and gambling. Not that Fox didn't enjoy carousing—sometimes too much—but literature, art, and intelligent conversation were also diverting.

"As the son of a knight, I spent much of my youth being educated in a monastery," he said. "The monks had a large selection of manuscripts, and Brother Anselm let me sneak in to read after vespers." The library was at its quietest after the church's evening services.

"So you've read more than just the Bible?"

"The Bible, histories, romances. Whatever I could find."

"In Latin? I noticed that's the language you speak to Zephyr."

Fox was amazed both that she knew Latin and that she had noticed that detail in the face of all that had happened.

"It was my brother James's idea. He thought training our horses to respond to Latin would help us in battle when all the other soldiers were shouting in English and French. But I do read French as well."

"You're a man of many talents, Sir Gerard. A fighter and scholar."

"Fighting is simply my profession."

"You seem to be quite good at it."

"It's what I trained to do when I wasn't reading."

"Have you fought in many battles?"

"Just one of note."

"Crécy?"

Fox turned to her in astonishment. "How did you know?"

"You're English. You're the right age. It's the only recent major battle of which I'm aware."

The five years since the Battle of Crécy seemed like a lifetime to Fox. Though outnumbered, he and his English compatriots had decimated the French forces with the aid of their deadly archers, securing a foothold in France and escalating a war that continued to this day.

He could still remember every detail of that battle. The sound of the screams from both man and horse as they went down under the withering hail of arrows. The feel of the thick mud in that sodden pasture. The coppery smell of blood and gore. The gut-wrenching pain of his losses.

He stayed quiet. So did Isabel.

Then she tentatively repeated, "How did you come to name your horse Zephyr?"

"I didn't," Fox said. "He was originally my brother's horse. I named my own horse Velox."

"Latin for 'swift'," Isabel said.

He was again impressed by her knowledge of the language and nodded. "Velox was the fastest horse I've ever ridden."

"And Zephyr?"

"The second fastest. James and I would race all the time. He was superior with both lance and sword, but he and Zephyr never beat me and Velox."

"Maybe you were simply the better horseman."

Fox smiled. "That's what I thought as well until we switched horses. Then he left me in his dust."

"He sounds like quite a man."

"He was."

Isabel noted the past tense and looked at Fox with sad eyes. "Crécy?"

Fox didn't answer. Instead, he changed the subject. "How did you escape from Lord Tonbridge? Surely he would have kept you on a tight leash if your wedding is imminent."

"*Was* imminent. It was Willa's idea. She suggested we take the carriage that Lord Tonbridge had gifted me to retrieve his mother for the wedding. Then Willa pretended to be ill. I asked for the carriage to be stopped and sent the two men who served as our escorts into the forest to look for some nightshade to treat her. When they dismounted, we fled with my loyal coachman, taking their horses in tow. We left them in a field sometime later."

"And the soldiers ran back to Tonbridge Castle to get fresh horses and reinforcements," Fox said.

Isabel nodded. "They caught up to us much sooner than we

imagined they could. We were traveling along a narrow river, and Tonbridge's men shot their crossbows at us from the other side, killing Willa and Reginald. I got out and jumped onto the lead horse to escape. I saw you only a little while later."

"You seemed very skilled on that horse for a lady."

She looked affronted. "Does that make me strange?"

Fox smiled. "Unusual, I would say."

"My father had a large estate. As children, Willa and I would ride through the forest hunting rabbits."

"Riding *and* hunting? You're a woman of many talents."

As they passed a stand of trees, a weathered stone church tower came into view.

"Ravenswood," Isabel said with a distinct note of dread.

"We'll have to move quickly," Fox said, prodding Zephyr into a trot that Isabel matched. "We don't have much time to bury the bodies."

He pointed at the dark clouds rapidly blowing toward them. A storm was coming.

"I'm glad you're with me," Isabel said. "It would be terrifying to be here alone."

"Then it's good I happened upon you."

"Yes, it is. Not every knight would have been as honorable as you to help someone in need."

"That is true," Fox replied. He could only imagine James's disappointment at how close he'd come to turning a blind eye to Isabel's plight and forsaking that vow.

# 6

*Five years ago*
*July, 1346*

## NORMANDY, FRANCE

As he kneeled on the high hill overlooking the beach of Saint-Vaast-La-Hougue, Fox could finally take in the huge armada that had begun assembling two weeks before in Portsmouth. The seven hundred ships surely made up the largest fleet in English history, carrying thousands of men and horses and tons of wagons and supplies that were being unloaded quickly onto the sand. The sight was awe-inspiring, and Fox could not imagine any army repelling such a strong invasion force. If the campaign went as planned, the war for the French throne that had started nine years ago might even be over by Christmastide.

Only light resistance had met them upon landing, so King Edward III led a contingent of soldiers to a ceremony that would mark his successful incursion. Fifty kneeling men, including Edward's son the Prince of Wales, were to be knighted. Fox, until that point merely a squire, was thrilled to be one of those chosen for the accolade.

Across from Fox stood his brother James, resplendent in his brightly polished mail and fresh tabard. He looked every inch the knight, from his strong chin and regal bearing down to the Damascus-steel sword named Legend on his hip and the golden spurs on his boots. He was a true contrast to the king's sixteen-year-old son, whose gleaming black armor set him apart from the others lined up beside him.

The king, draped in his royal robes and wearing a golden crown, spoke from atop his horse. He was saying something about his rights of conquest and a just war and the code of chivalry, but the words barely registered for Fox, who was finally getting his wish to be a knight like his older brother.

Then the king's bishop recited the three commitments of knighthood, and the men all repeated the vows in one voice.

"I will champion good against evil and act with honor, mercy, courage, valor, and fairness."

"I will faithfully serve God, my Church, and my lord."

"I will protect and defend the innocent, the weak, the poor, and ladies in need."

The king dismounted and stepped in front of the Prince of Wales, dubbing him a knight with great reverence and taking the time to recite all of his other titles. The prince got to his feet and was girded with his sword by an earl in front of him and fitted with his golden spurs by a squire behind him.

With the most important part of the ceremony completed, the king proceeded down the line. He couldn't have possibly known all of the candidates, so he depended on the man standing before each knight-to-be to give him the proper name. Fox, his head bowed, could only see the king out of the corner of his eye, but he didn't have to wait long for his turn. The king stood in front of him, and Fox's heart hammered against his chest at being so close to the sovereign. In a loud and clear voice, James said, "Gerard Fox, Squire of Oakhurst."

King Edward used his sword to tap on Fox's shoulders three times while saying, "Arise, Sir Gerard of Oakhurst. Be thou a good knight."

Fox had to restrain himself from leaping to his feet. He stood up, keeping his head bowed. By that time, the king had already moved on to the next man.

James stepped forward and circled his waist with his sword belt, signifying that he was now worthy of holding the weapon of a knight, even though it was the same broadsword he'd been using for years. At the same time, the squire behind him removed the silver spurs from his boots and affixed golden ones, the traditional symbol of a knight.

When the accoutrements were in place, James took his place by Fox's side. Although James was still an inch taller, Fox felt that he now deserved to stand beside him as an equal. Fox was near bursting to talk, but it would be a grave violation to speak while the king was still dubbing new knights. James gave him a knowing smile.

Finally, the last accolade was bestowed. The king remounted his horse and invited them all to a great feast that evening to celebrate their accomplishment, and the entire group cheered in response.

"Congratulations, Gerard," James said. "I hope you will be the knight everyone expects you to be. *Abhor what is evil; hold fast to what is good.*"

"Philippians?"

James rolled his eyes. "Romans Twelve."

"I was close," Fox said as they began the walk back down to the beach. "Do you think I'll get to fight with a lance now?"

"That's your first thought now that you have earned your golden spurs?"

"My *first* thought was how impressed all the maidens back home will be with them. *Then* it was about the lance."

"I doubt the king will want to give up your talents as a mounted archer."

"Maybe we could give him a demonstration of my skills this evening, you and I jousting just like we practice back home."

"After nearly a fortnight on the ships, the horses will need days of rest to recover before we can ride on. Zephyr and Velox are in no condition to fight right now."

"Perhaps you don't want the king to see how Velox and I can knock you into the dirt."

James held up a finger. "That happened *once.*"

Fox smiled. "Right before we left home. Does your backside still ache? Or just your pride?"

"Remember that I *have* won tournaments in the joust."

"And now that I am a knight as well, I will be competing

against you soon. Not scared of a little sibling rivalry, are you? Just a bit? Come, you can admit it."

Fox was trying to get James to crack a smile, but he became more serious. "You'll find that practice in our courtyard back at Caldecott Mote is quite different from a tournament, let alone a real battle. Your skills with the bow and sword are what this army needs."

"You really don't want to have a laugh today, do you?"

James rounded on him and shoved a hand against his armored chest plate.

"Did you hear a word of what the king said?"

Fox shrugged. "Most of it. Some of it. Well, a little of it."

"You may think this is a grand adventure, but war is serious business. I saw it myself at Sluys. You will be sick of the sight of blood by the time we return to England."

"We're here to defeat the French, aren't we?"

"No. We are here to slaughter them. Do you know what a *chevauchée* is like?"

Fox nodded. "Of course. We get to raid and plunder all we want until the enemy comes to stop us."

James's lip curled in disgust. "*Raid* and *plunder*. Those are such innocent-sounding words. They don't give a sense of the ugly reality. Our army will chew through Normandy like a pack of hungry wolves. Nothing within ten miles of us will be spared. Men and children will be butchered. Women raped and defiled. Crops eaten or razed. Whole towns stripped of their wealth and then burned to the ground. The king said no prisoners will be taken. He meant in battle, but the foot soldiers won't care. During the *chevauchée*, even nobles won't be ransomed. The army's bloodlust will be at a fever pitch."

"It is our duty to fight for the king."

"And we will. But you are now a knight representing the Fox family. We won't be able to put a stop to the ravages that we see, but we will not participate in them, either." James held Fox by both shoulders. "Remember the vows you just took. Are you prepared to honor them?"

Fox took a breath and nodded.

For the first time, James smiled. "Good. I'm proud to have you as my brother."

They continued walking. It suddenly occurred to Fox what the *chevauchée* would mean for the Normandy estate that their mother Emmeline had brought to the Fox family when she married their father Richard. It was located outside Saint-Lô, which lay just fifty miles to the south.

"What about Château de Beaujoie?"

James nodded grimly. "When the time comes, we will have to do what we can to keep it from suffering the same terrible fate."

It took just two weeks for Fox to see the worst that the army could do. James was right. Fox had been sickened by the sights unfolding all around him and left helpless by his inability to interfere. The sacking of Saint-Lô, one of the wealthiest trading posts in Normandy, was well under way as Fox and James raced through the city on horseback. By rights, they were abandoning their positions in the rearguard, but no one would miss them amidst this orgy of mayhem and destruction.

Fox caught only glimpses of the pillaging as they rode. A feeble old man whose throat was cut by a laughing soldier. Two screaming young girls dragged into a local tavern by a squad of men who were likely to do unspeakable things to them. A fire raging out of control in a stable as the horses were taken out while a group of townsmen was barred inside despite their desperate pleas for mercy. Fox had no doubt that the entire city would be a smoking ruin by the next morning.

Finally they reached the town gates on the south side, and Fox and James were able to put the horses into a full gallop. Fox spurred Velox, a black Arabian that was brother to Zephyr, to his fastest. James and Zephyr trailed close behind as they strained to keep up with Velox, who seemed to enjoy being allowed to sprint after so much marching.

They didn't know how far the spearhead of the army had gotten, but certainly companies of soldiers were already patrolling the countryside around the city in search of new treasures to loot. Château de Beaujoie would provide a bounty if Fox and James didn't get there first.

Before the war, the family had spent time at both estates, one in France and one in England. Fox had often visited Normandy during his childhood, learning to speak French like his mother, who was a native. And though as the second-born he would not inherit the family's patrimony, he expected James to let him oversee Beaujoie when he was not going off on knightly quests.

The horses didn't even seem winded when they arrived at the familiar fork in the road with the giant beech tree signaling that they were nearing the estate. They crested a hill and were stopped by two chilling sights.

The first, a half-mile in the distance, was a company of soldiers approaching the front gate of Château de Beaujoie, torches in their hands. It was clear that the guardians of the stately and elegant stone manor had fled to safety in the face of the encroaching army, and the unguarded wall and wooden gate didn't provide much protection against a determined force.

The second sight, much closer, was of another squad of soldiers encircling a frightened group of travelers with a wagon and a donkey.

"Come," James said and kicked Zephyr into a canter.

"I'm not your dog," Fox muttered, but he goaded Velox forward.

When they reached the nearer soldiers, Fox could see who they were menacing. It was Denis, the caretaker of Château de Beaujoie, and his wife, a son, and two daughters, one of them near marrying age. Denis had been at the estate for more than twenty years, a good and loyal *seneschal* of the Fox family. Seven men armed with pikes were advancing on them.

"Ho, there!" James yelled at them.

A couple of heads turned, but most of the men were so focused on their prey that they paid no attention.

James rode past them and placed Zephyr between them and the family. He drew Legend, the whorled pattern of the Damascus-steel blade flashing in the sun. Fox drew his own broadsword and took up a position on James's flank. Given the savagery in the eyes of these men, Fox feared that the first blood he would draw in this campaign would be from his own compatriots.

"Stop!" James bellowed.

The soldiers halted, but their pikes remained in a threatening stance.

"Who are you to keep us from our prize?" the man at the front said. He was one of the Welsh foot soldiers that made up the bulk of the infantry.

"You will address me as Sir James of Oakhurst. And these people and their possessions are not a prize. They are under our protection."

"We saw them first. We get to take what's ours."

"You wouldn't dare disobey a knight in your king's army." James turned to the family and spoke in French. "Are you all right, Denis?" When he saw Denis hesitate, he added, "Don't worry. This lot doesn't speak French."

Denis nodded. "I'm sorry to have abandoned the estate, but when we saw the army approaching, we had no choice but to escape."

"What about everyone else?"

"They fled long ago. We saved what we could. The most valuable items from the manor are in the wagon, including all the silver."

If the soldiers did speak French, Fox thought they might have attacked then and there.

"You're one of them?" the Welshman sputtered in disbelief at James.

"I speak French just as your king does," James replied. "Now leave immediately."

When the men hesitated, James pointed Legend at them. "My brother and I are more than capable of slaying every single one of you if you don't go right now."

James sounded resolute, but Fox knew that seven men with

pikes would give them a challenge. At the very least, one of their horses could be seriously harmed in the melee.

Thankfully, the intimidating presence of two knights on horseback was enough to make them grudgingly turn tail.

"Do you have any family south of here?" James asked Denis when the men had backed away. Still, they watched the family with hungry leers.

"I have a cousin in Vire," Denis said.

"Then you must head there immediately. The rest of the army will be coming through this way soon. We will not be able to protect you from them all. We will escort you south until you are no longer in danger."

Fox looked at the company of soldiers only yards from Château de Beaujoie. "James," he said in English, "if we accompany them, those soldiers will loot Beaujoie and burn it down."

"I know."

"It's our home."

"It's one of our homes."

"We can't let it be ransacked by that mob."

"You would fight them all?"

"If I have to." Fox pivoted on Velox, sword still in hand. "This is our land."

"Gerard, stop!" James shouted. "This is my decision, and I will bear the consequences when we tell Father upon our return. If we leave Denis and his family now, they will fall to the soldiers. You know what will happen then. You've seen it with your own eyes."

Fox watched the men battering at the gates of their home.

"You took a vow to protect the innocent," James reminded him.

Fox looked at Denis and his family huddled together in fear and turned to his brother. "I did."

James recited another Bible verse. "*Blessed are those who have regard for the weak; the Lord delivers them in times of trouble.*"

"Psalms?"

James smiled at him. "You got it right for once."

"I listen to you occasionally."

James spoke to Denis. "Gerard and I will take you to the next town. Then we must leave you and return to the army. Do not stop after that until you reach your cousin."

"Bless you, Sir James," Denis said as they started walking. "God will surely reward you for your nobility."

Fox wasn't so sure about that. Before they were out of sight of Château de Beaujoie, flames from the roof of the main house were already flicking at the sky.

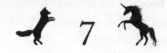

# 7

*July, 1351*

## RAVENSWOOD, ENGLAND

Fox had seen dozens of towns like Ravenswood over the past two years while he was supporting himself as a man-at-arms for hire, and the sight still made him shudder. The Pestilence had devastated Europe and exterminated the populations of entire villages during the event also known across the continent as the Great Mortality. The disease had been merciless, striking down young and old, the healthy and the already sick, the rich and the poor, the pious and the wicked. Fox was baffled by who was spared and who was taken. There was no rhyme nor reason to it, but the moment the disease descended upon a town, few escaped with their lives.

When the Great Mortality began, it seemed like the end of the world, the Apocalypse as had been foretold in the Bible's Book of Revelation. Fox had been in London when it first struck there. Hundreds died by the day, the corpses put into vast pits when individual burials became impossible. He could still smell the overpowering stench of the bodies, many of which decayed where they fell.

Only now, with the worst past, was life beginning to return to normal, whatever normal meant in a world missing half its inhabitants. There were still outbreaks of the Pestilence here and there, and people were wary of it coming back in force, but they believed that civilization would continue.

It was apparent that Ravenswood had been abandoned for at least two winters. The thatch roofs of the houses were rotted and crumbling, and ivy and weeds were already reclaiming the twenty buildings in the hamlet. A fire had torched the stone church so that it was nothing more than a burned-out hulk, but the largest building besides the church, a combined inn and tavern with a slate roof, had survived.

Isabel shivered as they rode down the town's main thoroughfare, which adjoined one of the primary routes to Canterbury.

"I don't know if I can stay here tonight," she said. "Aren't we at risk of being struck by the Pestilence?"

"I spent the night in Ravenswood, and I'm healthy," Fox said. "I think the danger is long past."

"This place is most unsettling."

"Would you rather sleep in the forest during a downpour?"

She took a deep breath and looked at him. "We'll leave at first light?"

Fox nodded. "The sooner we get you to Canterbury, the better." He could now see the cemetery. "Let's get your servants in the ground before the storm arrives."

Four new graves had been dug, but the remaining townspeople must have fled or died before any interment could take place, the corpses likely carried off by wild animals.

He found a shed with tools inside and took a spade. He carefully placed Willa and Reginald in the graves. He was about to fill the holes from the adjacent piles of compacted dirt when Isabel stopped him.

"I know we don't have a priest," she said, "but we can't bury them without saying a prayer."

She looked beseechingly at Fox, who stabbed the spade into the ground. He recited the first psalm of the Office of the Dead in Latin, as he did the last time he'd buried someone.

*"Dilexi, quoniam exaudiet Domine vocem orationis meae..."*
*I have loved because the Lord will hear the voice of my prayer...*

After he completed the psalm, Isabel's eyes brimmed with tears as she crossed herself before nodding to him. He picked up the spade and began shoveling.

The light was fading, and it would be dark by the time he finished.

"You should go build a fire. There's a hearth in the public house. We'll bring the horses inside with us."

When she didn't respond, he paused and saw her staring at him with an embarrassed expression.

"I don't know how to start a fire."

"Ah yes, you're a noblewoman. You don't have much cause to do anything for yourself."

She bristled at that. "I'm not useless."

"I didn't say you were. You could at least gather some dry wood before it starts raining."

"What do we have for supper?"

"I have a little salted fish and three-day-old bread." They hadn't eaten anything on the ride, and Fox's stomach was rumbling. "Didn't you bring anything?"

She shook her head. "We hadn't been able to pack food for the escape. It would have looked suspicious."

"Well, there aren't any chickens or other tame animals left. I checked last night. If any remained after the townspeople left, they must have been eaten by foxes."

She marched over to his saddle, removed his unstrung bow, and took two arrows and the bowstring from his bag.

"What are you doing? Put those back!"

With deft precision, she hooked the bowstring around one end of the bow, wrapped the bow behind her leg to bend it, and expertly looped the string around the other end to turn it into a weapon.

Fox was stunned by her display.

Isabel looked at him with a raised eyebrow. "Do you want hot food or not?"

She didn't wait for an answer and walked away toward the forest. Fox considered chasing her down, but he thought she'd be back as soon as she realized how strong the pull on the bow's drawstring was. It didn't require the huge muscles of the archers using the six-foot-long English war bows, but it was certainly not made for a lady.

He got into a rhythm tossing dirt into the graves and was

nearly done when Isabel finally returned. He stopped when he saw her triumphantly holding two dead rabbits by the ears.

She didn't say a word as she replaced the unstrung bow, both arrows, and string she had taken, but he could see she was pleased by his surprise.

"That's a fine weapon," she said. "I'll water the horses and gather the wood."

Fox looked at her in wonder as she walked away. Isabel was unlike any lady he'd ever met before.

Just as he put the last spade of dirt onto the graves, drops of rain began to fall. He hurried over to the inn and found Isabel inside the darkened main hall with the horses brought in for safety. She had removed their saddles, and they were contentedly eating from bales of hay that Fox had lugged into the inn the night before. Wood was piled awkwardly in the hearth, ready to be lit.

He took a bag from his saddle containing flint, steel, and tinder and handed it to Isabel, while he placed their belongings on one of the long tables.

"You, my lady, are going to learn how to start a fire without a ready flame."

She followed his instructions for placing the tinder by the kindling and striking the flint against the steel to create a spark. It took her several tries, but soon a blaze caught the dry wood.

She smiled broadly and gave his kit back.

"Thank you for teaching me that," she said. "I don't think I've ever lived in a home without a burning candle, stove, or lantern."

"You learn quickly."

Now that the hearth was ablaze, its smoke escaping through loose tiles in the ceiling, the interior was fully visible. Three-legged stools and benches were scattered around the trestle tables, and several half-burnt candles remained in their wall sconces. At night, the guests would have bedded down in the main room. At the far end of the room was a door leading to the small kitchen and the owner's quarters, and to the right of that was a door opening into a private back room for special overnight visitors.

"You must be used to sleeping on feather beds," Fox said, "but this is a simple inn. No fancy beds here. Why don't you sleep out here by the fire, and I'll sleep in the guest quarters. I'll make a hay pallet for you. There may be some moldy bits, but it's more comfortable than sleeping on the floor."

"I'll make do," Isabel said.

Fox skinned and cleaned the rabbits with a practiced hand. Using the spit he had fashioned the night before, he skewered them and roasted them over the fire.

When the rabbits were cooked, Fox and Isabel washed their hands with rainwater from a barrel outside and ate in silence. Fox noticed her eyeing him cautiously. She had likely never spent the night in the company of a lone stranger, and a man to boot.

"You don't have to fear me," he said.

"I'm not afraid," she replied, not quite convincingly. "To this point you've shown yourself to be a gentleman. I expect you to remain one. Does that make me naïve?"

"No. It makes you a good judge of character. But I would choose your future traveling companions carefully. Other men might not be so gallant."

With full bellies, Fox and Isabel retired to their respective sleeping areas. The rain continued to batter the roof, leaking through where the tiles were missing, but Fox found a dry spot for his pallet and removed all his clothes but his undertunic and braies. As he lay there alone in his room, he was haunted by the day's images of battle and death. It took him a long while to fall into a fitful sleep.

He was awakened sometime later by a noise from outside the room. Rain no longer pummeled the roof. At first he thought the sound was simply the wood in the fire settling, but a few moments later he heard another noise and realized that it was the light scuffle of feet.

He went over to the door, and through a crack saw Isabel wearing a linen chemise with her braids tucked up under a coif. He wondered if she, too, was having trouble sleeping because of the day's ordeal. She furtively glanced back to his room, but she was apparently unaware he was watching. Seemingly satisfied that she would be undisturbed, she continued with her task by the fire.

Isabel lit a candle from the smoldering hearth and went over to the messenger's *coffret* that lay on a table. She took a key from a chain around her neck to unlock the box, unlatched the clasps, and carefully raised the lid.

She paused and took in a deep breath at the sight of its contents, which Fox couldn't see because the box's lid blocked his view. After a moment of indecision, Isabel reached into the *coffret* and gently pulled out the object as if she were handling a delicate piece of glass. She carefully removed the obscuring layers of crimson silk.

Fox was surprised to see that the item she had insisted on bringing with them was a book.

But this was obviously a special manuscript, for the wooden binding was covered with thin sheets of gold, and precious gems were inlaid on the metal. The gold and jewels alone had to be worth a king's ransom.

Now Fox knew why Lord Tonbridge had been so eager to get his betrothed back.

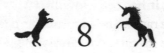 

## 8

Fox waited until Isabel had placed the manuscript safely on the table before he opened the door and spoke.

"I assume you'll say you didn't steal that, either."

As he expected, Isabel let out a tiny squeal and looked up, clutching her chest in fright.

"Goodness!" she cried out. "How dare you spy on a lady in her nightclothes like that!" She gazed at him with a mixture of curiosity and embarrassment, perhaps never having seen a man in such a state of undress.

"It's not your attire that intrigues me," Fox said before nodding at the book. "You've been keeping a secret from me."

Fox went over to get a better look at the manuscript, its cover glinting in the candlelight. It was larger than most books he had read, about half the size of a cavalryman's shield, and by its thickness he guessed it had hundreds of folios. The cover design was even more exquisite up close. A gold plaque with a sculpted image of the Virgin Mary was surrounded by pearls and gems forming geometric cruciform patterns. The fine detail and artistic flair meant this book had been created for someone of high nobility, perhaps even royalty.

"This is my book," Isabel said. "It's been in my family for generations."

"What is it?"

"It's called the Book of the Virgin."

"It's not a Bible?"

Isabel shook her head. "It's a Gospel book from Constantinople."

"That's a long way from here."

"It was brought back by a family member who saved it during

the Sack in 1204, otherwise it might have been destroyed in the pillaging. Ever since, it has been cared for by the first daughter of each generation." She ran her hand across the cover. "My older sister Catherine used to be its caretaker until she had to leave it behind when she became a nun. The manuscript is now my responsibility."

"Why does your betrothed want it?"

"He has made a bargain to trade it away. I couldn't let that happen."

"I imagine he could get quite a price for it." The gems alone would bring a princely sum.

Isabel watched him gazing at the book. "If you take it, you will never be able to sell it yourself without bringing down Lord Tonbridge's wrath."

Fox cocked his head at her. "Don't you have a higher opinion of me than that, Lady Isabel?"

"I know a covetous eye when I see one."

"As I told you, I am a lover of the written word. I am not a thief."

"That is good to hear."

"Why risk looking at it now?"

"I had to make sure it was not damaged in my flight from Tonbridge Castle."

Fox picked it up and turned it over. "It seems to be in good condition."

Isabel let out a squawk. "Please be careful with it. It's worth more than you know."

"May I look at some of the pages?"

She took the book from him. "Allow me."

She placed it on the table, unhooked the two clasps holding it closed, and opened the manuscript to the second leaf. Greek words written in gold faced a full-page illumination of a richly dressed woman being presented a book by a man who was kneeling as he did so.

"That is the scribe giving the book to the woman for whom it was made. She was a devout Eastern empress, and she commissioned it hundreds of years ago."

Fox leaned closer and shook his head. "I can't understand the patience it would take to paint this. The brushstrokes are so fine that the page looks like enamel."

When he pulled away, she closed the book, wrapped it in the silk, and replaced it in the *coffret*. "This was passed down to me by my mother and her mother before her. Tonbridge was going to trade it away to an important man in Paris for a kingship."

"A kingship?" That sounded like an odd thing to promise in exchange for a manuscript. Surely no book was worth that, and who would even be able to make such a trade? And what kingship could be appointed? Fox suspected Isabel had her facts wrong. "Do you know this important man's name?"

"No. But I got a short glimpse of the underling who had come to collect the manuscript from Tonbridge. It was to happen the day after our wedding. I couldn't let it leave the family."

Fox nodded. "I have a book my mother left to me. Only death would make me part with it."

As she closed the latches on the box, Isabel said, "What kind of book?"

"It's called the *Secretum philosophorum*, a book on the liberal arts. It also contains riddles, tricks, and arcane knowledge. She knew I would be fascinated by its contents."

"I would like to read that sometime."

"Perhaps I'll let you," Fox said. He looked at the box. "What do you plan to do with your book?"

"My cousin Claire will keep it safe while we think of a long-term plan."

Fox nodded in understanding. "That's why you're going to Paris."

"It's the only way to keep it out of Lord Tonbridge's hands."

"From what you've told me about him, he might want this back as much as he wants you."

"More," Isabel said. "I have no doubt of that."

"Then we must get you to Canterbury as soon as we can. We'll leave at dawn."

"How long will it take?"

"If we keep up a good pace, we should get there in the evening by vespers."

Isabel sighed and nodded, apparently relieved that she would not have to spend another night with him along the way.

"Sir Gerard, I trust you will keep the existence of this book to yourself?"

"Of course, Lady Isabel. Your secret is safe with me."

"Then I will bid you good evening."

From a darkened corner of the hall, Zephyr chuffed and stomped his foot, agitated by something. Fox put his hand out to stop Isabel from moving and cupped a hand to his ear.

Footsteps outside splashed through a puddle, followed by a whispered voice hushing someone.

Isabel looked at him with alarm when she realized what Fox had already guessed. Men were trying to sneak up on the inn.

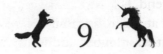 9

Fox slipped on his boots, hastened to his saddle, and drew his sword. He said to Isabel, "Stay inside."

There were only two voices. He pulled the door open and rushed out, his sword at the ready.

The men were twenty paces in front of him, their faces half-lit by the glow of the full moon struggling to get through the dissipating cloud cover. They were soaked from head to toe from the earlier rain shower and looked miserable. But they were also moving stealthily and had knives drawn, not the behavior of men simply looking for shelter on a stormy night.

"Who goes there?" Fox demanded.

The men stopped and looked at each other. The one on the left spoke, his voice weak and raspy.

"My lord, we have lost our way and are looking for temporary lodging. We saw the light from your fire and thought we might warm ourselves."

"Why do you have knives in your hands?"

"It's dangerous in these parts. You never know who you could come across."

That was true enough, but Fox thought there was something strange about them.

"Where are your belongings?" he asked. Neither of them carried so much as a satchel.

"Sire, we have none. We lost them in the storm."

The man on the left stepped forward, and the other followed.

"Hold!" Fox shouted, and they stopped. "Not one more step."

"Sire, we mean you no harm."

"Then put your knives away."

The man nodded at his companion. He slipped the knife into his belt, as did his friend. Fox kept his sword held in front of him.

"Why are you out at this time of night?" he asked.

"Our encampment was flooded and nearly washed us away."

Isabel poked her head out of the door, and that got the attention of the men. The silent one licked his lips.

"Look at them closely," Isabel said. "They're ill."

The clouds had parted, allowing the full moon to illuminate the men. They looked haggard, which was to be expected if one was chased from his sleep by a flood. But there was another reason for their bedraggled appearance.

The man on the right was bleeding from his nose, while the man on the left was shivering uncontrollably. Both men had blackened hands and ears, but not from dirt.

These men were infected with the Pestilence. Fox had seen its ugly effects before—swollen lumps in the neck and groin, fever, chills, vomiting, loosening of the bowels, and blackened noses, ears, hands, and feet, followed by insanity and death, sometimes all in less than a day.

Fox raised his sword higher.

"Stay away from us."

"Sire, please," the leader said pathetically. "We just need a place to lie down and be warm so we can recover our health."

Fox shook his head. "You'll have to move on."

Without a word, the leader drew his knife and rushed at Fox. Fox sidestepped him and slashed the sword across his chest. The man sank to his knees and pitched backward, his dead eyes shining in the moonlight.

Fox stepped away quickly, ready for an assault by the other one, but he didn't move and made no attempt to pull the knife from his belt.

"Do you also wish to die like him?"

He shook his head.

"Then drop your knife on the ground."

He did as he was told.

"Now you must leave," Fox said.

The man hesitated, as if wondering whether he could succeed where his companion had failed.

"Wait," Isabel said. "You can't just send him out into the forest."

Fox didn't take his eyes off the man as he spoke. "I know you mean well, my lady, but this man is not only infected with the Pestilence, but he is also a marauder. We cannot care for him."

"You misunderstand my meaning. If you send him out into the wild, what's to stop him from coming back and attempting to sneak up on us again?"

"You have a point. Are you suggesting I kill him where he stands?"

"I do have some sympathy for his plight. Perhaps there is another solution. Can we barricade him in one of the houses?"

Fox shook his head. "There are too many possible ways he could escape." Then he thought of a building that would be suitable. "The shed where we found the spade. It's small and sturdy."

He instructed the man to head to the church and ensured that he never strayed any closer as he staggered along. Isabel, who was still in her chemise, remained behind in the tavern.

Fox told the man to remove all of the tools from the shed, though he could barely accomplish the task in his weakened state. When he was done, Fox told him to go inside and close the door behind him. Fox drove three spades into the ground and wedged them against the door.

"At least you will be warm and dry here," Fox said. "If you attempt to break through the door, I will hear. Then I will kill you as surely as the sun rises. Do you understand?"

He gave an exhausted "Yes", and Fox didn't think he'd have any more trouble with him.

When Fox got back to the inn, he found Isabel still awake.

"Are we safe?" she asked.

"Yes," Fox replied as he carefully cleaned his sword. "But if it makes you feel more comfortable, I will remain out here the rest of the night."

"Thank you. It will."

As he walked past her to go get his clothes, he saw Isabel

looking at him, her blonde braids spilling out from her coif and shimmering in the dancing firelight. She shyly averted her gaze from him and lay down on her hay pallet before the fire.

Fox got dressed, strapped on his sword, and returned to the main room. He sat with his back against the wall and couldn't sleep, but now for a completely different reason. His gaze kept returning to Isabel's sleeping form across the room. He finally rose and saddled the horses when light was peeking under the inn's front door. While he did so, Isabel woke and took her things into the next room to change into her day clothes.

Fox led the three horses out to the pasture so they could graze. Then he went to release the bandit from his confinement.

Fox knocked on the door. "I intend to release you now. I want no contest from you."

There was no response. Fox leaned closer, but he could hear nothing, not even the man's hoarse breathing.

Fox drew his sword, kicked the spades aside, and yanked the door open. He was met by a rank odor. He knew well the pungent aroma that emanated from the dark interior, which he had experienced during the worst of the Great Mortality. It was a potent combination of sweat, vomit, excrement, and urine.

There was no mistaking the reek of death.

He glanced inside and saw the man lying on his back in a puddle of his own filth, his mouth slack and unbreathing.

Fox was backing away from the sight when Isabel, now dressed, rounded the church with an alarmed look on her face.

"What is it?" Fox asked.

"Armed men on horses are coming," she said. "Three of them."

Farmers or peasants wouldn't be mounted, and merchants would be riding wagons, not horses.

"Lord Tonbridge?" Fox said, instantly regretful that he'd left his bow lashed to Zephyr's saddle.

Isabel shook her head. "I've never seen them before."

Fox couldn't decide if that was better or worse.

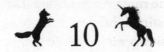

# 10

Fox accompanied Isabel back to the inn as three stout men rode up the main road. They had retrieved the horses from the pasture. One of them was holding the reins to Isabel's palfrey and the horse that had carried the bodies, and another held Zephyr's.

The man in the lead had a neatly shaven goatee and a scar on his brow. He wore a fresh russet tunic and a brown cloak.

He rode up to the body still lying in the middle of the street and stopped. He regarded Fox and Isabel with a steely glint.

"I am Sheriff Roland of Ashford," he said. "This region is under my authority. Who am I addressing?"

Fox didn't hesitate. "I am Sir Geoffrey Dacre, Lord of Elmhurst. This is my wife Lady Winifred."

Isabel bowed.

Roland gestured to the body, noting the bloody slash across the chest. "Can you explain this, Sir Geoffrey?"

"A bandit," Fox said. "He attacked my wife."

Roland dismounted and walked closer to the body.

"I would not approach too closely," Fox warned. "He was stricken by the Pestilence."

Roland stopped abruptly. The other men glanced at each other.

"Was there anyone else with this man?" Roland asked.

"One other," Fox answered. "He is also dead, but from the Pestilence itself. You'll find him in a shed by the church."

Roland nodded to one of his deputies, who handed off Zephyr's reins and rode away in the direction of the church.

"What business do you have in an abandoned town?" Sheriff Roland asked.

"We could not find suitable lodgings before the storm arrived. We made do with the meager accommodations here."

"What is your destination?"

"We intend to visit my family's estates near Rye."

Roland cocked his brow at Fox. "You travel lightly. I do not see any wagons."

"A wagon would only slow our progress."

The deputy returned at a trot.

"He was telling the truth about the bandit," the deputy said. "He is dead of the Pestilence."

Roland nodded. "You have done us a great service, Sir Geoffrey."

"How do you mean?"

"We have been on the hunt for these men. They robbed and killed a family of five on the other side of the county and were witnessed fleeing in this direction. Now that you've dispatched them, we can continue on our way knowing that travelers have nothing more to fear from them."

"There is something else you should know, Sheriff Roland," the deputy said. "There are two freshly covered graves at the church."

Roland raised an eyebrow at Fox. "More people have succumbed to the Pestilence?"

Fox shook his head. He had anticipated this line of questioning.

"Poisoning," he said smoothly. "My squire and Winifred's handmaiden. They were foraging in the woods for food a few days ago and mistook death cap mushrooms for the edible variety. They only began showing the effects once we arrived here."

Roland looked around him. "I see only three horses."

"The marauders chased off the maid's pony," Fox said. "We haven't been able to find it."

The sheriff seemed to believe his answer. "So you are traveling without servants now?"

"We hope to acquire some during our journey."

Roland peered at Fox with a careful eye. "It is against Church law to bury the dead in a churchyard without a priest present, but I will forgive your trespass under these circumstances."

"My thanks," Fox said.

Roland walked over to Zephyr, who tossed his head against the hold of his reins.

"A fine horse," he said. "I don't think I've seen its like." He ran his hand down Zephyr's distinctively curved face.

"It's an Arabian," Fox said. "A descendent of a breed my grandfather's father brought back from the Holy Land."

"Is this also from the Holy Land?" He plucked the double-curved bow from the saddle and weighed it in his hand before running his fingers along the layered wood and inspecting its intricate design. "It's much shorter and lighter than an English war bow."

"It's made for horsemen. It served me quite well at the Battle of Crécy."

That got Roland's attention. "You fought with the king?"

Fox nodded. "His Highness knighted me before our march through France. Crécy was a great victory for our countrymen."

"Indeed, it was." Roland seemed to be only a few years older than Fox, but he said nothing about fighting in the same campaign.

Roland replaced the bow and walked over to Fox. "Now that is a work of art. May I?"

He was speaking about Fox's sword, Legend. Fox would have rather run it through the sheriff than let him handle it, but he had no choice. He nodded and drew the sword from its scabbard to hand it over. The hilt was knurled leather for a better grip, the pommel was decorated with ivory, and the guards tapered into curved ends.

Roland took two swings. "It's well balanced and light." Then he looked more closely at the blade. "What is this swirl pattern in the metal?"

"It's Damascus steel. It holds an edge without dulling."

Roland raised an eyebrow at Fox. "Another acquisition of your forebears from the Holy Land?"

Fox nodded.

"Something wrong with English blades?" said the deputy looming over Fox.

"Or bows, for that matter?" his comrade said.

Fox didn't like their tone. This was turning ugly. His only armament was a dagger he concealed in his tunic. He prepared to throw the dagger at the nearest deputy and charge the sheriff to get his sword.

"Now, men," the sheriff said as he gave back Legend. "This is a knight and war hero. He fights on our side, and I'm all the gladder for it."

Fox relaxed. He was happy not to battle with the local lawmen.

When he got back on his horse, Roland said, "We have some business to tend to in Charing. Fare well and Godspeed, Sir Geoffrey and Lady Winifred."

Fox nodded, and they cantered away.

When they were out of earshot, Isabel turned to him.

"Nicely playcd, *Sir Geoffrey*. We don't want Tonbridge to know we came through here."

"I got the idea from you, *Lady Winifred*," Fox said. "You have commented many, *many* times about how improper it would be for an unmarried lady to travel with a gentleman and no chaperone."

"And the sheriff would obviously agree with me, so don't be too pleased with yourself. Now, it looks as if we will remain married for the day, but we have to come up with a different story for the monks when you leave me at the Canterbury guesthouse."

"We will have plenty of time to consider that while we ride."

Isabel nodded. They loaded their remaining belongings and mounted their horses. As they rode past the marauder's body and out of Ravenswood, Fox realized how lucky it was that they had buried the bodies the evening before. If the sheriff had seen the corpses pierced by crossbow bolts, he and Isabel would have been detained. Then Tonbridge surely would have caught up to them, and the underling of the important man in Paris would have acquired the manuscript he'd come so far to collect.

## 11

PARIS, FRANCE

Morning sunlight streamed through Notre Dame's south Rose Window, playing its rich colors along the walls and floor of the massive cathedral, creating the effect of jewels strewn across the stones. The church had only recently been completed, after more than one hundred years of continuous construction, and Cardinal Dominic Molyneux wondered if the funds would diminish now. He supposed not, as long as worshippers, landowners, and nobility continued to fear for their immortal souls. And for that, he was grateful, for his coffers overflowed from payments they hoped would secure their places in Heaven.

Molyneux's long scarlet robe whispered along the stone floor as he exited the choir. He was met by the commoners who didn't participate in the ritual Mass with the Church elite but rather stood in the central nave. They had been waiting for their hero to appear, and Molyneux didn't intend to disappoint them.

He soaked in the adoration they had for him as he listened to their pleas for a blessing or a kind word. He dispensed coins to the poorest or most infirm and laid his hands on all who wished for his holy touch. None of the other cardinals would deign to consort with this rabble, but Molyneux understood that being popular with the masses was key in his ascendancy to power. And he simply loved being loved.

"Molyneux, a word, if you please," said a reedy voice behind him.

Molyneux sighed. The person interrupting him would have been annoying to speak to at any time, but even more so when he cut short Molyneux's time with the people. He sent the crowd on their way with a prayer and a wave, then turned and smiled.

"What can I do for you, Jouffroy?"

A thin old man with pockmarked skin hobbled up to him. He was wearing the wide-brimmed hat and deep red robe that signified he was also a cardinal. The ancient cleric didn't have Molyneux's regal Gallic nose or strong chin, assets that Molyneux used to his best advantage.

"I want you to cease embarrassing the Church," Jouffroy said.

"I have no idea what you mean."

Jouffroy huffed. "You know exactly what I mean. You are selling your influence for the appointment of Church offices all over England and France and keeping the money for yourself."

"That's quite an accusation, Jouffroy," Molyneux said calmly. "I wouldn't go spreading such rumors if I were you."

"Is that a threat?"

"Not at all. It's your reputation I worry about. It would be a shame if our most senior cardinal were to make baseless claims that sullied his good name when they were not borne out."

"Baseless? I know of three bishops who bought their way into their positions."

"You have proof of this?"

"Not proof as such," Jouffroy admitted, "but these three men are utterly venal, and they were elevated on your recommendation above other priests who deserved the honor. I wonder why."

"Perhaps I know these men better than you do. I would never propose anyone to His Holiness that I didn't take the utmost care to evaluate personally."

That was true. Molyneux had two criteria that were most important in his selections: who had the most money for their "donation" to his vaults and who could keep their mouths sewn shut. The three bishops Jouffroy spoke of could be any one of a dozen men, but whoever they were, Molyneux had no doubt that they would keep quiet for fear of losing their positions.

Growing up as the third son of a minor noble, entering the

priesthood had been the only viable path to a better life for Molyneux. He'd steadily moved up in rank any way he could, whether through charm, bribery, or extortion. Thanks to his methods, Molyneux was now the wealthiest cardinal in the Church and he had the ear of the pope. He'd been carefully amassing influence during the past twenty years, but some of the elders were stubborn and resisted having their allegiance purchased. Jouffroy was the leader of that element.

"I know you crave the papacy," Jouffroy said. "I can assure you that will never happen."

"My ambitions are meager. I only wish to serve."

"Your ambitions are as swollen as your ego. I've heard you making discreet inquiries about the support that you might have amongst the other cardinals. I can tell you it will not be nearly enough, and I find it distasteful that you are even pursuing it while His Holiness still sits on the throne in Avignon palace."

"We all must be prepared for any eventuality," Molyneux said smoothly. "In fact, I hear Pope Clement has taken ill recently. In this awful time, one never knows what the Lord has planned for us."

Most of the highest officers in the Church had survived the horrors of the Great Mortality that decimated France two years ago, primarily by sequestering themselves at the first hint of the disease nearing them. Molyneux himself kept his various châteaus stocked with food stores to withstand weeks of such isolation. He'd seen enough of the scourge's effect to know it was the only thing on this earth that truly terrified him.

"You're just waiting for His Holiness to die," Jouffroy said. "Nothing will make me happier than seeing you voted down at the next Conclave."

*If you survive that long,* Molyneux wanted to say. But what Jouffroy said was true. Although Molyneux had his supporters, it was not yet enough to carry him to victory.

"I'm sure that God will choose the right man," Molyneux said.

"Though in public you put on the airs of a godly and ardent servant of the Church as well as the flock," Jouffroy said, "that is not who you truly are. I seem to be one of the few who know that your devotion is merely for show. I believe you are guilty of all manner of sins, including simony, swearing false oaths, and embracing violence. I find it abhorrent that you introduced Basquin at court."

"He's a trusted adviser."

"He's a brute who leads your private army, and he would carry out your most fiendish wish, if you so ordered it."

"Loyalty should be rewarded, don't you think?"

"Of course he's loyal. He's your bastard. Everyone knows it. I thank the Lord that you never tried making *him* a bishop."

Even if Basquin had wanted a bishopric, which he most certainly did not, Molyneux had more important uses for his son.

"I'm sure all of these insults have a purpose."

"I wanted you to know I'm not the only one who is on to you," Jouffroy said. "It doesn't matter how much money and land you acquire. Unless God appears to us in all His splendor and orders us to choose you, you've gone as far as you can in the Church."

"That is good to know, Jouffroy. I appreciate you taking the time from your busy schedule to inform me. Now, if you'll excuse me, I have other matters to attend to."

He nodded at the old man and walked away, leaving Jouffroy scowling at him. Molyneux wasn't a personally violent man. He preferred to let others do that work when necessary. But he silently prayed that God would see fit to clear his path to glory by ridding him of such irritating obstacles.

Molyneux met his attendant, Father Lambert de Bouzincourt, at the front doors of Notre Dame.

"You saw?" Molyneux asked.

Lambert nodded. "My apologies, Your Eminence. I tried to cut him off, but Cardinal Moretti cornered me in a discussion before I could get to him."

They exited into the sprawling neighborhood of houses and shops built around the cathedral. If he could, Molyneux would remove them so that the grandeur of Notre Dame could be appreciated without having to step through the filth ejected into the streets, but that would hardly help his popularity among the common people.

"What did Cardinal Jouffroy want?" Lambert asked as they walked to Molyneux's personal residence.

"To warn me. He will never vote for me, and he thinks few others will, either."

"You still have time to build your support before Pope Clement's time comes to an end."

"I will have their support. All of them. Even Jouffroy. When I have Lord Tonbridge's manuscript, they won't be able to deny me my proper place in history. How long until his marriage?"

"It is to take place today."

"Then Basquin will return with the manuscript soon."

"Have you decided how to introduce it?"

"Carefully and privately, at least at first. We must make it clear that it is *my* discovery, and mine alone. The nobles will fall in line one by one, as will the cardinals. When I have rallied my support, then I will reveal it to the world. The masses will clamor to see it and revere me for bringing it to them. Then my elevation will be assured."

"You're paying a pretty price to get it," Lambert said.

"If promising to make Tonbridge King of Jerusalem earns me the title of pope, it will be well worth it."

"You can't make him a king unless your crusade is successful."

"You worry too much, Lambert," Molyneux said as they entered his luxurious townhouse, a far cry from the hovels of the people who worshipped him. "Didn't the Holy Lance help us secure a victory at Antioch during the First Crusade?"

"Yes, Your Eminence, but the war—"

"The war between England and France can't last forever. When the nobles on both sides see what is in that manuscript, they will know that God is truly on the Christian side and will fall over themselves to conscript the largest army Europe has ever known."

They entered his private cabinet, and Molyneux took a seat on a velvet chair, his morning refreshment laid out on a table beside him. He picked a bunch of ripe grapes and bit into the sweet fruit.

"I have no doubt that we will wrest the Holy Land from the infidels once and for all," Molyneux said with assurance, "and I will rule a Christian empire that will etch my name in history."

# 12

## Charing, England

Lord Tonbridge and Basquin found the destroyed carriage on the road at midday. The horses, freed of their harnesses and saddles, were grazing in a nearby field. It was lucky they hadn't already been found by robbers. Tonbridge had counted the appropriate number of warhorses, but two of the white coach horses were missing. The slain men had been dragged into the forest. Isabel and her dead attendants were nowhere to be found, renewing Tonbridge's fury at her traitorous escape.

He ordered the twenty men he'd brought with him to split up and search in all directions. Basquin volunteered to go in search on his own, but Tonbridge didn't trust him, sending two of his men to accompany the Frenchman. Tonbridge owned a manor outside of Charing, and they would all rendezvous there at the end of the day to share news of their findings.

When Tonbridge and two of his soldiers arrived in Charing, it was late afternoon. They had searched all day, but hadn't found a trace of the fugitives. Soon the church bells would toll that it was time for vespers. They rode to the center of the village and saw a crowd gathered around a wooden platform.

A man was being placed in a pillory, his hands and head inserted into gaps in the framework. Tonbridge watched from his horse as the locks were latched, holding the criminal in a bent-over but still standing position. Several of the townspeople threw filth from the streets at the prisoner, whose miserable face was soon smeared with mud and worse. A scarred man with a goatee in a russet tunic and brown cloak was standing to the side and addressed the crowd.

"By the power invested in me by King Edward, I, Sheriff

Roland, do hereby sentence Michael of Hobshire to shaming in the pillory until nightfall for the crime of charging an unseemly daily wage. He tried to take more than his fair share in these tumultuous times, and he must now pay the price for violating God's law and taking advantage of his rightful overlord."

The sheriff, satisfied that the crowd had gotten the message, took note of his esteemed visitor and walked over to him.

"Good evening, sire," he said as Tonbridge dismounted. "As you have just heard, I am Roland, the sheriff in this county."

"I am Sir Conrad Harrington, Earl of Tonbridge."

Roland bowed his head. "My apologies, my lord. I did not know you were planning to visit your estate here. I am pleased to make your acquaintance at last. How may I be of service to you?"

"A troubling affair. I believe my betrothed has been abducted by marauders on the road between here and Tonbridge. We are tracking them down and would appreciate any help in their apprehension."

"That is indeed a tragedy," Roland said. "I wish you Godspeed in their capture and the safe return of your betrothed. But the only marauders I have come across recently did not have any woman in their possession, and they are now dead anyway. I maintain a strict code of justice in my jurisdiction."

Tonbridge nodded at the pilloried man. "What about him?"

Roland shook his head. "He is a local laborer who tried to overcharge for his toil. He thought that since there is a labor shortage, what with losing so many in the Great Mortality, that he could charge his landlord an outrageous fee for his work."

"I am glad to see you enforcing the king's authority," Tonbridge said. "The notion that peasants are free to sell their services to the highest bidder is a dangerous one. That might lead to revolts."

"Which is why His Highness was wise enough to begin tamping down such folly," Roland said. "This is an example to others who might be tempted. I don't think we'll have any more problems."

"Have you seen any strangers pass through this area in the last day or so?" Tonbridge asked.

Roland nodded. "As a matter of fact, I did, just this morning."

"Who were they?"

"A knight and his wife who said they were going to visit family in Rye."

"Perhaps this noble couple saw someone while they were on the road," Tonbridge said.

"Perhaps, but they left this morning. I suspect they are long gone by now. I wouldn't want to spend any longer than I had to in Ravenswood. The knight killed one of the marauders I mentioned earlier. The other died of the Pestilence."

"Ravenswood?" Tonbridge said. "The abandoned village?"

"Yes," Roland said. "And now home to four more corpses."

"Four? You said there were two marauders."

"Yes, it was a peculiar business. Sir Geoffrey and his wife lost their servants."

"What do you mean?" Tonbridge asked.

"Their squire and handmaiden. They ate some poisoned mushrooms."

That piqued Tonbridge's interest.

"You saw the corpses?"

Roland shook his head. "I saw no need. They were buried and weren't locals, so I left it."

"Can you describe the couple?"

"They were Sir Geoffrey of Elmhurst and his wife Lady Winifred. He was a large man with brown hair and a beard. She was blonde and quite fetching."

"And their horses. What were they riding?"

"We saw three horses, only two of them saddled. Two of the horses were white, while the gentleman had an unusual courser. He called it an Arabian. I'd never seen its like before. A strong stallion. Mottled silver in color."

Tonbridge felt a thrill arc through his chest at the mention of a lovely blonde woman and two white horses. The sheriff had actually come across Isabel, and now Tonbridge had a chance to find her.

"I think I should speak to Sir Geoffrey," he said. "Should I be able to locate him, can you tell me how to identify him? A notable scar, perhaps?"

Roland considered his description. "The simplest way to recognize him, besides his unusual horse, would be by the weapons he carried."

"How so?"

"He had a hunter's bow from the Holy Land and a sword made of something called Damascus steel. It's the finest blade I have ever held, with an ivory pommel and curved guards. Sir Geoffrey told me that he fought in the Battle of Crécy. I imagine it served him well during that campaign."

Tonbridge would make sure to take possession of this prized sword once he punished the man who helped Isabel escape.

"If we can find him and his wife," he said, "they might be able to share valuable information about my betrothed's whereabouts since they may have traveled the same road she did. Did you see which direction they went?"

"Though Sir Geoffrey said they were headed south to Rye, one of my men reported that he saw them traveling east on the road toward Canterbury."

Tonbridge remounted his horse. "You've done good work here, Roland. I will be sure to put in a word to the Crown on your behalf."

Roland bowed. "Many thanks, my lord. Should you need any more assistance, my deputies and I will be staying at the inn. We will be returning to Ashford in the morning."

Tonbridge rode off toward his manor to rest until Basquin arrived. Roland would not see him again, for Tonbridge expected to be at Canterbury's gates by the time they opened in the morning.

## 13

### Canterbury, England

Isabel and Fox made good time on the road, stopping only for a brief midday meal. The closer they'd gotten to Canterbury, the more pilgrims they'd passed, all of them heading for the Feast of the Translation of Saint Thomas Becket. The martyr was the most venerated saint in all of England, and the annual festival celebrating him brought visitors from all over the country, as well as many who came from Brittany, Normandy, and beyond.

By the time the walls of the city came into view, it was late afternoon, not much time to find lodging before vespers, and the two of them were in a full-throated debate about the details of Becket's murder.

"You are sorely mistaken," Isabel said. "Edward Grim's telling of the assassination of Saint Thomas Becket must be the definitive account. After all, he was injured in the melee."

"But he was no scholar," Fox retorted. "Surely William Fitzstephen, who was a clerk for the archbishop, would know the more complete story."

"Well, I've read both accounts, and if Fitzstephen wanted to be sure of his facts, he should have been in the church that night when the king set his hooligans on the saint."

"King Henry may have been mad at the saint for excommunicating the Archbishop of York, but he did not order anyone to kill the man."

"The king said, 'What miserable drones and traitors have I nurtured and promoted in my household who let their lord be treated with such shameful contempt by a low-born clerk!' That may as well have been an order to the four knights who came over from France and chopped the top of Becket's head off."

"You have amazing power of recall. You're also quite stubborn, do you know that?"

"I do," Isabel said. "That's why I often win my arguments. Like now."

Fox shook his head at her as she continued. "In any case, I'm happy that they translated Saint Thomas's remains to the shrine in July so that we have a feast in summer instead of December when he was killed."

"Lucky for you," Fox said. "It's much easier to travel during this time of year, so you should have no trouble finding travelers to accompany you on your journey to Paris."

As they approached the walls of Canterbury, the richly detailed limestone towers of the cathedral loomed in the distance, delicate yet imposing.

"Are you sure the stabler won't recognize this saddle?" Isabel asked.

Her gown was currently draped over it, hiding it from inspection while she was riding.

"It has no markings specific to Lord Tonbridge," Fox said. "I'll trade it for a saddle more suitable for a lady. You truly want to keep your horse? It's meant for pulling coaches."

Isabel patted the horse's neck. "I've grown accustomed to Comis. She's been a good traveling companion."

Fox was amused she had taken his lead and named her palfrey the Latin word for "friendly".

"And I think she likes Zephyr," Isabel added. "They seem to stick together whenever they graze."

"Perhaps we should give them some solitude to let them court in private," Fox teased.

Isabel just shook her head in mock exasperation.

At the city gates, there was an entry toll, one of the endless taxes assessed on travelers. Every lord, mayor, and bridge owner wanted their share of the bounty that rich visitors could afford, and there was no fighting it. Only the poorest pilgrims were allowed to enter without payment, and they were monitored carefully, to be thrown out of the city for vagrancy if they stayed too long. Rotting bodies strung up on the walls reminded those entering of the penalties for not obeying the law.

Armed guards kept watch from the turrets above as Fox paid the toll. It would raise eyebrows for Isabel to be the one to hand over the coins.

"Where would I find a reputable stabler?" Fox asked the toll clerk. "We also need supplies."

The man appraised Fox and Isabel, probably to take measure of their means.

"You'll want Bertram. He has the best stable in the city. He's at the end of the high street just before the turnoff for the cathedral grounds. Tell him that Charles the tollman sent you."

"And the monastic guesthouses?" Isabel asked. "My sister and her husband are meeting us here today, and they said they would stay at one of the monasteries."

"I'd start with Blackfriars. They have the largest guesthouse for pilgrims besides the cathedral priory, which has been full for almost a week already. North of Bertram's stable."

"Thank you," Isabel said, and they rode into the city. When they were out of earshot, Fox leaned over to her and said, "That was quick thinking on your part."

"It's becoming a habit," she replied, seemingly pleased with herself.

Canterbury was so bustling with activity that the horses had to walk slowly to keep from trampling someone. The city brimmed with merchants, nobles, pilgrims, and church clerics preparing for the principal feast the next day. The wide main street featured every kind of shop imaginable, with stone and wooden buildings two or three stories tall on either side.

Butchers had meat hanging from stalls, tanners displayed their leather wares, importers showed off fabrics and bolts of cloth for sale, and vegetables of all types filled baskets. Purchasers and tradespeople shouted at each other as they haggled over prices. The influx of pilgrims brought wealth to the city despite the famine ravaging many parts of the land as an after-effect of the Great Mortality.

Isabel goggled at everything, taking in each new sight with delight.

"Have you not been to the Feast of Saint Thomas before now?" Fox asked.

"The only city I've visited is Paris," she said, "and that was when I was a child. Have you ever been there?"

"Several times. I've been wandering Europe for some time now."

"Why?"

"It's a long story," Fox said, glad that she had not pursued this line of questioning earlier in their trip. "Sadly, we don't have time for it."

"I have only a vague recollection of Paris. Is it even more magical than this?" As she said that, a shopkeeper tossed a bucket of eel skins into the street in front of her.

"Magic isn't the word I'd use. But it has its wonders."

Isabel positively beamed at the prospect of seeing Paris again, and Fox had no idea why. He always found cities to be crowded, foul, smelly, and expensive. As soon as he had Isabel safely ensconced in the monastery, he would settle her business with the horses and then spend one night before leaving with his fee.

At the end of the high street, Fox saw the stable that the clerk had told them about. A large sign with a painted stallion hung above the main doors, and multiple iron rings for tying up horses were ranged along the front. Bertram knew how to advertise his services.

They turned and were confronted almost immediately with the magnificence of Canterbury Cathedral, which had been obscured by the local buildings until now. Up close, it was even more resplendent, designed to inspire awe by its sheer size. It was adorned with intricate finials, carvings, and sculptures surrounding the massive stained glass windows.

"Our church is but a cottage compared to this," Isabel said.

"You'll soon see it from the inside," Fox said as he looked to the sky. "It won't be long until they ring the bells for vespers. We're fortunate to have arrived before nightfall."

"Why?"

"The guards close the city gates after sundown. No one comes in or goes out."

"How many gates are there?"

"You're a curious lady, aren't you?" Fox said. "I should say seven or thereabouts."

Isabel nodded her head as if she were formulating something in her mind, but Fox didn't probe.

They circled the cathedral grounds, passing the archbishop's stately residence made out of a mosaic of different-sized stones, and headed north until they reached Blackfriars.

The monastic buildings were found on either side of the River Stour. The masonry walls led to a plain wooden door set into a larger gate that would allow horses and carts to pass, the exact opposite of the cathedral's ornamentation.

They dismounted as two monks exited the building.

"Pardon me, brothers," Fox said. "This young lady requires lodging this evening."

The two monks stopped and looked at each other. "We are quite full with pilgrims," the older of the two said.

"I'm sure Lady Isabel will be more than happy to make a generous contribution to your order if that would find her a place here."

The monk eyed Isabel's fine woolen kirtle, but looked in vain for her maid. "That would be a decision made by the guest master."

"Of course," Fox said.

It took some cajoling, but a loosened purse convinced the guest master to clear a private room in the guesthouse for Isabel. Fox made sure she was comfortably lodged with her belongings, including the *coffret* holding the gilded manuscript.

Isabel accompanied Fox back to the main entry as he remounted his horse.

"Your payment," she said. "I still owe you five shillings."

"And I intend to collect. But not until I take care of your horse. I will stop here in the morning before I leave."

Isabel gave Fox a winsome smile that made his heart skip. "Perhaps then I will hear your story."

"I doubt you will enjoy it," Fox said. "It's full of murder, intrigue, and treachery of the worst sort."

"That makes me want to hear it even more."

Fox shook his head in wonderment. "As I said before, you are a curious woman, Lady Isabel."

He turned Zephyr and led the horses away toward the stabler. He had the sense that Isabel was watching him leave, but when he looked back over his shoulder halfway to the cathedral, she was gone.

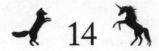

## 14

### CHARING

The light had faded by the time Basquin rode into Charing with his two minders. They had found no sign of Tonbridge's betrothed, and Basquin felt the need for some entertainment to fortify himself before meeting again with that pompous Englishman. If Basquin had to hear one more tirade about the sanctity of family bonds from a man who had been deceived and outwitted by his own intended bride, he might not be able to control his sword. He knew that family bonds could also serve as manacles.

He saw light and smoke rising from the nearby tavern, where he could make out the voices of carousing patrons and the high-pitched laughter of women.

"Ride on to the manor without me," Basquin said to Tonbridge's men. "I'm going to avail myself of some local color. I will see Lord Tonbridge later."

The soldiers looked at each other with concerned expressions.

"Our orders are to stay with you," one of them said.

Basquin sighed. "Where would I go? The manor is a short ride up the east road. It will soon be dark and I need a drink, even if it is swill you English pass off as wine."

"But Lord Tonbridge told us—"

"I have suffered your dull company the entire day. If you don't leave me alone for the evening, I will tell your lord that *you* were the ones who insisted on visiting the tavern instead of returning to the manor. Now go!"

The men knew that Tonbridge would not look kindly on his soldiers drinking when they were supposed to be on duty. They grudgingly turned tail and trotted off toward the manor.

Now that he was alone, Basquin tied up his horse and entered the tavern.

Cresset lamps lit the dim interior, which consisted of three trestle tables, most of which were occupied along their length. He enjoyed the attention of curious faces watching the handsome and clearly wealthy stranger saunter to one of the tables and take a seat. The eyes of every woman in the place were riveted on him, a sensation with which he was familiar.

The keeper came over and appraised the newcomer. "What can I get you?"

"A bottle of your best wine and whatever pottage you are serving this evening," Basquin said in his accented English.

The keeper raised an eyebrow but merely nodded and went back to the kitchen.

Two men in well-made cloaks took note of him as they entertained a couple of women. Another maiden by herself couldn't stop staring at Basquin. He winked at her, beckoning her to him.

The girl giggled and blushed. She walked over and sat across from him.

"Who might you be?" she asked.

"You, my pretty young thing, may call me Basquin," he said.

"I'm Mary. Your accent is funny. Where do you come from?"

Basquin took her hand in his. "I'm just a lonely man passing through on some very important business for some very important people. You wouldn't know how I might be able to find some companionship, would you?"

Mary leaned over the table, revealing a delicious amount of cleavage. "There are always ways to help strangers in need who have coins to spend."

The proprietor returned with the wine and pottage and set them down next to Basquin, who was focused on his next conquest.

The tavern door banged open, and a brawny man burst in while adjusting his tunic. He crossed toward the men in cloaks, then stopped abruptly when he saw Basquin talking to Mary. He wheeled around and stalked over to the table.

"What's this?" he said, glaring at Mary. His words were slurred from too much drink. "I leave to take a piss and come back to find you slobbering over this fool?"

"I was just talking to him while you were gone, Rafe."

"She obviously prefers to be with someone who doesn't make her sick to look at," Basquin said.

Rafe snickered. "You're not even English. I know a French accent when I hear it."

"Then you're not quite as stupid as you are ugly. Now leave us be." Basquin waved him away like he was an annoying gnat.

Mary tittered at Basquin's casual dismissal, which made her former suitor irate.

"Do you know who I am?"

"Yes," Basquin said, tired of the English arrogance he had encountered since landing at Dover. "You are the pest who is trying to spoil my evening. Now fly away or I shall have to teach you a lesson."

Rafe leaned down, putting both of his hands on the table. His foul breath puffed in Basquin's face. "Teach me, you French bastard."

If Rafe had called him any other name, Basquin might have tempered his reaction. But being reminded that he was in fact a lowly bastard, especially by an Englishman, enraged him.

Basquin reached forward, grabbed Rafe by the hair, and slammed his face into the table. Mary screamed and leaped off her stool to back away.

Rafe rose with a bent nose and a cut on his brow. He shook his head to clear it, then snarled like a mad dog. In his drunken state, he made the mistake of pulling out his knife and brandishing it in front of Basquin.

"I'll cut you for that, swine."

That was all the threat Basquin needed to hear. He drew the dagger from his scabbard with lightning speed and jabbed it through Rafe's chin.

As Rafe choked on his own blood, his two companions jumped

from their seats. Everyone else in the tavern went silent. Basquin withdrew the dagger, and Rafe slid to the floor.

"This doesn't concern you," Basquin warned the other two as he casually wiped the blade clean on Rafe's hose and resheathed it.

"I'm afraid it does," said the one with the scar on his face. "I'm Sheriff Roland, and you've just killed one of my deputies."

"You should control your dogs better, Sheriff."

Roland drew his sword. The remaining deputy did the same and circled around to flank Basquin. The other patrons edged to the far corners of the room.

"Drop your weapons," Roland said.

"You cannot touch me. I am a representative of Cardinal Molyneux. I can show you my writ of safe conduct."

"That doesn't apply to murderers. There will be justice in my jurisdiction."

"Only the Church has a right to judge me," Basquin said. "You are making a very grave error."

Roland nodded at his deputy, who charged toward Basquin. Basquin drew his sword and deftly parried the deputy's blow. With the same continuous motion, he slashed the man from belly to throat.

Even as the deputy fell dead, Roland crossed the distance in an attempt to surprise Basquin while he was distracted. He brought his broadsword down in what should have been a killing blow, but Basquin somersaulted over the table to evade it.

Roland was a large man, but Basquin was faster and more agile. He knocked aside each thrust and swing of the broadsword with patience as he waited for his opening to strike back. He quickly got a sense for Roland's fighting style. The sheriff's technique was adequate, but he depended far too much on brute force in the hope of wearing down his opponent.

Finally, Basquin bored of the minimal challenge. He waited for Roland's next swing, stepped out of the way as the sheriff's blow met nothing but air, and thrust his sword into Roland's gut, running him through.

When Basquin pulled out the sword, Roland went to his knees holding his stomach. His mouth moved, but no words came out.

At the same time, Lord Tonbridge marched in with the two soldiers whom Basquin had dismissed. The earl was just in time to watch Sheriff Roland pitch onto the floor and breathe his last.

"What the devil has happened here?" Tonbridge demanded in disbelief as he surveyed the carnage.

Basquin cleaned his sword on the sheriff's tunic and said, "We had a disagreement."

Tonbridge was apoplectic. "A disagreement? Do you realize what you've done?"

"Of course. The sheriff no longer disagrees with me."

Basquin could see that Tonbridge wasn't satisfied with his attempt at humor. As much as he abhorred doing it, he had to placate the earl to keep this incident quiet.

"Perhaps you're right," Basquin added with a nod. "This distracts from our mission. I won't let it happen again."

Tonbridge glanced around at the mute patrons.

"If anyone here breathes a word of what happened in this tavern tonight," he hissed, "I will know of it, and every single one of you will pay the consequences. Now go!"

All of them scrambled to make an exit. They would be eager enough to forget the evening's events in the face of their lord's wrath.

When they were alone, Tonbridge turned to his men-at-arms. "I told you specifically not to leave him alone, and now look what's happened. Take these bodies out to the forest and make it look like they were ambushed by bandits. Quickly!"

The chastened men began carrying the corpses outside, starting with the sheriff's.

"I'm still famished," Basquin said. He sat at the table, poured himself some wine from the bottle that remained upright despite his tumble across the table, and calmly began to eat.

"By all means, enjoy the rest of your meal," Tonbridge said in a mocking tone before turning serious. "But do it quickly. With the moon out, it is bright enough to ride. We leave for Canterbury at midnight."

"Canterbury?"

"Thankfully, I was able to speak to Roland before you got to him." Tonbridge explained about the traveling woman who fit Isabel's description and the man calling himself Sir Geoffrey of Elmhurst who owned the unusual weapons.

When Tonbridge mentioned the Damascus steel sword, Basquin sat straighter and whispered, "Legend."

"What's that?" Tonbridge asked.

"Damascus steel is quite rare and expensive. Blades made from it never shatter and hold their edges even after a pitched battle. I've only ever seen one in my entire life. That and Roland's description of the horse confirm the man's identity."

Tonbridge was shocked by the admission. "You know him?"

Basquin nodded. "I first suspected it when I recognized the uncommon fletching of the arrows in your soldier at Tonbridge. Only one person I know uses arrows with that design *and* owns a Damascus steel sword. His name is not Sir Geoffrey of Elmhurst. It's actually Sir Gerard of Oakhurst, otherwise known as Gerard Fox."

"I'm aware of Fox's fall from grace," Tonbridge said. "But why would he come to my castle?"

"He must think you know the truth about my mother Emmeline," Basquin said without a trace of emotion. "*Our* mother, I should say. Gerard Fox is my brother."

# 15

## CANTERBURY

By the time Fox returned to Bertram's stable, crowds of pilgrims were filing toward the cathedral for vespers while shopkeepers packed away their wares for the evening. He dismounted at the front gate and walked the horses inside.

There was a central courtyard surrounded by stalls on three sides, nearly every one occupied. The fourth side was reserved for the common rooms and the keeper's residence. A balcony ran around the second level where rooms for the inn were located. Grooms were busy feeding the horses and mucking out the stalls.

An older gentleman shuffled over to Fox, shouting orders to the workers as he walked.

"Oy! Rub down the wool merchant's saddle with oil like he asked. And see that the blacksmith stops by with new shoes for that carthorse." He stopped in front of Fox and regarded him with a curt nod. "Sire, how can I be of service?"

"You must be Bertram. I'm in need of lodging for me and my horses."

"I am Bertram, and as you can see, I'm short of room. Now that the Great Mortality has done its worst, there are more pilgrims here than ever for the Feast of Saint Thomas to give thanks for their deliverance and pray for continued health. Not even the war has stopped visitors coming over from the Continent."

Fox partially pushed aside his mantle and took some coins from the leather purse he kept securely underneath. "Would this be enough to free some space in your fine establishment tonight? Charles the tollman said this was the best stable in the city."

Bertram eyed the coins, and then Fox. "Not quite enough, but I might be able to find some for another half shilling."

Fox smiled. "You drive a hard bargain, but I accept."

He handed over the money.

"Most of this will go to taxes," Bertram grumbled.

"I've already paid some just to enter the city."

"And you'll pay more, believe you me. I wouldn't mind it so much if it went to things we need around here, but I fear the fees are mostly gilding the homes of the city officials. And we have a war going on. The French could invade any day, and the city walls are crumbling from neglect. There are holes big enough to ride a *destrier* through."

Surely the stabler exaggerated, but Fox didn't have time to listen to his problems.

"It's a scandal," Fox agreed. "Which is why I am in need of some funds." He nodded to the horse they'd used to carry the bodies. "I would be willing to sell you that rouncy for a good price."

Instead, Bertram gazed with admiration at Zephyr. "How much for this one?"

"He's not for sale."

"It's a rare breed by the look of it. I'd give you an excellent price."

"I'm sure you would. I'm not interested. What about the other one?"

Bertram nodded. "We can talk price, but I need to leave for vespers. We'll bargain in the morning." He waved for a groom to take the horses to their stalls. Fox removed his sword, bow, arrow bag, scrip holding his extra clothes and personal effects, and the leather pouch containing his book before they were led away. "I have a locked trunk where you can store those."

"And a bed for me?"

"All the beds are taken. But I will see an innkeeper at the cathedral who may still have space for you. I can arrange for you to speak to him there."

Fox hesitated. He hadn't set foot in a church in four years. Not since the day Cardinal Molyneux came to visit his father's estate and changed their lives forever.

"You can sleep with the horses if you'd rather," Bertram said.

"An inn would be preferable," Fox said.

They walked over to a huge trunk chained to the wall. Bertram unlocked it, and Fox placed his possessions inside. He would have liked to carry Legend with him, but a weapon of war wasn't allowed to stay on his person inside the city walls, let alone the cathedral.

When the trunk was locked, Bertram put the key in the purse at his waist along with Fox's payment. It appeared to be near bursting with coins.

When he noticed Fox looking, he closed the purse and said, "My yearly tithe. I always present it on the eve of the festival to avoid the crowds at the shrine during the feast."

Fox thought the old man was brave to venture out with such a princely sum until Bertram waved over the two largest grooms, their bulging muscles still running with sweat. They were to be his guards during the walk to the cathedral.

The four of them joined the throngs of pilgrims. Fox felt an odd unease about the prospect of entering a cathedral. The absence of the ritual and guilt over missing the liturgy had gnawed at him despite his anger at the Church for ruining his future. Even during the military campaign in France, he'd made sure to attend Mass at least once a week besides the daily offices he'd said on his own. Now he worried that lightning might strike him from the heavens when he stepped across the threshold, in retribution for his sacrilege at entering the holy precincts.

As they approached the cathedral's towering stone façade, Fox briefly considered telling the stabler that he would wait outside, but that would raise more questions than he would have answers for. When they reached the huge wooden doors that had been thrown open, Fox took a deep breath and went inside.

The soaring nave was crammed with townspeople, peasants, and pilgrims all the way to the choir screen. Beyond that was the choir and the altar, where the most important Church leaders, monks, and priests would chant the service and receive communion. Due to the importance of the occasion, hundreds of beeswax candles lit the dim interior, supplemented by the meager twilight straining to get through the stained glass windows. Despite the faint lighting, the brightly painted statues and banners were a feast for the eyes. The magnificent shrine of Thomas Becket could just be glimpsed by peering through the choir screen, and tomorrow people from across Christendom would line up for hours to file past the tomb and pray at the gilded coffin. The cavernous room echoed with the Latin prayers that were chanted by the cathedral's monks for vespers.

A long queue of people stretched from a set of stairs to the left that led down to a vestibule below.

"You can wait here if you want to get blessed where Saint Thomas was martyred," Bertram said.

"Perhaps tomorrow," Fox said.

They pressed on through the masses crowding toward the choir screen, and the smell from such a horde in an enclosed space was nearly overpowering. Walking through the packed cathedral was like threading a loom. Fox felt decidedly uncomfortable for many reasons, but at least he wouldn't be expected to take communion, which the laity only received once a year, usually around Easter. On crowded festival days such as this, commoners were lucky if they could see the elevation of the Host.

"The innkeeper is that way," Bertram said, pointing toward the choir screen. "Roger always likes to be at the front."

As they pushed their way forward, Fox was jostled by a blond boy whose beard had not yet begun to grow. He immediately realized that it was no accident.

Cutpurses enjoyed hunting in crowded situations like this, especially inside a church during one of the best-attended events of the year when rich out-of-town pilgrims were the most unwary. He'd seen them operating many times. Fear of God's wrath counted for little when so much coin-laden prey was about.

With Fox's purse protected by his mantle, any searching hands would have found nothing to acquire. But Fox knew Bertram hadn't been as prudent.

Fox turned just in time to see the boy slice through the tie on Bertram's purse with a small sharp knife as he shoved the stabler with his shoulder. The cutpurse expertly caught the pouch and passed it off to a red-haired boy. His accomplice.

Bertram noticed the loss of his purse immediately.

"Thief!" he cried, and pointed out the culprit to his large grooms, who snatched the blond boy before he could squirm away.

But Fox had his eye on the redhead and was already fighting his way toward the exit.

Behind him, Fox could hear the blond one protesting that he was innocent and that his accusers could search him if they pleased.

By that time, the redhead was exiting through the church doors. The pouch he was carrying held not only the stabler's annual donation to the Church but also the key to the lockbox holding Fox's possessions. If the boy disappeared from view, the purse was as good as gone.

Fox sprinted after him.

# 16

The redheaded boy was quick, but Fox kept him in sight as they dashed through the city streets, and with his long strides, he was closing the distance. The boy saw that he was being followed, but he couldn't shake Fox. He veered down a narrow alley.

Fox rounded the corner in time to see the thief disappear into the shadows of a seemingly dead end. Fox ran to it and saw that there was a gap between buildings barely wide enough for a man turned sideways. If he hadn't seen the boy duck into it, Fox might have thought he had gone into one of the doors.

Fox squeezed through and raced after the pounding footsteps, catching sight of red hair momentarily before each turn through the maze of the city.

He had entered yet another alley when he was confronted by the boy, who had stopped running. This time, the alley really was a dead end with no doors. Next to the redhead were three other boys, including the blond one who had snatched the stabler's purse. He must have escaped Bertram's grooms and taken a shortcut to arrive here so quickly.

None of them were more than three-quarters Fox's height or age. They looked like serfs who had gotten sick of tilling fields and found a better way to find money, and they seemed experienced at their trade. They wore bold expressions, for all of them held small daggers.

"Best you leave now if you know what's good for you," the redhead said.

"Listen to John," the blond cutpurse said. "You may be big, but we'll cut you for sure."

"No, you won't," Fox said.

"Walter's right," John said. "We don't give up our bounty for none, and you're not the first to try to take it."

"Just give me that purse back and I'll leave you in peace."

The four boys laughed.

"Or what?" John asked. "You'll go get the sheriff? We'll be long gone."

Fox shook his head, his arms hanging loose but ready at his sides. "Don't need the sheriff for help with four little boys like you."

They stopped laughing.

Walter came next to John and brandished his blade, which was shorter than Fox's longest finger. "Are you asking to get that pretty face of yours carved up?"

It was clear these boys wouldn't be intimidated by his age or size. They edged closer in a threatening gesture, but Fox didn't move, keeping his eyes on Walter, who seemed the most experienced with a knife even though John seemed to be the leader. The other two were a little younger, but they would certainly join in if their friends attacked.

Fox leaned forward as if he were about to say something, but he was done talking. He unleashed his fist on John the redhead, and it smashed the boy square in the nose, sending a torrent of blood gushing down.

The momentum of his lean let him strike with his opposite leg, giving a mighty kick to Walter's groin. The boy screamed and dropped his knife to hold on to his most precious possessions.

John made a half-hearted effort to stab Fox, but Fox grabbed his wrist and wrenched the blade from his hand. Fox kneed him in the stomach to take the rest of the fight out of him, and the boy collapsed to the ground.

The ruffians behind had no way to escape past Fox, and seeing how easily he had disarmed their comrades, they dropped their knives without a fight.

Fox reached down and took the stabler's purse from John's belt.

"I'll be taking the rest of your ill-gotten gains as well," Fox said.

The boys hesitated and looked at each other.

"That's all we have," Walter said, coughing and still bent over in pain.

"If you wish to have children someday, you'll want to rethink that notion. My boot can take a lot of punishment. More than any of your privates can, I imagine."

Reluctantly, the boys fished beneath their tunics and withdrew three other purses they'd collected that day. He could see them sizing up their chances with a distraction, so Fox headed off those thoughts.

"Toss them on the ground by my feet," he said. "Anywhere else and I'll see what this knife can do."

They did as he ordered, and Fox kept an eye on them as he bent to pick them up. All of the boys had dejected looks on their faces.

"Don't be so put out," Fox said. "You're not the first thieves I've cornered."

In fact, Fox had found that confiscating cutpurses' spoils provided a useful source of income when he was low on funds in a city.

When he had the purses stowed, Fox said, "You'll be wanting to leave Canterbury before they close the gates. I'll make sure the local watch is on the lookout for a redhead with a bent nose and his friends."

As the boys watched, seething at him, Fox backed out of the alley. It wouldn't be surprising if they regained some courage and attempted to get their coins back.

But as soon as they were no longer hemmed in, the boys took off toward the city gates. They'd seen enough of Fox's skill as a fighter.

When he returned to the cathedral, he found Bertram outside reporting his loss to the local officer. Fox handed him the stolen purse.

"You'll find every coin still inside," Fox said.

Bertram stared at him for a moment, wide-eyed, before he gushed his thanks. "Fair friend! I never thought I'd see this purse again! You are a true hero and gentleman."

Fox acknowledged the praise with a nod.

The officer went on his way, and Bertram gave Fox a grand smile. "The innkeeper was full, but no matter. You will be a guest in my home tonight. My wife tapped a barrel of fresh ale this morning and we have a fatty ham hock for supper."

"You're too kind," Fox said. "But I accept your gracious offer."

"Not at all, dear sir. After I complete my tithe, I want to hear all about how you captured the thief. Excuse me for a moment."

He returned to the church to make his donation. Fox was relieved that he wouldn't have to go back inside the cathedral. When Bertram returned, he put a friendly hand on Fox's shoulder to guide him back to the stable.

As they walked, Bertram showed off his new best friend like a prized steer to every acquaintance they passed and boasted that Fox was his personal savior. He wondered how the stabler would feel if he knew he was consorting with someone the Church had excommunicated and that Fox's crime was so severe that absolution could only be dispensed by the pope himself.

## 17

OAKHURST, ENGLAND

Although the journey to Fox's family estate south of London was less than ten miles, it was tricky to navigate the correct roads to reach it. Fox had been sent by his father to greet Cardinal Molyneux and guide his entourage to their estate.

The morning was overcast but warm, heralding a pleasant autumn. He was riding at the head of an impressive train of guards, clerks, and grooms, all of whom surrounded the most elegant carriage Fox had ever seen, which conveyed the cardinal himself.

The leader of Molyneux's retinue was a young blond man, though he carried himself with the assurance and experience of someone more worldly. His name was Basquin, and he rode beside Fox.

"Is all this land yours?" Basquin asked in French, waving his hand at the tracts of farmland around them.

"My father's, yes," Fox answered.

"But someday it will belong to you."

"I hope not for a long while."

"Are you the oldest son?"

"I am now. My brother is buried in France."

Basquin regarded him anew. "During the invasion? Then you must have fought at the Battle of Crécy."

"Does that bother you?"

"Not at all. I fought there as well."

"Without success. We slaughtered the French."

Basquin shrugged as if it had simply been an inconvenience. "Our leaders were fools. The Genoese crossbowmen were no match for your archers. We should have lured you onto more favorable ground."

Fox was surprised to hear Basquin speak so critically of his side's tactics, since the army was led by King Philip himself.

"Although we suffered mighty losses," Basquin continued, "I understand the English did have a few of their own casualties. Was that how your brother died?"

Fox's stomach tightened at the memory. "He took down half a dozen French knights before he was slashed from behind by a coward."

"That must have been terrible."

Fox was offended by Basquin's casual tone, but said nothing.

Basquin added, "Even though our countries are at war, honorable men such as ourselves don't need to be enemies."

"I don't think you'd be so well-received if you weren't representing the pope on this visit."

"Traveling with a cardinal does make it easier to tour England. We're still all Christians, bound by our devotion to the Church. I notice that you speak French without an English accent."

"We have property in Normandy," Fox said. "My mother was French."

"See there," Basquin said with a smile. "We have more in common than you knew." He looked ahead at the manor coming into view. "That must be your fine home."

Fox didn't trust the glib tone, so he was happy to be done with their journey. "Caldecott Mote. It's been in my family for seven generations."

The square stone manor with a dozen chimneys springing from the red-tiled roof was surrounded on all sides by a deep moat. A stone bridge, Caldecott Mote's only entrance, crossed to an archway where a portcullis could be lowered for defense. Today it was raised, and two guards stood at attention on either side of the gate. Pennants displaying the family arms of a rampant fox on a field of green waved in the breeze.

Fox led the entourage through the arch and into the large central courtyard. The estate's staff and men-at-arms were lined up at the far end. In front of them stood a tall man with dark, silver-flecked hair and a strong jaw. He was dressed in a fine wool cotehardie.

Fox dismounted with Basquin beside him and said, "Father, this is Cardinal Molyneux's representative, Basquin." To Basquin, he said, "My father, Sir Richard Fox, Lord of Oakhurst."

Basquin bowed. "My pleasure, Sir Richard. His Eminence has been enjoying the tour of this region, but he's been especially keen to see you again. I understand your first meeting happened before I was even born."

Fox's father had mentioned that he and Emmeline met Molyneux at Château de Beaujoie when Fox was just a child.

"I am honored that His Eminence remembers me from so long ago," Richard said in a deep baritone. "But I am surprised he is paying a most welcome visit to my humble home when there are wealthier landholders who can donate greater funds to construction of the pope's palace in Avignon."

"Do I detect a reluctance to contribute to such a grand project?"

"Not at all. I look forward to doing what I can to help."

"That is wonderful to hear," Basquin said. "I'm sure His Eminence will be pleased."

The carriage came to a stop in front of them. When Fox had arrived in London for the rendezvous, Molyneux was already in his carriage, so this was his first chance to see the cardinal. One of the grooms placed a step stool in front of the rear door before opening it. When everyone and everything was in place, the door was opened, and Cardinal Molyneux exited the coach gracefully. He was resplendent in scarlet robes and broad-brimmed hat, looking as refreshed as if he had been lounging in a salon instead of being jolted over rutted dirt lanes. He regarded his surroundings with steely eyes.

When Basquin went to his side, Fox noted a remarkable similarity between the two men. The same blond hair, the same Roman nose, the same piercing gaze.

Molyneux inspected Fox from head to toe. "I do see the resemblance," he said in a cryptic aside to Basquin. He held out his right hand, gloved and studded with gold and jewel-encrusted rings. "Sir Richard."

Fox's father stepped forward and kneeled, the signal for the Fox household far behind them to do the same. Richard was to kiss Molyneux's ring, the expected greeting when meeting a cardinal.

Richard leaned over to kiss it but stopped before his lips touched. Instead, Fox was surprised when he stood without completing the obeisance. Fox got to his feet as well.

"Where did you get that?" Richard said, pointing at the ring worn at the knuckle of the cardinal's middle finger. It was a gold band in the form of a hand holding a heart-shaped ruby.

"How dare you speak so rudely to the cardinal," Basquin said, although his offended tone seemed feigned to Fox. It was almost as if Basquin had been expecting the question.

"Perhaps we should discuss this inside," Molyneux said.

Richard's eyes seemed to be boiling. "It's a simple question."

Fox had no idea why his father was so incensed, but it immediately caused his muscles to tense, ready for action.

Molyneux looked at the men around the edges of the courtyard. He spoke loudly so they could hear. "Are you having second thoughts about your contribution to the Church?"

To Fox's astonishment, Richard leaned toward him and growled, "I want to know how you came to be in possession of a ring that I gave my wife. Emmeline was wearing it the last time I saw her."

"Lady Emmeline," Molyneux said wistfully in a lowered voice. "She was a beautiful woman, wasn't she?"

"You remember my mother?" Fox said, speaking out of turn.

"Boy, I knew your mother well. So well in fact that you stand next to your only living brother."

Basquin smiled broadly at the revelation. For a moment, the shock was so complete that neither Fox nor his father could say a word.

"I knew she wasn't slain by marauders on her journey back here from Normandy," Richard finally said.

"It was a crude but believable lie that allowed me to keep her as my companion," Molyneux said. "As soon as I saw her again, I knew I had to have her. I was so sad when she died in childbirth. So many lost years together."

Fox spluttered at the brazen infamy of what Molyneux had revealed. Such an atrocity was a scandal that could hardly be believed. He wanted to rip the cardinal's head off.

Richard bared his teeth like a snarling lion. "You will be defrocked for this."

"By His Holiness?" Molyneux said easily. "I think not. After all, who is the pope going to trust? A minor noble from England or one of his most beloved French cardinals?"

Fox balled his fists, his fury boiling at hearing how his mother had been taken from him.

"I know my Emmeline," Richard said. "She would have done everything she could to get back to me. You had to have kept her prisoner."

"Only until she understood that it was in her best interest to stay with me. Once she knew she was with child, returning to you would have brought great dishonor to your house, don't you agree?"

"You think you can get away with this?"

"Fair sir, I already have. And there is nothing you can do about it."

"Why reveal this to me after all these years? Just to be cruel?"

"I thought you should finally know that your wife found more comfort in my bed than she did in yours."

Molyneux's gloating and vulgarity was finally too much to take for Fox. All the years of resentment for growing up without his mother, and the truth was that she had been stolen from him by someone who should have been her spiritual protector.

Fox couldn't help himself. In his all-consuming anger, he launched himself at the smug cardinal, ready to beat him senseless no matter the cost to him. He grabbed Molyneux's robes, but before he could strike, Richard rushed over to push them apart. The cardinal stumbled backward with an astonished look on his face.

Fox was so inflamed that he charged forward again, but Basquin kicked him in the stomach, sending Fox to his knees. Fox grabbed the hilt of his sword, but before he could draw it, Basquin held a dagger to his throat, his eyes glittering in delight at the turn of events. Fox let go of the sword and stood up until they were eye to eye.

"You're a disgrace," Molyneux snapped at him in disgust as he composed himself.

The Fox men-at-arms and the cardinal's guards advanced on each other, preparing for battle.

In a flash, Fox's father drew his knife and put it under Basquin's chin.

"Hold right there," Richard said.

"You move well for an old man," Basquin said in appreciation.

"Let my son go or I will slice you open from ear to ear."

Basquin looked at the cardinal, who nodded. Basquin released Fox, and Richard released Molyneux's bastard son.

Fox was disgusted by how pleased Molyneux and Basquin seemed to be with the response their revelation had produced.

"I will kill you for this," he spat at them.

"Quiet, Gerard," Richard said, pulling Fox back.

The men on both sides halted when they saw Richard and Fox retreat.

"You all saw what happened!" Molyneux called out. "These Englishmen attacked a representative of the Holy See. He threatened to kill me. An attack on one of us is an assault on the entire Church."

He turned to face Richard and Fox. "I should have you both hanged. But as you did not actually cause me harm, the proper punishment is banishment from the rites of the Church. With the witnesses I have to your misconduct, I will have both of you excommunicated and your land confiscated. I'm sure the Church will find better uses for the property." He glanced pointedly at Basquin.

As the cardinal returned to his carriage, Basquin backed away slowly, his hand on his sword.

"We'll meet again someday, brother," he said.

"You had better hope we don't," Fox replied.

All of the family soldiers stayed ready to fight until the last horse left the manor.

Fox was outraged watching them depart unpunished. "You can't simply let them go!"

"What would you have me do?" Richard replied. "Hunt down and slay an emissary of the Church?"

"If that's what it takes!"

"And to what purpose? So that my only remaining son is executed?"

"Molyneux took Mother from us! He violated her!"

"Don't you think that destroys me?" Richard yelled back. "She was my love!" He opened his mouth to say more, but no words came. He swallowed hard, choking back his emotions. His face transformed from frenzied rage to profound anguish.

"And now Molyneux's admission has provoked exactly the reaction he hoped it would. He has all the evidence he needs to expel us."

Fox realized that their plight was the result of his reckless act. It felt as if his heart had been torn from his chest.

"I'm sorry, Father. I shouldn't have been so rash."

"It's not your fault, Gerard. If I had been younger and bolder, I would have killed him where he stood."

"But it *is* my fault that Molyneux now has the excuse to excommunicate us."

The gravity of the situation was only now hitting Fox. To be banished from the Church was a ruinous event. Even their close friends and family would consider them pariahs. They would lose their titles and lands. Even worse were the spiritual implications. By not being allowed to take the sacraments and facing a burial in unconsecrated ground, their souls would be damned. He thought of the images he had seen in church of bodies being tortured by demons and burned in hellfire, and he felt a shiver of terror run down his back. Unless they could somehow stave off the coming excommunication, life as they knew it was essentially over and an eternity of damnation awaited them.

"Clearly, that was Molyneux's plan all along," Richard said. "If he hadn't provoked you, he would have found another way to justify it."

"But we will be cast out of the Church! Everyone will treat us like lepers. And now he no doubt plans to hand over our lands to Basquin."

"Unless we can find proof that he kept your mother against her will."

"There must be someone who can testify to his crime," Fox said. "I will make it my mission to find them and bring them all the way to Avignon. The pope will have to rule in our favor."

Richard looked at Fox with a mix of pride and resignation.

"I admire your spirit, but you're not yet old enough to appreciate the way the world works. There is no more powerful organization on this earth than the Church. We can try to fight them, but it will be a long and bloody combat, and the odds are against us."

"That's what we were told at Crécy. We won."

"But at great cost to us," Richard said, shaking his head. "And that is our cross to bear."

His father was right. Losing James was a high price for victory, and now they had an even more daunting battle in front of them.

## 18

*July, 1351*

### CANTERBURY

After riding through the night, aided by a nearly full moon, Lord Tonbridge was exhausted, but when he spied Canterbury Cathedral's towers backlit by the rising sun, he felt newly invigorated. The main gate was teeming with farmers and merchants eager to enter the city to market their wares for the festival taking place that day. It only made sense that his betrothed had sought out the anonymity of this crowded city to hide herself, and he was more sure than ever that he would find her here.

First they checked Canterbury's only nunnery, which was outside the city walls. They found no trace of Isabel there and kept going toward the city gate.

"If she is in Canterbury, we cannot let her escape," he said to Basquin, who was riding beside him. Infuriatingly, the young Frenchman seemed as fresh as he had been when they'd set forth from Tonbridge Castle the day before.

"Will the local officials aid us in our search?" Basquin asked.

"I don't want their involvement and risk them discovering the manuscript, but I will tell them we are pursuing a fugitive, which will allow us to remain armed in the city. In any case, they don't know who to look for."

"Neither do I. I got only a brief glimpse of her and her handmaid leaving in their carriage when I arrived at your castle."

"You'll have my soldiers. They'll recognize her. Although she is willful, Isabel is also clever. She could be dressed in commoners' clothing."

"They should be aware that she may be in the company of a man."

Tonbridge nodded. "I've passed along your description of him and his unusual weapons."

"He's quite dangerous."

"I've shared that knowledge with my soldiers as well. They will not be surprised this time."

"You have twenty men," Basquin said. "That's enough to put two at every gate and still leave six to help us search the city. How shall we divide our efforts?"

"I will take two men and inquire at every inn and monastic guesthouse in the city," Tonbridge said. "If she is here, she will be staying at one of them. You take the rest of the men and split yourselves between the market and the cathedral."

"Do you want them alive?"

"Gerard Fox? No. I most certainly want him dead for his actions against me. It sounds like you'll be willing to carry out that task."

"I'll do whatever is required, and that's all you need to know," Basquin said testily. "What about your betrothed?"

Tonbridge thought about Isabel. She was a beautiful woman, one who might bear him handsome sons, but given her actions thus far, she would no doubt be troublesome from this point to her last breath. Isabel needed to be punished by his own hand for her disloyalty.

"Bring her to me unharmed," Tonbridge said. "If she does not have the manuscript in her possession when you find her, I will thrash its location out of her."

The night in the care of Bertram was pleasantly spent for Fox, although he did have to endure the stabler's constant and insistent praise for the recovery of his money. His actions also produced a healthy price for the horse he sold, so he had little to complain about. However, to avoid a morning bout of adulation, Fox decided to slip out of the house before the stabler arose.

His destination was the market, the perfect place to acquire supplies for his upcoming journey. The newfound funds from the cutpurses gave him more than enough money to fully outfit himself for a fortnight of travel.

He wandered through the crowded square that served as the center of the festival, passing all manner of entertainers—jugglers, musicians, storytellers, and acrobats. Spectators were gathered around pens cheering bouts of cock fighting and bear baiting, but Fox didn't partake of those types of brutal exhibitions. Although there seemed to be plenty of food for people with means, starving beggars who looked like little more than walking skeletons pestered anyone who passed for extra morsels. Fox was generous in handing out coins to them from the cutpurses' takings.

Most of the people spoke English, but Fox also heard pilgrims conversing in French, Flemish, Breton, Walloon, and a host of other languages. Blacksmiths hammering on anvils, goats and sheep bleating nonstop, and hawkers shouting about their goods added to the cacophony. The scent of newly baked bread and brewing ale mixed with the less savory odors of animal dung and butcher's offal. Colorful fabrics in silk, wool, and linen fluttered in the breeze.

Fox bought a bunch of carrots, amused as always that the purple color of this lowly root was the same favored by royalty. Most kings and queens didn't realize that they were obsessed with a dye made possible only by crushing snails in the ancient Holy Land city of Tyre, a process Fox had read about. All they knew was that the pigment was worth its weight in gold. Of course, different and less expensive colorants could be used to dye wool, but purple's association with power and wealth was well established.

He chewed on the decidedly non-royal carrots while he walked and bargained to fill his bag with salted meat, fresh vegetables, rye bread, a waterskin of ale, a new undertunic and braies, and a needle and thread to repair his pierced mantle. He packed everything in a linen scrip. He even bought a pilgrim's badge of the saint's shrine for Isabel to commemorate her visit to the city. It was a small token of their time together, but it seemed appropriate. Pleased with his purchases, he turned back to Bertram's stable to stow his goods before seeking out Isabel. For the first time in days, he felt at ease.

He was nearly at Bertram's when he saw two armed and mailed soldiers on horseback wearing scarlet and white tabards. He withdrew behind a display of leather goods and waited until they came fully into view. When he saw the crossed swords of Lord Tonbridge's coat of arms, he knew he had to find Isabel as soon as he could.

Once the soldiers passed, Fox ran to the stable and pressed several coins into the nearest groom's palm as he handed over his bag of purchases.

"Prepare my horses immediately and make sure this is hooked to my saddle."

The groom stared at the unexpected bounty for a moment before he said, "Yes, sire!" and ran toward the stall of Zephyr and Comis.

Then he found Bertram and had the stabler unlock the trunk in which his weapons were held.

"You seem to be in a hurry this morning, fair sir," Bertram said as he opened the box.

Fox yanked out the bow, arrow bag, and pouch holding his book and thrust them into Bertram's arms.

"Put these on my horse. I will be leaving shortly."

"I hope I haven't done anything to offend—"

"My good man, I count on your discretion if anyone comes searching for me," Fox said as he strapped on his sword and hid it under his mantle.

"Of course. It would be a small payment for my debt to you."

Fox didn't have time to further explain himself. He raced out into the street and toward Blackfriars.

 19

Twice on the way to the monastery, Fox had to put his head down to avoid the gaze of Tonbridge's soldiers. When he arrived, he was relieved to find the main door open on this busy day, but his hurried manner and wild eyes alarmed the young porter.

"Sire!" he scolded. "Your demeanor does not befit this place of peace. And you are wearing a weapon, no less!"

"Brother, I must see Lady Winifred immediately. It's most urgent."

"And you are?"

"Sir Geoffrey of Elmhurst. I escorted the lady here yesterday."

The porter's expression softened. "Oh, yes. Lady Winifred has spoken highly of you, Sir Geoffrey."

"I'm pleased. Where is she?" Fox resisted the urge to push him aside and search the guesthouse himself.

"That is the same thing Lord Tonbridge asked not long ago."

Fox was taken aback. "Lord Tonbridge was here? What did you tell him?"

"He was a thoroughly unpleasant man who claimed to be Lady Winifred's betrothed and demanded to see her most brazenly. Oddly, he said she might also be called Isabel. He was very rude and insistent, and I didn't care for him one bit. When he asked, 'Is she here?', I told him the truth—that she wasn't."

Fox was not only surprised that Tonbridge knew Isabel's false name, but also that a monk would lie so baldly to a noble. When he noticed Fox's astonishment, he gave an embarrassed smile and added, "He did not ask if she *was* here. He asked if she *is* here. She is not here now and was not then."

"You were right to conceal her whereabouts," Fox said. "Lord Tonbridge means to do her harm. Where is she now?"

"I believe she is at the cathedral preparing to take part in the Mass for the feast. She went with nuns from Saint Sepulchre's Priory. I was just leaving for the services myself."

"Lady Winifred and I need to leave Canterbury as soon as possible to keep her out of Lord Tonbridge's clutches. I will go to the cathedral to fetch her, but I must ask a favor of you. She is in possession of a *coffret*. It must be in her quarters. There is a stabler by the name of Bertram where our horses are kept. Would I be able to persuade you to take it there at once with her other belongings?"

"I know of Bertram. He is a decent man who has been kind to our order. But it doesn't seem right taking it there without a request from Lady Winifred."

"Please, Brother. This a matter of life and death. That *coffret* holds her most sacred possession, and if we have to return here to retrieve it, she may not make it out of the city alive."

The young monk paused, then nodded. "I will do this for you. But I'll be waiting there. I expect that Lady Winifred will confirm this request when I see you together."

"She will indeed. Thank you."

Fox rushed out of Blackfriars and back toward the cathedral. On his way, he looked down the length of the high street to the gate at the far end and saw two men in red and white tabards on horseback inspecting every passerby intently. Fox had no doubt that each of the other six gates would be similarly guarded. They would either have to hide themselves until Tonbridge gave up searching for them—an unlikely prospect—or they would have to find another way out of Canterbury.

By the time he arrived at the cathedral, it was even more crowded inside than the previous night at vespers. Before entering, Fox put the sword under his cloak and hoped no one would notice the scabbard poking out from the bottom.

As a noble in the company of nuns, Lady Isabel would most likely be invited to see the shrine before the Mass, which was situated beyond the choir and main altar. Fox snaked his way toward the altar, where one of the priests stopped him from passing through the choir screen.

"Where do you think you're going?" he asked in a haughty tone.

"I must see Lady Winifred."

"I know no one by that name."

"She is in the company of the nuns from Saint Sepulchre's Priory."

"The laity are not allowed into the choir right now. You should know that."

"This is a most urgent matter—"

"That is none of my concern," the priest said. "Besides, the nuns of Saint Sepulchre's are not in the choir at the moment."

"How do you know?"

"Because this time has been reserved for them to be blessed at the site of Saint Thomas's murder."

Fox remembered the stairway down to the small vestibule where Saint Thomas had been stabbed and the long line to get down there. It was near the front door of the cathedral.

He pushed his way back as fast as he could go until he got to the queue of worshippers ready to receive their blessing. He scanned the line for Isabel's blonde hair, but the nun's wimples obscured his view.

He finally found her waiting patiently on the stairs leading down to the site of the martyrdom. Isabel was a stunning sight next to the simply dressed nuns. Her braided hair was visible over her ears with a veil falling down her back, and she wore a beautiful green surcoat over a rose kirtle. There was enough commotion from his movements that she looked up to see what was going on and startled at seeing him.

He forced his way down the stairs to much complaint from the waiting pilgrims until he stood in front of her. He would have grabbed her arm and fled, but that might have raised some resistance from those nearby.

"Lord Tonbridge is in the city. We must go. Now."

Isabel's face turned ashen at Tonbridge's name. She seemed paralyzed by his pronouncement.

"How do you know?"

"I saw his men, and he came calling at Blackfriars. If he doesn't know where you are now, he will soon. Please come with me."

He held out his hand, and she took it.

As he led her up the stairs, she said, "How did he find me?"

"I don't know, but that doesn't matter."

"We must get the manuscript."

"One of the monks is taking it to Bertram's stable as we speak," Fox said.

When they got to the top of the stairs, Isabel came to an abrupt halt and her grip on his hand tightened.

"What's the matter?" Fox asked.

Isabel bowed her head as if to hide herself. "There is a man across the cathedral. He's the one who came to get the manuscript from Tonbridge."

"Who?" Fox said eyeing the crowd.

"I don't know his name. I only saw him from afar, but I recognize his clothes. He has golden hair and a strong chin and he's tall like you. He has to be helping Tonbridge."

Fox was about to hurry them out when he saw the back of a man's head with blond hair. The man turned, his eyes eager and searching. Fox froze.

"Basquin," he whispered.

"You know him?" said Isabel, shocked.

Fox didn't answer. At that moment, he locked gazes with his half-brother. Basquin didn't seem surprised at all to see him. He simply smiled, an expression that haunted Fox because it reminded him of his mother.

Basquin whistled, and two of Tonbridge's soldiers appeared from behind a pillar. The three of them began shoving people out of their way to get at their prey.

"Move!" Fox shouted as he dragged Isabel to the exit.

 20

Lord Tonbridge had checked every single inn and monastery in the city, and no one had admitted to knowing Isabel or her alias Winifred. He was convinced that someone was lying. He planned to go to each one again and demand to see the proprietor or abbot. But first, he would find Basquin to hear if the Frenchman had had better luck.

Accompanied by two of his soldiers, he entered the street in front of the congested cathedral entrance at the same time that Basquin ran out the door and stopped to survey the crowd with an intense expression. He was searching for someone.

Tonbridge looked around and saw a man and woman running away on the other side of the square. He could only see the backs of their heads. The man was tall with shaggy dark hair and a flowing cloak, and the woman had blonde braids and was wearing a bright green silk surcoat embroidered with gold thread.

Tonbridge recognized it instantly. He'd given it to Isabel as a betrothal gift.

"It's them!" he yelled to Basquin and pointed to where they'd disappeared onto a side street. Basquin nodded, and they both raced after the couple with the four soldiers close behind.

Basquin told his men to circle around to the north while Tonbridge told his men to do the same to the south.

As he and Basquin ran, Tonbridge said, "Was it Gerard Fox?"

"Yes," Basquin answered.

"Do you think he knows about the manuscript?"

"If he doesn't now, he soon will."

"There!" Tonbridge shouted.

He saw the hem of the green gown, now muddied from Isabel's flight. She was pulled around a corner by Fox and out of sight.

Tonbridge and Basquin ran even faster. There was no telling what Fox would do with the manuscript if he realized its true value. He might even barter it himself.

They followed their quarry's path onto the side street only to find it empty. They slowed and looked down every alley, but none of them had outlets. By the time they reached the end of the street, the four soldiers met them coming the opposite direction. One was holding Isabel's veil, but they had no prisoners.

"No!" Tonbridge shouted in frustration. "How could they have escaped?"

"They could be in one of these houses," Basquin said, nodding at the doors along the narrow street.

"And we will check every one of them." Tonbridge lowered his voice. "Did Fox see you?"

Basquin tilted his head as if that were the most simple-minded question he'd ever been asked. "Why do you think he ran?"

"Then he will suspect that Cardinal Molyneux is involved."

Basquin nodded. "And he will realize that you are in league with him."

"Then this is your fault. You and your father are responsible for this mess."

Basquin approached Tonbridge slowly until he was nose to nose with the earl. Tonbridge wasn't going to back down, not to a bastard he far outranked, not when he had four of his soldiers watching. But the broad Frenchman, an experienced war veteran who had easily cut down the sheriff and his two deputies the night before, was an intimidating presence. Tonbridge was an experienced strategist, but in a fight against Basquin, he knew he would lose.

The soldiers stepped forward, drawing their swords halfway from their scabbards.

"I don't think you want to test me," Basquin said quietly. "If you like, I will dispose of these four without taking a hard breath, and then I will ask you to say that again." He hadn't even laid a hand on his sword's hilt.

Tonbridge didn't back off, but he said, "I only mean to point out that this Gerard Fox is a formidable man."

"That he is," Basquin said, casually turning away. "Now, do you want to find him or would you rather that we continue to squabble like clucking hens?"

Tonbridge looked at the soldiers, regaining his air of command. "Search every house on this street. Knock down the doors if you have to."

Basquin walked away.

"Where are you going?" Tonbridge demanded.

"To check the stables," Basquin said without turning. "He won't be fleeing on foot, and no one else in this maze of a city has a horse like his."

If it hadn't been for the cutpurses showing Fox the way out of the blind alley the day before, he and Isabel surely would have been caught. They waited until the soldiers who had been trying to intercept them passed by, then backtracked and hurried to Bertram's stable.

"You said his name is Basquin?" Isabel said as they walked quickly, but not so fast as to draw attention.

"Yes," Fox said, looking behind him to make sure they weren't being followed. "He's the bastard son of Cardinal Molyneux. That must be who Lord Tonbridge was planning to sell your manuscript to."

Isabel's blonde hair was too noticeable. He grabbed a linen coif from a market stall as they passed and tossed a coin at the protesting shopkeeper.

He handed it to Isabel. "Put this on. And you'll have to remove your surcoat and just wear your kirtle. That green gown is like a beacon."

Isabel tied the coif around her head. "The cardinal has a son? And how do you know this?"

"Remember that long story I told you about? He figures in it. I might ask you what Molyneux really wants with that manuscript."

"What do you mean?" she asked unconvincingly.

"A cardinal of his wealth and power would not go to these extraordinary lengths to secure that manuscript unless it held something far more valuable than just gold and jewels."

Isabel looked at Fox with an expression that confirmed she had been hiding something else from him.

"It is also a long story," she said.

He threw her a withering glance. "If we survive the day, I should like to hear it."

They reached the stable and found Bertram in the courtyard. He approached them with an appreciative smile at the young lady with Fox.

"Now who might this lovely—"

"Forgive me, Bertram," Fox interrupted. "I have no time for courtesies. Are the horses ready as I requested?"

"They are," Bertram replied, "although they are accompanied by an insistent monk who refused to leave my premises until you arrived." He pointed behind them.

Fox turned and saw the same monk whom he had met at Blackfriars. He was standing next to a mule with the *coffret* and a scrip strapped to its back.

Isabel strode over to the monk. "Brother Gabriel, thank you for bringing my belongings."

"Then I was right to answer this gentleman's appeal?" Brother Gabriel looked at Fox, who was already moving the *coffret* over to Isabel's horse.

"Yes," Isabel said. "Unfortunately, I must depart sooner than I expected. I can never repay you for saving me from Lord Tonbridge."

"Your safety is all I require, Lady Winifred," Brother Gabriel said. "Good day and God bless you in your travels."

As the monk took his mule and left, Fox muttered, "We may have a very short way to travel. Tonbridge's soldiers guard every gate."

"Can't we disguise ourselves as common pilgrims?" Isabel asked, as she removed her green surcoat and threw on her traveling mantle.

Fox shook his head. "They will detain every couple leaving the city. The moment Tonbridge or Basquin sees us, the game is over."

Fox climbed onto Zephyr and Isabel did the same with Comis.

"Are you sure Tonbridge's soldiers are at every gate?" she asked.

"No, but we can't inspect them all without being caught."

"This is maddening. We must try *something*. You're an expert soldier yourself. I've seen your abilities. Can't you fight them?"

"Two of them possibly. But there are city guards at every gate to assist the tax collectors. They certainly would…"

Fox had a sudden thought. *Tax collectors.* The words reminded Fox of something the stabler had told him the day before.

He rode over to Bertram and said, "Yesterday you were complaining about the excessive taxes in the city." Isabel joined them and gave Fox a puzzled look.

Bertram nodded ruefully. "They're a scandal. I'd go poor if—"

"You said that the city wall is in disrepair," Fox continued, "that there are holes big enough to ride a horse through. Were you stretching the truth of its state?"

Bertram shook his head and crossed himself. "It's an honest fact as God is my witness. There is only one place in that condition, but I've seen it myself."

Fox glanced at Isabel with hope. They might have a chance after all.

He looked back to Bertram. "Tell me where."

## 21

During the Great Mortality two years before, Bertram quickly told them, the Great Stour River, which ran directly through Canterbury, flooded, causing the south arch of the city wall to collapse. It hadn't yet been rebuilt, so there was a gap between the river and the remaining wall barely large enough to ride a horse through.

The gap led to a large sheep pasture outside the city. It was far from the nearest gate, but it was also far from the road they needed to take to Dover.

"We're going to Dover right now?" Isabel asked as they rode toward the opening in the wall. Their pace was hasty but unremarkable. With most of the inhabitants and pilgrims still at the cathedral and its surrounding environs, the streets on the south side of the city were relatively empty.

"You said you wanted to go to France," Fox replied. "That means we need a ship."

"We? I can't continue to travel with you unchaperoned."

"I'm afraid you have no choice now. You can't wait for a pilgrim caravan to accompany you. Tonbridge would surely capture you before you could find one."

She studied him. "Why are you continuing on this journey with me?"

The face of Cardinal Dominic Molyneux flashed in front of Fox's eyes. "I have my reasons."

"I shall be intrigued to hear them."

As Bertram had described, the gap in the wall along the river was scarcely wide enough for a horse, and the footing was muddy and treacherous. Fox could see why no one used it even though it was unguarded. One slip, and a horse or pedestrian could tumble into the river.

Fox inspected the wall's ramparts, but he saw no patrol atop it. However, even if they were spotted by the city watch, there was no cause to stop them. Taxes were assessed upon entering a city, not when leaving.

"I'll lead the way," Fox said. "Make sure your horse follows Zephyr's path."

"Comis is sure-footed," Isabel said, patting her neck. "She won't let me fall."

Fox guided Zephyr past the broken wall where its arch had been undermined, and the stones that had tumbled into the river left an uneven, rock-strewn trail. Fox was careful to steer Zephyr so that he wouldn't catch a hoof and break a leg.

When he was past the worst of it, he looked back over his shoulder to ensure that Isabel made it safely through. She guided Comis with a steady hand and didn't seem bothered in the slightest by the uneven terrain. She must have spent more time rabbit hunting than he gave her credit for.

"I am duly impressed," he said.

He and Isabel rode east from the city as casually as they could until they were on the southern road to Dover.

There was a small village not far from the city walls that they had to pass through. Zephyr drew stares with his silver mottled coat and black mane and tail, and Isabel's fresh-faced beauty was of great interest to the men.

She noticed the attention as well.

"We're as conspicuous as a couple of barking dogs," Isabel said. "Tonbridge will surely know we've come this way. It's a long ride to Dover. They might catch us before we get there."

Fox nodded. She had a good point. Their head start was minimal at best. "If they don't overtake us before then, it's likely they'll arrive while we're waiting for our ship to depart."

"There's another port you must know. Sandwich. It's where the Flemish fabrics for my gowns come through." She lowered her voice and leaned closer to Fox. "What if we make it look like we're heading for Dover but turn off somewhere down the road and go to Sandwich instead?"

Fox nodded in appreciation of her suggestion. Isabel was clever, much more so than many of the knights he'd fought beside. No wonder she'd been able to escape from Tonbridge's men.

"If we weren't taking you to your cousin, I'd advise King Edward to make you a battle planner in his war against France."

When they were halfway through the village, he called out to a boy, "Is this the road to Dover?"

The boy nodded, and Isabel followed Fox's lead when he kicked Zephyr into a canter.

A mile down the highway, there was an intersection. Fox stopped to check that no one was around to see them and turned onto the road going northeast. Isabel rode beside him, matching his pace.

Fox didn't know anything of Tonbridge's deductive skills, but Basquin would be difficult to deceive for long. Spending the night in Sandwich while they waited for a ship to leave in the morning was too risky. They had to get there before the last of today's ships set out for France.

 22

Basquin rendezvoused with Tonbridge and his soldiers at Canterbury's West Gate.

"We didn't find him," Tonbridge said.

"I'm not surprised," Basquin replied. "I've just come from a stabler called Bertram. He claimed not to know Fox or your betrothed, but a few coins loosened the tongue of one of his grooms. The lad said he cared for Fox's horse and saw the two of them ride south not long after they eluded us."

"Then my men at the Wincheap Gate should have captured them."

As they rode for the southernmost gate, Basquin shook his head in contempt for his temporary ally. Although Tonbridge's resources and ruthlessness were commendable, Basquin was convinced of his own superiority as a tactician. If the Englishman's soldiers had Fox and Isabel in their grasp, surely they would have carried the good tidings to their master by now.

At the Wincheap Gate, the men-at-arms stationed there said they hadn't seen anyone fitting the description of Fox and Lady Isabel. They checked the only other southern gate, the Riding Gate to Dover, but the soldiers there hadn't seen them either.

Something wasn't right. Basquin could feel it. Fox wouldn't have ridden this direction knowing he would be caught at one of the gates.

"Is there any other way out of the city other than these gates?" he asked the gate's tax assessor.

The man shrugged. "Not if you value your life."

"What does that mean?"

"There's a small gap in the wall where the river goes through it, but many people foolish enough to use it fall into the water and drown."

Basquin didn't wait to hear more. He took off at a gallop through the gate and rode toward the river on the outside of the city. Tonbridge and his men trailed behind.

When they reached the place where the wall met the river, Basquin pulled his horse to a stop and put his hand up to keep Tonbridge and the other men from approaching more closely. He inspected the area between the crumbled wall and the water, and just like the tax assessor had stated, it seemed nearly impassable. But that wouldn't have stopped Fox.

Basquin peered at the ground. There were fresh hoofprints and mud in the grass. Tonbridge noticed them before Basquin pointed them out.

"Someone has come through here recently," Tonbridge said. "Two horses."

*At least he has a hunter's skills,* thought Basquin.

"It must be them," Tonbridge said, looking around in vain at the surrounding countryside. "It can't have been long ago."

"Does Lady Isabel have any family in this area?" Basquin asked.

Tonbridge shook his head. "Her guardian is still at my castle anticipating the wedding, so she won't go to him. The rest of her family in England are all dead from the Great Mortality. The only relations she has left are the Duvals near Paris and a sister who used to be at a convent near Saint-Quentin in the northeast of France, but I don't know where she is now."

"Then they must be intending to cross the Narrows."

"Isabel has the funds to buy passage. We have to find her before she gets on a ship."

"Which could be today," Basquin said.

"Don't you think I know that?" Tonbridge replied with an imperious tone. "I may not have crossed to France since the war began, but I've done it many times."

Having made numerous crossings of the Dover Narrows himself, Basquin knew well the conditions required for the trip. Since prevailing winds traveled from west to east, it generally took less time to travel from England to France than the other way around. A ship's captain wouldn't set out knowing he would still be in the open seas after nightfall, but the sun went down at a late hour this time of year.

Basquin looked down at the shadow he cast. It was still morning and there would be some time before the sext bells rang at midday.

"If they leave before the hour of nones," he said, "they could easily make it to France by this evening."

Tonbridge was incensed at the thought of his betrothed getting away again. "Dover is the closest port to France." He ordered one of his soldiers to gather the rest of the men from Canterbury quickly and meet him on the road to Dover.

They raced to the village outside Canterbury's southern gate and Tonbridge announced in a loud voice that he was looking for a man traveling with a woman and that the man's horse was a distinctive color. When none of the gathered villagers responded, he offered two pence to the first person who could tell him if they saw the couple.

A young boy sprinted over and claimed he saw them.

Basquin scoffed. "He'll say anything for two pennies."

Tonbridge ignored him. "What did the man's horse look like?"

"It was splotchy silver with a black mane and tail and a white swirl on his forehead," the boy said. "And the woman was blonde and very pretty. The man looked tall, like a warrior."

Tonbridge threw a smug look at Basquin before turning back to the boy. "Where did they go?"

"The man asked if this was the road to Dover. I said yes, and they galloped away."

Tonbridge looked pleased with his discovery and tossed two coins onto the ground. The boy snatched them up and ran away giggling at his prize.

"It won't take us long to catch up with them," Tonbridge said. "I doubt Isabel can keep up a fast pace. I should think we will get them well before they reach Dover."

Something about the boy's identification of them nagged at Basquin, but he bit his tongue since he couldn't put his finger on it.

When the rest of Tonbridge's men arrived, they tore off down the road. At this speed, Basquin calculated that they would be at Dover a little after midday.

Halfway there, they still had not seen Fox and Isabel, which made Basquin uneasy. He called for Tonbridge to stop.

"Don't you think we should have overtaken them by now?" Basquin asked.

"Maybe I underestimated the harpy's riding skills."

"Perhaps. But I think we should ask someone on this road to make sure they came this way."

When they rode into the next village, the formidable array of soldiers on horseback roused the residents' interest. As he had before, Tonbridge made an offer of two pence for anyone who could tell them about Isabel and Fox. When no one stepped forward, he raised the offer to a shilling.

A ragged serf came up to them and said, "My lord, I saw them surely."

"Where did they go?" Tonbridge asked eagerly.

"Straight on to Dover, methinks."

Basquin held up a hand. "Hold. Describe them."

"They was on horses and raced right through the town."

"I mean, what did they look like?"

The man faltered before saying, "The horses was black, and the man was dressed all in tattered clothes like a criminal. I didn't get no good look at the woman, but she was an ugly thing, I can tells you that."

Tonbridge snarled at the peasant, "Be off now before I slice your tongue out for lying to your betters."

The man gulped and stumbled backward before turning to run away.

At that moment, a knight traveling with several squires and servants entered town. Tonbridge waved him over.

"Good sir, I am Sir Conrad Harrington, Earl of Tonbridge."

The knight bowed in his saddle. "I am honored, my lord. I am Sir Godwin Cecil, Lord of Shropshire."

"Do you come from Dover?"

"Aye. I have just arrived this morning from Calais."

Tonbridge turned to Basquin and said, "Finally, an honorable man to talk to." He looked at Sir Godwin. "We are in search of two fugitives. A man and a woman. They would have been riding fast on this road from Canterbury. Have you seen them?"

Sir Godwin shook his head. "We've seen no couples at all on the road, let alone traveling quickly."

"You are sure?" Basquin asked.

"They might have passed earlier. We've only left Dover after morning Mass."

"Then you would have seen them."

"I'm sorry to be of no help. I hope you punish them for whatever crime they've committed against you." Sir Godwin nodded and rode on with his entourage.

"As I feared," Basquin said, "Fox tricked us."

Tonbridge slapped his leg in anger. "Then where have they gone?"

"The only other port they could reach today that might have a ship leaving this afternoon is to the north. Sandwich."

"Sir Gerard of Oakhurst fancies himself a clever man, doesn't he?" Tonbridge said through gritted teeth.

"Only because he is one," Basquin had to admit. "Let's go." He spurred his horse into a gallop back the way they'd come, and Tonbridge yelled for his men to follow. It wasn't far to the closest road north.

## 23

### SANDWICH, ENGLAND

As one of the busiest ports in southeast England, Sandwich always had a harbor full of ships trading wool and textiles with Flanders and transporting goods to the English-held city of Calais, which had been captured from the French during the military campaign that included the Battle of Crécy. Either destination would be fine with Fox if it meant leaving this afternoon.

Only two ships were alongside the quay loading cargo and supplies. One was a small cog that was used only for crossings to France, and the other was a much larger seagoing nava. Fox recognized it as a Genoese design.

He and Isabel rode up to the cog, and Fox asked a man wrestling with a barrel of salt if the ship was leaving soon.

"Aye," the man replied, gesturing at the barrels lined up next to him. "We sail for Antwerp just as soon as we get these loaded."

"Would you have room for two horses and two passengers?"

"Nay. We don't have any stalls to stow them, and if they were on the open deck when we ran into rough seas, they'd pitch overboard."

"What of that one?" Fox asked, pointing at the nava.

"I keep to my own business. You'd have to ask them." The man went back to loading his cargo.

Isabel gave Fox a look that reflected his worry. The Genoese ship was their last chance today.

They rode to the nava, and Fox saw a man ordering the crew about in an Italian dialect. He had to be the vessel's master.

"Hail, captain," Fox called out with a raised hand. "Are you preparing to leave?"

"Yes, we leave soon," the captain said in halting English. "My crew work too slow or I be sail already."

"We would like to be taken aboard your ship as passengers."

The captain appraised the two of them with squinting eyes. "People only?"

"Our horses come with us."

The captain shook his head. "No horses."

Fox would never leave Zephyr behind.

"You don't have stalls for the horses?" he asked.

"We have stalls, yes. But filled with wool."

To Fox's surprise, Isabel spoke up. "We can pay you double the normal rate." She was holding her bag of coins.

Fox leaned over and whispered. "You don't even know what the normal rate is."

"Does it matter?" she whispered back. "We need to get on this ship."

The captain squinted even more until his eyes were slits. "She speak for you?" he said to Fox.

"I am Lady Winifred of Elmhurst," Isabel said in a proud voice. "This is my manservant."

"Manservant? Is... how you say... appropriate?"

"Don't worry. He will be a gentleman and protect me from any men who might covet me." She looked pointedly at the crew. "You see, he's a eunuch. From the war in France."

Her statement stunned Fox into silence.

The captain was confused. "Unique?"

"Like a gelding," Isabel said and gestured like she was snipping off the stones dangling between his legs.

The captain looked at Fox's crotch, finally understood, and went into a fit of laughter. Fox felt the blood rushing to his face, but he said nothing.

When he finished guffawing, the captain said, "Is good. But where you go?"

"What is your destination?" Isabel asked.

"Honfleur first, then Saint-Malo, Saint-Nazaire, and Bordeaux. Then Espagna."

Isabel looked at Fox, who stared daggers at her.

"Saint-Malo," he said.

Isabel looked as if she were going to ask why there, but his expression quieted her.

The captain thought about it. "Twenty shillings for both and horses."

"Fifteen. Half now, half when we arrive."

"Yes, I take it," the captain said, likely surprised to get so much, but he didn't ask why. "I make space for you. We leave at the bells."

Fox nodded, and Isabel handed over the money.

"Welcome to my ship, *Bello Vento*. I am Giorgio." The captain walked away, pleased with this sudden windfall, and shouted at the crew while pointing at his two new passengers.

"I'm a eunuch?" Fox growled.

"It just popped into my head," she said, giggling. "I didn't want him to think we would sleep together on the voyage."

"From now on, we keep to the story that we're husband and wife."

"Fine. But I think my version is more fun."

Fox chuffed at that. Maybe more fun for her.

When the crew was ready, they dismounted and led the horses up the ramp and down into the cargo hold. After removing the saddles, Fox and Isabel backed Zephyr and Comis into their stalls, where the crewmen wrapped canvas slings under their bodies to steady them on the seas.

They were shown to the aft sleeping quarters, and they secured their belongings before going up on deck to watch the ship depart from Sandwich. The church bells for the hour of nones were ringing as they approached the wooden railing.

"Why are we going to Saint-Malo?" Isabel asked as the crew released the ropes from the quay. "Wouldn't it be better to go ashore at Honfleur to start our journey to Paris?"

Fox shook his head. "If Basquin and Tonbridge came to Canterbury to find you, they will follow us to France. We need help, and I think I know a place near Saint-Malo where we can find it."

As the ship pushed away from the quay, oarsmen began rowing them out of the harbor while other crewmen raised the triangular lateen sails on their masts. The canvas caught the wind immediately, and they made good speed to the harbor entrance.

As they approached the open sea, Fox saw a line of horses ride into town at full gallop. All the men were wearing Tonbridge's distinctive crimson and white colors except for a lone standout, who was a blond man on a white horse and dressed in a fine blue cotehardie. Fox couldn't resolve his face from this distance, but he knew it was Basquin.

The men fanned out to search the town and port. Basquin was the only one who watched the ship that was sailing away.

As the ship rounded the point and out of view of Sandwich, Isabel said flatly, "They will never stop searching for us."

"They might if all you were carrying was a manuscript," Fox replied. "But that *coffret* holds something more, I suspect." He turned to Isabel. "What could possibly be so desirable to a man as powerful as Cardinal Molyneux?"

Isabel sighed and looked around them to make sure no one was listening.

"After all you've done for me," she said, "I suppose you have a right to know. And I've come to trust you even in the short time since we met. But what I'm telling you now has been a secret kept by the women of my family for generations. That manuscript contains the most valuable holy relic in existence. That's why the cardinal wants it so badly. It could make him pope. He wants to possess the original Hodegetria, the only true image of the Virgin Mary and infant Jesus."

# Mont-Saint-Michel

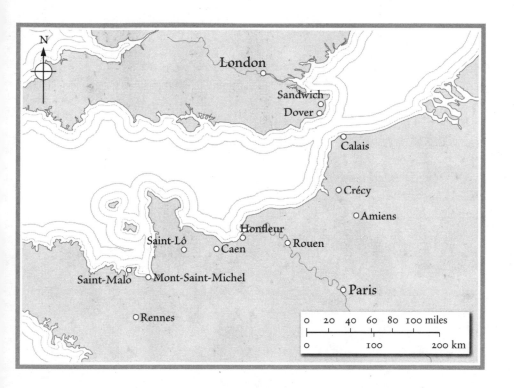

## 24

### THE DOVER NARROWS

Fox didn't have any dried ginger root with him, and that made the choppy ride across the Narrows a miserable experience.

Although he had traveled by ship since he was a boy, he was also prone to *mal de mer*. Chewing on a sliver of ginger root usually alleviated the seasickness enough to be tolerable, but he had none on this voyage given the haste of their departure. He spent nearly the entire trip hurling his innards over the railing. One sailor had snickered at him, but a deadly glare from Fox made the Genoese man scurry away.

What made the ordeal even more infuriating was seeing Isabel, who claimed she hadn't sailed on the sea since she was a child, happily sitting on the deck and watching the coast pass by without even a hint of illness. It was rare to come across a noblewoman who didn't complain about the hardships of travel.

In between his bouts of heaving, Fox asked Captain Giorgio when they would arrive at Honfleur so Fox could try to find some sort of medicinal preventative from a local merchant. He'd been hoping they could make the French harbor before the *Bello Vento* anchored for the night, but Giorgio said that because of the light winds they wouldn't get to port until the middle of the following day.

Instead, they dropped anchor in the estuary near Berck. Thankfully, the water was calm, and Fox's stomach finally ceased its rebellion.

He was sitting on the open rear deck breathing in the salty air when Isabel approached him with a tankard and bowl. The setting sun highlighted the contours of her cheekbones.

"How are you feeling?" she asked. There was no amusement on her face, just a look of concern.

"Better now that I'm not feeding every fish in the Dover Narrows."

She kneeled beside him. "Are you able to eat? I've brought you some ale and pottage."

Fox felt surprisingly ravenous, but he knew from previous journeys that guzzling the food and drink would not be a prudent idea. He took the dish and cup with a nod of thanks and sipped the ale. It tasted as good as the finest mead.

"I've got something for you as well," Fox said. He reached into his purse for the pilgrim's badge he'd bought in Canterbury and gave it to her.

She turned it over in her hand and seemed surprisingly touched by the gift. "That's quite thoughtful of you."

"I'm not sure you want to be reminded of our time there."

"On the contrary. It was a memorable experience. But now I am happy to be on this ship. Certainly happier than you are."

"You seem none the worse," Fox said, straining to hide his petulance.

"I didn't expect to enjoy it this much. Perhaps I should take to the high seas more often. Do you think Captain Giorgio has need for a washerwoman?"

"I wouldn't trust you with this lot for longer than the beat of a fly's wing."

"They've been quite kind to me today."

Fox grunted as he slowly began eating. He had no doubt that they wouldn't be so benevolent were he not aboard.

"What are you hoping to find in Saint-Malo?"

"I have some friends near the port at Mont-Saint-Michel," Fox said. "At least that's where I left them."

"I've heard stories about Mont-Saint-Michel. My mother was from Brittany, and she used to tell me stories about it as a way to teach me her native Breton. Is it true that Mont-Saint-Michel is an island only part of the day?"

Fox nodded. "Much of the time it is surrounded by a sandy

expanse that stretches a half-mile from the coastal marshes, but when the tide comes in, it is reachable only by boat."

"Can you walk to it during low tide?"

"Yes, but it can be treacherous without a guide. The flats are full of quicksand pits that can swallow a horse whole. It would be simple to stumble into them if you didn't know where they were."

"A monastery perched on an island," Isabel said with wonder, her eyes glittering at the prospect of seeing such a glorious sight. Then she snapped back. "How are your friends going to help?"

"Traveling across France by ourselves during wartime will be dangerous. We'll have safety in greater numbers. Besides, we need to convince Basquin and Tonbridge to give up their pursuit. Henri and Youssef are smart men, and together we can formulate a plan to do that. But first we need to divert Basquin from our trail to give us time to create our scheme."

"Do you think they'll be able to track us there all the way across the sea?"

"Basquin is relentless, resourceful, and intelligent. I believe he'd be able to hunt us all the way to the Holy Land if he had to."

"As would Lord Tonbridge," Isabel said. "That scares me, but it almost sounds as if you admire Basquin."

"I do, in a way," Fox said. Although his brother possessed a brutal and impetuous nature, Basquin was also a sharp and skilled warrior.

"How will we keep them from following us?"

Fox thought about the stories Isabel's mother told her.

"How good is your Breton?" he asked. Fox could speak English, French, and Latin, but he knew only a few words in Breton.

"I haven't spoken the language in years, not since my mother died, but I know it well enough to converse."

"Then I have an idea for how to use Basquin's cleverness against him." Fox finished the last bite of his food and rose to his feet. He felt exhausted but steady. "First, though, I want to see this treasure of yours."

She hesitated, then agreed that he deserved to see what he was risking his life for. After securing a lantern from one of the sailors, they went below deck to their quarters and made sure that all of the crew were outside before opening the *coffret*.

Isabel gently eased the bejeweled manuscript out of the box and laid it on its silk wrappings to keep it from getting dirty. She unclasped the cover and flipped through half the pages until reaching the Book of Luke.

"The Hodegetria," she announced breathlessly. "The one true Icon of the Virgin and Child."

Although he didn't gasp at the sight as Isabel did, Fox was nonetheless in awe of the delicate illumination that covered the entire page, which looked eons older than any other leaf in the book. There was a solemnity and timelessness to the image that created a sense of wonder.

The painting showed a hooded Virgin Mary holding out her hand to the baby Jesus, who was seated on her lap and wrapped in robes. A gilded halo surrounded His head, and the two of them looked out piercingly at the reader. The artist was clearly a master, and the whole illustration glowed in the light as if it were touched by the hand of God. Fox felt like a bolt of lightning was shooting down his spine. He had never seen anything so beautiful.

"We must destroy it," he said.

Isabel whipped her head around, aghast at his statement. "What?"

"Throw it overboard. Or better yet, burn it so that nothing is left of it."

"That's blasphemy! This is painted by the hand of Saint Luke himself as the Virgin and Christ sat before him. It is the only image of them drawn in their lifetimes."

"It's also likely a fraud," Fox said. "I've seen all kinds of holy relics in my travels. Pieces of the True Cross, the belt of the Virgin Mary, the fingerbone of Saint Thomas. Many of them were simply collected from a nearby trash heap and peddled as the true object. I've known charlatans who've made fortunes that way. This could be a counterfeit as well."

"This relic is no fake," Isabel said indignantly.

"And how would you know that?"

"You've heard the legend of how the Hodegetria was brought by Eudocia, wife of the Byzantine Emperor, to Constantinople from the Holy Land almost a thousand years ago? It's always been thought to be a painting on wood, but it's not. It's an illumination on parchment. A vision of the Virgin Mary herself told Eudocia that women were destined to protect the Icon, so she commissioned this manuscript to safeguard it." As she spoke she turned to the very end of the manuscript, to an inscription written in Greek.

"I don't read Greek," Fox said. "What does it say?"

"It's a letter written by Eudocia describing her vision and testifying that the manuscript holds the true Hodegetria. You can see the Greek word for Hodegetria here. This is her wax seal and the date is the thirty-third year in the reign of her husband Theodosius II." Apparently, she was even more adept with languages than he was.

Isabel flipped the page over and pointed to two columns of names on the back of Eudocia's testament. Fox leaned down and peered at them.

"Those are the names of every Byzantine Empress from Eudocia until the sack of the city in 1204 when it was brought to England," Isabel said. "And the names of each person from then on are the women in my family who have cared for this manuscript. It is only fitting that the Virgin's true image be protected through the ages by women and not be employed for power and wealth by men."

The last name on the list was indeed Isabel's.

Fox was not entirely convinced. "Still, we cannot let this fall into Cardinal Molyneux's hands. Europe has already endured the Pestilence in the last few years. He will bring nothing but bloodshed to its survivors if he uses this to become pope."

Isabel put herself in between him and the book. "I would die before I let you harm the Icon."

The thought of Molyneux's perverse pleasure at getting the Hodegetria in his hands almost caused Fox to push Isabel aside and rip the illumination from the book to light it on fire. Two things, however, stopped him.

One was the fact that Basquin and Molyneux would never believe it had been destroyed. They would torture both him and Isabel mercilessly to get them to admit they'd hidden it somewhere.

But the more compelling reason was the look on Isabel's face. He might not believe it was the one true Icon, but she most certainly did. Her family had protected this book for generations, and she'd given up everything to keep it out of the hands of those who would abuse it. It was her reason for being, and Fox couldn't take that from her.

He stepped back and said, "All right. We'll find another way to keep it safe."

Isabel breathed a sigh of relief. "Thank you. I knew you were a real knight and gentleman."

"How much gold money do you have left?" Fox asked her as she replaced the manuscript in the *coffret* and locked it.

"Very little, but I do have my jewels."

"What are they?"

She removed them from her bag. They consisted of several gold chains and rings, as well as a few gem-studded brooches and a golden fibula in the shape of an eagle.

"Lord Tonbridge made me clasp my cloak together with that garish thing at our last dinner together," Isabel said. "The rest are gifts from him. None of them mean anything to me. We could sell them."

Fox shook his head. "We need them."

"For what?"

He smiled at her. "To make Basquin think the manuscript is gone once and for all."

## 25

HONFLEUR, FRANCE

It didn't take long for Basquin and Tonbridge to discover that Gerard Fox and Lady Isabel were on the nava that left the harbor just as they arrived. Tonbridge attempted to hire a ship to chase them down, but none of the vessels in port were large enough to accommodate his men and horses.

The only choice was to ride to Dover, but the men were exhausted, and so were their steeds. They had to rest for the night and head south in the morning. Basquin learned the intended ports of call for the *Bello Vento* and was comforted that once their quarry was in France, he would have the advantage of his extensive contacts throughout the country.

The next morning, they arrived in Dover to find a ship suitable for them—one that was carrying the Bishop of Lisieux back from the Feast of the Translation of Saint Thomas. There was room enough only for Basquin, Tonbridge, and eight of the men-at-arms and all their horses, so Tonbridge sent the remainder back to Tonbridge Castle to await his return.

Basquin wanted to leave immediately, but rough seas and an extremely low tide delayed the sailing. Once they cast off the following day, the ship headed straight to Honfleur.

The French city sat at the mouth of the Seine River and was the quickest way to reach Paris. If Fox and Isabel were going there, Honfleur was the best place for them to disembark. But when their ship arrived, Basquin and Tonbridge found the Genoese nava long gone.

Basquin questioned the merchants and port workers who had offloaded its passengers and goods, and none of them reported anyone fitting Fox and Isabel's descriptions getting off the boat. Surely they would have noticed the couple and their horses if they had disembarked. Evidently, they must have stayed on the ship at least until Saint-Malo.

Still, he saw an opportunity and found a trader willing to be bribed.

After putting his plan into motion, he returned to the dock. He saw Tonbridge talking to the same man a short time later and was not surprised when the earl returned, barely able to contain his glee.

"I found a trader from Paris who claimed that he passed a couple leaving the city heading east, and they matched Fox and Isabel's descriptions. Finally, we have some blessings on our side. How long will it take them to get to Paris? They will have a day's head start."

Basquin suppressed a smile, but he was pleased that Tonbridge had bought the lie.

"Five or six days if they ride quickly, but I have made the ride in two days at a full gallop by changing to fresh horses."

"We lack such a luxury, but so do they," Tonbridge said. "We should have no issues catching them."

Although Tonbridge now had fully swallowed Basquin's claim that Fox and Isabel had departed from the ship, it also begged the question why they had remained on board.

*Where are you going, my brother?* Basquin thought.

Tonbridge called his captain of the guard and told him to get the men and horses off the ship.

"All but mine," Basquin said.

Tonbridge gave him a quizzical look. "You're not joining our hunt?"

Basquin shook his head. "I will continue on in the hopes of finding that Genoese ship, just in case Isabel is not actually planning to seek shelter at her cousin's estate. Perhaps the captain overheard details about their journey and destination. I will plan to meet you in Paris at my father's home if I find no further information."

Tonbridge regarded him curiously.

Basquin smiled with feigned innocence. "I expect you will already have conveyed the Icon to Cardinal Molyneux, and my jaunt will be for naught."

"Perhaps I should send some of my men with you."

Basquin didn't flinch. He thought Tonbridge would be suspicious, but he wanted to continue on alone. "If that is what you wish, but I had assumed you would want an impressive force with you during your ride. These are dangerous times while England is at war with France."

Tonbridge furrowed his brow. "You said that you would arrange for a writ of safe conduct for us."

Hostage-taking was a reliable source of funds during the war. Lord Tonbridge would be worth a tidy sum.

"The Bishop of Lisieux, our traveling companion, is loyal to Cardinal Molyneux," Basquin said, taking full advantage of his father's power. "He is drawing up a formal writ of safe conduct through the French kingdom. No one will be able to detain you without suffering the Church's wrath. In fact, you may enjoy the hospitality of nobility along the way to Paris if you so desire."

That seemed to appease Tonbridge. The far-reaching extent of the Church's authority wasn't limited by nationality, language, or borders.

"I appreciate your foresight," he said.

They found the bishop still loading his carts for the trip to Lisieux. The bishop obligingly affixed his seal to the writ his clerk had drafted and handed it over to the Englishman.

Basquin was pleased with his cunning. He now had free rein to track Fox on his own. With Molyneux's pervasive influence in the north of France, Basquin would be able to recruit local men to chase Fox down no matter where he left the ship. Then he would have the manuscript and Icon and could give it to the cardinal himself. Basquin would be knighted for his great deeds and loyalty and then gifted the lands that his father had been dangling in front of him for four years.

As Tonbridge mounted his horse, Basquin said, "I wish you

Godspeed in your search. I have no doubt that the Lord will guide you truly in your quest."

Tonbridge said nothing in return, dismissing him with a curt nod. The English lord launched into a canter, his men following closely behind him.

Basquin exhaled and went back to the ship, hoping to leave for Saint-Malo as soon as possible. If his instincts were correct, in a short time Lord Tonbridge would have no choice but to treat him as an equal.

# 26

Fox couldn't acquire any ginger in Honfleur, so he spent another wretched day heaving over the side of the ship during their transit to Saint-Malo. When they arrived, he felt completely drained. The only benefit was that his depleted condition would aid his plan with Isabel.

His stomach settled as soon as he led Zephyr onto the wooden pier. The air stank of fish and algae, but Fox didn't mind as long as his legs were steady.

With Isabel at his side, he talked to several of the locals working there to unload their ship. Fox spoke French in the accent of a native Norman thanks to his mother Emmeline. He asked mundane questions, like where to find an inn and who had the best ale in town. The answers didn't matter. They weren't staying long. It wasn't until the fourth inquiry that they found what they were looking for.

"*Toi là-bas,*" Fox said to the laborer. "*Où est le forgeron le plus proche?*" He didn't care where the nearest blacksmith was, but it was a common question.

The man looked at him in confusion and said, "*Ne Gomzan ket Galleg.*"

This was what they'd been hoping for. The Breton said he didn't speak French, not unusual in commoners.

Fox looked at Isabel and motioned for her to speak.

Isabel meekly spoke in Breton to the man. Although Fox didn't understand the language, he knew what she was going to say since they had scripted the entire exchange.

*We need to find a smith to shoe our horse,* she said with a smile. *Do you know of one nearby?*

The commoner nodded, bewildered at being addressed by a noblewoman. He pointed down a street and spoke briefly. Isabel translated.

"There's a smith not far in that direction," she said to Fox in French, which they would both speak from that point forward now that they were on the continent. "He says his cousin is the smith and will give you a fair price if you say that Erwan sent you."

Fox nodded. "Now it's time to make the 'mistake' we talked about."

Isabel turned back to Erwan. *"He's a skilled workman? My husband doesn't feel well, and we don't want to be stuck on the road with a lame horse. It's a long ride south to our next stop."*

Then he asked a question, and Fox knew Erwan had taken the bait because he said the word *Rennes*, one of the largest cities in Brittany and a day's ride south. He had jumped to the hoped-for conclusion that they were going to Rennes.

Isabel feigned a shocked expression. They wanted Basquin to think they were going to Rennes, but if she revealed their fictional destination too blatantly, he would see through the ruse. She pretended to quickly compose herself and smiled at Fox.

"He says we probably won't be able to make the city by nightfall," she said to him.

"Make it clear that's where we're going," Fox said. "We don't want to leave any doubt in Basquin's mind if he comes this way."

Isabel faced Erwan again. *"Please, fair friend, don't tell anyone that we're heading south. I wasn't supposed to let anyone know our destination. We're in debt and being pursued by creditors. My husband will thrash me if he finds out that I let it slip."*

Erwan peered at Fox as he replied.

Isabel took Erwan's hand and pushed a coin into it as if she were trying to hide it from her husband. She thanked him for his discretion, and he walked away, shaking his head.

Isabel said, "As we expected, he wanted to be paid for his silence."

"Of course he did," Fox said. "I could see that he thought a single English penny was an insulting amount for a bribe."

"Do you think he'll talk?"

Fox helped her onto her horse and then pulled himself onto Zephyr. "If Basquin and Lord Tonbridge are able to follow us. I don't know about Tonbridge, but Basquin will question every person here until he finds some useful information. Erwan strikes me as someone who will negotiate a much better price to reveal our whereabouts, just like we want him to."

Fox could have planted their false destination himself, but Basquin would never believe that Fox would make such an idiotic error. However, his half-brother didn't have such esteem for women's intelligence. He would undoubtedly find Isabel's mistake to be credible, especially if Fox hadn't been able to "understand" that she had made it in the first place. Further, Basquin would believe that she would hide her blunder from Fox, and that they would continue on to Rennes anyway.

"How far is it to Mont-Saint-Michel, do you think?" Isabel asked as they rode toward the smith Erwan had pointed them to. That was another part of the ruse. They would have to purchase a new shoe to complete the illusion.

"A full day's ride, I should think," Fox answered. The weather was fair enough that they could sleep on the highway if necessary, but an inn was always preferable. "And remember, wherever we stay, I am your husband, not your eunuch."

Isabel laughed. "Staying in an inn with a man I'm not married to? Such a scandal."

"Better a scandal than continuing to play your neutered manservant."

"But you did it so well."

Fox scowled at her. "Would you like me to leave you with your new friend Erwan?"

"All right," Isabel said in mock surrender. "You win. We pretend to be married. But I'm still quite noticeable in these noblewoman's clothes."

"Which makes it more likely that Basquin will swallow our

trick when we are spotted going out the east gate of Saint-Malo instead of the south gate toward Rennes. He'll think we're using the same deception we employed in Canterbury to throw him off the scent, but this time we really will be heading east."

"I need new clothes after that," Isabel said. "Ones that aren't so recognizable."

"I agree," Fox said. "We'll take care of that tomorrow when we get to Mont-Saint-Michel."

"And then we actually go to Rennes?"

Fox nodded. "Once my friends help me figure out a way to gain our freedom by having Basquin and Tonbridge watch your manuscript burn to ashes."

## 27

MONT-SAINT-MICHEL, FRANCE

Mont-Saint-Michel rose out of the sea like something from a fantasy. Fox and Isabel had been able to see it from miles away, but now that they were directly across the tidal flats, the monastery looked even more spectacular and magical.

The abbey itself dominated the top of the rocky islet, its spires jutting into the sky. Stout stone walls below the peak's Norman church were dotted with five levels of windows. A village clung to the sloped base of the island, rising all the way to the entrance of the abbey on the eastern end. The red roofs of the houses that were jammed together to maximize the use of the space contrasted with the blue-gray roof of the monastery. The shores were surrounded by formidable battlements that looked strong enough to repel any attack. The entire image was so reminiscent of an illumination in a romance story that Fox might have expected a dragon to swoop from the sky and land on the abbey's pinnacle.

He had only been to the island once before. He couldn't imagine the effort it took to build the place. Since construction began five hundred years ago, it must have taken generations to haul all those stones across the tidal flats from wherever they were mined. But the builders had achieved the desired effect. Pilgrims from across the continent—like the group of ten that idled nearby—flocked here to bask in its magnificence and invoke the powerful protection of Saint Michael the Archangel.

Fox and Isabel were both standing beside their horses. He looked over to see her staring at Mont-Saint-Michel from under her hood. The expression of wonder on her face somehow made her even more attractive.

"What do you think?" he asked.

She couldn't tear her eyes from it as she spoke. "I never imagined I would see something so extraordinary." Then she finally cast her gaze down at the vast stretch of sandy ground around the island. "How shall we cross?"

Although the tide was out, the flats were riddled with gullies and rivulets of water. The footing didn't look very firm.

Fox pointed at a group of travelers, some on horseback and the rest on foot, picking their way toward them across the flats in single file from the island. They were being led by a large, boisterous man in a cloak. Even this far away, Fox could hear his booming voice, though he couldn't yet understand what the leader was saying.

"We must wait for a local guide who knows the lay of the land." He then nodded at the waiting pilgrims near them. "That's why they have not attempted the crossing yet."

When the group departing the island arrived and climbed up onto dry land, the guide waved goodbye and surveyed his next customers. He was a barrel-chested Frenchman with auburn hair, blue eyes, a thin beard, and a wide smile. When his eyes settled on Fox, the guide spread his arms and rushed over, grappling Fox in a hug fit for a bear, lifting him off his feet.

"Gerard, my old friend!" he bellowed. "I never thought I'd see your face again!" He planted a kiss on each of Fox's cheeks.

Fox returned the embrace, and he couldn't help but laugh at the clamorous greeting. "Henri, I knew it was you from the moment you set off from Mont-Saint-Michel. Your voice likely carries all the way to Paris."

Henri let out a belly laugh. "That is why I am a guide instead of a monk." He pushed Fox back, gripping his shoulders to look him up and down. "You seem stronger than the last time I saw you. Your injury has healed well since last year?"

"Good as new," Fox replied. "And your hand?"

Henri flexed his fingers, but Fox noticed he could barely make a fist.

"Not good for much now except raising a pint or tying laces," Henri said.

"As long as you can still drink," Fox said with a smile. "I wasn't sure you would still be at Mont-Saint-Michel, but I'm happy to find you here. What of Youssef?"

"*Oui*, he is here as well. We are only here a year, and he has somehow maneuvered himself into becoming master brewer for the island."

"After getting to know every tavern between here and Paris at his side, I'm not surprised he would find a way to make sure he was well supplied inside a monastery."

"You would not believe the elixir he has concocted."

"I look forward to sampling his ale."

"Ale, he calls it." Henri chuckled mysteriously, as if there were more he was not letting on. "In any case, we owe you a debt for making our positions here possible."

"And that is why I have come. I'm afraid it is time to collect."

"Anything for you, my friend. Neither of us would be alive were it not for your cleverness and courage. What brings you here?"

"She does," Fox said, gesturing to Isabel. "May I present Lady Isabel of Kentworth."

Isabel pushed the hood of her cloak down and smiled at him. Henri gasped aloud at seeing her face and glided over to her. He gracefully kneeled on one knee. "*Damoiselle, que Dieu vous octroie la santé et bonheur.*"

"*Et vous aussi.*"

"May I inquire as to the purpose of such a beautiful lady's visit?" Henri asked as he stood.

She glanced at Fox, who said in a lowered voice, "That will have to wait until we all meet with Youssef in private."

Henri gave a mischievous grin and spoke for the first time in a whisper. "You have me intrigued."

He turned and announced to the assembled group, "We must get going before the tide begins to roll in. My payment is one sou per person to guide you through the flats."

One of the pilgrims, a boy not yet full grown, grumbled about the fee. "One sou each? Why should we pay that?"

"Because without my aid, you may never reach the island. The flats are teeming with pockets of quicksand. I've seen the ooze swallow an entire wagon. They're nearly invisible, and it takes an experienced eye to spot them, so you would be wise to follow closely in my footsteps."

The boy gulped and paid without further complaint.

Once he collected the payments, Henri began walking, with everyone else following him in single file. As he gave a history of the island and monastery, Henri peered intently at the ground and steered them around obstacles that looked no different from any other part of the sand to Fox's untrained eye. Wind whipped their hair as it swept across the flats, but Henri's thundering voice could still be heard. Halfway across, Henri looked into the distance and picked up the pace. Fox could see why. Water from the ocean was flowing toward them.

The tide was coming in.

"Not to worry," Henri said. "We will make it to the island long before the sea does."

The boy pilgrim must have been more worried about the incoming water than Henri because he walked even faster, passing by Isabel.

"You there!" Henri shouted. "Fall back in line."

But it was too late. The boy suddenly collapsed. Since Isabel was nearest to him, she reached out to steady him, and the boy, shrieking in terror, would not release her grip.

He was not falling. He was being pulled into a quicksand mire. The more he thrashed, the quicker his legs were gulped down. The sand was already up to his mid-thigh.

The men and women in the pilgrim party added to the clamor by screaming and shouting, but none of them dared approach.

Henri rushed to him, careful to avoid the same trap, but Isabel had already managed to press the reins of her horse into the boy's hands. She pulled hard on the bridle and said "Back, Comis!"

The horse responded by slowly retreating from the screaming

boy. The teen was strong and held fast to the reins. He wasn't being sucked down any longer, but neither was he rising.

"Boy," Henri said in a suddenly soothing voice. "Boy, calm yourself. It's the only way you're coming out of there."

The teen stopped screeching and nodded. "What do I do?"

"Swirl just one leg around."

"Swirl?"

Henri made a mixing motion with his hand. "Like a mortar in a pestle. You see?"

The boy nodded and began moving his thigh in a circle, tight at first and then wider and wider until it was free of the muck. He was able to raise his foot out, but his boot remained in the quicksand. He still had hold of the reins.

"Now the other," Henri said. "Hurry."

The boy repeated the motion with his other leg, and soon Isabel was able to back Comis enough to take the boy to the safety of solid ground.

The boy dropped to his knees and began a prayer of thanks.

Henri pointed at Isabel. "You should thank her as well as you thank God, boy."

The boy stood and said, "I humbly thank you, my lady."

"I'm just happy you're safe now," she replied. "You're a brave young man."

The boy blushed and got back into his place in line.

Henri continued walking and turned to Fox. "She's clever, that one."

"I am well aware," Fox said in admiration not only of her quick thinking, but also her generosity and kindness. He'd never met a woman remotely like her. "Lady Isabel is full of surprises."

 28

Most of the pilgrims who visited Mont-Saint-Michel stayed in the monastery's guest hall or in one of the several inns in the village at the base of the island. However, with Fox and Isabel both being nobles, they would be afforded more comfortable quarters in the monastery away from the commoners. The only stable was located near the main gate, so they had to leave Zephyr and Comis in the care of a young groom there. With Henri by their side, they began the long trek up the steep and winding path leading to the monastery entrance.

As they ascended, Fox carried the *coffret* and Henri regaled them with stories of his stay on the island, including the time that a ship foolishly tried to come into Mont-Saint-Michel just as the tide was going out. It got stuck on a shoal for three weeks until a storm came along and blew it away.

A cart being hoisted by rope from a portal high up in the monastery's wall caught Fox's attention. Piled high with large sacks tied to iron rings, it was rolling slowly up a nearly vertical ramp.

"What is that?" Isabel asked.

"That is the ingenious way the abbey receives supplies," Henri said. "Vegetables, grain, building materials, tallow, anything the monastery needs for daily life. On the way down, it is filled with leftover cooked food, bread, and ale for the poorer pilgrims, who are forced to leave the abbey after one night's stay."

"The cart has room for all that?"

Henri laughed. "It is much bigger than it looks from here. I'd wager you could fit six men on it."

"A good tip," Fox said to Isabel. "Never gamble with Henri. He's an expert at raffle."

Henri mocked offense. "How dare you accuse me of playing at dice. You know the Church frowns on games of chance."

Isabel was still curious about the cart system. "How does such a large cart get raised up that steep incline?"

"By a windlass."

"What is that?" Isabel asked.

"It's a large wooden treadwheel, twice the height of a man," Fox explained. "A man stands inside it and walks. As the wheel turns, it winds the rope around a spool. That's how cranes raise and lower stones when they construct great cathedrals like the one at Canterbury."

Isabel's eyes glittered with curiosity. "I should like to see it in practice."

"It is no place for a woman," Henri said. "Especially one as fine as you. It is backbreaking work that makes sweat pour from your brow. I spent one awful day on that endless walk in the windlass. Never again."

They stopped in the village to buy a simple gown and head covering for Isabel, which she would change into later, then proceeded to the monastery. There was a single entrance, which required them to ascend a steep set of stairs. Once inside the foyer, Henri spoke to a monk to arrange lodging for Fox and Isabel. Then he took them to see Youssef down a series of passages lit only by the sunlight streaming through the windows. They passed the scriptorium filled with monks writing and illuminating manuscripts, then eventually into the massive kitchen, where workers were preparing the evening supper. Huge ovens were stuffed with baking bread, and the aroma made Fox's stomach rumble.

Men were carrying sacks in from one of two doors at the opposite end. They glanced at the odd sight of Isabel visiting such a workplace in her finery but said nothing.

"That's where the windlass is," Henri said. "They must have raised the cart all the way up by now."

The second door was closed, but Henri breezed through, ushering Fox and Isabel inside before shutting it behind them.

The room was half as big as the kitchen and was dominated by a brick fireplace. Brewing equipment and casks lined the walls, and the smell of barley mash, yeast, and ale mixed with the odor of smoke.

The room's sole occupant was a thin man bent over a complicated set of interconnected ceramic vessels in and around the fireplace. He was so focused on his task that he hadn't noticed them entering.

Suddenly, Henri's voice echoed through the chamber. "Youssef, get your nose out of your alchemy and greet your visitors."

The man spun around, grabbing his chest. He was the same age as Henri, but with dark skin, black hair, and high cheekbones dusted with a smattering of whiskers. "You oaf! You'll cause my heart to stop, surprising me like that. Now, I'm quite busy, so if…"

His eyes went wide when he recognized Fox, who set down the *coffret* and opened his arms in a welcome. "Still dabbling in your unusual enterprises, I see."

Youssef rushed over and gripped Fox in a forceful embrace. "My dear Gerard, you're alive!"

"No thanks to the Devil. He's tried his best to do me in since I last saw you."

"And now you've come to bless us with your presence while you give thanks to Saint Michael?"

"I'm afraid not. I've come to ask for your help."

"Anything for you, Gerard. Now stop being rude and present me to this noble lady."

"This is Lady Isabel. She is the reason for my visit."

"And what a wonderful reason she is. My name is Youssef, as you have already heard." He bowed his head.

Fox had seen many others react negatively to his dark-skinned friend, so he was pleased to see Isabel nod in return and ask, "You have an uncommon accent, Youssef. From where do you hail?"

"Egypt, my lady. But I am no Moor. I'm a Christian like you, but Coptic."

"And the monks care not a whit," Henri said. "Not when Youssef brews the best ale in Normandy. Now he's been expanding his craft. Give Gerard a taste of your medicine."

"Yes, yes!" Youssef picked up a jug next to the apparatus on the fire and poured a small amount of liquid into a cup. "It's a wonder you survived the Pestilence without my elixir to ward it off."

He handed the cup to Fox, who took a sip. The liquid was lukewarm, but it nonetheless burned his tongue and he coughed as it went down.

"What is that?" Fox asked as he made a face.

"I named it burned wine. It's a process called distillation. I learned it from a master brewer in Avignon who brought it back from Egypt, but it's not well known in Europe. It concentrates the fermented grapes into spirits. I've also been experimenting with wheat and barley using the same method." He nodded to a large barrel next to the ale casks.

"That one really kicks you in the stomach," Henri added. "But after a few draughts, you won't mind at all."

Fox didn't care for the taste. "If I come down with the Pestilence, I'll try it again." He tossed the remaining liquid from the cup into the fire. Youssef put out his hands to stop him and shouted, "No!" but it was too late.

The moment that the burned wine hit the fire, it sent a geyser of flame spurting up the chimney. They all stepped back from the heat and watched to see if there was any reason to flee. The flames quickly died back down, and no damage seemed to have been done.

"The grain elixir is even more flammable," Youssef said.

"If the monks knew," Henri said, "they'd never let you make it."

"But they don't, so let us keep it that way, shall we?" Youssef leaned over to Fox. "I make quite a pretty income selling samples to the pilgrims who pass through."

"With me as his main salesman, of course," Henri said.

"I'm sorry to intrude on your successful business venture with our predicament," Fox said, "but you are the two craftiest men I know. We need your help in planning an intricate ruse that will require precise execution."

"We owe you our lives," Youssef said. "Aiding you in this scheme is the least we can offer."

Henri nodded in agreement. "What is it you would have us do?"

Fox looked to Isabel, who took the *coffret*'s key from around her neck and opened the box, pulling aside the silk covering. The gold and gems in the cover of the manuscript dazzled them as they reflected the firelight.

Youssef and Henri stepped closer, gawking at the beautiful book.

"*C'est magnifique*," Henri said.

"I've seen the monks create many books over my years here," Youssef said in wonder, "but I've never seen one that is so remarkable. Have you come to donate it to the library's collection?"

Fox shook his head. "We need your help in destroying this book."

"Obliterate such a masterpiece? Are you mad?"

"He is not," Isabel said. "We have to make it absolutely clear and certain that this manuscript has been incinerated."

"But why would we do such a thing?" Henri asked, incredulous.

"Remember the promise I made," Fox said solemnly, "that I would come back when we could get some measure of justice against Cardinal Molyneux and Basquin?"

Henri and Youssef nodded.

"My friends, today is that day."

## 29

*One year ago*
*May, 1350*

### CHÂTILLON, FRANCE

Thunderclaps and flashes of lightning punctuated the drone of pouring rain. Fox delighted in the wretched conditions as he led an ox pulling a cart full of firewood. Although he'd been planning this escapade for over a month, the storm was a stroke of good fortune. He walked stooped over with a pronounced limp, same as he'd done for his three previous visits to Château de Riquevert. The castle only a few miles south of Paris's walls was Molyneux and Basquin's country retreat outside the city, and today Fox was finally going to get the evidence he needed to clear his family name and prove that his mother Emmeline had been abducted by the cardinal.

Fox took advantage of the fact that since the Great Mortality, laborers were in short supply, so peasants had taken to traveling around looking for paid work instead of living as tenants eking out a living on their lord's property. When a group of such itinerant workers had arrived at Château de Riquevert, Fox was among them. He volunteered for the task of collecting firewood for the castle.

In the evenings he'd dispensed with his disguise and frequented the local tavern until he met one of the castle guards. Fox had plied him with wine to get him to reveal the information needed for a successful infiltration, including the layout of the castle.

Fox limped over the moat's drawbridge and up to the front gate, where he found two men sheltering under cover in the entryway near the portcullis located on the outer side of the thick barbican that served as the castle gatehouse. The heavy iron and oak grating with spikes at the bottom was suspended in grooves so that it could be brought down at a moment's notice. A second portcullis was located thirty feet away on the inner side of the barbican's portico. Fox shuddered to think of both slamming down to trap enemies between them, where the men could be slaughtered at will by crossbowmen shooting through murder holes.

The two barriers were a fresh reminder that Fox would need to be stealthy. If anyone spotted him out of place, any escape would be impossible once one or both were dropped.

The guards were used to him by now and they waved him in with barely a glance, loath to leave their warm places by the brazier in the face of the downpour outside. Nobody else in the castle would care about him, either.

Fox trudged through the central courtyard and stopped the cart at the usual spot behind the stables. He always unloaded the stack of firewood into the nearby storage room. Although the ox would be visible, the cart was out of sight of any patrolling guards, so he would have plenty of time to carry out his plan unnoticed.

He moved a quarter of the logs, making sure that no one was watching him. When he was sure he was unobserved, he took off his sodden cloak and the wooden pattens that protected his boots from the mud and left them in the cart. Now he wouldn't leave any tracks during his trek through the castle.

He'd chosen this time based on his previous visits because most of the workers were eating their midday dinner. The corridors should be deserted long enough for him to complete his task.

His destination was Cardinal Molyneux's private cabinet next to his bed chamber, the office where he conducted business while at the castle and thus the most likely place for the locked chest that Fox was hoping to find.

He padded through the halls, warily checking each corner for anyone in his path and stopping regularly to listen for approaching footsteps. Only once did someone come near him, but the man was in too much of a hurry heading to the privy to notice him.

Fox got to the door and held his breath as he listened outside. He heard no sound from within and pushed it open.

Weak light shone through the windows. The lack of lit candles confirmed that the room was currently unoccupied.

Fox spotted the massive lockbox behind the clerk's writing desk. He closed the door behind him and crept over to it, removing a pair of thin metal prongs from their hiding place within his boot.

He inserted them into the lock as he'd learned from an entry added to his copy of the *Secretum philosophorum*. It was a practice that had come in handy more than once since his excommunication. It didn't take him long to hear the click of the mechanism springing open.

After replacing the prongs in his boot, he lifted the lid and saw a wealth of deeds, proclamations, and other official Church documents, rolled and sealed. But one item stood out. It was a flat leather case.

Nothing else in the lockbox could have held the letter Fox was looking for. He gingerly lifted the case and opened it. Inside was a single piece of parchment. His hands started to tremble when he recognized the seal at the bottom.

It was his mother's emblem pressed into red wax. Next to it was her signature. Emmeline Fox, Lady of Oakhurst.

He scanned the delicate handwriting and saw that it was the note that he'd been searching for. During his year-long investigation leading up to this moment, Fox had discovered the location of a defrocked priest named Lucien who used to be the confessor for both Molyneux and his clerk Lambert. Fox had gone to the destitute Lucien with bribes of wine and gold, hoping to get him to reveal the confessions of Molyneux, who was responsible for Lucien's downfall. It turned out that Molyneux had never confessed any heinous crimes.

But Lambert had.

Molyneux's clerk had disclosed the tale of how he had assisted in Emmeline's capture, how she had been impregnated by the cardinal, and how she had died in childbirth while bearing him a son. Of course, Lucien's testimony would be worthless in a court, but he had provided one final detail that Lambert had shared.

Emmeline had written a letter for Molyneux. It stated that Lambert was the one who had fathered her child by raping her. She wrote it only under Molyneux's threat of harm to her first two sons. The letter, signed and sealed with Emmeline's unique emblem in wax, was held in secret under lock and key at Château de Riquevert as a safeguard against any future accusations. Lambert feared for his life if he tried to steal the letter, which was why it was still in Molyneux's possession.

As he read it, Fox smiled when he recognized the same substitution cipher his mother had taught him as a child. He knew she would have taken advantage of any chance to leave evidence of her plight for her husband or sons to find. To his eye, it was clear that the hidden message blamed Molyneux, not Lambert, for her abduction and rape. Once he showed the deciphered message to the cardinal's rivals at the Papal Palace, Fox thought he would have a good chance of disgracing Molyneux, being absolved of his excommunication, and earning back his stolen lands.

He carefully tucked the parchment into his tunic, locked the chest, and quietly left the room. He retraced his steps, put his cloak and pattens back on, and was diligently unloading the rest of the firewood by the time the courtyard was bustling with post-dinner activity.

When his cart was empty, he took the ox's reins and headed back for the entry gate, elated for the first time since his father's passing. Even the rain had abated for a few moments, which Fox took as a good omen.

But he wasn't halfway across the courtyard when a bone-chilling sight met him. Riding through the gate was Basquin, returning a week earlier than Fox had been expecting. Two other riders trailed him.

Fox put his head down and pulled his cloak farther over his eyes. It was too late to return to his spot behind the stables unnoticed, but he didn't think Basquin had seen him, so he kept limping along.

"I'm famished," Basquin said to the others as he hopped from his horse.

"Perhaps this peasant will give us his ox for our dinner," one of the men said in a joking manner.

The other of Basquin's companions rode over to Fox and jumped down in front of him.

Fox stopped walking.

"How much is this sad-looking beast worth?" the man said to Fox.

"I doubt we could get much meat off of it," Basquin said.

"You can part with it, can't you?" the man-at-arms said with a laugh.

"Only if you don't need any more firewood," Fox said and immediately cursed himself for talking back.

The man stopped laughing. "Maybe I'll make you haul the cart by yourself."

"I'm sorry, sire. No disrespect intended."

Despite Fox's apology, the man-at-arms cuffed him across the cheek, and the hood of his cloak flew back. Fox locked eyes with Basquin, who recognized him instantly.

Fox seized the sword from the man-at-arms' sheath and slashed a killing blow along his torso. As the man fell, Fox leaped onto the soldier's horse.

Basquin's other comrade galloped at him with sword drawn, but Fox parried a strike and thrust his sword through the man's chest.

Basquin didn't move. Fox kicked his horse and turned toward the entryway. All Basquin did in response was yell, "Drop the portcullis!"

Fox hadn't even reached the archway leading through when the heavy gate slammed down, its chain rattling as it fell. The spikes buried themselves in the dirt. Fox's exit was cut off.

"Crossbows to the ready!" Basquin shouted.

Fox spun around, looking up at the battlements. Six crossbowmen leaned over the parapets, their weapons aimed at Fox.

Basquin appraised him. "Those were two of my best men, but that's a price I'm willing to accept for you delivering yourself to me like this. Now, if you'd rather have me present your dead body to the cardinal, by all means stay on that horse and keep your sword in hand."

Fox had no choice. He dismounted and threw the sword to the ground. A half-dozen guards surrounded him. Basquin sauntered over.

"I told you we'd meet each other again. But why on earth would you sneak into the cardinal's castle?"

Fox said nothing.

"You must have come for something valuable. Let's make sure you're not armed."

Basquin ran his hand over Fox and found the hidden parchment. He read it, an amused look on his face.

"You thought it was worth risking your life to get this?" Basquin asked when he was done. "I'd love to see that sniveling clerk removed from the cardinal's service in disgrace, but the scandal wouldn't be welcome, so let's just make sure the temptation is gone forever."

He walked over to the entryway where a torch was burning. He held the letter up to the fire. Fox watched in helpless fury as the proof of Molyneux's crime burned to ashes in front of his eyes. Despair twisted his stomach at seeing the last piece of evidence left by his brave and ingenious mother disappear.

With obvious delight, Basquin said, "Cardinal Molyneux will be here tomorrow. I can't wait for the two of you to meet each other again."

Basquin watched closely as the guards shackled his prisoner in a room above the gate, which was the most heavily fortified part of the castle. Basquin even tested the manacles himself. When he was satisfied they were firm, he looked down at Fox with a smile.

"I'll see you in the morning. I promise it will be a glorious day."

The door closed, and only a pale light shone through the slit windows. Fox squinted as his eyes adjusted to the darkness. He could make out two other men chained to the same stone wall.

"Lovely fellow, isn't he?" one of them said. Fox could just make out red hair and a burly frame.

"For some reason, he doesn't like me," Fox replied. "But younger brothers can be like that sometimes."

"He's your brother?" the other man asked in disbelief. He had a strange accent, and Fox couldn't be sure in the dimness, but he seemed to have unusually dark skin and raven-black hair. "If that's your blood relation, I'd hate to see how your friends treat you."

"I don't have any friends, really."

"If you're in here with us," the redhead said, "then you must be a friend of ours. I'm Henri of Carcassonne. This is Youssef. As you might have noticed, he's from a bit farther away."

"And I wish I were in sunny Cairo right now," Youssef said.

"A pleasure to meet you both. I'm Gerard Fox of Oakhurst."

"An Englishman in Paris?" Henri said. "From your French accent, I would have thought you were a Normandy native."

"It's complicated."

"We might not last past morning when Cardinal Molyneux arrives," Henri said, "so you might as well tell us your story now."

With his hopes of vindication gone up in flames, Fox saw no harm in telling them everything. They both nodded as he related the tale, obviously not surprised in the least about what had happened to him.

"Just when I thought Molyneux and Basquin couldn't be any more evil," Youssef said. "We seem to have a common foe."

"Why are you here?" Fox asked.

"My misfortune is because of my love for a woman. My beautiful Eléanor. After her parents died in the Great Mortality, we fell in love. I was willing to convert from the Coptic faith to marry her, but Cardinal Molyneux craved her lands, so he concocted a charge of sorcery against me and sent her to a nunnery, taking her holdings as a dowry for her entering the convent. I expect a short trial and a burning in the courtyard of this castle."

"I'm sorry to say that I just delivered the wood that will be used. But it was very wet, so you may have more time than you think. What about you, Henri?"

"My tale is much duller. Until a time not long ago, I was a clerk accounting for money going in and out of the Church's coffers in Paris. I discovered that Basquin was stealing a portion of the funds with Molyneux's knowledge. Basquin found out that I was going to report his thievery and leveled the same accusation at me before I could reveal his fraud. A capital crime, of course, but I'll be hanged instead of burned."

"Your mistake was being an honest man working within Molyneux's reach," Fox said.

"My mistake was not wringing Basquin's neck when I had the chance."

"I'm not sure that would have worked, my new friend. Basquin is a trained fighter. When we escape from here, it had better be without him noticing. If we could only get out of the castle, my horse is tied up in a stable not far from here where we could liberate a couple more horses for you two."

Henri laughed at that. "Are you mad? We can't even get out of these manacles, let alone out of the castle."

"When Basquin searched me, he didn't find these." Fox was barely able to reach into his boot and remove the metal prongs stashed inside. "I'd better work fast. They'll lower the portcullises at nightfall."

Henri and Youssef looked at him dubiously as he worked at the locks on the manacles. Thunder crashed regularly, reverberating through the stone room.

"Even if you're able to open those, we can't get out of this chamber," Henri said.

"The guards will open the door for us." There was a small barred hole for the guards to look through, but no one was watching. "It'll just take a bit of sorcery."

After Fox told them his idea, Henri said, "You are a resourceful man, Gerard. This is risky, but it might work."

"It's certainly better than waiting around to be executed," Youssef added.

"The only problem is that we can't steal any horses from the castle," Fox said. "We'd be caught by the time we reached the stable. We'll need to make a quick escape, and we won't get very far on foot before Basquin chases us down on horseback."

"I know how we could bring down the portcullis behind us," Youssef said, getting into the spirit of their escape plan. "If we can tie a thin rope around the winch lever, we can lower it through the groove where the portcullis slides down. Then we can pull it as we escape and have it drop behind us."

Fox nodded in appreciation. "Excellent idea. What do we use for the rope?"

Youssef began tearing his linen tunic into thin strips. "I'll need yours as well to make it long enough." Henri and Fox ripped off their outer garments and handed them over.

"They can simply raise it again after we're gone," Henri said. "It would only take a few moments."

"It looks like you have a thought for how to prevent that from happening."

Henri happily nodded. "They can't turn the winch if the handles have been destroyed."

"Then, my friends," Fox said, "it sounds like we have a plan."

Because of his awkward position, it took quite a while to unlock the manacles, but Henri and Youssef's eyes went wide when the first of them sprung open.

Fox didn't have time to unlock Henri and Youssef because it was close to sundown, so they immediately put their scheme into action. He crouched beside the door, out of view of the peephole above.

He nodded to Henri and Youssef, who began shouting in terror.

"He's gone! What is this sorcery! Guards! Guards! Save us!"

Fox could see the torchlight cast by a guard appearing at the door.

"What's with all the noise, you swine?"

Henri breathlessly babbled, "The new man. He must have been a sorcerer. He made an incantation and then just vanished into thin air in front of our eyes!"

Fox's manacles dangled from the wall still locked together.

"What the blazes!"

The key rattled in the lock, and the door was yanked open. Fox didn't wait until it was fully ajar. He put his shoulder into the door and threw it back into the guard, who went sprawling to the floor.

Fox leaped atop him, plucked the dagger from his belt, and plunged it into his heart.

Another guard was watching in shock. Before he could cry for help, Fox flipped the dagger over and hurled it with all his might. It embedded to the hilt in the man's throat. He fell forward without a sound.

Fox took the manacle keys out of the first guard's hand. He tossed them to Henri. He and Youssef looked at him with stunned admiration.

"Hurry," Fox said quietly.

He dragged the guards into the cell. He took the two men's swords and handed one to Henri when he had freed himself. Youssef was soon unshackled, too, and took the remaining dagger.

"The winch room is this way," Fox whispered.

They crept down the corridor. The falling darkness helped conceal their approach. A guard called out.

"What were those lowly turds going on about?"

Fox came into a large room with two winch mechanisms for raising and lowering the portcullises. A pair of guards were lounging with their backsides on the floor. One was cutting a turnip with his knife and gnawing on the slices. Their halberds leaned against the wall. Neither could scramble to their feet before Fox and Henri cut them down.

They didn't know how many more guards were in this section of the castle, but they might enter at any time, so Fox kept watch as Henri and Youssef quickly completed their tasks.

Each portcullis was suspended by chains over pulleys. The

chains wound around drums turned by four wooden handles. There was a counterweight to make raising them easier. Once a portcullis was fully raised, it was locked into place by a ratchet, but a single throw of a lever would allow the gate to drop all the way to the ground with no further action.

To Fox's relief, both portcullises were still raised.

On the release lever of the portcullis closest to the drawbridge, Youssef tied the thin rope of linen. Youssef made sure the rope was secure around the lever and then threaded it down the groove where the portcullis would slide. It would take an attentive observer below to see it.

At the same time, Henri took one of the halberds and used the axe head to hack at the wooden handles of the winch, striking whenever he heard a thunderclap outside. Soon there were only nubs left, making it impossible for anyone to wind the portcullis back up.

"We're pressing our luck by staying here," Fox said. "We have to go now."

Henri and Youssef each took one of the halberds while Fox wedged the second sword against the winch chain of the inner portcullis so that it wouldn't fall even if the lever were pushed.

The next moments would be the most dangerous part of the escape. They had to make it down the stairway and out the entryway before anyone could intercept them. And even the guards at the entrance wouldn't be their last obstacle. Any men on the walls above would shoot at them with their crossbows as they fled, although the rain would dampen the strings, significantly reducing the weapons' range.

They were just halfway down the stairs when a shout came from above them.

"Alarm! Alarm!"

The dead bodies had been discovered. Fox hoped their sabotage hadn't been noticed in the furor.

The need for stealth was gone. They sprinted down the stairs to the courtyard.

As they rounded the corner to the castle entryway, the gate

guards almost barreled into them as they ran toward the cry for help.

Henri and Youssef were obviously not trained fighters, but the long halberds kept the guards from striking them with their swords. Henri, the taller and stronger of the two, was able to muster enough of a swing to catch one of the guards in the body with the axe head, but as he did the guard was able to slash his hand, causing Henri to drop the weapon.

The second guard knocked Youssef's halberd aside with his sword, the point catching Youssef across his ribs. The distraction was enough to give Fox a chance to put his sword into the man's stomach.

"You certainly know how to cause trouble, don't you?" said a voice behind him.

Fox whipped around and saw Basquin shaking his head not ten feet away. More guards were charging across the courtyard, and Henri and Youssef were no longer in any condition to fight.

"Run!" Fox yelled, and motioned as if he were going to follow them as they bolted for the drawbridge.

But Fox's honor made him stay behind to cover their escape. This was finally his chance to face Basquin. He backed into the entryway, his sword at the ready.

The guards behind Basquin were rushing to help him.

"Leave this one to me," Basquin said to them. "Get the horses and prepare to run those two others down!" The men obeyed his order and ran to the courtyard stable.

"You plan to take me down on your own?" Fox said. "You must get your arrogance from your father."

Basquin smiled. "You mean my confidence."

Fox shrugged. "I suppose you depend on him for everything, don't you?"

Basquin's smile evaporated. With a quickness Fox didn't expect, he swung his sword around so fast that Fox nearly missed blocking it. He staggered back from the blow and spun around to stay on his feet.

He struck back, but Basquin expertly parried him. They

exchanged a furious set of thrusts and slashes, but it was obvious who was the better swordsman, and it wasn't Fox. He'd practiced the discipline all his life, and against most challengers he was far superior, but it seemed as if Basquin moved twice as fast. Every time Fox thought he had the upper hand, Basquin would easily counter him.

Fox was losing, and Basquin knew it. He was enjoying the game, toying with Fox. As the vicious pummeling continued, Fox backed up toward the portcullis they had sabotaged. On the next strike, they got into a clinch. Fox needed to get some separation between them, so he shoved Basquin hard. The push temporarily made Basquin stagger back, giving Fox the space he needed to escape.

Before he could turn to pull the rope, Fox cried out as he felt an agonizing pain in his thigh. He looked down and saw a crossbow bolt protruding from the side of his leg. He buckled from the injury but didn't go down.

Basquin's face contorted into a mask of rage. He turned, pointed his sword at a crossbowman behind him, and took two steps in that direction.

"You fool, I wasn't in trouble! You'll die for that!"

Fox's excruciating injury would have allowed Basquin to best him with two more flicks of his sword. He hobbled to the linen rope and yanked on it, releasing the lever. The portcullis shot down.

At the sound of the wood grinding against stone, Basquin turned back around. He ran toward Fox, who wished he'd try to roll under it and get pierced by the spikes. But it was too late. The portcullis crashed into the dirt, separating the half-brothers.

Fox pulled the bolt from his leg and pressed his hand against the wound.

Basquin was so angry that Fox thought he'd foam at the mouth.

"Your father will be very disappointed in you," Fox said.

Basquin's cheek twitched only slightly, but it was enough to see that the comment hit a nerve. "This isn't over, brother."

"It's over for now."

Fox turned and lumbered off across the drawbridge. This time his limp was real. Every step took his breath away.

"Raise the portcullis!" Basquin screamed behind him. "Immediately!"

A call came down from above. "It has been disabled!"

"Then raise the drawbridge!"

But Fox was already across the moat and joined Henri and Youssef, who were crouched in a ditch. His two new friends were nursing their own injuries.

"That went well," Henri said.

"Are you actually complaining?" Youssef asked.

"Bicker while we run," Fox said, although the best he could manage with his wounded leg was a hasty shamble.

By the time Basquin came to his senses and yelled for his crossbowmen to begin shooting from the battlements, the three of them were lost in the rain-soaked twilight.

## 30

*July, 1351*

### SAINT-MALO

As soon as Basquin arrived in Saint-Malo and discovered that a couple fitting the descriptions of Fox and Lady Isabel had been seen departing the *Bello Vento*, he sent out word that he would need a cadre of men loyal to the Church and Crown to join him on his quest. Then he set about questioning the locals to see if he could find out where the two of them went.

He wondered why they had traveled all the way to Brittany if their final destination was Paris. Not only did it mean more days on the ship, but it significantly extended the travel time to the French capital. Perhaps Isabel had relatives here as well. Without further clues, he would be riding blind into a very large country.

Several of the dock workers had spoken to Fox, but he'd simply asked about the town's amenities. No one had any information about where he was going. It seemed as if Basquin would need to take a chance and guess as to the direction they were heading when two young men nervously approached him.

"Sire," the taller one said, "My name is Gaël, and this is Erwan. We have heard you are inquiring about the man and woman who arrived here two days ago."

"I am. Do you know their whereabouts?"

"I don't, but Erwan might."

Basquin looked at Erwan. "Then tell me."

"He does not speak French, sire," Gaël said, "but I can translate for you."

"Then ask him."

The two of them spoke several sentences in Breton while Basquin waited impatiently.

Finally, Gaël said, "How valuable is this information to you?"

Basquin squinted at them. "If you give me something useful, I'll pay you a sou."

"Three sous," Gaël said without hesitation.

"Don't get greedy. Two sous, and if I find you have tricked me, you'll go through the rest of your lives without tongues."

Gaël gulped and repeated what Basquin had said in Breton. Erwan nodded emphatically. He spoke quickly while Gaël interpreted for him.

"They are going to Rennes."

"How do you know that? Is that what the man told you?" Fox couldn't be that careless.

Erwan shook his head. "The woman let slip that they were heading south after they visited the smith, who is my cousin."

"The woman?"

"The man didn't speak Breton, so he had the woman translate. Her accent was English, but she could speak the language very well."

That had to be Isabel. "Why were they going to Rennes?"

"I don't know. But she seemed very nervous. And she didn't want me to tell anyone that I knew, including the man she was with."

"And yet you are telling me."

Erwan glanced at Gaël. "She said creditors were after them and that you were sent to bring them to justice."

Basquin smiled.

"You are quite right that I am pursuing them. But what they are wanted for is stealing. And you no doubt noticed that they traveled alone, an improper arrangement for a single man and woman."

"She called him her husband," Erwan said.

"Did she? She is therefore only adding to her lies. Did you see how they departed the city?"

"I didn't, but my cousin said they headed toward the East gate of the city when they left the smith."

Basquin nodded, guessing it was a ruse similar to the one they had used when leaving Canterbury. They must have turned south not long after leaving sight of Saint-Malo.

He couldn't help but smile. Fox's downfall was his faith in people, despite everything that had happened to him. Now he'd made a grave error in trusting a woman. The fairer sex made for good playthings, but they were far too simple to entrust with valuable information. Better that Fox kept his plans from her, but it wasn't in his nature. Basquin relished taking advantage of his brother's flaws. It made his task so much easier.

He fished the coins from his purse and handed them over. Gaël and Erwan split them and hurried away.

Basquin spent several more hours gathering his troops, six in all. More than enough to handle Fox once he was found.

Basquin laid out the mercenaries' rules of engagement. He wanted Fox and Isabel alive if possible, but the *coffret* holding the manuscript was the most important item. They had to recover it no matter the cost.

When Basquin described Fox and Isabel, the most experienced of the men, Cyprien, cleared his throat.

"Are you sure they went to Rennes?" Cyprien asked.

"That is the best information I have. Why?"

"Because two days ago I saw a man and woman with horses that sound like the people you seek."

"Where?"

"I was leaving Mont-Saint-Michel. They were waiting with a group of pilgrims to follow the guide to the island, though the couple looked like nobles. I didn't get a look at their faces. Their horses were in the way of my view as I passed, and the lady was wearing a hood."

As Basquin put all of the information together, he got the sinking feeling that he'd nearly been misled yet again. "Did one of the horses carry a wooden box with iron clasps?"

Cyprien nodded.

"And the man's horse. Do you remember it?"

"It was unusual, a mottled silver."

Basquin cursed. "That's them, all right. How well do you know the island?"

"Quite well. I go there regularly to protect the traveling clerks collecting payments for the Church. If they are still there, we will be able to corner them without a problem."

"Then my information was wrong. We ride east."

Basquin despised being manipulated, and Fox had nearly succeeded at doing just that again. Perhaps the woman was as dim-witted as any, but she had played Fox's cunning deceit to perfection.

Clearly, Basquin had providence on his side. Fox might have been a capable trickster, but it was Basquin who had the luck.

# 31

PARIS

Lord Tonbridge's first visit to Paris had been as a young squire accompanying Lord Hartwell of Lancashire. It was common for nobles to send their sons to other peers for training, and Hartwell enjoyed traveling. Tonbridge himself did not share the enthusiasm for voyages, but he would certainly make an exception when Cardinal Molyneux made him King of Jerusalem. However, to make that happen, he still needed to acquire the Icon of the Virgin and Child, and the ride from Honfleur had been fruitless.

During their journey, the writ of safe passage had been useful more than once as they encountered French units wary of any strangers, especially a band of Englishmen. But the bishop's letter, which invoked the name of Cardinal Molyneux, had cleared a path for them. Some parts of the countryside had seemed untouched by the war, while other towns they had ridden through were burned-out husks left that way after the English *chevauchée*. Other villages were intact but abandoned as a result of the Great Mortality. The French nobles who had hosted Tonbridge and his men for the night had been quite curious about the state of England during the war, but the earl was reluctant to share any information that might aid the enemy.

At no point did Tonbridge and his men come across anyone who could definitively say they saw Isabel and her escort, so Tonbridge was beginning to wonder whether he'd been deceived by Basquin. Now that he was in Paris after the hard ride from the coast, he had no choice but to go to Molyneux to tell his version of events before Basquin arrived with his own.

Tonbridge entered the cardinal's residence, and he presented himself to the cardinal's clerk Lambert, who showed him through a luxurious apartment adorned with sumptuous tapestries, polished pewter urns, vases filled with flowers, and velvet-covered furnishings. When he reached the solar, Tonbridge kneeled. But instead of approaching him to receive the kiss to his ring, Molyneux didn't rise from the elaborate carved wooden chair placed next to the hearth.

He gave Tonbridge a thin smile and gestured to the smaller chair next to him, "Sit, Lord Tonbridge."

Tonbridge took his seat. When Molyneux said nothing more, Tonbridge cleared his throat. "Your Eminence, thank you for receiving me into your home."

"I was not expecting to see you at all. Have you come to deliver the manuscript personally?"

Molyneux's eyes pointedly dropped to Tonbridge's empty hands.

"I am afraid that I don't yet have it in my possession. Have you word from Basquin?"

Molyneux tented his fingers. He seemed imperturbable. "He doesn't accompany you?"

"We were separated at Honfleur."

"And why have you come all this way? Was the wedding completed?"

Tonbridge sighed. He loathed to share his failures, but the tale was better coming from him rather than Basquin. The cardinal listened quietly and attentively.

At the end of the story, Molyneux shook his head in open contempt and contemplated the news silently for an agonizingly long time. Finally, he said, "This will not do."

"Never fear," Tonbridge said hastily. "We will have the manuscript soon."

"What makes you so confident?"

"Because Isabel has relations in Paris. This must be her destination."

"What relations are these?"

"A cousin. Her name is Lady Claire Duval."

Molyneux tilted his head in recognition. "The wife of Sir François Duval, whose estate is at Saint-Jacques?"

"Do you know him?"

"Yes. You say that it's likely your betrothed will call on them for help?"

Tonbridge nodded. "I will go there personally and determine whether Isabel has paid her a visit."

Molyneux stood, his ruby robes cascading around him. "We will go together."

Tonbridge quickly rose to his feet. "Now?"

"Do you have another more pressing engagement at the moment?"

"I know you are a busy man, Your Eminence. I do not wish to intrude on your time."

Molyneux stared at him so icily that Tonbridge had to stifle a shiver. "Do you think *anything* is more important right now than acquiring what you promised me?"

"Of course not. Forgive me."

With a flourish, the cardinal breezed out of the solar and told Lambert to have his carriage prepared.

Tonbridge's men followed the coach while he sat inside with the cardinal. The ride to the south of Paris took them past wagons transporting huge limestone blocks toward the city. In an effort to fill the chilly silence, Tonbridge commented that they must bring in a pretty penny.

"Those stones come from the same mines that were excavated to build Notre Dame," Molyneux explained as they passed peasants heaving one into an oxcart. "This entire area is strewn with more tunnels than a mole could dig in a lifetime. They crisscross under many of the estates built in this area, including Sir François's. Income from these mines is what makes the Duval land so valuable."

After passing through the town of Saint-Jacques, they traveled a hundred yards down a drive that ended at a stately château surrounded by a moat. They crossed a drawbridge under a large stone carving of a rampant griffin standing on the hind legs of a lion and baring an eagle beak and talons for attack with its wings spread. The carriage came to a stop in the central courtyard. At the front of the manse, they were greeted by a retinue of servants as well as a man and woman in noble attire. They had no doubt been notified of Molyneux's imminent arrival by a messenger sent ahead of them. It wouldn't do to appear without the proper reception from the hosts.

When Tonbridge and Molyneux alighted from the carriage, the whole household dropped to one knee and bowed their heads. Although the *chevalier* was a strapping man with a strong chin and a prominent nose, he was having trouble lowering his leg to the ground. He and his wife kissed the cardinal's ring and then rose back to their feet.

"Sir François," Molyneux intoned.

"Your Eminence," François said, "your visit is unexpected but most welcome. I believe you remember my wife, Lady Claire." She was a handsome woman dressed in the latest style.

Molyneux nodded at her. "How could I forget a woman blessed by the Lord with such lovely cheekbones?"

Claire smiled tightly, but said nothing. Tonbridge noted that she seemed uncomfortable in Molyneux's presence.

"And you may not know his face, but surely you know him by name and reputation. This is Sir Conrad Harrington, Earl of Tonbridge."

That produced surprised looks from them both.

"I understand you were to marry Lady Claire's cousin," François said. "I trust the nuptials were well met. Will she be joining us shortly?"

Molyneux looked at him silently for a moment, then said, "That is what we are here to discuss."

François held his arm out. "Your Eminence, my house is prepared for you if you would accept our hospitality."

They went into the château and were seated in the great hall where chairs and a table had been placed for them. Claire oversaw the delivery of food and wine. After fulfilling her duties as hostess, she left the men to talk. Molyneux didn't partake, so Tonbridge didn't either.

"How does the summer treat you, Your Eminence?" François said awkwardly.

"There is no need for pleasantries," Molyneux said. "I will get straight to the point. Have you seen Lord Tonbridge's betrothed, Lady Isabel?"

"Betrothed?" François looked in confusion at Tonbridge. "Are you not yet married?"

If he was pretending, Tonbridge couldn't detect it.

"She betrayed me and stole something that was rightfully mine," he said.

"I'm very sorry to hear this. She has dishonored us both by her actions. I'm sure Lady Claire will be quite upset that her family character has been besmirched. Where is Lady Isabel now?"

"That is what we were hoping you could tell us," Molyneux said.

"I would surely help you if I could, but I have never met her, and Lady Claire has not seen her for many years."

"And if Lady Isabel does call on you?"

"Then I will contact you immediately. I will not have a traitor in my midst."

"Good. If she does come, she may be in the company of a scoundrel named Gerard Fox of Oakhurst, and they will be in possession of a very valuable item. Above all, you must make sure this object is transferred to us safely."

"May I ask what this item is?"

"It is a *coffret* with a strong lock," Tonbridge said. "The box's lid is carved with a lady and a unicorn."

"Do not attempt to open it," Molyneux said. "I have the key. If you attempt to force it open, it may damage the contents, of which I can say nothing further."

The key had been sent by courier to Molyneux before the

wedding. That way, the *coffret* could be transported by Basquin and opened only upon its arrival in Paris. What the cardinal did not say was that Isabel held the original key.

Molyneux leaned forward. "Sir François, you still owe me a great debt, one that must be repaid to me soon if you do not wish to forfeit your property to the Church."

Tonbridge raised his eyebrows and listened to the conversation with even more interest.

François nodded. "And I intend to pay."

"How? I understand you have been having trouble making your mining quota, what with the distressing number of laborers struck down by the Great Mortality."

"It has been difficult lately, yes, but my standard will be represented in the king's tournament to be held at Château de Tournoël in four weeks. The one who wins the honors of the tournament receives the Crusader's Chalice. I trust handing it over to you will be more than enough to settle my debt."

The famed drinking cup, chiseled from solid rock crystal and adorned with pearls, gems, and gold bands, had been given to Saint Louis as a diplomatic gift after the crusade he led.

Molyneux seemed amused by François's proposal, perhaps because it sounded so unlikely to occur. "I have always admired the chalice as a symbol of crusade. If you win and give it to me, your debt will be cleared."

Tonbridge glanced at the French knight's leg. "And how do you intend to participate?"

"I have hired a champion to fight in my stead. He is quite good."

"Be that as it may," Molyneux said, "if you turn over Tonbridge's betrothed and her *coffret* to us, I shall also consider your obligation fulfilled. If your champion then wins the match, the Crusader's Chalice will be yours."

François looked shocked by the statement. "You are too kind, Your Eminence."

With no other business to conduct, Molyneux stood, as did Tonbridge, and François made his obeisance.

After they left and were settled in the carriage, Molyneux gave a withering look to Tonbridge.

"I am not pleased that your betrothed may cost me Sir François's debt. Until this matter is settled, you serve me, do you understand? Like Sir François, you made a bargain, and I intend to hold you to it."

Tonbridge nodded. "I will deliver what I promised."

"I'm glad to hear it." Molyneux eyed François's château. "I don't trust this *chevalier*. Post two men on the road leading to his house at all times to watch for visitors. If we can intercept Lady Isabel before she meets with her cousin, I will get both the manuscript and this valuable estate."

## 32

### Mont-Saint-Michel

After several days of planning, Youssef, Henri, Fox, and Isabel all agreed that they were ready to head to Rennes. Basquin should have arrived in Saint-Malo by now, so it was time to carry out their scheme to dupe him. To prepare for their departure from Mont-Saint-Michel, Isabel volunteered to join Youssef in the stable to get the horses ready this morning. As she helped him connect a cart to his horse's harness, he delighted her with tales of Egypt and the Holy Land. She seemed scarcely able to believe his recounting of the size of the pyramids of Giza and wondered aloud if he was exaggerating for effect, but she was so enthralled that she rarely interrupted otherwise. He also told her of exotic animals like elephants, lions, and camels, as well as the Roman Colosseum and the ruins of the Forum.

"It all sounds so adventuresome and magical," she said, tying together the harness's leather straps as Youssef had taught her. "You should write your tales for others to enjoy. I know I would delight in reading them."

"Writing stories is for monks and nuns," Youssef replied. "As Gerard knows, I prefer making things with my hands."

"I have been curious. How did you come to know Sir Gerard?"

"That is a tale in itself, although I don't know how much he would want me to share."

"At least a little," she pleaded.

Youssef smiled. "Your charm can't be ignored." He told the story of his and Henri's imprisonment before meeting Fox and escaping from Cardinal Molyneux's castle.

"I'm glad that your injury healed."

"It was a small price to pay for my freedom, but the wound was insignificant compared to my true loss."

"Eléanor?"

He nodded.

"What happened to her?"

The memories were painful, but Youssef put on a brave face. "She is safe, and resigned if not happy. A nun at an abbey in Reims."

"I'm so sorry."

"As you can see, we all have reason to despise Molyneux and his bastard." He buckled the belly band to finish harnessing his horse. "I need to return to the abbey now and prepare my elixir for travel. My spirits should fetch a good price in Rennes."

"I can't thank you enough for helping us."

"You're very welcome, though it is not necessary. I'm glad Gerard has given us an opportunity for retribution. Besides, Henri and I have been confined to this island for too long. It will be good to stretch our legs."

Isabel picked up the saddle for Comis, carrying the bulky object awkwardly. Youssef helped her lift it onto her horse's back.

"This is no work for a lady," he said.

Isabel looked down at her plain brown gown and sleeveless overtunic, a far cry from the fine fitted kirtle and silk surcoat she'd arrived in. "Look at me. I'm no lady."

"I understand the need for disguising yourself, but to carry out men's manual labor as well?"

"It's the least I can do."

Together they lifted Zephyr's larger saddle into place, then the one for Henri's horse. Youssef would be driving the wagon.

"I can bridle the horses and cinch the saddles," Isabel said. "You should go tend to your business."

"I must say you seem comfortable here," Youssef said. "No offense intended, my lady."

"None taken. I've spent many a lovely day with horses."

"Then I'll leave you to it. I'll be back down with Gerard and Henri once we've lowered the spirits with the windlass. Then we'll finish packing our things."

"You seem a bright man, Youssef. Do you think our plan will really work?"

He smiled at her reassuringly, trying not to reveal his doubts. "There are some details remaining to figure, but we will have a long ride to Rennes to work them over."

"If Basquin and Tonbridge are actually there."

"Gerard seems to think they're still following you. I trust his instincts. And I agree that this might be the only way to set you free from your betrothed once and for all."

She gave Youssef an enigmatic smile, and he left her in the stable humming a haunting melody that slowly faded as he made his way up the serpentine path to the monastery.

"How do you know the monks won't miss the book?" Fox asked Henri. He was carrying the *coffret* on the outdoor terrace along the north side of the abbey. Inside the secured box was a manuscript lifted from the monastery's library to replace Isabel's own book, and Isabel's key for its lock was around Fox's neck. They had already rolled the barrel of spirits from the brewery to the room with the windlass cart and were to meet Youssef there. Fox would send the *coffret* down on the cart with the spirits so that they wouldn't have to carry it all the way to the bottom of the island on foot.

"The librarian will surely miss it at some point," Henri said. "Monks visiting from all of Christendom scour the library looking to copy texts their libraries don't have. But this Greek manuscript has clearly lost many of its leaves, making it useless for transcription."

The stolen book was the right size, which was why Fox had originally chosen it, but when he realized what text it was, he thought it would make the ideal substitution. Too bad Molyneux would never know. Their plan was simple in conception, but difficult in execution. Molyneux wanted the manuscript badly, and Tonbridge and Basquin wanted to recover it for him. If they believed the manuscript no longer existed, they would have no reason to pursue Fox and Isabel. Surely, Tonbridge would be upset about his matrimonial betrayal, but he could keep his betrothed's lands and possessions if she were a fugitive, so what would be the point of chasing her across the country?

The key was making them all believe that the manuscript—and the Icon with it—had been utterly destroyed. One of them had to see it happen. Tossing it into the ocean or a river wasn't possible because the wooden *coffret* might float even if weighted down. They had to burn it.

"This smith you know in Rennes," Fox said, "does he have a loose tongue?"

Henri shook his head. "But he needn't know of the details of our plan. For the right price, he'll let us toss the *coffret* into his furnace no questions asked."

"Our timing will be critical. Basquin must see it placed into the fire, but he can't remove it before it's burned beyond recognition." The parchment pages would ignite once the box had caught fire, but the gold placed in the box to simulate the cover would take longer to melt.

"Don't worry," Henri said. "Those furnaces can turn iron to liquid. It will only take a few moments for the box and its contents to be reduced to ashes."

"As long as Basquin is convinced that it's the *coffret* he's after. If he has any doubts that it's the same one, they will continue to seek us no matter how far we venture."

Henri stopped along the balustrade and looked at Fox. "Us? You *are* smitten with her, aren't you?"

Fox looked away. "I don't know what you mean. My only interest is in depriving Cardinal Molyneux of his precious prize."

"If that were true, you would have obliterated the manuscript long ago. But you haven't, because of Lady Isabel."

Fox sighed. "I'm simply helping a damsel in distress."

Henri huffed in disbelief. "Even after all this time away from you, my friend, I can tell that you're taken with her."

"That's absurd," Fox said, clearing his throat. "She is my charge. I have a responsibility to get her and her possessions to safety. Despite some rather dubious escapades in my past, I like to think that I have some chivalrous instincts left. Now can we leave this island?"

Henri looked out toward the ocean. "Blast!"

"What's wrong?"

"We're too late." Henri pointed at the flats far out between the island and the ocean. "You see that line of water crossing the bay? That means the tide will be in soon. It took longer than I expected getting Youssef's spirits prepared this morning. We will have to wait until mid-afternoon for the next low tide."

They crossed the west outdoor terrace and were about to go inside the abbey when Henri continued on to the south balustrade and clucked with annoyance.

"Fools! Crossing the flats without a guide? And on horses, no less! Serves them right if they become mired."

Fox hurried next to him and looked down where Henri was staring.

Seven men on horseback were trotting across the sand in the vague footprints left by the last pilgrim group. From this far away, their faces were but needlepoints.

Fox nonetheless went cold when he saw them. In an instant, he knew that all of their planning had been for naught.

The second man in line had flowing blond hair and a blue cotehardie that Fox had last seen when they were sailing away from Sandwich.

Somehow, some way, despite Fox and Isabel's deception, Basquin had discovered their true location. And with the tide coming in, they would all soon be stuck on the island with no escape.

 33

When Basquin's party reached the sole gate to Mont-Saint-Michel, they dismounted. Riding up the steep streets and stairways of the village to the monastery would be impossible. He posted men to watch for anyone trying to get away while he and Cyprien took the horses into the stable. Just as he'd hoped, he found Fox's horse inside. Mottled silver, white swirl, sloping Arabian nose. Unique and recognizable. Fox's pathetic dedication to the animal was pure weakness. The horse was already saddled, which meant Fox was preparing to leave, though his weapons were nowhere to be seen. Thanks to Cyprien's observation, they had arrived just in time to block the escape.

A pretty blonde maiden rather than a groom was tending the horses. She saw Basquin and then quickly looked away in shyness.

"Girl," Basquin said, "where is the owner of this horse?"

The maiden continued looking at the floor and said something in Breton.

Cyprien translated. "She says she doesn't speak French."

"Then ask her."

Cyprien did so, and the girl mumbled something and shook her head.

"She doesn't know."

"Tell her to watch our horses," Basquin said.

When Cyprien told her, the girl bowed her head and they left the stable.

"We will search every house on the way up to the abbey," Basquin commanded. "If anyone resists, they are to be considered heretics and may be slain on the spot."

As they began the methodical hunt for Fox, Cyprien said, "I

wish I had seen that lass when I was here before. I would have shown her what a real Breton was like."

Basquin stopped. "What do you mean?"

Cyprien shrugged. "I would have noticed such a beautiful girl when I was here a few days ago. Besides, she's not Breton. Her accent is off. She wasn't born there."

Basquin thought back to her blonde hair…

"Come with me. The other men will keep looking."

They returned to the stable as the woman was trying to leave. She nodded as she attempted to pass them, but Basquin grabbed her to pull her back inside.

"Where are you going?" he asked in French.

Cyprien began to translate into Breton, but Basquin put up a hand to stop him.

"She understands very well what I just said, don't you, Lady Isabel?"

A look of fear crossed her face momentarily before transforming into one of contempt.

"Why aren't you in Rennes?" she said.

Basquin could hardly contain his relish at capturing her. "I almost did go there, but Cyprien here was eagle-eyed enough to remember seeing Gerard's horse when he was leaving Mont-Saint-Michel. That timidity you showed earlier was merely playacting."

She tossed her head defiantly. "I recognized you as soon as you walked in."

"Your disguise is convincing—common clothes, simple hair— but you should have pretended to be French."

"The accent revealed me, didn't it?" She shook her head in anger at her mistake.

"Speaking Breton was clever, as was your deceit in Saint-Malo, but I am not a man easily fooled. Now, where is the manuscript?"

"Very well hidden."

"Perhaps Gerard has it. His location?"

"I don't know."

"It doesn't matter. I'll find him. And after that, I will take you to your betrothed in Paris where he is waiting for you. I'm sure he will be delighted to see you again. Perhaps Cardinal Molyneux will even conduct the marriage ceremony himself while you're there."

"I will never marry that pig-nosed knave."

"We'll see about that," Basquin said as he went to the stable door. "Stay with her, Cyprien, and be watchful. As you've seen, she can be quite cunning. And remember, she is Lord Tonbridge's betrothed. If I find that you have touched her, I will strike you down myself. Do you understand?"

Cyprien nodded. He drew his sword, pushed Isabel into a corner, and sat her down.

"Don't worry, my lady," Basquin said. "I will be back soon enough."

Then he exited to join the search for Fox and the manuscript.

Fox had been watching the stable and town gates from the ramparts of the abbey. When he saw Basquin and his hireling exit and then re-enter the stable, he knew Isabel had been discovered. Only Basquin emerged, evidently leaving his man behind to guard her.

"What shall we do?" Henri asked. "Fight them?"

"With what? You know the abbey doesn't allow weapons to be carried inside. My sword and bow are locked in a chest in the stable, and I count five men ascending to the monastery with Basquin. Knowing him, the mercenaries he has hired are both skilled and brutal, and they certainly won't be adhering to the ban on weapons in the abbey."

"But how can we escape? The tide will be in soon. There are no boats here right now, so your brother will have hours to hunt us down before we can possibly leave the island."

A moment later, Youssef joined them, out of breath from running.

"I saw the armed men," he said. "I couldn't go back to Lady Isabel without getting caught. Are they here for you?"

Fox nodded. "Basquin must have seen through our ruse in Saint-Malo and came here instead of going to Rennes."

"Then our plan won't work. We can't burn the box now."

Fox looked at the *coffret* and then realized that the abbey's kitchen was not far away.

"The baking ovens," he said.

Henri shook his head. "They are not nearly as hot as a smith's furnace."

"It's all we have." He looked at his friends with regret. "I apologize for bringing this danger here to you."

"We are your brothers," Henri said, "perhaps more than he is."

"I couldn't agree more," Youssef added. "But we still need to get away from Basquin. I'm just sorry we have to leave my spirits behind."

The thought of Youssef's barrel of elixir that they were going to lower on the cart gave Fox an idea.

"Does the room with the windlass have a lock?" he asked.

"The windlass?" Youssef asked, dumbfounded by Fox's suggestion. "You're not serious."

"It's our only chance."

"The door has a padlock," Henri said, "but to secure the items within from outside."

"Then we'll have to barricade the door from the inside to give us time to lower the cart and then climb down the rope."

Henri held up his crippled hand. "Won't work, my friend. I couldn't grip the line."

"Then Youssef and I will run the windlass, and you can ride down in the cart. We'll follow after it's at the bottom."

"And they'll follow us down the rope," Youssef said.

Fox thought of Youssef's barrel of elixir currently waiting to be lowered.

"I think we can keep them from coming down after us," Fox said. "But first, we need to get them all the way up here as fast as we can. Stay back so he doesn't see you."

He leaned over the rampart and saw Basquin a hundred feet below him on the pathway leading to the abbey entrance.

"Ho there, brother!" Fox yelled down. "Is it me you're after?"

Basquin looked up and smiled wickedly. "What a pleasure to face you again, Gerard."

"I see you've brought help with you."

"They're only here to protect my rear. I will be happy to fight you alone."

"I'm sure you'd rather have this." Fox held up the *coffret*, making sure that Basquin got a good look at its distinctive lid.

"I already have Lady Isabel. If you give me the box, I will give you her life."

"What do I care for her life? She's nothing to me. Besides, I wouldn't trust your word farther than a snail's length."

"I know. But I was required to make the offer as a gentleman."

"A bastard is what you are. The product of your father kidnapping and raping my mother."

"So *you* say. But you could never prove it, could you? And why would anyone believe an excommunicated heathen such as you?"

"All I want is for you to fail in bringing this to Cardinal Molyneux," Fox said. "And I will see it destroyed before you get your hands on it."

That wiped the smile from Basquin's face. He barked orders for his men to speed up, and they sprinted up the stairs toward the abbey.

Fox took off for the kitchen with Henri and Youssef close behind.

"Basquin sounded as mad as a badger," Henri said as they ran.

"I know I enjoyed hearing that," Youssef replied.

"I hope making him angry was the right move," Fox said. "If the ovens aren't already stoked, this could all be for nothing."

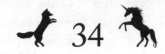 34

Basquin and his five mercenaries ran up the stairs to the abbey. He posted two at the entrance to make sure Fox didn't get around him and rushed inside, ignoring the objections of the monks at the main gate to the abbey.

He heard pounding footsteps somewhere ahead and ran toward the sound, his sword drawn in defiance of the monastery's ban on weapons. Even if he were confronted by a brave priest or monk, he bore Cardinal Molyneux's signet, which would silence any objections.

He spotted Fox carrying the *coffret* as he ran through a door and slammed it behind him.

"Where does that go?" he asked one of the mercenaries who was familiar with the abbey.

"The kitchen."

"Is there any other way out?"

"Yes, a stairway that leads up to the refectory."

"Take a man and circle around that way," Basquin said with satisfaction. "We have him cornered."

He gave the hireling a few moments to run to the other exit with his companion, watching the door in case Fox decided to backtrack. When he was certain that they were in place, he took the final mercenary with him and yanked open the kitchen door.

The kitchen workers, who were busy making the midday dinner, glanced up in surprise at seeing armed men burst into the room. Heat from the ovens made the interior stifling.

Fox was at the opposite end, but nowhere near the stairs. He was empty-handed, and there was no sword on his belt. The other two mercenaries came into the room from the stairs as the workers fled past them, cutting off Fox's only avenue of escape.

"You're finished, Gerard. Tell me where the *coffret* is, and I might spare your life."

Fox scoffed at the proposal. "That offer is worthless coming from a deceitful weasel like you."

Basquin shrugged. He had no intention of honoring the proposal.

"Have it your way." He advanced on Fox, warily keeping his guard up. Fox was skilled enough to be dangerous, even unarmed.

"If you want the box, I hope Cardinal Molyneux will be satisfied with ashes."

Fox turned and dashed through the open door behind him, slamming it shut. It was followed by the sound of it being barricaded from within.

"What room is that?" Basquin demanded of a cook.

"The windlass room," the man answered. "For raising the cart."

Basquin fumed at what that meant. "He's trying to escape! Break down the door! Now!"

He dispatched one of the men to go get the two stationed at the abbey entrance to join them in trying to burst the door open.

Basquin was still curious about Fox's last taunt. *Satisfied with ashes?*

He'd said earlier that all he wanted was for Basquin to fail in bringing the manuscript to the cardinal, that he would rather destroy it than give it over. Either he didn't know what the manuscript actually contained or he didn't care if the Icon was annihilated.

And how would he do it? He could tear it to pieces or he could burn it…

The ovens. With horror, Basquin finally understood. He whirled around and saw the *coffret* in one of the ovens. It was already on fire.

He sprinted to the oven. Using his sword, he knocked the box toward the opening, but it caught on something and wouldn't come all the way out. He dropped the sword. With his gloved hands, he grabbed the iron clasps and screamed in pain as the searing heat penetrated the leather. Despite the pain, he pulled on the red-hot metal until the *coffret* was free.

It clattered to the floor, still burning. In agony, Basquin picked up a bucket of water and splashed it on the box, extinguishing the flames. Then he thrust his hands into another bucket to soothe his scalded fingers under the charred gloves.

Any longer in the oven, and the *coffret* could have been completely destroyed. The surface was scorched, but it didn't look as if the thick wood had burned all the way through. The contents likely hadn't suffered any injury. He'd managed to save it in time.

He didn't dare force it open and potentially cause his own damage to the Icon, since the box was still basically intact and locked. That honor would have to go to Cardinal Molyneux, who held the key.

Basquin peeled off the ruined gloves to reveal blistered fingers. He picked up his sword but could barely grip the hilt because of the pain. Although his quick action saved the manuscript, he was in no condition to fight. He gingerly placed the sword back in his scabbard and wrapped his hands in linen kitchen cloths.

By this time, the two remaining men had arrived and were battering the door to the windlass room with the other three.

"Stay here until that door is open," Basquin commanded. "Then kill anyone inside. Follow them down if you have to, but I don't want them to reach the island's gate."

He turned to the lead mercenary and pointed at the *coffret*. "Bring that and come with me."

The mercenary stuffed the blackened box into an empty flour sack, slung it over his shoulder, and followed Basquin out of the kitchen.

Basquin hated to leave, but if his men didn't finish off Fox, he'd be facing his brother alone, unable to hold a sword properly. His highest priority was to get the manuscript to Molyneux. His father would no longer have reason to deny him the Fox family lands and knighthood he deserved if he delivered it intact.

He had to get off the island before the tide fully surrounded

Mont-Saint-Michel. Then no matter what happened, he would have an insurmountable head start back to Paris, where he would present the manuscript to the cardinal and receive his just reward.

As he exited the abbey, he looked at the cart coming down the steep ramp. There was only one man aboard it. He couldn't make out the man's face, but it clearly wasn't Fox.

 35

Fox had never operated a windlass, but the principle was simple enough. Shaped like an enormous hollow barrel turned on its side and mounted on an axle, the treadwheel was connected to the winch rope. The rope extended over a groove in the window where it was attached to a cart with wheels that rode against a sharply pitched ramp. The treadwheel was wide enough to hold two men walking to turn it, but Fox was the only one inside. It had taken a few tough strides to start it up, but now it was turning more easily. Fox, who was already breathing hard, had to brace himself and walk steadily to keep the cart holding Henri from dropping out of control, and there was no stopping until it reached the bottom.

"How far to go?" he asked Youssef between breaths.

Youssef briefly paused what he was doing and looked out the window.

"It's more than halfway down."

Youssef continued generously ladling clear liquid from his spirits barrel onto the rope as it spun past him.

The creaking of the wooden windlass didn't mask the heavy pounding on the room's lone door. With each blow, the barricaded door shook a little harder. It was but a matter of time before Basquin's mercenaries broke it down. If that happened before the cart reached the bottom, Fox and Youssef would have little chance of surviving.

"Almost there!" Youssef called out.

Moments later, the rope went slack. Fox came to a stop, then reversed direction until the rope tightened. He hopped out, wiping the sweat from his brow, and locked the treadwheel in place with a block.

At the window, he could see Henri at the bottom waving up at them while he held a torch in his good hand. Fox looked around and caught a glimpse of Basquin exiting the abbey and hurrying down the stairs into the town. A man with him was carrying a large sack.

"Basquin has something," Fox said, cursing in frustration. "It must be the *coffret*."

"Never mind that now," Youssef replied, pointing at the trembling door. "We need to leave!"

Fox pulled on his gloves. "Is the rope slick?"

"No, the liquid isn't oily, and the fibers are rough. Our grip should be fine."

"Then go."

The lithe and agile Youssef climbed out the window, keeping his hands on the rope, which was as thick as a ram's horn. He braced his feet against the ramp and began descending.

As soon as there was space, Fox joined him on the line. Instead of putting his feet against the ramp's stones, he wrapped his legs around the rope and lowered himself hand over hand.

They had competing pressures driving them. If they lost their grip for even a moment, it was a long and lethal fall to the rocks below. But if they went too slowly, they could then be stuck high on the rope when the door finally gave way. The mercenaries could either simply cut the rope to kill them or pull the cart up using the windlass in order to capture them.

"Hurry!" Henri yelled, as if they needed any prodding.

Fox didn't say anything, concentrating on his hold, and Youssef failed to respond as well. Fox could hear the wind whistling over his heavy breathing in addition to Youssef's occasional grunts of effort. The spirits soaking the rope gave off a pungent and acrid scent that burned his nostrils.

At one point, Fox caught up to Youssef, so he took a moment to look out at the flats. The water was already racing across the sand from the ocean, and it wouldn't be long before the tide engulfed the island.

When they were only a few yards above the cart, Henri shouted again.

"They're through!"

Fox looked up and saw faces peering over the edge of the window. The men seemed to be arguing about what to do.

He looked down at Youssef. "Jump!"

Youssef pushed himself away from the wall and let go. He was only a few feet above Henri, who caught the smaller man and cushioned his fall.

Fox loosened his grip and slid quickly down the rest of the rope until his feet came to rest on the top of the cart.

He hopped to the ground and peered up at the window. Fox was worried they would simply leave the room and run back down the monastery's stairs as Basquin had done. But their employer must have commanded them to follow their quarry at all costs because they did exactly what Fox was hoping they'd do.

Seeing how easily Fox and Youssef had made it down, the four men climbed out onto the rope to make the same descent toward the island's base.

Fox waited until the topmost man was well away from the window, then said, "Let's see if this works."

He took the torch from Henri and touched it to the rope. Just as Youssef had claimed, the rope burst into flame, and fire raced up its length. Fox, Henri, and Youssef stood back, knowing what was to come.

The mercenaries cried out in terror at seeing the blaze tearing toward them. They scrambled to climb back up to the window, but the effort was far greater than going down.

In moments, the fire caught them, and one by one the men let go as the flames shot up the rope and erupted in their faces. They screamed and plummeted to the ground, landing with sickening thuds. Broken and bloodied bodies littered the stones. None of the men so much as twitched.

"Those are powerful spirits," Fox said.

"It's no wonder the elixir burns up the Pestilence inside you," Henri said.

"You can also use it on wood to make a cooking fire light more quickly," Youssef said proudly as the rope continued to burn. "I guarantee no one else will be coming down that way."

"Then our rear is protected," Fox said, turning toward the gate, which was still a good hundred yards below them.

Despite their rapid speed down the rope, they were too late to intercept Basquin. Through a gap in the buildings, Fox saw him and his companion entering the stable.

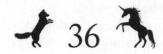 36

Basquin kicked open the door to the stable and found Cyprien and Isabel exactly where he had left them. She gave him a poisonous glare from her seat in the corner.

"What have you done to Gerard?" she demanded.

"He'll be dead soon enough," Basquin lied. He'd seen what had happened to his men climbing down the rope.

"Then why do I see fear in your eyes?"

He ignored her and turned to the mercenary carrying the sack with the *coffret*. "Lash that to my horse." Then he looked at Cyprien. "Take her with us."

Cyprien grabbed her arm and wrenched Isabel to her feet. She struggled, and Cyprien slapped her across the face to quiet her.

Basquin pointed at him. "Do that again, and I'll run you through. She is to be unharmed and unblemished when we return her to Lord Tonbridge."

Cyprien's lip curled in derision, but he nodded. He took her toward his horse.

As the mercenary began to secure the *coffret*, the saddle suddenly tilted to the side and slid off. He barely caught the sack before it fell to the ground.

The strap underneath the horse had been let out three notches.

"She must have loosened the girth," Cyprien said, raising his hand over her again but restraining himself when he saw the incensed look Basquin shot him.

"I can see that, you simpleton," Basquin said. "Check our other horses."

The mercenary looked under the saddles.

"They've all been let out."

Basquin cursed Isabel's foresight in loosening all of their saddles as soon as he had left her alone in the stable. She was much keener than he'd originally thought.

"We don't have time to tighten them again and check for other sabotage." Not with Fox on his way and the tide rolling in. He looked around the stable and saw that Fox's horse and two others had already been saddled.

Basquin pointed them out to the mercenary with the *coffret*. "Use one of those."

The mercenary approached Fox's horse, but it lunged at him with teeth bared.

"He's too difficult," Basquin said, not wanting to fight the horse all the way back to Paris. "That one."

The mercenary lashed the sack to a brown horse while Cyprien lifted Isabel onto a white palfrey with him.

When the bag was secured, Basquin got on, wincing as he held the reins with his injured hands. He looked at the mercenary. "Stay here and kill anyone who enters the stable." Before the man could protest that he would then be stuck on the island, Basquin dropped a hefty pouch of coins at his feet.

The mercenary's eyes bulged at the bonus payment. He picked up the pouch, drew his sword, and nodded.

Basquin kicked hard. The horse whinnied and charged forward.

As they exited the stable doors, Basquin saw Fox running toward them only a dozen yards away, but he wasn't close enough to be a threat.

Basquin smiled and waved as he galloped out onto the sand, the tidewater coming in from both sides. Judging by how fast the water was flowing, he estimated they would barely make it across to dry land. Even if the mercenary he'd left behind didn't manage to kill Fox, by the time his brother could follow, they'd be long gone.

Fox seethed as he watched the jubilant Basquin ride away, with Isabel in the clutches of his hireling close behind on her horse Comis. Fox needed Zephyr to launch a pursuit.

He had seen a different man exit the stable with Isabel than the one he'd seen entering, so he knew someone was still inside the building. He crouched and eased the door open, a butcher's knife from the abbey's kitchen in his hand. He peeked inside.

A sword smashed into the jamb where his head would have been. Fox sprang to his feet and jabbed the knife through the mercenary's neck. The man collapsed backward, his sword clattering to the floor.

With no time to retrieve Legend from the lockbox, Fox snatched up the mercenary's sword and vaulted onto Zephyr.

He didn't wait for Youssef and Henri. He shouted, "*Oppugna, Zephyr!*" and took off out of the stable.

He raced through the open gates and saw Basquin and Isabel a quarter of the way across the tidal flats. Water gushed toward them from both sides and would first meet at the lowest point halfway between Mont-Saint-Michel and the mainland.

Isabel was riding sideways, held tight in front of the mercenary. When she looked over his shoulder and saw Fox behind them, she began wrestling with her captor. He smacked her in the face to stop her resistance, but she persisted. He was about to strike her again when she leaned forward and bit deeply into his cheek.

The man howled and knocked her aside. The motion unbalanced both of them and they went flying to the ground. Instead of following Basquin's horse, Comis stopped when she felt the pull on the reins.

Isabel and the mercenary plunged into a mire of quicksand. They were immersed to their waists in moments.

Basquin heard the shouting behind him and turned to see them stranded in the muck. With the tide rapidly approaching, he didn't even slow. He kept going without looking back again.

The water was nearing Isabel, but she didn't panic. While the man next to her screamed in terror, she pushed with her arms on the firm sand next to her and methodically used the technique

Henri had taught them when the young boy had become trapped. Despite her hampering skirts, she rocked her leg back and forth until it was free.

She had fallen off not quite halfway across the flats, and the tide was coming in fast. It wouldn't be long until Isabel was in its clutches. Fox galloped toward her at full speed, watching her with dread.

Isabel called to Comis. The horse came toward her and stopped when its hooves sank a little into the sand, but the dangling reins were close enough for Isabel to grab onto. Once she had a hold of them, she clucked with her tongue for Comis to back up. The horse dutifully responded, and Isabel was pulled from the quicksand.

She climbed onto Comis. The mercenary shrieked as the water rushed toward him. There was no time for Isabel to help him even if she wanted to. She kicked Comis into a gallop and met Fox a hundred yards from where she'd fallen.

"Are you all right?" Fox asked as he arrived beside her.

She nodded as she caught her breath.

"Go back to the island."

She looked at him, then at the retreating Basquin. "You can't go after him! You'll drown!"

The two tongues of seawater finally met in the center of the tidal flats. The water covered the head of the trapped mercenary, and his screams gurgled into silence as he was swallowed by the sea.

Even though he wanted to continue the chase, Fox stared at where the mercenary had just disappeared and knew she was right. Drowning futilely was no way to die.

"Come on!" he shouted and took off back toward the island with Isabel next to him.

Zephyr and Comis raced to stay ahead of the surging tide. Fox was worried that they had delayed too long in making the return trip. The water finally caught up to them when they were just a hundred feet from Mont-Saint-Michel's gate. It was up to Zephyr's knees in seconds. He could feel the pull of the current nearly knocking them over. But then they reached the shallows and were able to make it back onto dry land, where Youssef and Henri were waiting.

"That was close, my friend," Henri said as Fox climbed down. "I've seen horses swept away by smaller tides."

Youssef helped Isabel dismount and said, "You have blood on your mouth, my lady."

She spat and wiped her face on her sleeve, but said nothing about it. "Thank you for your instructions about the quicksand, Henri."

"My pleasure," Henri said with a slight bow. "I'm pleased they were useful to you."

Fox watched the far shore and saw Basquin rise above the tide before coming to a stop. The lucky bastard had managed to avoid any pits of quicksand all the way back. He turned and waved. He was too far away for Fox to see his expression, but Fox could imagine nothing other than an arrogant grin.

Basquin rode off at a trot and soon disappeared from view behind some trees.

They went back into the stable, and Fox opened the lockbox. Next to his sword Legend was the gilded manuscript encased in a leather pouch waxed to repel water.

"How long until the tide goes out enough for us to cross?" Fox asked as he unpacked the box.

"For one this high?" Henri said. "Not until the bells for nones at the earliest."

Isabel came over to Fox. "Basquin has a sack with him."

"Did you see what was inside?"

"No."

"It must be the *coffret*," Fox said. "We'll never catch him with the head start that he has."

"Was the manuscript inside it destroyed?" Isabel asked.

"I don't know. If the box has not been breached, he will open it as soon as he gets to Cardinal Molyneux in Paris."

"Then we must go there and find out whether it was burned."

"If it wasn't, we can no longer leave the real manuscript with your cousin," Fox said. "Molyneux will be expecting you to go to her."

"Still, we must see Claire anyway," Isabel said.

"Why?"

"There is one other person to whom I can safely entrust it. My older sister Catherine. She is a nun who used to serve at a convent near Saint-Quentin. The three of us corresponded by letter, and the last I heard from Catherine was that she was sent away from her convent after the crisis of the Great Mortality, but I don't know where. Since Claire is in Paris, she may have received a letter from Catherine more recently."

"You're going to Paris?" Henri asked.

"It seems we have no choice," Fox said.

Youssef glanced at Henri and said, "Then we are going with you."

"I can't ask you to do that now," Fox said. "I've caused you more than enough trouble."

"You don't have to ask," Youssef said. "And you obviously need help."

"I'm sick of this place," Henri said. "Besides, I don't know if the monks will be happy to let us stay after the damage we caused."

"Thank you, my friends," Fox said.

"There is only one problem," Henri said. "If Cardinal Molyneux suspects that you will attempt to visit Lady Isabel's cousin, it will be dangerous to call on her."

Youssef nodded. "He'll likely place a watch on her manor. They will catch you before you ever see her."

"I spent a summer at Claire's family estate, which was gifted to her husband in the dowry," Isabel said. "It's surrounded by a moat and high battlements, but I can get us in without being seen."

"Do you have a way for us to walk through walls?" Fox asked.

"Not through them," Isabel replied. "Under them."

# Paris

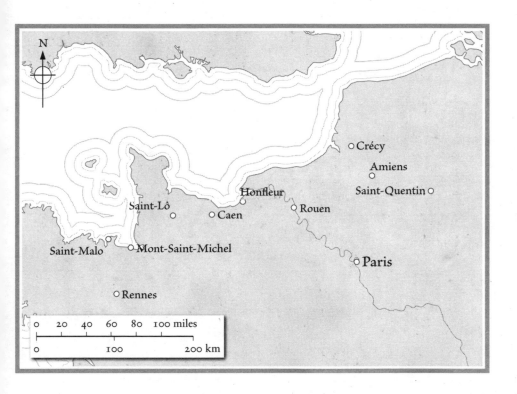

 37

PARIS

Basquin rode fast, stopping only to sleep and change horses. The traverse of northern France took five days, half the normal time. When he arrived in Paris, he went straight to Cardinal Molyneux's residence, the sack carrying the locked *coffret* held carefully in his hands.

The guard at the door recognized him and immediately ushered him inside. The cardinal's assistant, Father Lambert, met him in the lavish entryway. Basquin knew well that the prim clerk had a low opinion of the cardinal's bastard son, and Lambert barely made an effort to hide his disgust at Basquin's dirty appearance.

"Is he here?" Basquin asked.

Lambert gave him an icy stare. "Cardinal Molyneux is in a meeting in his chambers at the moment. I'm sure he won't be long. Perhaps you would prefer to change your clothes before calling on him."

"Perhaps you would prefer to be transferred to a parish in the wilds of Scotland." Basquin started walking through the great hall without asking permission.

"I will see if he's willing to be disturbed," Lambert said as he tried to keep up. "Shall I tell him what is so important?"

"I have what he's been waiting for," Basquin said, indicating the sack.

Lambert's eyes went wide. "I see." He dashed forward, opening the door to Molyneux's solar before Basquin could burst through it. Molyneux sat at a round table. Tonbridge was in a chair across from him.

"Your servant Basquin to see you, Your Eminence," Lambert said, with snide emphasis on the word "servant".

"I'm not blind, Lambert," Molyneux said, bemused by Basquin's disheveled appearance.

Basquin settled into the chair beside Tonbridge. "Lambert, be a good man and bring me a tankard of ale. I'm parched from my ride."

Lambert eyed him with contempt for omitting the proper honorific "Father", but Molyneux nodded at the priest, and he left to do Basquin's bidding.

"Why are you soiling my furniture with your filthy clothes?" Molyneux asked calmly.

"I think you'd rather ask what I have in this filthy bag," Basquin said, barely containing a smile.

Tonbridge stared at the sack in confusion, then sat up straighter when he understood what Basquin meant. "You found it?"

Basquin stood and removed the *coffret*, placing it before the cardinal triumphantly. The unicorn on its lid was blackened but recognizable.

"It's a little charred," Basquin said, "but I rescued it from complete incineration, at some small cost, I might add."

He held up his hands for his father to see. They were healing but still raw from the burns he'd received. The cardinal noted his injuries without comment and then went back to inspecting the *coffret*.

Tonbridge got to his feet and ran his fingers across the wood. "I expect our pact will still be honored," he said to Molyneux.

"I am a man of my word," Molyneux replied. "I don't care who delivers the Icon to me."

Basquin bristled at this casual dismissal.

Tonbridge turned to him. "What of Isabel?"

"The last I saw of her, she was at Mont-Saint-Michel."

"Our agreement was that you would bring her to me if you found her."

"Do you think she's more important than the Icon, Tonbridge?"

"Lord Tonbridge to you!"

"Enough!" Molyneux narrowed his eyes at Basquin. "When you left Isabel there, was she still with Gerard Fox?" His father knew exactly how to twist the knife for maximum effect.

"Believe me, I would have preferred to kill him. I promise you that the next time I see him, he will meet my sword."

"I suppose bringing me the Hodegetria redeems your other failure," Molyneux said, turning the *coffret* to face him. "If you ever want the knighthood you crave, you'd better pray that it is intact."

Basquin had become familiar with his father's contemptuous tone over the years, but it smarted nonetheless.

Molyneux removed a key hanging from a cord around his neck. It went into the lock without trouble, and it clicked open with a turn.

Molyneux took a breath and raised the lid, which stuck only slightly. For a moment, he simply stared at the contents without expression or comment. He reached down and opened the cover of the book inside. Then he looked at Basquin and said, "I hope this is not your idea of a jest."

He turned the box, and Basquin went cold when he saw what the *coffret* held.

Instead of an elegant manuscript with a gilded and bejeweled cover, the book was bound in plain leather. The opening lines were written in red, identifying the first text contained in the book: *Meditationes ethicae*, Aristotle's famous work on ethics.

It was a well-known Greek commentary, translated into Latin, on how men should strive for moral lives. Basquin felt Fox's pointed jab, even if his half-brother perhaps never intended him to see it.

Next to the manuscript was a pile of gold jewelry and gems that would have been indistinguishable from the ones decorating the cover if the box had been destroyed in the fire and melted the contents within.

"That brazen harlot," Tonbridge said, reaching into the box and removing a large gold fibula in the shape of a noble eagle studded with garnets. "This clasp was given to me as a mark of esteem by the Archbishop of Canterbury. I let Isabel wear it at our last dinner together." He removed the simple one from his cloak and pinned it closed again with the eagle.

Basquin looked up to see Molyneux staring at him, obviously disappointed by his son's efforts. The withering glare made Basquin feel like a child again.

"I am eager to hear your explanation for your rush to deliver this useless book to me," Molyneux said.

"Fox attempted to deceive me."

"Indeed, he seems to have succeeded."

"He intended to completely burn the *coffret*, so that I would think that the manuscript had been destroyed and the Icon along with it. The melted gold and remaining jewels would likely have convinced me. Now we know the manuscript is still in their possession."

"Then I suppose we should thank you for revealing this deception," Molyneux said, "even if it had to be done in this embarrassing manner."

Tonbridge chuckled softly. A sharp look from Basquin caused it to die in his throat.

"They will have departed soon after you did, so they could be anywhere," the cardinal said. He looked at Tonbridge. "You mentioned that Isabel has a sister. Where is she?"

"I don't know," Tonbridge said. "Isabel said the last she knew, Catherine had been sent away from Saint-Quentin, but she didn't know the eventual posting. My betrothed hadn't heard from her since shortly after the Great Mortality ravaged France."

"Then she could be dead," Basquin said.

"Very possibly. Even if she is alive, Isabel doesn't know her current whereabouts."

"I'll have Lambert check Church records to see if we can determine where she is, either above or below ground," Molyneux said. "But it sounds unlikely that your betrothed could go see her in either case. Which leaves…"

"Her cousin, Lady Claire," Tonbridge said. "I have my men

watching her husband François's estate day and night. If Isabel and Fox attempt to make a visit, we'll have them."

Molyneux looked pointedly at Basquin, who struggled not to shrink under his scornful gaze. "You'll be truly blessed if they are so foolish."

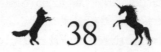

## 38

### The road to Paris

Youssef sat with his back to a large elm tree as he wrote in Fox's book. An inkpot was on the ground next to him, and he dipped his quill in it as needed. They'd been riding for six days straight at a brisk pace, so his backside was thanking him for the spell on soft ground.

"May I ask what you are writing?" Isabel asked.

He looked up, startled by her presence. "I'm sorry. I didn't hear you approach."

"I apologize. I should have announced myself."

"Not at all. Please." He waved for her to join him, and she sat on the grass. "I thought you were watering the horses with Gerard and Henri."

He pointed at the two of them standing beside the horses drinking from a nearby stream.

"I was more interested in your book," she said. "I love reading, but I've always wanted to write."

"It's not mine. It's Gerard's. His mother gave it to him." He held it out to show her the opening lines written in red on the first page.

*Iste liber quem per manibus habemus vocatur Secretum philosophorum.*

Isabel translated the words out loud. "This book, which was written by hand, we have called the *Secret of the Philosophers.*"

Just above the first line was an inscription in French.

*God keep you, my clever little Reynard. Your mother, Emmeline.*

"I'd never heard of the *Secretum philosophorum* before Gerard mentioned it," Isabel said. "Can you tell me more about the text's contents? It sounds fascinating."

Youssef was impressed at her easy translation of the Latin and her curiosity about the manuscript. He was beginning to see why his friend Fox was going to such lengths to help her.

"This book describes all manner of applied science, practical tricks, and riddles. It has sections on methods of geometry, the ways of conjuring and deception, recipes for pigments and invisible inks, examples of weasel words to disguise your meaning, and many other things."

"I know he values it highly, especially because I now see it was a gift from his mother. I'm surprised he allows you to write in it."

"His mother had it rebound for him and added several empty quires at the end for him to insert new information," Youssef said. "Some items at the end were even written by Emmeline. Since Gerard saw how useful my elixir could be in a fight, he asked me to record my formula for creating more of it. I wanted to get it down before I could forget."

"So the book isn't just sentimental?"

"The contents of this book got us out of more than one predicament after we fled Basquin and the cardinal. And I know that the formula will be safe inside because Gerard would never part with it, just as he would never go without his family's bow and sword. Devotion is one of his defining traits, and it usually serves him well. Why do you think he's so attached to his horse?"

"Zephyr is a fine animal," Isabel said. "Fast, obedient, loyal. He snapped at Basquin's mercenary."

"There's more to it." Youssef looked in the direction of Fox and Henri before lowering his voice. "Gerard doesn't mention it unless he's drunk, but Zephyr is his last reminder of his brother James."

"Who was killed in the Battle of Crécy."

Youssef was taken aback. "I'm surprised he told you the story."

"Just a little part of it."

"I'm sorry, but it's not my place to tell you the rest."

The fact that Fox had mentioned James at all to her struck Youssef as a sign of sincere trust.

"I understand," Isabel said. "Can you tell me about his book of tricks instead? I should very much like to read it sometime."

"I think it's all right to show it to you now. The distillation formula can wait."

Youssef put the manuscript between them, eager to share the book's secrets with a kindred spirit.

"This is one I added myself after our escape from Molyneux's château. Do you know how to pull something open from afar using a hidden rope or string?"

Isabel shook her head.

"Allow me to explain." Youssef began to read.

While Zephyr and Comis grazed in the pasture, Fox and Henri stood with the other two horses as they finished their drink.

"How long do you think until we make it to Paris?" Henri asked, massaging his sore rump.

Fox and Isabel could have traveled more quickly, but Youssef and Henri needed more frequent rest as they had not spent much time on horseback lately. The horses also needed to take a slower pace, given the number of consecutive days of travel.

"Another four days," Fox said, "assuming we don't run into any more *routiers*."

Gascon mercenaries were plundering the towns and countryside of Normandy on the side of the English. During their ride, they'd steered clear of most of the raiding parties, but they were surprised by a company of twenty men outside of Mortain. Only Henri's quick wit saved them from certain death.

"My brother Albert would be proud," Henri said. "I bet he never thought teaching me Gascon drinking songs would save my life one day."

"I hope we don't have to depend on that a second time."

"I'd like my chances in that situation better than yours and Lady Isabel's sneaking into her cousin's estate. If the replacement manuscript wasn't burnt up in that oven, Basquin and Molyneux will still be searching for you and Isabel, and Claire would be the obvious person to give her sanctuary."

"That's why I'd like you and Youssef to find out whether anyone is waiting for us at her house. Basquin didn't see either of you at Mont-Saint-Michel, so his men won't be looking for you."

"Lady Isabel hasn't been there since she was a child," Henri said. "Do you really think you'll be able to get into the château if it's being watched?"

Isabel had explained to them all that there was a maze of tunnels carved out of the limestone mines under her cousin's estate, the source of her family's wealth. When Isabel had visited all those years ago, she and Claire had spent an entire summer exploring the tunnels, eventually finding a secret path from the manor to the crypt of a nearby church. It had even been marked by notches in the wall. It was only when Isabel was much older that she realized the route might have been used by Claire's father to conduct secret affairs.

"If the church hasn't been altered," Fox said. "If Molyneux does not have the church under observation as well. If the guiding marks are still on the walls. If there haven't been any cave-ins that have blocked the passages." He shrugged. "If all that, it might work."

"That's a lot of ifs, my friend. And you don't know how her cousin will receive her. Lady Claire could very well turn you both in to Molyneux if he has offered a reward for your capture."

"There's nowhere else to turn, and we've already come this far. What other choice do we have?"

"I know the lengths you've gone to help her," Henri said. "Pretending to be her husband so she can travel without a chaperone must be a real burden for you."

Fox scowled at him. "You know that we don't share a bed."

"At least not on the nights we've all spent sleeping in the same room," Henri replied with a wink.

Fox could see Isabel sitting with Youssef, studying his book. She leaned back and laughed with abandon at something he said, causing the sun to glint off her golden hair. It took great effort for Fox to pull his eyes from her.

"I'm a gentleman," he said, attempting to brush off Henri's insinuation. "Our traveling arrangements are simply a matter of necessity and convenience. I have no feelings toward her."

"Is that so?" Henri said, following Fox's gaze.

"A woman like that would have no interest in being with a vagabond excommunicant like me."

"Just because she's a lady doesn't mean she wants a dull life."

"No, but someday the Hodegetria will be safe, and then she'll find someone worthy of her."

"Well, my friend, you might ask her what *she* wants."

Fox didn't answer. Instead he said, "We should be going soon. I'll go tell them to pack up."

He left Henri with the horses and walked over to Youssef and Isabel.

"What are you hens cackling about?"

Isabel smiled up at him. "Youssef was just telling me a delightful story about a monk who drank too much of his burned wine and wandered through Mont-Saint-Michel stark naked."

"I hadn't even gotten to the part where he mistook the abbot for a donkey."

She and Fox both laughed at that.

"I hope you don't mind that we've been reading the manuscript your mother gave you," she said as she closed the *Secretum philosophorum*.

"Not at all, Lady Isabel," Fox said. "You've entrusted me with your book. I trust you with mine. Now, I think it's time for us to move on."

While Fox helped Isabel to her feet, Youssef stood and said, "I'll go put my writing utensils away." He left them standing under the tree.

Isabel handed the book to Fox. "It's an honor that you're willing to share this with me. I know how much it means to you."

Despite its light weight, the book felt heavy from the memories it contained.

"Youssef also mentioned how important Zephyr is to you. I remember that you told me he came to be yours after Crécy, but Youssef didn't divulge anything further."

"He may enjoy telling stories, but he knows how to keep a confidence."

Isabel took a step closer to him. "I want you to know that I am also a friendly ear. If you ever feel the need to unburden yourself, I will listen."

He remained quiet for some time, the pain of that day fresh even five years later. Finally, he said, "Maybe someday, when Youssef has plied me with some of his burned wine."

Isabel nodded in understanding and said nothing. She turned and walked toward the horses.

Fox stood there for a moment by himself, wondering if there were enough spirits in the world to make him recount that terrible event ever again.

## 39

*Five years ago*
*August, 1346*

NORMANDY, FRANCE

It had been six weeks since the English army landed on the coast of Normandy. King Edward chose high ground outside the small town of Crécy for his defensive position in the long-awaited battle against the French. His tactical genius was now apparent to Fox as he rode back and forth on Velox behind the lines. The wide valley below was a killing field.

It was nearing sundown. The fight had been raging since late afternoon following heavy rains that had drenched the ground. Genoese mercenary crossbowmen, five thousand strong, had been the first into action against the three thousand Englishmen wielding longbows. The archers, safe behind a barrier of wagons, could loose arrows at a greater range and five times as quickly as the unprotected Genoese could with their slow-to-reload crossbows. Stone cannonballs firing from deafening bombards added to the mayhem. The few enemy crossbowmen who weren't wiped out in the barrage retreated toward their French employers, who slew them without mercy for abandoning their positions.

The following charges by the French went no better. The muddy ground slowed down the horses, and although the men-at-arms were clad in mail, their steeds were not. Entire rows of racing knights were felled in a hail of arrows that darkened the skies. The men behind were then further hampered by the growing number of horse and human corpses littering the wide valley.

Still, even as the English casualties remained minimal, the

French continued to rush headlong to their doom until finally the English archers simply ran out of ammunition as the sun was reaching the horizon. Runners were sent for more sheaves of arrows, but it would take time to rearm them, allowing the French to finally make a successful charge.

James and the other English knights were on foot with lances and swords to protect the archers, their horses safely ensconced in a protective circle of supply carts at the rear of the army. Only a few mounted archers like Fox were on horseback, going to wherever they were needed to shore up the lines and function as runners. Fox was given the honor of serving in the vanguard led by the Prince of Wales, the sixteen-year-old getting his first real taste of battle.

Seeing that the relentless French knights were going to make it all the way to the English lines, the prince turned to his men and yelled, "Follow me, men! God and Saint George!"

The brash prince in his obsidian-colored armor then did something Fox thought very unwise. He raced around the barricades, along with the knight carrying his banner, into the open field as the French knights bore down on them.

Fox, who was behind James, exclaimed in disbelief, "Is he mad?"

"Yes, he is," James replied. "But the Black Prince is our leader, and it's our duty to protect him."

With that, James ran out onto the field as well. Soon the melee was at full pitch, swords clashing and lances piercing armor and horsehide.

Fox rode out and began loosing arrows at any knight where he had a clear opening. He soon realized that even if the archers were resupplied, they'd never be able to bring their weapons to bear at this close range without endangering their own side, including the prince himself.

As the battle thundered on, more French knights arrived to reinforce their brethren. Fox could feel the tide turning even before he saw the prince go to his knees under a withering assault by a knight on horseback. His standard-bearer threw his banner to the ground to protect his prince. Fox launched his last arrow, which caught the Frenchman in the shoulder. The knight fell from his horse, and the prince got back to his feet and finished him off with a thrust of his sword. The standard-bearer triumphantly raised the mud-covered banner again.

The Earl of Warwick, one of the prince's top lieutenants and the marshal of the army, desperately waved to Fox, who galloped over to him.

"The prince will not admit it," Warwick said, barely able to catch his breath, "but we must have reinforcements or I fear we will be overrun if the French are able to mount another charge. Ride to the king and ask for his aid. Go!"

Fox nodded and took off, spurring Velox to his fastest speed up the steep slope, heading for the windmill where he knew the king was overseeing the mile-wide battlefront.

He saw the king's flag and raced toward it. He came up quickly and stopped in front of the king, who was atop his horse, and bowed his head without dismounting.

"Sire, the Earl of Warwick has sent me to ask for your aid. The Prince of Wales and his battalion are under severe assault. If the French press the attack with more men, they may be annihilated."

"Is my son dead or wounded?" the king said dispassionately.

"No, sire."

"Is he on his back?"

"No, sire. He was beaten down to his knees, but he had battled back to his feet when I was sent to you."

The king considered this for a moment. Then he said, "If he is still in the fight, he will get no reinforcements. The prince will have to earn his spurs."

Even though Fox was aghast at the cold-hearted statement, the command was final, and he didn't question His Highness.

"Yes, sire."

Fox turned Velox and raced back to deliver the bad news.

When he reached the lines again, the battle was being fought just as viciously before, and as feared, a new wave of French knights was bearing down on them. Fox found the Earl of Warwick and informed him of the king's response. The earl simply nodded and returned to the side of the Black Prince, who was organizing his men into a fresh line to beat back the upcoming attack.

Fox looked for James and had trouble spotting him in the chaos. But finally he saw the Fox family arms on James's tabard. He was engaged with a Frenchman, both of them on foot, their swords connecting with furious speed.

James was so fixed on his adversary that he didn't register a knight on horseback bearing down on him with a lance as he charged across the field from the French side. Even if James defeated his opponent, the charging knight would run him through.

Fox reached for his arrow bag and found nothing but air. He had used his final arrow on the knight attacking the prince. From this far away, yelling at James to beware was pointless amid the noise of the battle.

An English man-at-arms was running past Fox to join the battle, and Fox yanked the lance out of his hands, causing the man to curse a streak at him.

"Get another one!" Fox yelled. "*Oppugna*, Velox!"

He shrank the distance quickly, but it would be close. The French knight was initially so focused on James that he didn't spot Fox racing toward him. When he finally noticed Fox, he shifted his aim, the needle-sharp steel tip of his lance glinting in the fading sun.

Velox passed only feet away from James when the chargers met each other. Fox had been pointing his weapon at the knight, and his lance plunged into his enemy's chest, throwing the man from his horse. But before the Frenchman died, he had lowered his lance, aiming not at Fox but at his horse.

The tip pierced the neck of Velox, causing him to fall to the side as if a cord holding him upright had been cut. Fox, unable to free his feet from the stirrups, was still in the saddle as they went down. His horse's full weight landed on his left leg. Though the thick mud cushioned the impact, he was trapped.

Velox shuddered from the mortal blow. He let out a last anguished whinny and went still.

Fox had no time to mourn the death of his beloved horse. He struggled to free his leg, but he was stuck, unable to move. A dismounted French knight saw an easy kill and stalked over to Fox, who couldn't even draw his sword. The Frenchman raised his sword for the final stroke, and Fox could only stare at him in contempt for such a dishonorable action.

But the knight didn't complete his swing. James came from nowhere and dispatched the Frenchman in one stroke.

He bent down to assist Fox from his predicament, but two more knights were advancing on them.

"Behind you!" Fox yelled.

James turned in time to ward off a strike from the first man. The second battered James in his non-sword arm, causing James to stagger to the side. The mail armor kept James from losing the arm, but Fox could see the pain etched in his face. He knew his brother's arm must have been broken by the blow, but James didn't go down.

Instead, the injury seemed to spur him on. As Fox kept trying to extricate himself, James viciously fought back against both knights at once in a dazzling display of expert swordsmanship. One of the Frenchmen would thrust at him, and he would parry the blade even as he was swinging his next strike. The flurry was almost too fast for Fox's eyes to track.

But Fox could tell that his brother was tiring. He'd been in battle for a long time now, and the fatigue was setting in. He needed to finish the fight quickly. Fox felt helpless as he watched. He called for help, but no one was near enough to hear his cries or they were too engaged with their own battles to come to the rescue.

James finally was able to hit one of the knights in the side of the helmet with Legend, breaking the man's neck with his strength. The other Frenchman attacked James while he had his back turned. Fox gasped when he saw the blade slash into James's legs. Blood poured in a river below his tabard.

James fell to his knees only a body length away from Fox. To anyone else he would seem utterly defeated, but Fox knew his brother. James waited for the knight to close the distance. As the Frenchman raised his arms for the lethal finish, James thrust Legend up through the mail's weak point under the armpit. The sword sank deep into the Frenchman's chest and neck. When James withdrew it, the French knight toppled over dead with a look of surprise in his eyes.

James fell onto his side facing Fox, who remained pinned. The blow to the back of his legs must have been deep, hitting a vital spot, because Fox could see the life ebbing from his brother's eyes.

"You must stanch the bleeding," Fox said.

"My arm is broken," James replied, "and I have nothing to tie it with."

"You can't give up. Use Velox's reins." Fox held them up and beckoned James over.

James tried to crawl over to him, but he only got to within an arm's reach before he collapsed from exhaustion. His sword Legend had never left his hand.

Fox strained to reach out and drag him the rest of the way, but by the time he was able to grasp James's hand, the awkward angle meant he had no leverage. No matter how much he pulled he couldn't get his brother to budge. Nothing would stop the deadly blood loss.

Fox didn't release his grip on James, who gave him an amused look despite his mortal wound.

"I thought using that bow had made you strong."

Fox tried to smile. "If you hadn't been eating all of that French bread for the last few months, maybe you wouldn't weigh so much."

"They do know how to bake well here."

"It's probably the real reason the king invaded. He couldn't stand English food."

That brought a weak chuckle from James. "You were always funny, Gerard, but you can't play the rogue anymore." He patted Legend. "This will be yours now. You will be the Fox family heir."

"I don't like this talk—"

"We are men and knights, Sir Gerard. We mustn't surrender

when there is still hope, but we must also accept the inevitable with grace. Do you remember your oaths?"

Fox nodded solemnly. "Yes, Sir James."

"Good. Father will expect you to honor them. As will I. I'll always be watching over you, even if you won't be able to see me."

Tears welled in Fox's eyes. "I know."

"I'm sorry about Velox. You will need to look after Zephyr for me now. He's a fine horse." James's voice was starting to weaken.

"I will. James?"

James's eyes were closed now. "Yes, Gerard?"

"You are the best man I have ever known."

"Don't let Father hear you say that."

"It's true."

"You're a good brother," James said in a breathy whisper. He could barely get the words out. "One day... when you truly realize... who you can be... you'll become... a great knight."

James's fingers went limp, and his chest stopped moving. Fox knew that his brother was gone, but he didn't let go of his hand.

They lay next to each other like that for a long time.

# 40

*July, 1351*

## SAINT-JACQUES, FRANCE

It wasn't difficult for Youssef and Henri to find Saint-Jacques, the town closest to the Duval estate. All they had to do was follow the trail of oxcarts carrying blocks of limestone from the mines south of Paris.

The remainder of the journey to Paris had been uneventful, but they needed to be careful now that they were in Basquin and Molyneux's territory. Even though Paris was the largest city in Europe, they took precautions so they wouldn't be recognized. Because Youssef's dark skin would stand out, he was dressed in a hooded cloak, while Henri wore robes that made him look like the clerk he once was.

Their mission was to investigate access to the estate of Lady Isabel's cousin to see if it would be safe for her and Fox to make a visit. If it was being watched, the soldiers would be on the lookout for a man and woman, not two men the likes of Henri and Youssef.

Although Henri had lived in Paris for much of his life, he had never ventured into the mining region. The village of Saint-Jacques outside the stout walls of the city was the main center of the underground quarries. Most of the mine entrances opened straight into the town's hillsides. The stones on the carts were huge but crudely hacked out of the mines' walls. Skilled masons would shape them into building blocks like the ones used to construct Notre Dame Cathedral, where Lady Isabel and Fox had gone to see if they could find out the fate of the *coffret* while Henri and Youssef scouted Saint-Jacques.

According to Isabel's information, several estates in the area controlled the valuable mines. Lady Claire's father had been one of the most prominent landowners, and he had bequeathed the Saint-Jacques estate to the nobleman Sir François Duval in her dowry.

When they drew near the village, Youssef and Henri tied up their horses and went the rest of the way on foot so they wouldn't draw undue attention. They stopped at the southern edge of town. An expansive manor sat more than a hundred yards down a lane leading south from Saint-Jacques. It was the only road to the estate amid the farms around it.

"That must be it," Youssef said.

Henri nodded. "I can make out the carving of the griffin above the entrance, just as Lady Isabel said."

The two-story Duval château was made of the local limestone and bordered by high walls flush with the buildings surrounding a central courtyard. The structure had just the single gate, and the entire property was surrounded by a wide moat.

"There's the chapel," Henri said, pointing to a cross-shaped window at the front of the manor.

He began to walk out of the alley to get a closer look, but Youssef tugged at his robes and pulled him back to the cover of the building.

"There are watchers," Youssef said. He nodded at three men standing next to warhorses on the main road leading to the gate. They had been out of view until Henri and Youssef had exited the alley.

"Do you think they're Lord Tonbridge's men?" Henri asked. They weren't wearing the earl's coat of arms or mail armor, but they had the unmistakable bearing of soldiers.

Youssef shrugged. "Molyneux's, Tonbridge's. Does it matter?"

"Not really. They're not doing a very good job of disguising their observation."

Youssef and Henri watched for a while to see if they went on patrol, but the men simply stood there, talking and laughing, making no attempt to keep a low profile.

The men abruptly quieted, and Henri felt his stomach tighten when he saw why.

"Basquin," he spat.

Henri's old nemesis rode out of the shadow of the buildings, his blond hair waving in the breeze. He yelled at the men, obviously displeased with their lazy methods. He pointed at the second floor of a nearby building. The chastened men nodded and led their horses away.

"Basquin is telling them where they should be watching from," Youssef said. "Out of sight, with a good view of the château's gate and anyone approaching it."

"It's the wiser choice. Better to trap Fox and Lady Isabel than scare them off. One man rides for reinforcements while the others keep their quarry from fleeing."

Not long after the men left with Basquin, an elegant coach appeared. In front of it was a majestic nobleman on an expensive black stallion. His horse's caparison was blue with a white rampant griffin embroidered into the covering. A retinue followed, including a knight and squire with shoulder badges featuring the same arms. The entire group went down the road and through the gate of the Duval estate.

"That's why Basquin is here," Henri said. "While Tonbridge's men watched the château, he was shadowing the Duvals. They must be coming back from their townhouse in Paris."

"Then Basquin rode ahead to make sure the watchers wouldn't be noticed by the Duvals."

"If Gerard wants to call on them, he and Lady Isabel certainly can't go in through the front entrance."

Youssef nodded. "The only way to do it unseen is to take their chances through the mines."

"Let's go to the church and see if Lady Isabel's route is still intact."

They ducked back down the alley, walking to the center of Saint-Jacques where the church was situated. They approached it from the rear, walking along its flank. It was a grand structure, much larger than would be expected for a town of this size, a testament to the region's wealth and the Duval family's generosity to the Church.

Because it was mid-morning, the noon Mass was hours away. The church should be empty, allowing them to explore it without being seen.

Just as they reached the corner at the front of the church, it was simply poor luck that Basquin rode into view behind them down the street. Basquin looked in their direction, turned away, then stopped his horse as if something had caught his attention.

"By God's bones!" Henri hissed, and turned his face away. "I think he recognized me. Is he looking at us?"

"Yes. And he's coming this way."

"Don't make any sudden movements. Follow me."

They rounded the corner and calmly entered the church into a long nave flanked by pillars on either side. A lone priest with his back to them was tending to the altar at the other end. Then he went through a rear door into the sacristy, leaving the nave empty for the moment. Youssef and Henri hurried to the stairs by the altar that led down to the crypt. Henri didn't take the time to light the candle he'd brought with him.

When they got to the bottom of the stairs, they could hear the soles of leather boots clap on the stone floor above.

They were trapped. Neither of them had a weapon, not that it would have mattered against Basquin.

"Quick," Henri whispered. "We must find Lady Isabel's secret passage."

"She said to look for a stone marked with a rampant griffin."

The door to the hidden passage could be opened only by pressing on a stone to unlock it. Isabel couldn't remember exactly where it was in the crypt, but she knew it was etched with a griffin, just as it appeared on François's coat of arms.

They split up, Henri taking one side of the crypt and Youssef the other. Only the meager light streaming down the stairway and from several openings in the ceiling lit the chamber. While he waited for his eyes to adjust to the dark, Henri had to run his hands across the stones to feel for the etching.

Basquin's commanding voice called out above. "*Bon Père!*"

The sacristy door creaked open, and the priest shuffled toward him. "You can't wear that weapon in here."

"I represent Cardinal Molyneux. I thought a familiar-looking man might have entered the church. Have you seen anyone?"

The priest's tone changed at the mention of the cardinal. "Pardon me, sire, but I was in the sacristy and didn't see anyone come in. You're free to look for them."

It would only be a matter of time before Basquin completed his survey of the nave and made his way to the crypt, which had no other exit.

As they searched, a shadow fell on one of the holes in the ceiling to let light through, and the boots went quiet. Basquin had to be looking down the hole and listening for movement. Both of them froze until the shadow disappeared and Basquin continued walking.

He was heading toward the stairs.

By now, Henri's eyes had adjusted to the gloom, and he could see the stone face more clearly. Tamping down his rising panic, he scanned the wall quickly.

His accelerated pace made him nearly miss what he was looking for. He felt a subtle change in the smooth wall as his fingers brushed across it. He stopped and focused on the spot. The shape of a griffin was barely visible.

The sound of Basquin's boots was almost to the stairs.

"Here," he whispered.

Youssef rushed over, glancing at the stairway. Henri pushed on the griffin etching, and to his relief, the stone receded into the wall. As Isabel had instructed, he put his shoulder into the large vertical stone next to it, which pivoted on its axis, revealing an opening just large enough for a man to squeeze through.

He motioned for Youssef to enter as he took one last look at the stairs. Basquin must have stolen a candle from the altar because a light began to grow at the stairway.

Henri ducked inside, and they eased the door closed again as silently as they could. When it was shut, he felt around in the darkness until he put his hands on the stone he'd pushed to open the door. He could feel the griffin etching on this side as well. He pushed it back into place, where it settled quietly into a groove that locked the door in place. An iron handle driven in the stone would allow him to pull it back out to open the door again.

He and Youssef breathed as softly as they could while the sound of the boots grew louder. Through the crack at the bottom of the stone door, they could see the light getting brighter.

Basquin was thorough. Perhaps he'd heard the noise of the door closing. He circumnavigated the crypt and certainly would have found them if they had tried to hide behind one of the stone sarcophagi.

Finally, the light dimmed as he went back up the stairs, leaving Henri and Youssef in pitch-black darkness.

"Basquin is patient and clever," Henri said as he took a deep breath. "He might leave someone behind to watch for us. We should wait until noon Mass so we can mingle with the crowd as we leave."

"He can't be sure it was you he saw."

"Let's hope he thought I was a phantom of his imagination."

"At least we know this part of Lady Isabel's passage is still here."

"True," Henri said. "Fortunately for us. But we don't know if the entrance in the chapel of the Duval estate is still there, and without a light we can't verify it. Gerard and Lady Isabel will have to come here and discover that for themselves."

 41

PARIS

Befitting its stature as one of the most important churches in France, Notre Dame Cathedral towered over the Paris skyline. Fox had seen its exterior before, but he had never been inside the hundred-year-old building until this moment. The crowd streamed in for midday Mass, and Fox escorted Isabel inside at the tail end. The altar was so distant that there would be no way for Molyneux to recognize Fox if the cardinal made an appearance.

Fox had worried he would feel uneasy inside the cathedral, as he had in Canterbury. But the imposing space imparted a calming effect, one that made his future descent into Hell seem less certain. He could tell that Isabel was drinking in every inch of the magnificent interior, and her heartfelt devotion also gave him comfort. For the first time, he had the blasphemous thought that reconciling with the Church might not be the only way to express faith.

With some effort, he dragged his mind back to the business at hand.

If Tonbridge were still in the city, he'd be attending the service. No visiting nobleman of his stature would forgo Mass at Notre Dame, especially if he were trying to gain favor from Molyneux. If Tonbridge didn't show up, however, they could assume that he and Molyneux believed the manuscript and Icon had been destroyed in the fire. But if he were still in Paris, then they hadn't given up on finding it, and Fox would know that the ruse hadn't worked. Once they had their answer, they'd meet Youssef and Henri back at the inn where they were staying.

As the parishioners continued to enter, he and Isabel found a spot near a pillar midway down the nave, far enough to maintain their low profile but close enough to see the entire cathedral clearly.

Footsteps and chatter resonated in the vaulted space. While they waited for the service to commence, both of them gawked at Notre Dame's immense proportions, the details in the stained glass windows, and the colorful painted carvings that adorned most surfaces. The rich decorations were meant to entertain and educate the commoners during the Latin service that would be unintelligible to most of them.

Isabel tapped Fox on the shoulder and pointed at a relief sculpture in a nearby pillar.

"Look at the fox on that capital. Why is it wearing a cleric's robes?"

She indicated several figures embedded in the stone. A fox dressed as a bishop was preaching to an audience of geese.

"That's Reynard, the trickster," Fox said. "He's pretending to be a cleric to lure the geese close enough to catch them. Haven't you read that story?"

"It sounds vaguely familiar, but I spent most of my time reading histories."

"There are many tales of Reynard, who always uses clever deception to get out of trouble. All of the characters in the stories are animals, like King Noble the lion, Bruin the bear, and his archenemy Isengrim the wolf. Isengrim would steal from Reynard and then falsely accuse him of crimes to the king. It was only through Reynard's quick thinking that he was able to escape execution."

"Your mother must have liked those stories," Isabel said.

"Why do you say that?"

"Because of the inscription in your book. Youssef showed it to me. Your mother called you her 'clever little Reynard'."

"I got myself into trouble a lot as a child, but I usually talked my way out of it. My mother called me Reynard when she played with me."

"And the book?"

"She knew I would enjoy the intrigue of the *Secretum philosophorum*, encouraging me to read more in the future. She gave it to me before I left our estate in Normandy to go back to England. She stayed behind to care for her sick mother. That was the last time I saw her."

"How old were you?"

"Seven."

"And that book is the only thing you have left from her?"

Fox nodded. "That and my memories."

"I'm so sorry. What happened to her?"

"Let's keep looking for Tonbridge," Fox said to avoid the question as the monks began chanting, indicating that the service was beginning. Instead of quieting, the crowd continued to gossip and share news of the day during what to them was a social gathering.

While the ritual was familiar and soothing to Fox, it was also a painful reminder of what had been taken from him. He believed in the message of justice and salvation conveyed by the ceremony's holy words, but he was appalled that some members of the Church, like Molyneux, did not adhere to those ideals. When it was time for the elevation of the Host and the congregants went silent, he looked away. Though Isabel took notice of his odd behavior, she said nothing.

At last, the people received their benediction. Even though the service was short, it had seemed interminable to Fox. While the crowd filed out, Fox and Isabel stayed near the pillars as they walked toward the choir screen. If Molyneux were present, their best chance of seeing him was at that location.

Fox had almost given up hope when he glimpsed the crimson robes of a cardinal appear from behind the choir screen following several priests and bishops. As the cardinal exited, he was immediately swarmed by a group of admirers, obscuring him.

When they began to disperse, another man approached from the front of the congregation. He was dressed in the rich clothes of a nobleman, compact but barrel-chested with graying hair.

"That's Lord Tonbridge," Isabel said with a gasp.

As the cardinal turned to Tonbridge, Fox could finally see his face, and he felt as if drenched with icy water. It was Molyneux, who smiled at the earl. Fox hadn't seen the cardinal in years, but hate coursed through him as if their last meeting were yesterday.

Basquin was nowhere to be seen.

"He's wearing it," Isabel said in a whisper.

"What?"

"Tonbridge. See that gold fibula in the shape of an eagle that's pinning his cloak closed? It was his favorite. We put it in the *coffret*."

Fox could barely make out its shape from this distance, but it did look like the one they'd stashed inside the box so that it would melt and simulate the gilded cover of the book.

"Then it didn't work," Fox said, cursing silently.

Isabel looked around at the thinning crowd. "Soon there won't be many people left in here to blend in with. We have our answer. We should go."

Fox wanted nothing more than to march over to Molyneux and strike him down where he stood, but it would do Isabel no good. Besides, he didn't have Legend with him. Not to mention that he was inside a hallowed space. Despite all that had been done to him by the cardinal in the name of the Church, Fox still respected the sanctity of holy ground.

To sear the image into his brain, Fox took one last look at the cardinal enjoying the fruits of his position. Then he grabbed Isabel's hand and led her out into the afternoon sunshine.

Once they were outside, he took a deep breath, as if the air inside the cathedral had been suffocating him. He couldn't walk fast enough to get away from the church.

"You hate Molyneux even more than I hate Tonbridge, don't you?" Isabel said. "I could see it in the way you looked at him. If eyes could kill, the cardinal would have burst into flames."

"I despise him more than you could imagine."

"What did he do to you?"

"It's not what he did to me," Fox growled. "It's what he stole from me."

Isabel yanked him to a halt. She looked at him, her gaze both caring and curious. "You can tell me. What did he steal from you?"

"Everything."

Fox took a deep breath and told her the whole story of Molyneux's visit that led to the excommunication of him and his father.

42

When Fox and Isabel returned to the inn where the four of them were staying, Youssef and Henri confirmed the existence of the secret passage and recounted the story of how they hid from Basquin in the dark until they heard the chants of the Mass. During the service, they had slipped out of the passage, resealing it behind them, and crept up to the nave, separating so that they wouldn't be marked as a duo by anyone watching for them as they exited the church with the congregation. They didn't see Basquin again, so Henri and Youssef thought he must have been convinced that his eyes were deceiving him.

The inn was outside the city of Paris, so Fox and Isabel didn't have to wait until the gates opened the next day at dawn to head toward Saint-Jacques. Isabel had changed back into her fine rose kirtle and bright green silk surcoat for her presentation to Claire.

The church was quiet when they arrived just after the bell for prime. Fox had a candle and torch with him for the journey through the subterranean labyrinth to the Duval estate. He lit the candle from one of the altar's flames, and they headed down to the crypt.

They found the stone with the griffin on it, and the door opened just as Henri had told them. They went in and closed it behind them.

Since Youssef and Henri had no light when they'd hidden from Basquin, they couldn't tell Fox and Isabel what to expect. Fox lit the torch from the candle and held it high.

On the other side of the secret door was a short passage carved out of the rock. The air was cold and damp, and it had the musty smell of an ancient tomb. They walked until it ended at a long corridor that disappeared into the darkness in both directions. Fox knew that the Duval manor was toward the left, but that didn't mean it was the correct passage to take.

"We're looking for X's chiseled into the stone with a knife," Isabel said.

"There they are," he said, pointing to two of them at eye level. One identified the passage they'd just come down, the other marked a left turn. Whoever had blazed this trail made sure they could find their way back.

Fox gave the candle to Isabel and took the torch as they started down the wide corridor, which was bolstered at regular intervals by stone pillars left behind to support the roof. Every so often, they came to an intersection and searched for the marker, turning whenever it was indicated.

"I hope none of them have been erased," Isabel said.

"If they have, we'll have to turn back," Fox said. "We don't want to get lost down here."

"If we don't contact Claire somehow, the Icon will never be safe." At Isabel's insistence, the manuscript with the Hodegetria was slung on her back in a satchel. She had no intention of leaving it in a strange inn.

"We'll figure out a way to keep Molyneux from getting his hands on it. He's not using it to become pope if I can help it."

"Because you want revenge for what he did to your family?"

Fox had felt surprisingly at ease sharing his history and secrets with Isabel. She had taken the news of his excommunication far better than he had expected. When most people found out, they turned away in disgust or even fear, as if they could catch it like the Pestilence. Isabel's initial shock had quickly turned to sympathy for his plight. She too had experienced the capricious and vile whims of someone in authority over her.

"I don't want Molyneux to have the Icon for the simple fact that he is evil," Fox said. "If he ascends in power, his corruption of the Church will be complete, and he will plunge all of Europe into a dark age. I may not get my lands back, but I can get some satisfaction from seeing him fail."

"Is that what your father would have wanted?"

"My father was a man of high morals who was respected by everyone." Fox could taste the sickness in his throat as he recalled how they were treated once Molyneux excommunicated them. "Despite the good reputation he had spent a lifetime building, most of the people we knew were appalled by our crime against the Church and shunned us. We were outcasts in the town we had called our home. We had to skulk away to London in shame. When he fell ill with the Pestilence, he died in fear of what waited for him in the afterlife. I will never believe that such an honorable man could suffer for all eternity when he was the one wronged, no matter what the Church says. But my father never gave up on getting justice for my mother and our family. I truly think he could have formulated a plan to convince the pope that we were unjustly condemned."

"And you couldn't do it yourself?"

"I tried to find evidence of my mother's kidnapping that would have supported our case. But my investigation was discovered by Basquin, and he locked me in the dungeon with Henri and Youssef. We managed to escape, but he destroyed the proof I needed. Then recently I found a clerk who gave me an old communiqué between Molyneux and Tonbridge about Emmeline. I wrongly thought Tonbridge might be my savior, the person who could finally be my witness against the cardinal. If I hadn't come across you on the road, I'd likely be dead now."

"So in a way, I'm your savior, just as you've become mine."

"Don't exalt me yet. Let's wait to see what your cousin has to say. Or if she'll even talk to us. You haven't seen each other since you were girls."

"She and I are still very close. Claire is my connection with Catherine. The three of us regularly communicate by letter."

"With the war, the Great Mortality, and marauders on the roads, that can't be reliable. It's a miracle any of the letters get through."

"I admit, the couriers are not always able to deliver them, but we keep trying. Catherine sends letters to Claire that she forwards to me, and then I write back the same way. It lets us all stay in touch."

"And you think Catherine will safeguard the manuscript?" Fox asked.

"I know she will, if we can locate her. She was its original keeper, after all. But I fear it might be an even longer journey than the one we've already taken."

Fox held her eyes for a few moments as they walked. "Lady Isabel, I will take you anywhere you want to go."

Isabel blinked back tears. "Thank you."

"Now let's go find your cousin."

They continued through the maze of passages. At one juncture, they could hear the distant clang of pickaxes and shovels wielded by miners digging new tunnels.

Finally, they reached a set of steps carved into the rock. It led up to what looked like a dead end, but it was marked with another griffin etching. It was clearly the door into the Duval château chapel. An iron handle stuck out from the wall. Fox pressed his ear against the crevice. He heard nothing.

He extinguished the torch, but left the candle burning and set it down out of the way. He pulled on the handle, and the door came free. He pried it ajar so he could look out.

The door was hidden at the end of an alcove in the chapel, so all he could see was the altar. Still, there was no sound.

He opened it enough to slip out. He scanned the small room. The chamber was unoccupied.

Fox confirmed there was a griffin symbol that would show them which stone to press to reopen the secret door, then beckoned for Isabel to join him. She closed the door behind her, leaving the torch and the burning candle in the hidden passage in case they needed to make a hasty escape.

It was Isabel who now led Fox since she knew the layout of the manor. They had to get to the second-story solar unseen. That was where Claire spent her mornings embroidering and reading.

Isabel knew of a hidden spiral staircase leading from a little-visited storeroom near the chapel up to the second level, another reason she had come to the conclusion that the secret passage through the tunnels was for sneaking people in and out of the château. They quickly made their way to the storeroom stairway.

When they reached the top of the stairs, they almost ran into a washerwoman carrying an armful of linens, but they were able to duck into a side chamber before they were seen. As soon as the hall was clear, they raced to the solar.

It was empty.

"Where is she?" Fox said, closing the door behind him.

"It's still quite early. She must be dressing. She'll be here."

The clang of steel drew Fox to the window. In the courtyard below, two swordsmen wearing full mail were sparring with each other. One was a huge man dressed in the tabard of a knight, the other obviously his squire. The squire's passable technique was no match against the giant, who relied primarily on his size and strength to overpower his opponent. He looked impressive and intimidating, but a skilled swordsman would have his way with the behemoth.

"If that man is François," Fox said, "he'd better never go to war."

Isabel looked down. "I've never seen him, of course, but that can't be Claire's husband. François has a limp from when he was thrown from a horse."

The solar door creaked, and a petite woman Isabel's age in a fine woolen kirtle entered. Behind her was a younger woman in plainer clothes carrying a square of fabric and tambour, silk thread, and ivory needles. The two stopped when they saw the room was occupied.

"Who are you?" the noblewoman said.

Isabel stepped forward and spoke in French. "Claire, it is I, your cousin Isabel."

Claire was openly astonished. "Is it really you?"

Isabel pulled a jeweled pendant on a gold chain out from under her dress. It was a small enameled reliquary surrounded by tiny emeralds and sapphires.

"You gave this to me the last time you saw me. It holds the

hair of Saint Isabella of Portugal. For luck on my journey back to England."

Claire looked at the pendant then at Isabel and rushed to her, throwing her arms around her cousin.

"My dear Isabel, when François told me what Lord Tonbridge claimed you did, I could not believe it."

Isabel pushed her back and glanced at Claire's maid. "It's worse than you can imagine. May we have some privacy? I think it's better if no one else hears the details."

Claire eyed Fox warily. She would not be accustomed to having unknown men in her private chambers.

"This is my guardian, Sir Gerard of Oakhurst. He has brought me safely to you. I owe him my life."

Claire and Fox bowed, then she looked at her attendant. "Leave us, Justine, and do not speak of this to anyone, especially my husband."

Justine looked at the three of them with curiosity and said, "*Oui, madame.*" She shut the door behind her.

"Please, sit."

Claire pulled Isabel to a chair next to hers while Fox took a seat opposite them.

"How did you get in here?" Claire asked. "Why weren't you announced?"

"We couldn't come in through the front gate," Isabel said. "We used our old secret passage in the chapel. Lord Tonbridge would have me killed if he knew I was here. You know how the women in my family have been entrusted to protect the Icon of the Virgin and Child?"

Claire nodded.

Isabel removed the manuscript from her satchel. She opened it to the Hodegetria, and Claire gasped at the sight.

"*Mon Dieu!* You brought it with you?"

"Lord Tonbridge wanted to hand over the Icon to Cardinal Molyneux in exchange for a title and riches. I couldn't bear to see that happen, so I fled before our wedding. His men killed Willa."

"Your maid. I remember her fondly. The three of us played

together during your summer here. I know how much she meant to you, Isabel. I'm so sorry."

"The only reason I was able to complete my escape was because of Sir Gerard's quick action."

Claire looked at Fox. "Then I have you to thank for bringing Isabel to me, sir."

"I just happened to be in the right place at the right time," Fox said. "But you must credit Lady Isabel. She is a clever woman."

"Ever since she was a child." She turned back to Isabel. "But how can I help? As soon as Lord Tonbridge finds out you're here, he will drag you away. I will have to hide you until we know what to do. I must say, now that I have met him, he certainly fits your description."

Isabel nodded but said nothing.

"Tell Sir Gerard how you described your betrothal." Claire smiled as if they were sharing a joke.

"Our betrothal?"

"In your last letter to me."

Isabel hesitated, so Claire prompted her. "Like he was a snake in the tall grass slithering toward you, and you were the frightened rabbit?"

Isabel looked flustered. "Oh yes. Of course."

After that faltering response, Claire's demeanor changed. She sat up straight and focused on Isabel with a furrowed brow. Fox tensed at her reaction.

"Did I say something wrong?" Isabel asked, suddenly alarmed.

"In the letter, you made a jest regarding Lord Tonbridge's appearance," Claire said icily. "What did you call him?"

Isabel looked at Fox, searching for the right answer to the test. "That he was ugly, surely."

Claire shook her head. "You called him a toad. A hairy toad."

She snatched Isabel's left wrist and pushed up the sleeve, looking at the underside of her arm. The skin was smooth and pink.

"My Isabel tore her arm open when she fell on a sharp rock while we were playing in the woods during her visit here," Claire said. "It was such a long gash that it had to be sewn together. It was an ugly wound on a beautiful girl. But you have no scar."

Isabel sputtered, "I can explain…"

Claire cut her off. "You both looked very much alike. So much that you could have been sisters. But now that I know who I'm looking at, I can see the difference. Isabel had a more angular face and a slight dimple in her chin. You have a heart-shaped face and no dimple."

Claire looked at Fox. "Did you know?"

"Know what?" Fox asked innocently, even though he thought he already saw what was coming.

"That this isn't my cousin Isabel. This is her maid Willa."

## 43

### Kentworth, England

Willa stepped lightly, bow in hand and arrow nocked. Isabel, armed as well, tilted her head, indicating two rabbits grazing in the sun-dappled forest glade. This was Willa's favorite time with her lady. Her parents had died years ago, so the two of them had grown up almost as sisters, despite the difference in rank. Isabel's mother even noted how much they looked alike. When Isabel had lost her whole family in the Great Mortality, they had grown even closer.

The breeze was coming from the right, so Willa pointed to the left where they could get downwind. Their kirtles were hiked up to ensure they didn't rustle leaves as they walked. When they were in position ten yards away, Isabel nodded, an unspoken agreement. She would aim for the rabbit on her side, and Willa would take the other.

At the same time, they loosed their arrows. Willa hit her rabbit dead center, but Isabel just missed hers, scaring the rabbit back toward its warren. Willa quickly nocked another arrow and struck the rabbit in stride.

"That was mine!" Isabel cried out.

Willa smiled cheekily at her. "If it was yours, you would have hit it, wouldn't you?"

"I know I had it in my sight. What am I doing wrong?"

"You're still jerking your hand slightly as you release. Try again. I'll watch you. Concentrate on steadying the hand on the bow and easing your breathing."

Isabel inhaled as she pulled back and then held her breath as she launched the arrow. It sunk into the dead rabbit next to Willa's arrow.

"Now it's mine," Isabel said with a smile.

"Of course it is, *my lady*."

As they walked to collect their prizes, Isabel said, "You know, any other lady might take your words as insolence."

"Then aren't I lucky I don't serve a different lady?"

Isabel grinned at her. "Indeed you are. And I'm so very glad that you don't."

They carried the rabbits back to the meadow where their horses were tied up. They decided to take a rest before going back to the castle, and Willa clapped her hands together when Isabel reached into the saddlebag and took out the book she'd brought.

"What reading is it today?"

"William of Tyre's *Historia*."

Willa nodded in excitement. "I love hearing about the Crusades. Which volume?"

"The capture of Ascalon."

"May I read today, Isabel?"

"Please do," she said, handing over the book. "I'm happy to lie in the grass and listen."

She lay back and Willa read aloud about the siege of the city, how an Egyptian fleet almost destroyed the Christian army, and the breach that finally allowed them to take Ascalon. She marveled at the brilliant illuminations that adorned the beginning of each chapter, bringing the text to life. She felt like she was outside the massive fortress of Ascalon, a knight valiantly scaling the walls amidst a hail of arrows.

When she reached the part where the city surrendered to the Crusaders, Willa said, "I wish I could write books like this."

"Perhaps someday you will."

"You're jesting. What would I write about?"

"About hunting and rabbits and riding horses and whatever you like."

"That's not very exciting. I want to write about battles and far-off lands and sights that will amaze the people reading about them."

"You've been to Paris."

"Only when we were children. Besides, you have to be a nun like Marie de France or a queen like Eudocia to make great books."

"You know Eudocia didn't write the manuscript containing the Hodegetria. She only passed it down for safekeeping."

"But I'm so happy she did. Thank you for letting me share your secret. It touches my heart every time I see it."

"I wouldn't trust anyone with it more than you. Now, we must get back to the castle for dinner. I'll race you. First one through the gates gets the loser's piece of honey cake."

They scrambled onto the horses and urged them to full speed. Although Isabel was praised for her beauty and elegance, Willa was more accomplished at physical pursuits, including horseback riding. Willa could have easily taken the lead and beat Isabel back to the castle, but she knew how much her lady loved sweets. Still, she didn't let Isabel win by much.

When they came to a stop inside the castle courtyard, they were greeted by an unusual sight. Isabel's distant cousin and guardian Sir Eustace was standing beside a squat older man dressed in a fine woolen surcoat. Several mail-clad men-at-arms stood behind them with horses bedecked in full regalia.

Willa and Isabel dismounted, handing off the horses and rabbits to Reginald, Isabel's loyal groom and coachman. The stranger was obviously of noble rank, so they walked over and bowed, with Willa behind her mistress.

Eustace, in his sixties and fairly doddering, shuffled over to Isabel, beaming.

"Happy news, Isabel! I have found you a suitable husband. This is Sir Conrad Harrington, Earl of Tonbridge. Lord Tonbridge sadly lost his wife and three children to the Pestilence, and he is in need of a young and loyal wife to help him ensure his family's legacy."

Tonbridge stepped forward and looked Isabel up and down as if he were inspecting a prize cow. Once he was done, Tonbridge broke into a wide smile, which made him look somewhat charming. Although he was graying and twice Isabel's age, at least he had all his teeth.

"Sir Eustace, you were quite correct. Lady Isabel, you are an exquisite creature. I will be delighted to sign the contract."

Willa couldn't see Isabel's face, but she knew her lady was taught not to reveal her true feelings even if she were disgusted by the thought of marrying him.

"God save you, Lord Tonbridge," Isabel said. "It is truly an honor to be presented to Your Lordship."

"I knew this was a fine arrangement," Eustace said, delighted at how the introduction had gone. "There is no better match for you in all of Kent. Now let us break bread together to formalize the alliance."

As they walked together to the great hall, Isabel shot Willa a look of distress at the sudden turn of events, but Willa could only acknowledge her concern with a nod. Willa guessed that Sir Eustace had been planning this betrothal for weeks, even months. To catch an earl in need of a wife would be a feather in his cap and lead to a valuable increase in social standing for him.

The benches and tables were already laid out. Willa sat with the other servants while Isabel took a chair at the head of the hall next to Lord Tonbridge and Sir Eustace. Although the hall was alive with chatter and the rattle of tableware, Willa could hear the conversation between them.

"I am sorry to hear about your family, my lord," Isabel said as she ate her meal.

"Yes, the Great Mortality was a terrible blow to all of us. My son was so strapping and virile that it was a shock when he succumbed so quickly. Now I have no one to leave my estate to, which is why I have come calling. Sir Eustace tells me that you're healthy and that your parents' death to the Pestilence left you as the sole heiress."

Willa remembered that night well. Isabel's parents had died within hours of each other. It had been nearly unbearable to see her in such pain from the loss. With Catherine gone to the continent to become a nun, Willa had the task of comforting her. Except for Reginald, who had been with the family even longer, she really was the only family Isabel had left.

"It was a difficult time," is all Isabel said.

"What happened to your siblings?"

"Two of her sisters were stillborn," Eustace said. "Her brother died as a boy when he was trampled by a horse. A third sister, Catherine, went to Saint-Quentin in France to become a nun. We don't know her current whereabouts or indeed if she is still alive."

"That is sad to hear," Tonbridge said as his eyes wandered to the roasted pheasants being served. "But I am glad to know that you come from a good line of child-bearing women. I'm sure you'll agree that raising a family of strong boys is important for carrying on the name, and as Lady Tonbridge, you'll have all the appropriate gowns and jewels, I assure you."

"That is certainly comforting to know. Do you have any diversions that interest you, my lord? Books, perhaps?"

"Books?" Tonbridge laughed. "For enjoyment? No, although I wouldn't mind having the gold on some of the bindings I've seen. I prefer manly pursuits like hunting."

Isabel perked up at that. "Oh, I like hunting as well. I was out just this morning with—"

Tonbridge patted her hand. "Well, thankfully that will all be over for you. I'll bring in all the necessary game. Wouldn't want to risk my future sons, would you? But you will have a fine castle to live in. And books as well, if that's what delights you."

"That is kind of you."

"You will soon learn that nothing is more important to me than loyalty, and I will always be true to you. Together we will bring renown to the Tonbridge family line. I look forward to sealing our betrothal tomorrow."

Isabel glanced at Willa with a piercing gaze. Tonbridge looked to her as well, so Willa couldn't do what she wanted, which was to purse her lips in distaste. But she knew Isabel had no choice. Her guardian had complete control over her fate.

Isabel turned to Tonbridge and gave him a heart-melting smile, although Willa could see resignation, not joy, in her eyes. "Lord Tonbridge, our betrothal makes me very happy."

"Your guardian has chosen well, my lovely lady," Tonbridge said to her. Then he pounded the table, stood, and raised his goblet. "To my future bride!"

Everyone else rose to their feet. Shouts of "Hear! Hear!" and "Huzzah!" rang through the great hall.

The only ones not cheering were Isabel and Willa.

## 44

*July, 1351*

### SAINT-JACQUES

Willa had been dreading this moment since the day she met Gerard Fox, but in a way it was a relief. She'd been pretending to be someone else for weeks, and the constant fear of being discovered weighed on her every minute.

"It is true," she said to Fox. "My name is Wilhelmina, but everyone calls me Willa. You have to understand that I would never do anything to dishonor Isabel. My mother was maid to her mother, and I grew up with Isabel, first as her playmate when we were young girls, then as her attendant. We became even closer when her parents died in the Great Mortality. She was everything to me."

"And you dare pass yourself off as her?" Claire snapped. "You thought you could fool me?"

"She almost did," said Fox, who seemed to be taking the revelation in his stride. "She convinced everyone between Canterbury and Paris that she was a noblewoman."

"I suppose it helps that she was raised with one. She seems to have fooled you as well."

"I had my suspicions."

"What do you mean?" Willa said, shocked.

"The day we met, you braided and arranged your hair very easily, as if you'd done it that way all your life. A noblewoman would have little experience braiding her own hair. Very little experience doing anything for herself, for that matter. And from what I've seen, you are quite capable."

"So you are practiced at deception," Claire said. "Where is Isabel?"

"Lord Tonbridge's men killed her," Willa said, tears streaming down her cheeks. The anguish at being unable to grieve Isabel's murder properly for so long finally poured out. "It really was her idea to flee. I only wish I had devised a better plan of escape. Instead of being buried in an unmarked grave in an abandoned village, she might be alive to see you herself if I had."

"You've lied once already. Why should I believe you now? Why shouldn't I call for my husband this instant?"

"You know how much Lady Isabel and I loved each other. Why would I come here and risk capture if not to carry out her last wish in protecting the Hodegetria?"

Claire stared at her. "How can I know this terrible news is true?"

"I saw her body myself," Fox said. "I was the one who laid her to rest."

"You may have been the one to kill her for all I know."

"To what end? To steal from her? If we were thieves, we would have fled, not crossed the Dover Narrows to come to the house of her cousin. Lady Isab… Willa is right. We would have no motive to come here other than to safeguard this manuscript."

Willa was touched by Fox's support despite his knowledge that she had been deceiving him. Once he had revealed to her what had happened to his family, and how he had suffered as a result of his excommunication, she had felt even worse keeping her true identity from him. Now at least they knew each other's greatest secrets.

"All I want is for the Icon to remain safe and out of the hands of Cardinal Molyneux," she said. "He has been aiding and protecting Lord Tonbridge every step of the way and plans to use the Hodegetria in his own pursuit of power. Lady Claire, I know you revere the Icon as much as Lady Isabel did. If it will be secure with you, then I will leave it here and we will be on our way."

Fox looked alarmed by her proposal, but he remained quiet.

Claire considered the offer. She seemed to be softening.

"You say Lord Tonbridge is responsible for my cousin's death?"

Willa nodded. "Once he learned of the Hodegetria, that was all that mattered to him. Lady Isabel became an afterthought. While trying to recover the Icon, his soldiers put a crossbow bolt through her heart. If Sir Gerard had not been there, they would have done the same to me."

"Why did you pretend to be Isabel?"

Willa glanced at Fox and thought back to that awful day.

"When I saw that Lady Isabel had been killed, I was in a panic. I didn't think a knight would stoop to assist a commoner, and I wouldn't have been able to evade Lord Tonbridge's men on my own. Lady Isabel and I had exchanged clothing to make it look as if I were the lady and she were the maid in order to disguise our identities from any nobles we encountered during our escape across England. We knew they wouldn't even bother to look at a maid. I was wearing her gown when Sir Gerard asked who I was, so I blurted Lady Isabel's name. I had no plan to do so. It just came out in the moment. He seemed to believe me, and I have responded to her name ever since."

Looking back, Willa realized that at first she hadn't wanted Fox to know the truth because she feared he would abandon her. But she had gradually come to dread more the thought of losing his good opinion, either because she really wasn't a lady or because she lied about it. Now was the moment of truth. Would he stand by her or not?

Although Fox was addressing Claire, he looked at Willa as he said, "It has been my honor to escort her this far. She has constantly put the Hodegetria first, and I believe she has been a true caretaker, no matter who she is."

Willa took a deep breath and faced Claire, who seemed to accept the situation.

"I merely want to be sure that I'm not entrusting myself to a pair of charlatans."

"I have as much reason to help Willa defy Cardinal Molyneux as she does," Fox said. "I will avoid going into the details, but he has grievously harmed my family. My father was taken by the Pestilence before we could find justice."

"You are not alone," Claire said. "François's brother Rémy was a priest in Paris when the Pestilence arrived. Molyneux fled to the shelter of Avignon, but he forced Rémy to stay in the city even though we offered to let him retreat to our manor."

"I take it Father Rémy did not survive."

Claire shook her head. "Just as Isabel's parents were killed by the scourge. And now I find that Cardinal Molyneux is the reason for her death as well."

"Then you believe us?" Willa asked.

Claire's lip quivered. "I thought the danger had passed when I heard that Isabel lived through the Great Mortality." She sniffled at the thought. "I know my sweet and faithful cousin. She would have protected this manuscript with her life, as it seems she has. From all I know of her and Cardinal Molyneux, I take you at your word."

Willa felt a wash of relief at completing her task for Isabel. "Will you safeguard the manuscript?"

Claire sighed and handed the book back to Willa. "I dare not. François is in debt to the cardinal. He would surely turn you in to pay it off. Cardinal Molyneux and Lord Tonbridge called on us not long ago to make just that offer. Besides, it is Isabel's family that cared for it."

Willa was crestfallen at Claire's refusal, but she had committed to safeguarding the Icon for Isabel. Her quest was not over. She replaced the manuscript in the satchel and steeled herself for the journey still to come.

"Then the only other person who can protect it is Sister Catherine," she said. "According to Lady Isabel, she didn't even know if her sister was still alive. Please say that you have heard from her."

"As it would happen, I received a letter from Catherine two weeks ago. I was planning to send the note on to Isabel along with my congratulations on her marriage."

"Thank the Lord," Willa said, crossing herself. "Where is Sister Catherine now?"

"At an abbey in Piedmont. Near Turin. It is called La Sacra di

San Michele. Most of the monks were killed by the Pestilence, so it now serves as a convent. Catherine has been made abbess."

Fox shook his head at the news. "Turin? It might be safe from Molyneux in such a remote place, but it will take weeks of riding to get there."

"Then you must go at once," Claire said. "Leave the way you came. Men have been watching the entrance to our estate."

"Which is why we came through the tunnels," Fox said.

"I can provide you with what funds I have at hand, but it is not much." She stood, and Fox and Willa did as well. Claire retrieved a purse from a cupboard and gave it to Willa.

"My lady, I am so sorry to bring you such sad tidings," Willa said, "but I promise you that I will do everything in my power to carry out Lady Isabel's final wish."

"My cousin could not have a more loyal servant," Claire said. "God keep you on your journey."

"If it's not too presumptuous," Fox said, "I would ask you to burn the letter from Sister Catherine. We cannot let Molyneux know what our destination is."

Claire nodded and looked at Willa. "Your secret is safe with me, *Lady Isabel*."

Willa clasped Claire's hands. "Thank you. You have been most kind to me."

"I only wish I could have done more. Now, Lady Isabel, Sir Gerard, I will see you out."

As they turned to the door, it flew open. A courtly gentleman was standing in the doorway.

Claire gasped. "François?"

"Sir Gerard and Lady Isabel will be going nowhere," he said before shouting, "Guards!"

## 45

Fox thought about pushing François aside and making an escape attempt with Willa, but guards came running from both directions down the corridor, their swords drawn. It would be a bloody battle, and even if they could return to the chapel, there would be little chance of getting out of Saint-Jacques alive.

"François," Claire said, drawing him into the room by his arm, "I think you should hear what Lady Isabel and Sir Gerard have to say about Cardinal Molyneux and Lord Tonbridge." She closed the door behind him, leaving the guards outside.

François shrugged her off and limped away from her. "Why would I care? If I turn them in to the cardinal, he will forgive my debts."

"Do you really believe that, Sir François?" Fox said. "Have you ever known Molyneux to be honorable in his dealings?"

"He and Lord Tonbridge told me that Lady Isabel stole something valuable and that you are aiding her flight. Should I believe you, a stranger, over such illustrious figures?"

"Sir François, Cardinal Molyneux and Lord Tonbridge have killed my servants and tried to murder me as well," Willa said, keeping up her façade as Isabel. "They have concocted false charges against me. Claire has told us of the mistreatment of your brother by the cardinal. Do you want to reward him now?"

"I have no choice. It is true that I loathe him, but the cardinal wants you both, and I must turn you in."

"He will kill my cousin," Claire said. "That is why Sir Gerard had to escort her here in secret. I beg you, François. Let Sir Simon fight for you in the tournament as we had planned. He will win us the money we need to pay off your debts."

"Why would the cardinal have Lord Tonbridge's betrothed killed?" François asked.

They couldn't reveal the existence of the Hodegetria to him. Willa's recent revelations made Fox admire her even more for her quick thinking and devotion. He knew he could trust her to come up with something in this situation, so he gave her an encouraging nod.

Her eyes caught his meaning and she said, "Because I know the truth about the cardinal. I was going to inform the Archbishop of Canterbury about Lord Tonbridge and Cardinal Molyneux's scheme to acquire land by putting the owners in debt or excommunicating them. I know the intimate details about how they carried out their plots."

"That's just what the cardinal has done to you," Claire said to François.

"Molyneux hopes to buy his way into the papacy," Fox said. "Lady Isabel's testimony would have put an end to their business dealings."

It was an effective lie because of how close it was to the full truth.

François considered what they'd said, then shook his head. "I would like to help you, but I can't. If I don't pay my debts by the end of the summer, the cardinal will take possession of my estate."

"But the tournament…" Claire began.

"Is not a sure chance. Sir Simon is tall and strong, but there are many experienced knights entering the tournament."

Fox turned to the clanging outside the window and realized he was speaking of the man who was sparring in the courtyard.

"Tell me about this tournament, Sir François."

"It is to be held in a fortnight at Château de Tournöel."

"Where is that?"

"It is a castle in middle France that used to belong to King Philip the Fair, not far north of Clermont-Ferrand. Now that the worst of the Great Mortality is past, our new king wants to bring together his best knights to prove themselves worthy of carrying on the war against the English. Noblemen throughout this country and beyond will be participating for his favor."

The French King John II had been crowned at Reims just the year before and had yet to bloody himself in battle against his enemy. With an invasion from England possible in the near future, it would make sense that he'd want to be assured of the fealty of the nobility under his reign.

"And you plan to pay off your debts through ransoming in the melee?" Fox asked.

"I have never attended a tournament," Willa said. "What are the rules of a melee?"

"Two sides of knights fight each other in a great battle on the field with blunted weapons," Fox said. "Knights who are unhorsed and defeated can be taken captive by the victors and ransomed for their freedom."

François shook his head at Fox's proposal. "My debt is too great. The ransoms would not provide enough funds for my payment."

"Sir Simon would have to be named champion of the tournament," Claire said. "The prize is the drinking chalice of Saint Louis, known as the Crusader's Chalice, donated from the king's personal treasury."

"Not only is the crystal cup set in gold and encrusted with jewels," François added, "but it is also thought to bring good luck to whoever possesses it. I know that the cardinal covets it. If the knight fighting under my coat of arms wins the chalice, and I turn it over to Molyneux, he will be forced to forgive my debt. But I only made that plan in desperation."

"You must let Sir Simon try, my dearling," Claire pleaded. "It is our best hope for paying off our debt."

François eyed Fox and Willa. "Not anymore." He turned to leave.

"I agree," Fox said.

François stopped and looked at Fox. "You agree with what?"

"That you will never win the chalice if Sir Simon, the knight I saw clumsily fighting outside, is to be your champion. He may be large, but he has little ability as a swordsman."

"Then I have no other option than to hand you and Lady Isabel over and hope that Cardinal Molyneux is true to his word."

"That is not the only option. *I* will fight for you."

Willa was taken aback by his offer. "Sir Gerard?"

Fox continued looking at François, who hadn't dismissed his proposal out of hand. "If I enter the tournament as your champion and win the Crusader's Chalice for you, will you shield us from Cardinal Molyneux?"

"What makes you think you can win?"

"I didn't lose once at the three tournaments I attended in England."

"But how do *I* know you can win?"

Fox went to the window and saw Simon swinging his sword wildly. He was a hand taller than Fox, with the strength to match, but his technique was lacking.

"I can fight Sir Simon now as a demonstration of my skills."

"And if you lose?"

"If I lose, you may turn me and Lady Isabel over to Cardinal Molyneux and Lord Tonbridge without protest from either of us."

Willa began to say something, but Fox put his hand up.

"But if I win," he went on, "you will register me as your champion in the tournament. Under an assumed name, of course."

"What if you lose the tournament?"

"Then you can claim that I deceived you and hand us over at that time. I give you my word as a knight and a gentleman."

François held his gaze for a moment. Then he said, "I accept the challenge, as I'm sure Sir Simon will after I inform him of your dubious assessment of his skills as a warrior. I assume you are willing to have the outcome decided by custom."

Willa regarded Fox with a worried expression as he nodded and said, "First blood."

# 46

The courtyard was warm and bathed in sun, but Sir Simon didn't seem overheated or winded from his sparring. As he listened to François recount Fox's comments about his fighting skills, the towering knight scowled at Fox, who was watched by François's men to keep him from making any attempt at escape. The thought hadn't entered Fox's mind. Willa and Claire watched from the solar window above. Seeing how Simon stood half a head taller than Fox, both of them looked worried about the prospect of victory.

"What is this puny dog's name?" said Simon, whose face featured a broken nose, thin lips, and bushy eyebrows. "I want to know who I will be thrashing this morning."

Before François could speak, Fox said in perfect French, "*Sire Guillaume d'Amboise, à votre service, mon sire.*"

"Your only service to me will be to fall beneath my blade. Do you dare to admit that you called me clumsy?"

"Absolutely not," Fox replied. "I said your sword fighting was clumsy. I thought calling it pathetic would be too harsh a word."

Simon slashed his massive longsword back and forth, the air whistling from the menacing attempt at intimidation. "I will enjoy hearing you attempt to insult me again when I've smashed your teeth and cut your throat."

"Sir Simon," François admonished, "this match will be to first blood, not to the death."

"After how he has dishonored me? I demand satisfaction. The fight will be over when I say it's over."

"As you wish," Fox said calmly.

"No," François said. "Sir… Guillaume needs to survive the duel. You must swear to it."

Perhaps he was worried that Molyneux wouldn't forgive his debt if he delivered a dead body.

Simon nodded reluctantly. "I swear. But how long he survives his injury, I cannot promise."

"Very well. Do you accept these terms, Sir Guillaume?"

"Sir Simon is very generous with his otherwise empty offer," Fox said. "Therefore, I, too, promise not to kill him."

Simon's face was flushed with rage from the continued needling. Fox wasn't playing the overconfident fool just to get a rise out of his opponent. He needed to make sure that François would be convinced that his skills would lead to him being crowned tournament champion. But Simon was well-muscled, with arms as thick as oak branches, and could easily slay Fox if he wasn't careful.

"Swords will be the weapon of choice," François said. "Since Sir Guillaume does not have his equipment, there will be no armor. Prepare yourselves for battle."

While Simon removed the steel *bascinet* from his head, along with the mail tunic and gauntlets, Fox crossed himself and drew Legend, taking a few practice swings to get his blood moving. The wave-like pattern of the blade's Damascus steel glimmered in the sunlight.

"I am ready," Simon announced. He stood like the Colossus of Rhodes, with his legs apart and the tip of his gigantic two-handed broadsword planted in the dirt. The hilt was even with Fox's eye-line.

"Let the duel commence," François said as he stepped back to watch.

Simon smiled wickedly and picked up his sword with one hand as easily as if he'd plucked up a piece of straw. Each of them circled the other, their swords held in front of them. Having observed Simon's sloppy technique, Fox knew that the giant relied on brawn to win his battles. The key was using Simon's own body weight against him.

Fox held still, his body relaxed but ready. He was giving Simon the perfect opening.

Simon took it. He launched himself at Fox with a howl and a mighty overhead swing of his sword, which would have cut Fox in half if it had connected.

Fox simply stepped aside and swung Legend so that its tip sliced into Simon's exposed forearm. Blood splattered onto the sandy ground.

"That is first blood," Fox said as he withdrew from Simon's reach. "It looks like I am the victor."

Fox glanced at François, who was agog at how fast Fox had won.

"You are the victor," François said.

"It is *not* over," Simon shouted. "He cheated."

"By not allowing you to strike me?" Fox said. "I think it's simply that I'm deceptively fast."

"Sir Simon, you must stop!" François yelled.

Simon paid no attention. He charged at Fox, swinging his sword at Fox's waist, hoping to cleave his torso in two.

Fox deflected the blow, then brought Legend down with immense force on the flat of Simon's blade. The brittle metal snapped in half from the impact of the more pliable Damascus steel.

Simon staggered back with half his sword, which was now the same length as Legend. It still had an edge sharp enough to kill, so he ran at Fox again.

This time, Fox let Simon take his full swing, jumping back instead of parrying the blow. As Simon followed through, he became unbalanced. Fox kicked him as hard as he could in the back of his knee. Simon went sprawling on the ground face down, his sword skidding across the paving stones.

Fox made sure to stay out of the reach of Simon's hands. If Simon got him on the ground, he'd have to depend on François ordering his men to keep Simon from strangling him, a risk Fox wasn't willing to take.

Instead, he laid Legend's razor-sharp blade against the back of Simon's calf just above his boot.

"Do you yield?" he asked.

Simon didn't answer. He moved as if to get to his feet, but Fox forced Simon's foot back down.

"I won't kill you," Fox said, "but you will never walk without aid. I ask again. Is the fight over?"

Simon pounded on the ground with his fist and nodded. "I yield."

Fox released him and backed away, keeping his eyes on Simon for any treachery as his opponent got to his feet. But he doubted Simon would sacrifice his reputation as a knight. It would be a grave violation of his honor if he broke his word and continued to fight after he had yielded. His nobility would be forfeit.

"Leave at once, Sir Simon," François said. "Sir Guillaume is my new champion and will compete in the tournament under my banner."

Simon's bravado was gone. Fox expected a defiant retort, but all he got was a chastened and embarrassed look as Simon and his squire gathered his belongings and skulked away. If he'd had a tail, it would have been between his legs.

When he was gone, Fox sheathed Legend and walked over to François. "I will be honored to fight under your banner, Sir François."

"You have certainly impressed me, both with your skill and your honorable behavior. If you can best Sir Simon so easily, you should have no trouble winning the tournament. If I can pay my debt and keep Cardinal Molyneux from gaining something he so ardently desires, I will also be a winner."

"May I make a request?"

"Of course."

"I have a squire and attendant who are staying at an inn not far from here," Fox said. "I would like them to assist me at the tournament. They can join us when we leave."

François nodded. "I will send a man to inform them of your wishes. Do you have your own armor?"

"I do not."

"No matter. We are nearly the same size. I will let you wear mine."

"That is most kind of you."

Willa and Claire entered the courtyard with broad smiles on their faces.

"Sir Guillaume," Claire said, prudently using his alias for the benefit of anyone listening, "that was a most extraordinary display of expert swordsmanship. Lady Yvette and I were quite dazzled." Apparently, they'd already settled on a sobriquet for Willa as well.

"My thanks, Lady Claire. I'm happy you are pleased with the outcome. May I speak to Lady Yvette for a moment?"

"Of course." She withdrew to talk to François, leaving the two of them some privacy.

"I was so worried for you," Willa said in a low voice. "But since you defeated that huge man so quickly, you will surely be crowned champion at the tournament."

"Maybe. But I will have to train constantly on our way there."

"What do you mean?"

"Zephyr and I have been through much together, but remember that he was originally James's mount. The last time that horse fought in a tournament was with my brother riding him. The joust is the competition that determines the champion. Zephyr and I don't have any experience jousting as horse and rider."

"You told us you won three of them," Willa said with a concerned look.

"I said I didn't lose," Fox said.

"But you've been in tournaments before. Please tell me that you have."

"I've been *to* tournaments. Three, in fact. I've just never fought in one."

# Château de Tournoël

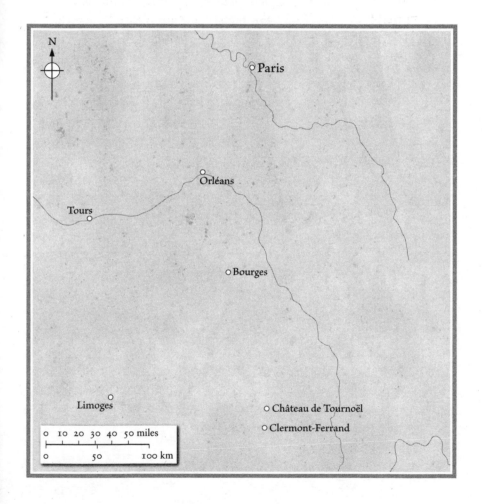

## 47

A morning fog embraced the city of Saint-Quentin so completely that Lord Tonbridge could barely make out the cathedral towers as he and Father Lambert passed through its gates with two of Tonbridge's soldiers. Known throughout Europe for its production of wool textiles, Saint-Quentin was a well-traveled trading hub and its merchants had grown rich. Their wealth was reflected in the extravagant timbered design of the city's buildings. Its streets were noisy with the shouts of vendors and braying donkeys carrying goods to market.

Despite the gloomy weather, Tonbridge was glad to be on horseback again. He had grown bored in Paris waiting for Isabel and Fox to make an appearance at the Duval estate. François and his men had left for the king's tournament at Château de Tournöel nearly a week ago, taking several wagons of supplies with them but leaving the more comfortable carriage and his wife Claire behind. It seemed the perfect opportunity for Isabel to call on her cousin, but no one matching her description had entered or exited the manor since then.

The only other person she might trust with the manuscript was her sister Catherine, and Molyneux's latest information was that she'd been serving as the prioress at a convent east of Saint-Quentin before reassignment to another city after the Pestilence struck. Tonbridge wanted to do something more proactive in the search for his betrothed, so Molyneux had suggested the visit to

Saint-Quentin. Tonbridge brought only two of his men with them since they were far from any possible war zone and needed the rest of the men to watch the Duval estate day and night. The three-day ride from Paris had been uneventful thanks to the writ of safe conduct carried by Lambert, acting as Cardinal Molyneux's local representative.

They passed a huge cemetery.

"How do we know Isabel's sister doesn't lie in a pit of Pestilence victims?" Tonbridge asked Lambert.

"According to our records in Paris," Lambert said, "Sister Catherine was alive as of last year when she was sent away, but we don't know her new assignment. The bishop at the cathedral should be able to tell us her destination."

Tonbridge nodded at the bustle of workers. "Then the Great Mortality didn't strike this area so hard?"

"On the contrary. It is said that Saint-Quentin lost more than ten thousand of its citizens two years ago. When the cemetery we passed was full, they hauled bodies to be buried outside the gates. But now that the Pestilence is past, the unquenchable desire for fabric across the continent is responsible for its recovery."

"I ask my question again, how do we know that Sister Catherine is not dead?"

"Her convent at Origny-Sainte-Benoite experienced a miracle. Despite being dispatched to the city to care for the sick and dying, the nuns lost only one of their number. Like some of her sisters, Catherine was later transferred to another convent, likely one that wasn't so blessed."

Tonbridge grunted at Lambert's confidence. It would be just his luck that Catherine was the sole nun to die.

When they arrived at the cathedral, Tonbridge told his men to wait outside while they called on the bishop.

A short time after a young monk took their request, an ancient woman with a round face greeted them instead of the bishop.

"Father, my lord, I am Sister Agnes, the almoner of the convent. I understand you wish to inquire about our nunnery. How may I help you gentlemen?"

"This is Sir Conrad Harrington, Earl of Tonbridge. I am Father Lambert, personal aide to Cardinal Molyneux. We have come to ask for assistance about an urgent matter. We require information about one of your sisters."

Tonbridge chafed at Lambert's formality.

"We have come all the way from Paris to find Sister Catherine," Tonbridge said. "Where is she now?"

Sister Agnes's face registered disapproval at Tonbridge's blunt question, but he didn't care.

"You are an Englishman?" she asked.

"What does that matter?"

"One doesn't meet English nobles in Saint-Quentin very often," Sister Agnes said dryly.

"You may consider him a representative of Cardinal Molyneux," Lambert reassured her.

"Is Sister Catherine still alive?"

Sister Agnes paused as she appraised Tonbridge further, then said, "I served under Prioress Catherine, and she was alive when last I saw her."

"Then she is not here?" Lambert asked.

Sister Agnes shook her head. "Her presence was requested elsewhere. We have not heard tell of her since she left."

"Where did she go?" Tonbridge asked.

"Avignon. I do not know if she remains there."

"You are sure that was where she was sent?" Lambert asked.

"Quite sure," Sister Agnes said. "We were all sorry to see her go, but it was the will of the Church. She was a capable healer and ran the convent efficiently under the abbess during our dismal time with the Great Mortality. If you'd like, you can visit the abbey to confirm the information."

"No," Tonbridge said, turning to Lambert. "Come. Let us take this news back to Paris immediately."

"Bless you, Sister Agnes," Lambert said. "Cardinal Molyneux will remember the assistance of your abbey fondly."

Lambert proposed that they at least stay for midday Mass, and Tonbridge agreed, thinking it was a proper time to give thanks to the Lord for this clue to finding the Icon. As soon as Mass was over, they exited the city, riding hard toward Paris.

In late afternoon on an isolated section of road where thick forest closed in on both sides, the horses of the two soldiers in the lead suddenly screamed in pain and bucked their riders off. As the distressed horses danced around and whinnied, each held one foot in the air. Metal spikes jutted from their lame hooves.

Caltrops had been carefully hidden under leaves strewn on the road. The iron devices, used frequently in battlefields, had four sharp points arranged so that one would always point up no matter how it was laid down.

It was a trap.

He and Lambert turned to flee back the way they'd come, but their path was blocked by more than a dozen grubby men with rudimentary spears and rough knives. It was a band of marauders meaning to rob them.

Tonbridge drew his sword and ordered his men to come to his aid. The soldiers ran around and put themselves between the earl and the highwaymen, their weapons at the ready.

"We are here by order of His Eminence Cardinal Molyneux!" Lambert cried out, his voice quavering with terror. "I have his writ of safe conduct. You must let us pass."

The largest man in the group laughed, and the rest of them joined in.

"What do we care about some piece of parchment?" the leader shouted back. "Even if what you say is true, none of us can read. It doesn't matter anyway. Church law means nothing out here. The Pestilence has done far worse to us. We'll take those fine weapons and eat heartily tonight. Horsemeat will fill our empty stomachs well."

"I order you to get out of our way," Tonbridge said. "Otherwise, we will kill every one of you and your souls will spend eternity in Hell."

"Do you hear that Englishman speaking French, boys? We have an enemy trying to tell us what to do. His rich clothes betray how much he is worth. I'll wager he is carrying a handsome sum of money with him."

That brought a rousing shout from the men, who greedily eyed Tonbridge's expensive trappings and luxurious cloak. With a war cry from the leader, they rushed at Tonbridge's soldiers.

Even without their horses, the two men fought valiantly. One of them was able to kill two of the bandits before being speared in the gut. The other soldier stabbed a marauder through the chest, but a half dozen knives took him down.

Seeing that they were hopelessly outnumbered, Tonbridge attempted to charge through them. He would have made it but for a spear that impaled his horse's neck. They both went down.

Tonbridge leaped to his feet, his sword held in front of him as five men edged toward him.

"Careful, boys," the marauder leader said with a gleam in his eye. "We can't sell his clothes if they're covered with blood."

Lambert was also trying to make an escape. As he rode by, Tonbridge hit him with the flat of his sword, knocking him from the horse. Tonbridge grabbed the reins as he slashed two of the marauders with his sword and climbed on. He kicked the horse and galloped down the road.

Over his shoulder, he saw the remaining marauders surround the priest.

"You can't harm me!" Lambert screamed from the ground as he cradled his cross. "I am a man of God and an officer of the Church!"

"God has already punished us, Father!" the leader yelled back and brought his spear down on the clergyman. A wicked cheer was the last thing Tonbridge heard as he rode over the next hill and left the bandits behind.

Once he caught his breath after that ordeal, Tonbridge checked Lambert's saddlebag. The writ of safe conduct from Molyneux was there. Then he patted his midsection and was relieved to find his purse heavy with coins still strapped to his waist. Lambert's loss was a pity, but necessary in service to a greater cause. Surely Cardinal Molyneux would understand when Tonbridge told a slightly altered story of the encounter, one in which they had all bravely fought, with Lambert's tragic death cast as a heroic sacrifice.

But to do that, Tonbridge had to return unscathed. He rode fast back toward Saint-Quentin to hire an entire squad of mercenaries to escort him safely to Paris.

# 48

### THE ROAD TO CHÂTEAU DE TOURNÖEL, FRANCE

After more than a week on the road to Clermont-Ferrand, François's entourage was nearing Château de Tournöel. Since they hadn't been set upon by Tonbridge or Basquin, Fox was fairly certain that their ruse had worked.

When François took his own men out the front gate of the Duval estate, he'd purposely left the carriage and Claire's maid behind at Fox's suggestion. Claire had accompanied Willa and Fox through the tunnels they had used to enter the estate to join Henri and Youssef. The five of them had then ridden far south of Paris to rendezvous with the remainder of the group. Fortunately, Claire seemed to be nearly as comfortable on horseback as Willa, and they'd made good time on the route.

With just a few more days until the tournament began, Fox had been spending every moment of their rest stops practicing for the joust. This afternoon, he had ventured far afield with Willa, Henri, and Youssef to get away from François's prying eyes so that the Frenchman wouldn't get a sense of how suspect Fox's skills were. He made the excuse that he needed his full concentration without distractions to practice properly.

It had been years since he'd held a lance, and his inexperience at jousting with Zephyr didn't help. Fox was still trying to understand why they were having so much trouble together, and time was running out.

Henri, a squire before he worked for the Church as a clerk, would serve in that capacity for Fox during the tournament, and Youssef would be his attendant, preparing him for battle and tending to the equipment.

They had set up a crude *quintain*, a pole set into the ground with a spinning target atop it. The object was to hit the target board representing the opposing knight with the tip of the lance. Fox and Zephyr lined up for yet another run at it, the blunted lance upright in the crook of his arm.

"Try it again," Henri said, the exasperation in his voice evident. "You can't miss it every single time."

"Shame, Henri," Youssef said. "I have faith in our friend."

"Thank you, Youssef," Fox said.

"There's no reason to think he can't miss it every time," Youssef added.

Fox wasn't in a jesting mood. "All right. Just reset it."

While Henri and Youssef worked on the *quintain*, Willa walked up to him and patted Zephyr, whose coat was wet with sweat. After practice, Fox would have to ride yet again in the wagon so that Zephyr could cool off unsaddled while they walked.

"Thank you for letting me join you," Willa said. "I wasn't sure you would want to carry on helping me after finding out how I'd deceived you."

This was the first opportunity Fox had had to talk to her alone about the admission of her true identity.

"You did what you had to do," Fox said. "I'm impressed that you carried it off so well for so long."

"You know, I thought about telling you the truth many times after you proved what an honorable man you are."

"But you didn't because you thought I wouldn't continue on our quest?"

"No, it was because I was afraid of what you might think of me."

"Whether you are called Lady Isabel or Willa, my opinion of you is just the same."

"And what is that?"

"That you are like no woman I've ever met. And for that, I am very glad."

She flashed a radiant smile that set Fox's heart racing. "You are a true gentleman, Sir Gerard. And for that, I am very glad."

Henri and Youssef finished setting up the target and began walking back to them, focusing Fox's mind again on the task at hand. "What I need to be is a jousting expert by the upcoming tournament."

"Are you certain you're up to it?" she asked.

"Zephyr and I are starting to understand each other," Fox said, overstating his confidence. "I'm sure with another day or two we'll be old hands at this. Besides, what choice do we have?"

"We could make a run for it. Escape in the night."

Fox shook his head. "Then we'd have François's men after us and soon all of France. But it doesn't matter. I gave my word of honor to François. I must carry this through to the end."

"Even if it means *our* end?"

"I won't let that happen."

"Do you swear on your mother's love?"

"I swear on my heart that I will fight for you until my dying breath."

Willa was rendered mute by his declaration, and he could feel something profound pass between them.

After a moment, she composed herself and stepped back.

"Then try again. After all, you can't miss every single time."

He shouted "*Oppugna!*" and Zephyr charged forward. Fox lowered the lance. As they approached the stationary pole, Zephyr slewed away from it to the side despite Fox's prodding legs. Fox adjusted his aim at the last second, and the tip of the lance barely grazed the target, causing it to lazily turn.

Willa, Henri, and Youssef let out whoops of joy.

"I stand corrected, my friend," Youssef said. "You *can't* miss every time."

"And who doesn't have faith in him now?" Henri said.

Their celebration was cut short by the sound of hooves beating their way. François and Claire were leading a group of men unfamiliar to Fox. One of them was on a huge *destrier* and carried a lance.

As opposed to Zephyr, a courser that was light, fast, and strong, *destriers* were the most expensive of horses—heavy, powerful, and used by only the richest men in battle and sport. Its rider must have been a man of some repute. But why he was riding the horse out here, Fox couldn't guess.

François came to a stop with a gleeful look on his face.

"Sir Guillaume," he said to Fox, "Sir Danckaert van Hoecke has come all the way from Flanders for the tournament and happened upon us during our rest."

Danckaert was the epitome of a gallant knight, with tailored clothes, a well-coiffed beard, a square jaw, and brown eyes that lingered with interest upon Willa.

"A pleasure to make the acquaintance of a future opponent," Danckaert said in a deep bass. "And who might this delightful creature be?"

"She is my companion for this adventure," Claire said. "Lady Yvette de Loches."

Danckaert's smile got even wider. "May God save you, lady."

Willa blushed and bowed.

Danckaert turned his attention back to Fox. "I am told you are a great fighter for Sir François. He is quite sure you will be named champion of the tournament."

Fox glanced at his "patron", annoyed about the bragging. They didn't need any more attention.

"Sir François is too kind."

"Not at all," François said. "I have seen him fight myself, and he is a brilliant warrior."

"Of course, some of us wish to believe we will be named champion ourselves," Danckaert said. "Which is why I was happy to make a wager with Sir François on a contest this very afternoon."

Fox couldn't believe the temerity of François, who seemed eager to collect coins on what he thought was a sure bet.

"What is the contest to be?" Fox asked. "Swords?"

Danckaert laughed. "Since we will be facing each other in the joust," Danckaert continued, "and we don't want to risk injury on a friendly game, I proposed that we tilt at rings." He nodded, and one of his men rode over to the *quintain*. On each side of the spinning board, the man attached three metal rings of increasingly smaller diameters.

"Whoever pierces the most rings with the point of the lance wins the wager," François explained to Claire.

"Now that I have met your wife's charming companion," Danckaert said to François, "I have a counter-proposal. If your man should win, I will pay the agreed amount. But if I win, I will have the favor of Lady Yvette by my side at the tournament's opening banquet."

Willa was aghast. "I am not a prize to be wagered."

"I beg your pardon," Danckaert said, amused as he looked at François. "Do you often let women speak for you? That is not our way in Flanders."

Before Fox could object, François rested his hand on Willa's shoulder and said, "Of course, she will gladly accept your terms, as do I."

"Splendid," Danckaert said, beaming, and rode to a spot in front of the *quintain*.

Fox could not withdraw from the bet without seeming cowardly, so he lined up next to Danckaert. The entire retinue from both sides had gathered to watch.

"I would be honored if you took the first tilt," Fox said.

"You are a true gentleman, sire," Danckaert said.

Without another word, he kicked his horse, and the ground thundered under the massive *destrier*'s hooves as he sprinted toward the target.

Danckaert lowered his lance and the point went through the dead center of the largest ring. Applause and hoots of approval erupted from his side.

As he rode back, he favored his adoring fans with waves and smiled at Willa, who kept her eyes on Fox.

The target board was turned so that Fox's rings were now on the right side. He dug his heels into Zephyr's flanks, and they took off.

This time, Fox tried to overcorrect for Zephyr shying away from the pole. He aimed straight for it.

Zephyr wasn't having it. He edged away no matter how much Fox adjusted him. But with a lunge of his lance, Fox was able to spear the ring as they passed. It wasn't pretty, but it got the job done.

François, Claire, Willa, and the rest of the Duval clan cheered wildly.

Henri and Youssef met him back at the start, grabbing on to Zephyr to steady him.

"Now that was a surprise," Youssef said.

"You looked like you almost fell off trying to spear that ring," Henri said.

"I did," Fox said. "I have to figure out why Zephyr is shying from the target or I'll be out of the tournament after the first tilt."

They watched as Danckaert captured his second ring with ease. Even louder applause this time.

"You'd better figure it out quickly," Henri said.

Fox charged again. This time he got closer to the pole, but his lance hit the edge of the smaller ring, and it fell to the grass. His side groaned at the miss, and François glowered at Fox as he rode back.

"I thought you were a great champion," François hissed. "I'm being made to look like a fool."

"You should have asked me before making this wager. But I will be ready for the tournament."

"You had better be, or I'll sell you off to Molyneux without a second thought."

"Two rings to one," Danckaert said with glee. "This round will decide the tilt."

He took off, his face etched with concentration as he aimed at the tiny ring. Once again, the tip of the lance slipped through the circlet without any difficulty.

"That's the match!" the victorious Danckaert shouted from the opposite end of the field. He turned and trotted back toward his admiring crowd with the outstretched lance still holding the three rings he'd speared.

Fox didn't wait for him to return. He kicked Zephyr into

motion and shouted the battle cry, "*Oppugna!*" hoping to save some of his honor by capturing a second ring.

As he neared the pole, Zephyr veered right, heading straight for Danckaert, who was still waving to his fans and ignoring Fox's futile effort to score.

Fox suddenly understood what was happening. Prodded to attack, Zephyr thought Danckaert with his pointed lance was the enemy. The horse was well trained by his brother James to charge into battle. The *quintain* pole, on the other hand, was simply a stationary object to be avoided. Fox and Velox had always been James and Zephyr's sparring partners before tournaments, so Zephyr had never learned to charge at a *quintain*. He likely equated the pole with a tree, which he would naturally avoid.

Seeing that he was in danger of blindly impaling Danckaert, Fox dropped the lance and pulled back on the reins, stopping Zephyr's charge.

Danckaert turned and saw his opponent standing motionless.

"I hope to face you in the joust, Sir Guillaume," he said with barely contained contempt. "Any victory is to be savored, even if it will be an easy one."

He rode over to François. "This has been a wonderful diversion after a long journey." He turned to Willa and bowed. "Lady Yvette, I look forward to our evening together."

He handed the lance to one of his men and galloped back toward the road, leaving both Willa and François fuming.

"Do you know how much that cost me?" François sputtered.

"Nothing but some coins that were never yours," Willa said, equally put out. "Because I am the one who is to fulfill the bargain."

Despite their anger, Fox was elated at his discovery. It was clear Zephyr knew what to do when he had a proper opponent, exactly what they would encounter in the tournament. Fox was newly filled with hope that he and Zephyr had a chance to win.

## 49

PARIS

Still smarting about being duped by Fox into bringing the *coffret* with the replacement manuscript to his father, Basquin had spent most of his time pacing as he watched the Duval estate. He wanted to be the one to capture his half-brother and the Icon. He'd seen François leaving for the tournament and immediately dismissed the idea of following them. Claire was the bait, and she remained at the manor, though Basquin was beginning to wonder if she had taken ill, as she hadn't been out of the château since François had departed.

Molyneux had told him about Tonbridge's expedition to Saint-Quentin to learn the location of Isabel's sister Catherine, but the obnoxious earl hadn't returned after a week. Basquin could only hope he was dead. Besides, if the nuns didn't know where she was, he thought it was unlikely that Isabel did either. He was sure that, sooner or later, Fox would deliver Isabel to her cousin. All Basquin had to do was wait.

One afternoon as he watched the front gate of the Duval estate from the second-story window of an abandoned townhouse, he listened to two of Tonbridge's men talking. They chattered like ravens all day long, but their conversations staved off his boredom.

"When does the king's tournament start?" Guy said.

"Tomorrow, I hear," Paul answered.

"Even if it's a bunch of Frenchmen, I would give anything to attend. I haven't seen a good melee in years."

"They say all the best knights of France will be there. Trying to impress His Highness, of course."

Basquin's stomach turned as he looked down at his fully healed hands. If he'd been a noble instead of a bastard, he'd be there, too. And he knew he would win champion standing.

"Not Sir Simon," Guy said.

That brought a laugh from Paul. "Apparently he's better at lifting a tankard than a sword."

The mention of Sir Simon caused Basquin to turn. "Sir Simon? He is François's champion in the tournament, I've been told." He hadn't seen Sir Simon with the entourage and assumed the knight had joined them on the road.

Guy shrugged. "He's not fighting anymore."

"Seems he was replaced with a new champion," Paul said. "Simon's been grousing every day since Sir François left. He won't shut up about it."

Basquin had a sinking feeling in his gut. "Where does Sir Simon do his complaining?"

When Basquin walked into the only tavern in Saint-Jacques, he saw the giant silhouette of Sir Simon drunkenly regaling two men about a boar hunt while sloppily gripping a half-empty tankard of wine.

"And then I had my hands around its throat..." Simon paused when he noticed Basquin standing beside them.

"Leave," Basquin said quietly to the two listeners.

The men looked at each other and laughed derisively.

"Who's going to make us?" one of them said with a sneer.

Simon peered at him and said, "Is that you, Basquin? I haven't seen you since Crécy!"

The sneers disappeared at the mention of Basquin's name. "Sorry."

"We were just on our way."

The men scrambled away, and Basquin took a seat.

"You're supposed to be at Château de Tournöel," Basquin said.

"You heard about that?" Simon said before taking another swig of his wine.

"Why are you still here?"

"I was beaten in a duel. Right there in the courtyard of Château Duval. Cheated, actually."

"By whom?"

"Sir Guillaume d'Amboise."

"Do you know him?"

"I do now. But no, I'd not seen him before."

"What did he look like?"

"Tall, but not as tall as me," Simon said. "No one is as tall as me. I should have won."

"His face."

"Brown beard, brown hair. Almost as pretty as you. At least the ladies seemed to think so."

"What ladies?" Basquin asked with rising dismay.

"The ones watching from the window. Sir François's wife—I forget her name—and her companion. A blonde maiden. Never seen her before, either, but I'd like to see her again."

The knot in Basquin's stomach was growing tighter.

"Were you defeated in a duel of swords?"

"Yes, but I was cheated. He had some kind of magic sword. Broke mine in half." Simon drained the tankard and called for another.

"This sword of Sir Guillaume's," Basquin said. "Did the blade's metal have swirls in it?"

Simon's eyes went wide. "You've seen a sword like that?"

Basquin didn't answer. Without another word, he stood and left Simon calling behind him.

"If you ever see Sir Guillaume again, tell him his magic sword won't save him every time."

Basquin ran from the tavern, climbed onto his horse, and rode for Paris with the taste of bile in his mouth. He would have to tell his father he'd been duped yet again.

Basquin burst into his father's chambers unannounced. A young clerk was standing by Molyneux's side at his writing table. A hiss from Basquin drove the attendant from the room.

"I hope this interruption is important," Molyneux said.

"I know where Fox and Lady Isabel are."

Molyneux leaned back in his chair and pursed his lips. "And I assume you are here to tell me you have captured them and they are now on their way here with the Icon?"

"Not yet. I will need men…"

"You need. You require. You demand. Yet, you do not produce anything of substance." Molyneux shook his head. While he spoke, Basquin stood there like a scolded boy. "I sent you to England to carry out a simple task to bring me the manuscript that I was owed, and since then I have heard nothing but reasons and excuses for why you have failed over and over again."

"If Tonbridge had not let his betrothed escape—"

"You see?" Molyneux interrupted with a hand leveled at him. "It was someone else's fault. Namely Lord Tonbridge, who still has not returned from Saint-Quentin. Now I've had to send someone in search of him and Lambert."

"Perhaps he has fled back to England with his tail between his legs."

Molyneux shook his head. "I know him too well. He does not give up so easily, especially with his family honor and a royal coronation at stake."

"And my knighthood? Formally legitimizing me in the eyes of the Church? The land you promised me?"

"So far, I see nothing you've done that is worthy of those honors. And at this point I'm beginning to doubt if I ever will. Sometimes I wonder what the use is of having a tame bastard at my beck and call."

Basquin felt the comment like a slap in the face. At that moment, he determined to obtain the Icon on his own and be free of his father's tenterhooks once and for all. He'd been waiting long enough.

"Father, I pledge not to waste your time again. I have to verify that what I've heard is true. Once I do, you will be the first to know."

"Very well," Molyneux said. "Now get out of my chambers and send that clerk back in. I have real business to conduct."

Basquin stalked away, waving the waiting attendant inside.

With the tournament starting the next day, he would have to ride fast to get to Château de Tournöel before it ended. On the way there, he'd have time to develop a plan that would secure the Icon and make him a noble.

Basquin would prove to his father that he could get what he deserved without him..

 50

RIOM, FRANCE

Château de Tournöel crowned a rocky outcrop above the town of Riom in central France with a commanding view of the Limagne plains. Fox could see it well from the tournament field. With thick stone walls, a high turret for crossbowmen, and steep slopes surrounding it on all sides, the castle was said to be impregnable. The king and his court had appropriated the fortress for the duration of the festivities, and the banquets would be held in the great hall.

The opening ceremony was a parade across the lists, the field where all of the events would take place. Large stands had been constructed for the spectators, with a place of honor in the center for the king and his court. Next to them were nobles and other people of importance, including the families of the participants. Claire and Willa sat far down from King John's left hand. Finally, the commoners stood behind barriers and cheered as the banners of their favorites passed by. Even more viewers watched from empty tree branches, from the hills overlooking the field, and from any other vantage point they could find.

François led his segment of the procession, with his standard-bearer by his side carrying the griffin-embroidered flag of the Duvals. Fox rode behind him atop Zephyr in full armor, shield on his arm and lance held at attention. Only his great helm was absent. The suit fit him well enough, but the shiny steel baked him like a loaf of bread, and sweat dripped down his face. When he passed Willa, he nodded at her, and in response she waved a white silk kerchief fringed in silver thread.

When they circled for the return pass, Danckaert trotted by

smartly on his *destrier*, the horse clopping its hooves in tandem as if it were marching. The crowd went wild for the display of horsemanship. When Danckaert saw Fox passing, he raised his lance in salute and gestured to Willa, not too subtly reminding Fox who had bested him.

When he got back to the staging grounds, he grumbled to Youssef and Henri as they helped him doff his armor.

"I can't take much more of Danckaert's gloating."

"You'll have to," Henri replied. "From what I've heard from the other squires, he's the one to beat. He was named champion at four tournaments before the Great Mortality, and he is itching to add another now that the games are starting again."

"I was thinking more about the banquet tonight."

"Lady Yvette is only doing this because she has to," Youssef said, trying to reassure him. Although Henri and Youssef had taken well the revelation that she was not a noble lady and was in fact a maid named Willa, they were all using her false name while they were at the tournament in case they were overheard.

"It doesn't make the taste in my mouth any less sour."

"You should be more worried about your stench," Youssef said with a wrinkled nose as he removed Fox's breastplate. "I've smelled fresher pig sties."

"That reminds me," Henri said. "When Sir François gave me clothing of his for you to wear at this evening's celebration, he insisted you be clean before putting on his finery. He even sent you some herbs to add to your water. They are all back in your tent."

"Along with some soap," Youssef added helpfully as Fox trudged away to wash up.

After a thorough scrubbing, including his hair and beard, Fox put on the garments François had lent him, which consisted of a splendid blue tunic embroidered with gold, brown hose, and fashionable shoes that were so pointed it was difficult for Fox to walk.

When he rendezvoused with François and Claire, she gushed over him.

"*Magnifique*, my lord! You are quite handsome tonight."

"You as well, my lady. Where is Lady Yvette?"

Claire exchanged a knowing glance with François.

"Sir Danckaert has already come for her," François said. "We will see them at the banquet."

"I think he wants to make a noticeable entrance," Claire said. "But don't worry. He had a chaperone with him."

"His aunt." François grimaced at the memory.

Trumpets blared across the valley, signaling that the attendees were to head to the banquet. They were supposed to be at their tables for the king's grand entrance.

Fox was not prepared for the extravagance of the affair. When they entered Château de Tournöel's great hall, he was slack-jawed at the grandeur of the decorations. Beeswax candles throughout the hall provided plenty of light to see the array of flowers set on tables that were arranged in a horseshoe shape around a wide expanse meant for the dance. The king's table was on a raised dais at the head of the horseshoe. Poles had been erected to simulate trees with leafy branches jutting from the trunks. Minstrels played music to entertain them while they waited, but the food and wine would not be served until the king was in his place.

Servants showed them to their seats on one side of the hall a good distance from the king's table. Although François was a noble, apparently he was not one of the wealthier families who had maneuvered for positions closer to power.

Danckaert was one of the last knights to arrive, and he sauntered in as if the event were being held just for him. But it was Willa who took Fox's breath away. Claire had gifted her a dress for the banquet, a crimson silk surcoat edged in pearls over a deep blue kirtle with decorative buttons running down both sleeves. The silver-fringed kerchief poked out from her left cuff.

Her golden hair was artfully braided in spirals over her ears, and the sun-kissed skin of her cheeks looked as soft and smooth as the finest silk.

She was the most beautiful creature Fox had ever seen.

And she was on the arm of Sir Danckaert.

The nervous look on her face as she'd entered was replaced with awe as she surveyed the ornamentation. Danckaert looked especially pleased with himself as he guided her to a place of honor much closer to the king on the opposite side of the hall. His lip curled in a smile when he spotted Fox, who wanted to tear his eyes away from the spectacle, but couldn't.

He was saved by the sound of trumpets marking the imminent entrance of the king. All who had been sitting rose to their feet, the minstrels stopped playing, and the crowd all fell to one knee and bowed their heads as the king made his entrance.

King John swept in, resplendent in blue robes lined with ermine. Now Fox had a much better look at him and saw that the monarch wasn't much older than he was, with a short beard and shoulder-length reddish-brown hair. His new queen, Joan, accompanied him. Even the king had not escaped the ravages of the Pestilence, losing his first wife two years ago before he ascended to the throne.

He stood at the far end of the hall and raised his hands in greeting, allowing the attendees to rise to their feet.

"Thank you all for joining me in this celebration of life. We have been through much hardship these last few years. The Lord has tested us, and we have His beneficence to thank for us being here to praise Him tonight. And now that the Great Mortality has passed and the famine is ending, it is time to renew ourselves with food, wine, merriment, music, and dancing. Then the real enjoyment begins. I wish all the knights here an honorable and victorious fight, and I look forward to crowning a worthy champion when the tournament is done."

The crowd chanted, "God save the king! God save the king! God save the king!"

Once the king sat, the minstrels began playing again, and

servers filed into the hall bearing platters heaped with food and jugs full of wine. It was the most sumptuous meal Fox had ever experienced, with seven full courses. Normally he would be salivating over treats like venison flavored with cloves and gilded sugar plums, but his mouth felt as dry as sawdust.

Although he didn't have much of an appetite, he knew he needed to eat if he was going to get through the upcoming tournament. While François and Claire made conversation with others around them, Fox chewed and drank in silence through course after course, trying not to watch as Danckaert plied his charms on Willa. Halfway through the meal, she took the silver-fringed kerchief from her sleeve and gave it to Danckaert, who kissed her hand in thanks for the favor.

Claire leaned over and said, "You'll stare a hole in him."

Fox was startled that someone was speaking to him. "Pardon?"

"You know he's just doing this to drive you mad."

"It's working."

"I've heard that Danckaert does this at every tournament. He finds his most formidable rival and then needles him until his challenger loses all focus, handing him an easy victory." She looked around and lowered her voice. "If he knew Yvette's true identity, he would be absolutely mortified at having consorted with her."

Fox looked at Claire. "You don't seem to be offended by her status."

"I admire what she has done in my cousin's memory. Not many women would have the fortitude to accomplish what she has. I only wish I were as brave."

Willa was not only courageous, but also had a true sense of honor. Fox was reminded of James and the lessons he had imparted about what was important in life. Willa embodied those same qualities.

The minstrels quieted, and a herald read a selection from a romance by Marie de France. It was a story about four knights competing for a beautiful lady's love at a grand tournament. Willa kept glancing at Fox during the reading, as if to note that they were now re-enacting the plot in real life. Fox didn't appreciate the climax of the tale, though, when it was revealed that three of the knights died and the surviving one was rendered impotent.

After the reading ended, the minstrels played a jauntier tune, the signal for the dancing to begin. The knights and their consorts entered the dance floor, arranging themselves in circles of a dozen or more couples.

Danckaert stood and put his hand out for Willa. She smiled wanly and took it. They made their way to the floor.

Fox turned to François. "May I have the honor of having this dance with your wife?"

"Please, François?" Claire said. "I don't often get this opportunity."

François nodded. "You might as well. I can't take her out there on this leg."

Fox escorted Claire to the floor in time to take a spot next to Willa. He took her hand as Danckaert shot him a haughty look.

The music began, and they went through the steps of the dance. In, out, around, twirl, step one, two, three times. Despite not being a noble herself, Willa didn't stumble once.

"You are quite good at this, Lady Yvette," Fox said under his breath.

"I practiced nearly daily with my maid," Willa replied.

The song ended and everyone applauded. Danckaert turned to Willa.

"If you'll forgive me, Lady Yvette, I must pay my respects to His Highness."

As Danckaert left her for an audience with the king, Fox excused himself from Claire and took Willa's hand, leading her behind a faux tree for privacy.

"Why did you give Danckaert your kerchief?" Fox asked bluntly.

"Why, I have had a lovely evening, thank you for asking."

"It's been agony watching you from across the hall."

"Are you jealous? I'm just amazed to be here in the first place. A maidservant eating in the presence of the king!"

She seemed rather amused by the whole affair. Fox was not.

"And the kerchief?"

"What of it?"

"You gave it to Danckaert."

"Is that why steam is shooting from your ears? He asked me to bestow a favor upon him. I couldn't very well turn him down. It would have been unladylike."

The explanation didn't help. Fox was still infuriated.

"The kerchief was a gift to Isabel from Lord Tonbridge," Willa added. "I was glad to be rid of it."

That took the air out of him.

"But I am happy to know you care," she said.

Fox smiled for the first time tonight. "May I ask you for my own favor?"

Without hesitation, Willa unhooked the gold chain from her neck and placed the Saint Isabella reliquary in Fox's hand.

"Isabel's pendant?" he said. It had to be Willa's most prized possession.

"*My* pendant," Willa said. "Claire doesn't know, but Isabel gave it to me years ago. It's my only reminder of her. Keep it safe. I want to see it again after the tournament."

They stared at each other for a moment that seemed to last an eternity. Then Fox kissed her lightly on the cheek. When he released her, she flushed.

"I must go before that Flemish popinjay returns," she said. "May God grant you good fortune on the field tomorrow. I will be watching."

"It will give me strength knowing that," Fox replied.

Willa hurried off and snatched Claire's hand to leave. By the time Danckaert turned around from his talk with the king, they and François were gone.

"Where is the lovely Lady Yvette?" Danckaert asked Fox as he returned to the dance floor.

Fox shrugged. "I think she was feeling ill and left. Something must have caused her stomach to turn."

He grinned at the nonplussed Danckaert and left him standing there alone.

## 51

The first day of the three-day tournament was the melee. Since the champion would be crowned based on the joust only, Fox would have preferred not to participate, but François insisted that his banner be represented in the mock battle.

The two sides were selected by lot and placed at opposite ends of the field for the start of the melee. The knights wore colored shoulder badges to indicate allegiances, red for Fox's side and blue for their opponents. They were equipped with blunted lances and swords, so Fox would have to fight without Legend and instead use one of François's blades. Even with these precautions, wounds and deaths were not uncommon, and Fox's primary goal was to avoid injury to Zephyr, who was clad in nearly as much armor as Fox.

The rules of the melee were simple. The two sides would charge each other with lances lowered. The intent was to knock as many of the opponents as possible from their horses on the first strike. Then the riders remaining would form up and turn as a unit, the crowd-pleasing *tournée* that gave the tourney, or tournament, its name. The opposing teams would race at each other again, repeating the attacks until the fight broke down into individual battles.

The goal was to defeat knights on the other side and take them captive. In the past, that meant taking possession of their horses, weapons, and armor. Now the vanquished were simply ransomed, providing great incentives to be a victor.

By chance, Fox ended up on the same side as Danckaert, who rode to a stop next to him as the riders lined up for the initial charge.

"Sir Guillaume, what a pleasure to see you on my side," said the affable Danckaert, wearing a bright blue and gold tabard draped over his chest plate and mail. He cradled a crested helmet in the crook of his arm, the better for his adoring fans in the stands to identify him. Willa's silver-fringed kerchief was tied to his arm brace to display her favor. Fox could feel her pendant pressing against his chest, a hidden source of strength.

"Good morning, Sir Danckaert," Fox said with a nod. "I would have thought you'd prefer me as an opponent."

"Nonsense. We are all gentlemen here. Besides, I'm well aware that Sir François is having trouble with his debts. Your ransom would bring a pittance."

"And after my loss in our tilt, you no doubt think that I make an easy target, which would draw our opponents away from you."

Danckaert gave a mock gasp. "Fair sir, the thought never crossed my mind."

"I wouldn't blame you," Fox said, feigning resignation to his fate. "I will be happy enough to get through today's melee with my head on my shoulders."

"It would be a pity not to face you again when the joust begins tomorrow."

Fox surveyed the opponents lining up far across the field.

"There are surely many nobles over there who will bring a much more hefty ransom than I would," Fox said.

Danckaert smiled at the prospect. "I've made a princely sum at tournaments in the past. You see the knight with the bright yellow plume in his helm?"

Fox spotted him astride a *destrier* even more formidable than Danckaert's and nodded. "Do you know him?"

"I know *of* him. His name is Sir Cosson. Well equipped and strong, but young, inexperienced, and impulsive. He's also the heir to a duchy in northern France. His capture will not be as valuable as the Crusader's Chalice after I win it as tournament champion, but the ransom I receive for him will fund my future travels nicely."

Fox now had his target. He wasn't going to let Danckaert get the biggest prize of the melee. "Then I wish you good fortune."

"That is kind of you, Sir Guillaume," the Flemish knight said. "And try to stay in formation. It may allow you to remain on your horse longer."

Danckaert rode away and took his place of honor in the center of the line.

The horn sounded, indicating that they should ready themselves for the charge. Fox lowered his cylindrical great helm over his *bascinet*, the smaller helmet that was connected to the chain mail protecting his neck. Then he made the sign of the cross—helmet, bollocks, shield, and sword—and whispered a prayer.

The horn blew again, and the crowd cheered as the riders began a slow trot toward each other, picking up the pace until they were galloping at full speed, lances pointed forward.

Cosson was in the middle of the pack, and Fox was near the end of the line, so he wouldn't be near enough to unhorse him on the first pass. Today they'd likely get only two charges before the battle devolved into the namesake melee.

Fox focused on the opponent directly ahead of him, holding Zephyr back from racing ahead of the line. There was no hint of him shying away this morning.

As the two lines crashed together, Fox hit his man squarely on the shield, sending the knight flying off the horse and breaking his own lance into splinters. The other man's lance barely grazed his shield before impaling in the soft ground of the field when its owner fell.

Considering it the spoils of battle, Fox dropped his broken lance and plucked the intact lance out of the soil before riding on to catch up with the rest of the line. The dozen or so men who'd been unhorsed scrambled to get out of the way of the next charge as the two lines made the *tournée* to the sound of raucous applause from the gallery.

Fox took the place of a man who'd fallen and left an open space next to Danckaert. Cosson was still atop his horse on the opposite side.

"You made it through, Sir Guillaume!" Danckaert called out in surprise when he saw Fox sidle up to him.

"Only by the grace of God," Fox replied.

"We'll see how long His grace lasts."

They charged again. If the lines remained intact, Danckaert would have a direct angle to hit Cosson. But this time, Fox kicked Zephyr to his full speed, leaving Danckaert and his stronger but slower *destrier* behind.

"You fool!" Danckaert shouted from behind him. "You'll be crushed!"

Fox raced ahead despite the risk. Through his helm's eye slits, he focused solely on Cosson's yellow feather fluttering toward him.

His and Cosson's lances hit their shields simultaneously. Fox's lance flew apart, and he rocked backward, straining to keep his feet in the stirrups. He dropped the remains of the lance and regained his balance in the saddle.

He pulled Zephyr around and saw that Cosson had fallen to the ground. The yellow feather was caked with mud.

Fox raced over and leaped from Zephyr, drawing his sword in the same motion. While Cosson was unsteady on his feet from the fall, Fox swung the blunted weapon, knocking Cosson's sword from his grasp.

"Yield, Sir Cosson," Fox said.

But Cosson didn't answer. Instead he bent to retrieve his sword, so Fox struck him in the helmet, causing it to fly off so that it dangled from the chain anchored to his chest plate. The ruddy cheeks and pocked skin of a knight barely out of boyhood were revealed, as were eyes brooding with anger.

"Who are you to defeat me?" Cosson spat.

"I am Sir Guillaume d'Amboise fighting under the arms of Sir François Duval. Do you yield?"

"A mere knight? I will be a duke!" Cosson grabbed his dangling great helm and attempted to use it as a cudgel.

Fox was getting tired of his bluster. He struck Cosson in the body twice with the sword, then kicked him in the chest, sending him onto his back. Fox stood over him, the blunted point of his sword in Cosson's face.

"You're not a duke yet, young knight," Fox said. "And if you wish to have all your limbs intact for the joust, I suggest you yield now."

Cosson nodded, and Fox held out his hand to help him up. Cosson refused the aid and got to his feet on his own.

"What is your price for my ransom?"

Fox looked around at the individual fights now raging across the field. Seeing that none were nearby, he removed his great helm and looked at Cosson. "Two hundred gold *livres* seems fair."

"That's outrageous! I could buy a new warhorse for that amount."

"Your father can't afford it?"

"Don't be absurd. He's one of the richest lords in northern France."

"Then he will be eager to pay my price for your freedom."

Cosson dithered under Fox's resolute gaze.

"I *could* take that fine *destrier* and feathery helmet of yours," Fox added.

Finally, Cosson said, "You will be paid your ransom."

"I have your *parole*?" The *parole* was a knight's word that his ransom would be paid as soon as possible. Once he gave his promise as a gentleman, he would be allowed to safely leave the field of battle.

"You have it," Cosson said.

"Then see to it that the funds go directly to Sir François."

Fox picked up Cosson's sword and handed it to him. Cosson snatched it away and stomped toward his horse without another word, only glancing over his shoulder to throw Fox a nasty look as he left.

As Fox remounted Zephyr, a rider approached from behind him. His sword at the ready, Fox turned to see Danckaert coming to a stop and removing his helmet.

"That was a brave feat, Sir Guillaume," Danckaert said with a smile. "The grace of God *does* seem to be with you."

"As is Cosson's ransom."

"Then congratulations are in order. His father's coffers are overflowing. Now if you'll excuse me, I have some more of my own ransoms to collect." He replaced his helmet. "Save some of your fight for me in the joust." He rode off toward the main body of the melee.

Both of them knew the same thing about the joust. They were destined to meet again.

 52

It was the first morning of the two-day jousting match. For the moment, that was all Fox could recall. His jaw hurt and his head felt like it was stuffed with wool. He saw nothing more than a bright light, and a high-pitched whine rang in his ears.

Suddenly, hands were grabbing at him. They were tugging at something he was holding. He pulled away from them until he recognized Henri and Youssef through the slits in his helmet. They were looking up at him and taking the shield and remnants of a lance out of his grip.

Fox was surprised to find that he was sitting in Zephyr's saddle, though he was leaning far to the side.

"That's one way to win a joust," Henri said, shaking his head and pushing Fox upright in the saddle again.

"I won?" Fox said.

"I didn't think you'd stay on your horse after that blow to your head," Youssef said.

Fox pulled off his helmet and let it dangle by its chain. That's when he noticed the crowd cheering. He looked around and saw them clapping from the stands as well as from behind the fences that surrounded the lists on all sides, which was possible now that the competition was limited to two jousters at a time. The only unenthusiastic applause was coming from Willa, whose face was etched with concern. Fox gave her a half-hearted wave.

Then he heard a groan. In front of him was a knight writhing on the ground. His riderless horse was being led away, and his squires were attempting to get him to his feet.

Now it was coming back to him. He had been paired with a

knight from Alsace. On the first pass, they'd both missed. Then on the second pass, they'd each hit the other's shield, but neither of them fell. The third pass would decide the victor.

Apparently, it was him, although he had no recollection of the actual impact responsible for his triumph.

"What happened?" Fox asked as he dismounted onto shaky legs. The three of them walked Zephyr back toward the stables to make way for the next set of tilts.

"What happened?" Henri repeated incredulously. "Did that Alsatian knock the sense out of you?"

Youssef looked Fox in the eye and shook his head. "He's addled, all right. I've got some *sal armonyak* that will bring him around before his next match."

"Will you tell me what happened?" said an exasperated Fox.

"Your lance hit him dead center on his shield," Henri said as he relished the tale. "Threw him back off his saddle like he was yanked by a string."

"His lance, on the other hand, went high," Youssef said. "Hit you square on the helmet. You leaned so far back from the blow that I was afraid you'd go legs up."

"But somehow you managed to stay in your seat," Henri said. "The stands went wild. Even the king rose from his throne. I think you made an admirer out of him."

"Wonderful," Fox said, massaging his aching forehead. "If he ever asks me about it, now I can recount the experience. Who am I fighting next?"

"That young blockhead you captured in the melee," Henri said. "Sir Cosson."

Youssef whistled his appreciation for the man. "He's going to be a tough one. He may not be smart, but he makes up for it in power. Unhorsing the other contender on two straight passes like that in his first tilt? The judges didn't even need to see a third to decide the match in his favor."

"His opponent won't be able to sit up straight for a week," Henri concurred. "You can't fight him with cloudy vision."

"I appreciate both your candid assessments," Fox said.

After some food and ale, Fox felt fit again, though the back of his neck would likely throb for days.

When it was time for his afternoon match, he climbed onto Zephyr and rode back to the field, paced by Henri carrying two lances with his good arm and Youssef holding the third lance and his shield. They watched as Danckaert easily defeated his opponent and acknowledged Fox with a salute.

Then it was his turn again. When his name was announced, Fox rode to the middle of the field to meet Cosson. They both dismounted to honor the king.

"You won't surprise me this time, Sir Guillaume," Cosson said under his breath as the herald presented them to the crowd.

"That's fairly obvious, you simpleton," Fox replied. "Was it difficult to clean the mud out of your helmet's feather? By the by, Sir François appreciates your father's prompt ransom payment."

Cosson did not respond, but his lip curled in unrepressed malice as they bowed to each other and remounted their horses to begin the match.

"It looks like you made him mad," Henri said as he handed over one of the lances.

"Impulsive and impetuous was what Danckaert told me," Fox said. "Let's see how he keeps his focus after that."

"When this is over," Youssef said, "remind me to tell you the story of the boy who poked the bear."

"If the boy had a lance, he likely came out unscathed," Fox said with a smile. Youssef only shook his head again.

The field was strewn with hay and sand to minimize the amount of dust as the repeated tromping of the horses tore the grass to shreds. Otherwise, the field was unencumbered. As in battle, there was nothing to separate the horses. No fence, no guiding rail. Two horses, two men, and nothing but the weapons they carried. It was not unknown for horses to collide as they raced headlong toward each other.

Fox and Cosson took their starting positions. When the signal was given, they charged. Fox steered Zephyr with his knees as he lowered the lance. He aimed for the center of the red band on Cosson's shield that slashed diagonally across a field of gold crosses on a blue background.

Their lance tips struck at the same time, but Cosson was able to withstand the hit and remain on his horse. Fox, on the other hand, took the full brunt of the impact, knocking him off Zephyr. He landed on his backside to a mix of groans and cheers from the audience.

Youssef and Henri rushed over and helped him to his feet.

"How do you think Cosson's focus is now?" Youssef asked.

Fox caught his breath. "Maybe I should hear the ending to that story about the bear poking."

"Too late for that now. But another tilt like that, and your time in the joust will be over."

"Maybe a favor from Lady Yvette will strengthen your spirits," Henri said. "She's waving to you."

He pointed, and Fox saw Willa standing at the front of the stands, dangling a kerchief for him to retrieve. Fox clambered back onto Zephyr and rode to the edge of the balcony where she was leaning out.

"Another favor, my lady?" he asked. Her pendant was around his neck under the armor.

Willa placed the kerchief in his hand and leaned closer.

"Sir Cosson's stirrups are not at the proper length for his long legs, so he's not riding securely in the saddle."

Fox kissed the kerchief, his eye on the crowd watching them. "Why are you telling me this?"

"He is unbalanced. Hit him low on the shield."

She coquettishly waved to him as she returned to her seat, but her eyes were deadly serious.

Fox tucked the kerchief into his belt and rode back to Henri and Youssef.

"It looked like the lady was whispering a love poem to you," Henri said enviously.

"She thinks Sir Cosson is unbalanced in his seat and a low blow on the shield is where I should aim."

"She's a better rider than I," Youssef said. "She may have observed something we did not."

"It couldn't hurt to try a different approach," Henri said.

Fox returned to the starting position with a new lance. Most men would discount any woman's opinion about battle, but he had seen what a sharp tactician she was. He might as well try it.

The herald gave his signal, and Fox spurred Zephyr into action. He raced at Cosson, who must have been smiling under his helmet at the thought of another easy victory. This time, Fox leaned forward and aimed at the lowest cross.

When his lance hit, it levered Cosson out of his seat, tossing him backward to the ground while his lance glanced off Fox's shield. The crowd erupted at the surprising sight.

Fox turned to the stands, removed his helmet, and nodded his appreciation to Willa, who gave a slight bow in response.

He returned to his side of the field, and Henri cried out, "*C'était magnifique!*"

"Perhaps Lady Yvette should be your trainer," Youssef said.

"If it helps me win, I'm happy to take her instruction," Fox said.

"You've still got one more," Henri said. "This tilt will decide it."

Fox took the third lance and once more raced at Cosson. The young Frenchman seemed to be using the same tactic as Fox because his lance was aimed lower as well. But Fox's seat was as secure as he could make it, so he wouldn't be catapulted out as Cosson had been.

When their lances smashed into each other, Fox's leg greave caught the full force of Cosson's lance, knocking it out of the stirrup. Fox tried valiantly to remain on Zephyr, but his weight took him over the other side, and he fell to the ground. He looked up to see that Cosson had adjusted his seating position and remained on his horse. He threw off his helmet and raised his arms in triumph.

The judges were about to name him the winner until Zephyr turned around to trot back to Fox, revealing to both him and the crowd why Cosson had won.

Splinters of Cosson's lance jutted out of the armor on Zephyr's shoulder. That's why the lance had struck Fox in the leg. Cosson had aimed at Zephyr instead of Fox.

Fox limped over and withdrew the lance head from between the plates. He checked for a wound. There was blood, but the laceration wasn't deep. A poultice from Youssef would stop the bleeding.

Fox turned, furious at Cosson. He was ready to draw his sword and demand a duel, but the call of the lead judge stopped him.

"For the unchivalrous act of striking his opponent's horse, we rule that Sir Cosson has been disqualified from the match. Sir Guillaume is declared the victor!"

Youssef and Henri dashed over and slapped him on the back for his victory.

"That dishonorable cheat didn't deserve to be on the same field as you," Henri said. "Only three more tilts to go to win the chalice."

"How is your leg?" Youssef asked.

"There will be a mark, but I'll be ready for the next joust," Fox said. "I'm more concerned about Zephyr."

"Don't worry, my friend," Youssef said, taking the reins. "He is a strong horse, and he's in good hands."

"Thank you." Fox turned to the stands and mouthed the same words.

Willa, who was clapping wildly, nodded to him. But it was François next to her who captured Fox's attention. His grim expression made it clear that he was dismayed by the near loss. Fox had no doubt that if he didn't win the whole event, François would be sure to turn him over to the king, revealing him as an English fugitive to settle his debt with Cardinal Molyneux.

## 53

PARIS

It was mid-afternoon when Cardinal Molyneux's carriage entered the town of Saint-Jacques. He was on his way to Château de Riquevert south of Paris to get away from the noise and smell of the city. He still hadn't heard from Tonbridge or Lambert and was beginning to wonder if they'd suffered some kind of setback in Saint-Quentin.

Molyneux sighed at the thought. This entire affair had brought him nothing but disappointment so far. He should have had the Icon in his hands by now and been preparing for his candidacy at the next papal conclave.

Instead, his son had failed him on several occasions, and his English ally and his personal attendant had gone missing. Even the messenger he'd sent to Saint-Quentin to find news of Tonbridge hadn't returned.

Since he was passing through Saint-Jacques anyway, he decided to get an update from Basquin, whom he hadn't heard from in days. The cardinal didn't hold out much hope. Basquin wouldn't dare call on him again unless he had something positive to report.

He sent one of his aides to fetch Basquin from the house where he was watching the Duval manor. While he waited, Molyneux considered how he would use the estate once François defaulted on his debt. The knight's ridiculous bid to settle his obligations using the Crusader's Chalice was doomed to fail. When that happened, Molyneux could expand his holdings in this region considerably given that the Duval estate abutted his own vast acreage.

When the aide returned, Basquin was not with him.

"Your Eminence," the man said nervously, "Basquin is gone."

"Gone where?"

"To the king's tournament at Château de Tournöel. The men said he left days ago."

Molyneux sat back as he ruminated about what could have made Basquin ride all that way. There was only one answer. He'd discovered information that led him to believe Fox and Isabel would be there with the manuscript.

So when Basquin had come to his residence, his son really did have useful information.

But why would he think that the two fugitives would go to meet with François at the tournament instead of coming here to see Isabel's cousin? Since Molyneux was already in Saint-Jacques, he could ask Claire himself.

He patted the side of the carriage and said, "Take me to the Duval manor."

When they arrived, they were allowed through the gate immediately. But when the coach came to a stop in the central courtyard, where he could see the Duval's own carriage still in the stable, he was not met by the lady of the house. Instead, an older man with a white beard stood outside by himself.

Molyneux stepped out of the carriage and looked at the man, who bowed his head and kneeled. The cardinal didn't bother to hold out his ring.

"Who are you?" he asked.

The man stood. "Your Eminence, it is an honor to have you visit this estate. I am Arnoult, Sir François's *seneschal*."

"Why do I not see Lady Claire before me?" Molyneux asked.

"I am afraid that she is not available to speak to you. Perhaps I can relay a message to her?"

"You may relay the message that I will wait in this very spot until she does me the courtesy of coming to meet me."

Arnoult's face twisted in a pained expression. "I cannot do that, Your Eminence."

"And why is that?"

"Because she is not here."

"Your obtuseness is trying my patience, Arnoult. Where is Lady Claire?"

"Forgive me, Your Eminence. I was instructed not to reveal that she was gone."

"Where!"

"She went to the king's tournament with Sir François."

Molyneux narrowed his eyes at the Duval coach, which had remained behind, no doubt to disguise her departure.

"Was anyone with her besides her husband and his entourage?"

"Just Sir François's champion and Lady Claire's companion."

"Companion?"

"A lovely blonde woman. Lady Yvette de Loches was her name."

"And this champion? Was it not Sir Simon as I had been led to believe?"

Arnoult shook his head. "Sir Simon was defeated by this new champion, a knight by the name of Sir Guillaume d'Amboise. He was a skilled warrior to beat a giant so easily."

So that's what led Basquin away on his chase. He believed the newcomers were Gerard Fox and Lady Isabel.

Molyneux turned to get back in the carriage.

"Please, Your Eminence," Arnoult called to him. "Do not tell Sir François that I disobeyed him."

From the steps of his carriage, Molyneux said, "Never fear, my son. The fault is Sir François's for entreating you to bear false witness to one of God's servants."

As the carriage exited the estate, a man on horseback galloped to a stop beside it. Molyneux was astonished to see that the horseman was Lord Tonbridge. Two of his soldiers trailed him.

"Your Eminence, your *seneschal* told me you would be here," Tonbridge said. "I must speak to you."

"Where is Father Lambert?"

"It is with deep regret that I inform you he is dead. We were ambushed by bandits on our way from Saint-Quentin. Father Lambert performed admirably in helping me escape with my life. It took me some time to hire enough capable men to escort me back to Paris safely."

"Did you find the information you went there to retrieve?" Molyneux asked.

Tonbridge nodded. "Isabel's sister, Prioress Catherine, was sent to Avignon after the Great Mortality decimated Saint-Quentin. From there I don't know where she went. I was hoping you would have a way to find those records."

"Not in Paris. Only in Avignon will we discover her final destination. She could very well still be there, which may be even more important now."

"Why?" Tonbridge asked.

"Because it seems that Lady Isabel has already made an appearance in Paris. Somehow, she has come and gone under our noses."

"Then we must ride to Avignon at once. I will gather my remaining men."

"I concur. And I will go with you. But we will stop at Château de Tournöel along the way."

"Why would we do such a thing?"

"Because Basquin is there. He seems to think Fox and your betrothed may have gone there with Sir François and Lady Claire."

Tonbridge looked alarmed at that prospect. "The manuscript truly belongs to me. If Basquin recovers it, I still expect to receive my kingship."

Molyneux put up his hand to appease him. "Our arrangement has not expired."

Although the title of King of Jerusalem had been claimed by several nobles since the fall of Acre in 1291, it was merely ceremonial. Lord Tonbridge would earn it. Molyneux fully intended to wrest the Holy Land back from the Mamluks. Even before the army was raised, he would designate Tonbridge as the leader of this new crusade. With the Hodegetria and God on their side, the infidels would surely fall, Jerusalem would be theirs, and Tonbridge would be rewarded with the royal moniker that was so dear to him.

The answer seemed to reassure Tonbridge only partially. "My men and I will ride with you just the same."

"Of course. It is late, and we must prepare for the journey.

We will stop at my country estate tonight and ride south in the morning to find Basquin."

The cardinal shook his head at the impetuous nature of his troublesome son. He had always been that way, even as a child. Perhaps if his mother were still alive, she could have tempered his brashness.

A smile crossed his face as he remembered Emmeline. No one could withstand her charms, especially Molyneux.

## 54

*Twenty-three years ago*
*June, 1328*

NORMANDY, FRANCE

Dominic Molyneux woke with a start. The carriage's rocking motion had lulled him into a deep sleep. He was exhausted from the long ride to Normandy after attending the coronation of Philip VI in Reims and then participating in the ceremony to receive his bishopric in Avranches. Now he was on a tour of noble estates in his new domain to receive their obeisance and deliver his blessing upon them.

When he opened his eyes, he saw the two men accompanying him on the journey. The first was his clerk Lambert, an aspiring priest who was not yet out of his teens. The other was Sir Conrad Harrington, the son of Tonbridge, who insisted on being called by his family name even though he had not yet risen to the earldom. He and Molyneux had met long ago during Tonbridge's travels in France as a squire.

He looked out of the carriage, but all he could see were fields on either side. The sun's position indicated that it was late morning.

"Where are we?"

"Approaching the château of Sir Richard Fox, Your Grace," Lambert said.

"Very well," Molyneux said. "I don't want to stay long. We will have better accommodations at our next stop. The Marquis de Bayeux, I believe?"

"Yes, Your Grace."

"He has a lavish château and feather beds. We will take a

refreshment and a short tour of Sir Richard's estate and then leave. Understood?"

Lambert nodded.

Molyneux looked at Tonbridge, who brushed at his surcoat to remove horsehairs. "How is it that an English nobleman has this château?"

"His family seat is in Oakhurst, England, but he acquired the lands here in a dowry from his wife's family, Your Grace. I only know him from a few tournaments that we attended together in Kent. He's a bit older than I, and a celebrated fighter who has won his fair share of jousts."

"What of his nature?"

Tonbridge looked thoughtful. "He is renowned for his honesty and charisma. If you can charm him, Richard will extol you to the other nobles in the area. Your stature as the new bishop will be secure."

"That's enough," Molyneux said, waving off any additional information. He didn't need to hear more. The rituals over the past fortnight had become drearily familiar. He'd arrive at the estate, the family would dutifully kiss his rings, he'd take a meal or refreshment with them, and then continue on to the next estate until it was time to bed down for the night at whatever noble house he found himself. Most of them couldn't stop talking about themselves and how devoted they were to the Church, so he didn't need a preamble from Tonbridge.

He supposed he should be glad for his position. As the third son of a minor Norman *seigneur*, Molyneux had no hope of inheriting land, and becoming a warrior knight held no interest for him. He'd had two choices: marry into money or enter the priesthood. He'd tried the former without success, so he entered the safety and comfort of Church life. He soon discovered that he had a talent for acquiring the riches and power the Church had to offer.

While serving as a parish priest in Caen, he'd worked hard to develop a reputation as a man of the people, who loved him as much for the trinkets and coins he handed out as for the reassuring words he offered to them in times of difficulty or when they asked forgiveness for sins. But rapport with his superiors was lacking. No matter how diligently he tried to ingratiate himself with them, they would not promote him. They looked down on him for his humble origins and bestowed their favors on those with more useful connections. Molyneux knew he was destined for a higher purpose, but nothing he had done had helped his ascension, until two years ago.

That's when he turned to what he knew would work. Money.

When a distant cousin died, Molyneux was made responsible for overseeing the small estate on behalf of the Church, and by milking it dry, had parlayed its modest returns into a growing treasury. From Tonbridge, he'd gotten the idea to use his status to blackmail nobles who did not want their secrets aired. Eventually, Molyneux planned to expand the scheme into taking estates wholesale, but that would have to wait until he had the power necessary to carry out such a plan. In the meantime, the extortions allowed him to buy the adoration of the peasantry and bourgeoisie, but more importantly, they provided him the means to bribe those in power above him.

And thus he came to be a bishop at such an early age. He had learned which cardinals were corrupt enough to take payment for bestowing their influence for bishoprics, and he took advantage of that knowledge. Now he was enduring the tedium required of his position as Bishop of Avranches before he began focusing on how to ascend to archbishop. Rouen would be his preferred seat.

The carriage went through the front gates of Sir Richard's estate and came to a stop in the central courtyard. Molyneux waited as Lambert and Tonbridge exited. He heard Tonbridge greet their hosts.

After an appropriate amount of time, Molyneux stepped out, making sure to take in his surroundings before continuing, to give himself an air of inscrutability and authority.

As he surveyed the manor, he felt an odd sense of familiarity. Of course, many of the châteaus looked alike because of the stonework, but it seemed as if he remembered this place.

He gave a slight smile when he noticed Richard Fox watching

him with curiosity. He was about to move toward him to receive the kiss on his ring when he was stunned into immobility by the sight of Richard's wife standing beside him. To his shock, he knew her, and quite well. That's why this château looked familiar. He'd been here many times in his youth. Though structural changes had been made since he lasted visited, he now realized that it was Château de Beaujoie, and Richard's wife was Emmeline. This was her childhood home.

Molyneux had to clench his teeth together so that his mouth didn't fall open. He hadn't laid eyes on her in ten years, and she was even lovelier than she had been then. She wore a dazzling emerald green surcoat over an embroidered blue kirtle that revealed a voluptuous figure, and her high cheekbones, full lips, and deep brown hair bound up in plaits highlighted her intelligent blue eyes.

Apparently she had been more prepared to see him than he was to see her. She wore a welcoming expression that held no surprise.

The old feelings of rejection and shame resurfaced in an instant. Emmeline had been the one woman Molyneux had truly adored when he was growing up in Normandy. He became completely obsessed with her beauty and elegance, and though many suitors pursued her, Molyneux thought his looks and charm should carry the day.

She was not lured by his winning manner. She was kind and friendly to him, but no matter how many times he asked her, she would not accept his proposal. Since he was a younger son, her father had backed her and finally ordered him to have no further contact with her. Although there were other women Molyneux could have settled for, Emmeline's persistent rejection had been unbearable, a blow to his manhood. That was the moment he'd decided to join the clergy.

But that was long ago. Molyneux gathered himself, concentrating on Richard, and walked over to them. The husband and wife kneeled, and Molyneux held out his hand so that they could kiss it. Richard took it with a strong hand and gave his ring a quick peck. Emmeline then grasped his hand with gentle fingers.

The only adornment on them was a gold ring shaped into a tiny hand cradling a ruby. She gave his ring a perfunctory kiss, and he imagined what it would feel like on his lips.

Once the obeisance was concluded, Lambert said, "It is my duty and honor to present His Grace Dominic Molyneux, Bishop of Avranches. My lord, I am honored to introduce Sir Richard Fox, Lord of Oakhurst."

"Sir Richard," Molyneux said, "I am so pleased that you have invited me to visit your beautiful manor this fine day." The manor that should have rightly been his.

"The pleasure is mine, Your Grace. May I present my wife, Lady Emmeline."

Molyneux turned to her. "Charmed as always, my lady."

"I am pleased to see you again, Your Grace. My husband and I are quite honored that you have chosen to visit us. I trust your journey was safe and untroubled?"

Molyneux forced down the fiery rage that threatened to consume him. She purposefully emphasized that Richard was her husband, as if she were rubbing his nose in that fact.

"It has been a long and fatiguing trip, but I'm glad to be here." He searched for even a flicker of emotion from her.

"I see that you have done well since we last met. We were only children then, but you seem to have blossomed in your new position."

Molyneux was crushed at how lightly she dismissed his fervent courtship, implying that it was a childish infatuation.

"I have been blessed indeed," Molyneux said, doing his best to endure her slights.

"I hope you will join us for our midday meal, my lord," Richard said. "We wouldn't want you to continue traveling until you've built your strength again."

"Sir Richard always enjoys a hearty meal, but we've prepared something special for Your Lordship today. Suckling pig and pheasant."

"I must credit Lady Emmeline with the dining choices. You are extraordinary, my dear."

They exchanged cloying smiles with each other. The thought of Emmeline enjoying her dinner with this undeserving Englishman made him sick. Molyneux should have been the one opening these château doors to entertain important Church officers and noblemen, with his doting wife at his side. He had never understood her refusal of him, and now her choice infuriated him anew. *He* should be the focus of her affection.

Without warning, two young boys ran from inside the manor and rambunctiously gamboled about, smacking each other with wooden sticks fashioned into makeshift swords. They screamed and shouted until Richard spoke a single word.

"Quiet!"

The boys immediately stopped playing, noticed the gathered retinue, and went stock-still.

A nursemaid flew out a moment later, apologizing profusely to Emmeline.

"Forgive me, my lady. They left my sight for the blink of an eye."

"I know what a handful they are, Marie. James, Gerard, go back inside and take your dinner with her. I will join you later for our reading."

"Do as your mother says," Richard commanded.

The boys replied, "Yes, sir," without hesitation and marched back inside with the nursemaid. The sight of Emmeline's sons, strong and vibrant, further twisted the knife in Molyneux's soul.

"My apologies, Your Grace," Richard said, belied by his proud smile. "Those two have overabundant spirit, but they will make fine knights someday."

Molyneux composed himself and faced Richard again, but he could still steal a glance at Emmeline from the corner of his eye. He saw her shift uncomfortably, as if aware of his surreptitious gaze.

"That's quite all right, Sir Richard." He put on a weary affectation. "Your dinner invitation is most kind. I suspect that would do well for the extended trek we have ahead of us. I'm not sure we will reach Bayeux by sundown with the state of my carriage. One of the wheels has given us a harsh ride since Vire."

"We wouldn't hear of you setting off on such a long voyage this late in the day," Emmeline said with a trace of hesitation. "You must be our guest at Château de Beaujoie tonight. After you have been refreshed, you can continue your journey."

"That is thoughtful of you, my dear," Richard said to her with an adoring gaze.

Richard wrested his eyes from Emmeline and back to his guest. "And I am happy to have the local wheelwright inspect your carriage and make sure it's in proper working order by morning."

Molyneux pretended to brighten up at the invitation he'd extracted from them.

"That is too kind of you, Sir Richard. Lady Emmeline. I would be delighted to accept your gracious offer."

"Very good. I will be leaving for England with James and Gerard in the morning so I can travel with you for part of the way to your destination."

"Will Lady Emmeline not be joining you?"

Richard shook his head. "She is staying at Beaujoie for the sake of her mother, who is unwell. Emmeline will join us by the end of the summer, God willing. I suspect each of the boys will be a head taller by then."

"No doubt. My sincere condolences about your mother's ill health. I would be happy to offer her a blessing after dinner."

"That is most kind of you, Your Grace," Emmeline said. "Shall we retire to our meal?"

"Perhaps I can have a private word with my aides to discuss our arrangements before I join you for dinner."

"By all means, Your Grace," Richard said. "My chamberlain will be standing by to show you where you can perform your ablutions. My wife and I will be waiting for you in the great hall."

As the couple moved away, Lambert looked at him with a puzzled expression. "I thought we were to stay only a short time and then leave, Your Grace."

"I have changed my mind," Molyneux said sharply and then cooled his temper. "I think it would serve me well to spend more time with a man as distinguished and influential as Sir Richard."

"And I don't object to spending more time in the company of his wife. She is quite a beauty. Sir Richard is a fortunate man." Before Molyneux could unleash his fury at that comment, Tonbridge added, "I didn't detect anything wrong with our carriage ride."

"Perhaps you are not used to the comforts of luxurious travel," Molyneux said. "Lambert, see to it that the coach is completely sound before we leave tomorrow."

"Yes, Your Grace." Lambert scurried off.

"Tonbridge, I have a task for you."

"However I may serve you, Your Grace."

Molyneux lowered his voice. "Find out more about the travel plans of both Sir Richard and his wife. But discreetly."

"Why?"

"That doesn't concern you."

"I will do my best, Your Grace."

They walked toward the main hall, the chamberlain coming out of the far shadows to escort them.

Molyneux couldn't get Emmeline out of his mind. She had denied him the life, the château, and the sons he deserved, and even worse, she seemed to remember him as a child rather than a serious suitor. But now he realized he could rectify her error in judgment. As a bishop, he had the means and power to take what should have been his all along.

No matter the risks, no matter the cost, he would finally have her.

 55

Basquin arrived at Château de Tournöel on the final afternoon of the tournament. He found the Duval banner flying over the family's collection of tents, guarded by some of François's soldiers. No one else was around. He could have killed the guards and ransacked the tents to look for the manuscript, but he had a grander plan.

The sound of cheers, applause, and clashing armor was carried by the breeze along with the smell of horse manure and the body odor of the masses gathered to watch. Basquin followed the noise until he saw the spectators crowding both sides of the tilting field.

He wended his way through the throngs of commoners until he squeezed himself into a spot at the railing relatively close to the action, opposite the king's viewing throne. The balcony was packed with nobles there to experience the event of the summer. Dressed in his fine clothes, Basquin would have been allowed to join them, but he wanted to observe the gallery first without being noticed.

He spotted François in the front row not far from the royal box. And there was his wife Claire sitting next to him, just as he'd expected. He was even happier to be proven right when he saw her cousin Isabel sitting beside her. Though Fox was nowhere to be seen, he couldn't be far.

Basquin turned to the man next to him, a commoner who had the rough hands and hearty scent of a tanner.

"How many more jousts until the tournament is over?"

The man looked him up and down, appraising his attire.

"Where have *you* been all day?" he asked with a laugh.

The woman beside him nudged him with her elbow. "Pierre, you shouldn't say things like that to your betters."

"This man comes out of nowhere and suddenly wants to know what's going on, Jaquette?" Pierre said. "I think it's a proper question."

"I have just arrived after a long journey," Basquin said.

"Then you've missed a fine tournament," Pierre said. "But you're in time for the championship joust."

"It's going to be thrilling," Jaquette said. "Pierre is cheering for Sir Danckaert of Flanders."

"Why shouldn't I? He is the clear favorite."

Danckaert's renown was undeniable. Basquin had even seen him win a tournament before the Pestilence arrived.

"That may be true," Jaquette said, "but I'm partial to his challenger, Sir Guillaume d'Amboise."

Basquin's interest was piqued at hearing the name of the knight who had defeated Sir Simon.

Pierre waved his hand dismissively. "Don't listen to her. Sir Danckaert has the better horse, and he's won every tilt easily. Sir Guillaume has some skill, I admit, but he only got this far by being luckier than a skinny pig at slaughter time."

"It isn't luck at all," Jaquette argued, swatting Pierre on the arm. "He's got a way of using his wits and vigor to win. Just you see."

"I look forward to it," Basquin said.

The herald came forth, and the crowd hushed.

"My lord king, noble knights and ladies, behold the challengers for the final tilt. King John will be presenting the famed Crusader's Chalice to the winner at this evening's feast."

The herald motioned to the stands, and an attendant beside the king lifted a silk cloth with a flourish, revealing a tall drinking chalice carved of rock crystal, set into gold and adorned with gems. The crowd gasped aloud at sight of the valuable object.

"Now that we can see what is at stake," the herald continued, "allow me present the contenders for the prize. From Flanders, I present to you, Sir Danckaert van Hoecke!"

A massive cheer went up, and Sir Danckaert trotted out of the holding area and onto the field with half a dozen squires running alongside as they carried his lances and shield. Atop his majestic *destrier*, Danckaert obviously enjoyed the attention and rode up and down the stands to receive his adoration. When he was quite through, he stopped his horse directly in front of the king and bowed his head.

"And now the challenger from Touraine, I present to you, Sir Guillaume d'Amboise!"

An even louder cry went up for the newcomer, who seemed to have a large portion of the crowd behind him.

As soon as he emerged, Basquin recognized François's coat of arms draped around the horse, which was covered with armor and a sumptuous caparison nearly nose to tail. But the silver color of his legs and black tail drew Basquin's eye, and he knew his instincts to come had been right.

Sitting on the familiar horse was Fox, his face grim with determination, a marked contrast from Danckaert's joyous demeanor. Basquin leaned down and covered his brow with one hand on the slim chance that Fox looked in his direction. He didn't want his surprise to be ruined.

But it was the two squires trotting next to Fox that truly stunned Basquin. One was a dark-skinned man, an unusual sight among the pale faces. The other, a burly fellow with reddish-brown hair, was Henri, the clerk who'd nearly revealed Basquin's scheme to skim money from the Church. Both of them had escaped from Château de Riquevert with Fox's help. Now Basquin realized that his mind hadn't been playing tricks on him back in Saint-Jacques. He really had seen Henri there.

Basquin didn't know how or when Fox had enlisted their help, but the sight of them started an idea churning in his head that would make for an even better plan than the one he'd created earlier.

Fox and Danckaert put on their helmets and went to their

starting positions to await the sound of the trumpet. Basquin noticed Fox cross himself as he readied for battle.

At the signal, the two knights raced at each other. Basquin knew that Danckaert was an expert jouster, but he was equally impressed by Fox's form as their lances broke upon each other's shields at the same time. Although Fox was rocked backward by the blow, neither of them fell off their horses, much to the crowd's disappointment.

Pierre slapped the railing. "What did I say? Guillaume is fortunate yet again to be upright."

"He's steadfast and true," Jaquette replied. "What you call luck, I call blessed by the Lord."

On the second pass, Danckaert's lance broke upon Fox's shield, sending it flying, while Fox's lance merely grazed Danckaert's and remained intact. The judges awarded a point to Danckaert, drawing a dismayed groan from Jaquette.

Another result like that, and Danckaert would be named champion. To win outright on the third try, Fox would need to unhorse the Fleming.

Either way, the plan that Basquin was formulating would work, but it would be so much more satisfying if Fox were named champion of the tournament.

Despite their antagonism toward each other, Basquin found himself rooting for his older brother.

"Danckaert will win for sure now," Pierre said.

"Would you like to wager on that outcome?" Basquin asked him. Of course, the commoner wouldn't have much to bet. "I've got three sous that says Sir Guillaume emerges as the victor."

"I don't mind taking a week's wages from the likes of you," Pierre said with a smile.

"Don't, Pierre," Jaquette protested. "Sir Guillaume can do it."

Pierre waved her off and agreed to the terms.

Before Fox returned to his starting position, Basquin noticed him remove his helmet and ride over to the stands. As he took a kerchief from Isabel, it appeared as if she were telling him something. Once their short conversation was finished, Fox kissed her hand and tucked the kerchief into his armor.

"It's just like in the romance stories," Jaquette swooned. "Her favor always gives him the strength he needs to win."

Danckaert looked put out by Isabel's gesture, but he composed himself to wave at the crowd before he put on his helmet and took a fresh lance from his squires. It was the confidence of a man who knew he was about to claim the king's prize.

Fox, on the other hand, rode quickly back to Henri and Youssef. He had them adjust his stirrups, and as a result, Fox seemed to be leaning farther forward in his saddle. With the weight of the armor he was wearing, it must have taken great strength to keep the position, perhaps just long enough for one more pass.

The trumpet sounded. Fox kicked his horse and shouted, "*Oppugna!*"

The silver Arabian galloped forward at top speed. It was clear Fox was going for maximum power, even if it sacrificed accuracy.

As they approached each other, Fox leaned even farther forward, his lance far out over his shield.

When they collided, Fox's lance was the first to hit. It rammed directly into Danckaert's shield, and the impact jarred it upward, redirecting the lance. Not only did Danckaert miss completely, but the force of the hit ejected him from his saddle. He fell to the ground, and his helmet flew off. He sat up immediately with an astonished and pained expression.

The crowd went mad. Hats flew in the air, the spectators cried with joy and disbelief, and trumpets blared, signaling Fox's champion status. Even the king stood to applaud.

Basquin clapped for his brother and turned to Pierre, holding out his hand for his payment. Pierre grimaced as he extracted the coins and dropped them in Basquin's palm, then walked away without a word. Jaquette followed, beating him around the shoulders for losing their food money.

Tonight there would be much merriment and celebration, but for Basquin it would be the time to set the wheels in motion for his own triumph.

He put the coins in his purse and headed back toward town. He had to go find a brothel.

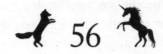 56

A temporary outdoor tavern had been put together at the tournament to cater to the squires and commoners not invited to the lavish championship celebration at the castle. A full moon added light to the torches scattered around the tables. Henri thought it was a beautiful night, improved significantly by the free beverages that flowed for him and Youssef. As the attendants to the winning knight, they were enjoying rounds of wine bought for them by other squires trying to learn the secrets to Sir Guillaume's improbable victory.

"It was me, you see, who taught him where to strike Sir Cosson," Henri bragged. "It's all in where to aim."

"Yes, but it was me that came up with the idea of tightening his stirrups against Sir Danckaert," Youssef said. "The riding position is just as important."

Henri clinked his tankard of wine against Youssef's to toast their perceptive ingenuity. "Sir Guillaume is a knight of rare talents, but I think it's safe to say that he would never have won if it weren't for us."

None of the others knew that their covert adviser was a pretty blonde woman. Henri and Youssef normally wouldn't have taken the credit, but Willa had told them to feel free to brag of the achievement as their own since no one would have believed the truth.

Two women carrying full tankards edged their way into the group and handed them to Youssef and Henri as they sat, a lovely raven-haired girl beside Youssef and a striking brunette next to Henri. Both of them seemed experienced and comfortable with approaching strange men in taverns.

Henri glanced in surprise at Youssef, who shrugged with a crooked smile at the unexpected development. The benefits of winning the tournament just kept getting better. Henri drained the rest of his drink and gladly took the new one offered. Youssef didn't seem to mind the drink or the company, either. The other squires knew when they weren't wanted and dispersed.

"Thank you for the hospitality," Henri said. "And who might you lovely maidens be?"

The brunette said, "My name is Margot. This is Geneviève. We wanted to thank you for such an entertaining joust the last two days."

"That's awfully kind of you," Youssef said. "Who are we to turn down a measure of gratitude? Don't you agree, Henri?"

"It would be downright rude is what it would be."

As they continued drinking, Henri and Youssef entertained the women by repeating their tales of insight into the joust. Then the conversation turned more personal.

"Oh, no," Margot said, holding Henri's scarred right hand. "What happened to you, you poor dear?"

"That?" Henri said. "It's just a battle wound."

"Tell me about it!" she pleaded.

"If you insist." He told the tale of their escape from captivity but embellished the story by saying that he single-handedly fought off a trio of English *routiers* and saved a maiden in the process.

"And I want to hear about where you got this delicious dark skin," Geneviève said to Youssef as she caressed his arm. "You must have traveled from amazing, faraway lands to get here."

"I come from a place called Egypt," Youssef said. "There are structures there so magnificent that they are twice the height of Notre Dame Cathedral."

"You lie," Geneviève said, so Youssef went into a description of the pyramids of Giza that Henri had heard many times before.

Margot tickled Henri's cheek and whispered in his ear. "It's such a wonderful night out, perhaps we should let them alone and take a walk. I want to visit the royal box at the tilting fields."

"I would be delighted to show it to you," Henri said. He patted Youssef on the shoulder as they stood to go, but his friend was so deep into his conversation that he barely acknowledged that Henri was leaving.

Henri was soused enough that he had to lean on Margot as they left, but he was sure that the flesh would be as willing as the spirit once they were alone on the grass under the moonlight.

The sound of the drinkers faded as they reached the tournament field. Margot smiled seductively and led him to the stands where the king's platform was located.

"I think you'll be very happy with my surprise," she said.

"I know I will," Henri replied.

When they reached the rear of the stands, she stopped and gave him a kiss on the cheek.

"This is the place," she said.

"You didn't really lead me out here to see the king's chair, did you?" Henri asked.

"No, I didn't."

"No, she didn't," someone behind Henri said.

His blood froze in recognition of that arrogant voice. He turned slowly to see Basquin standing there in front of him. The bastard was smiling, just like he had been the day he locked Henri in the cell with Youssef.

"Your friend wanted to surprise you," Margot said.

Basquin nodded. "I've come a long way just to see you."

Margot walked over to Basquin and held out her hand. Coins clinked as they fell into her palm. Then he leaned over and whispered something to her before giving her a small scrap of parchment.

She waved goodbye to Henri. "This was fun, love." Then she turned and trotted off in the direction of Château de Tournöel.

"What do you want?" Henri asked. His hand rested on the dagger sheathed in his belt.

Basquin's hands dangled by his sides, but his sword was within easy reach. "To talk. And don't bother making up one of your famous stories about why you're here. I know Gerard is masquerading as

Sir Guillaume. I saw him win the tournament. You can imagine my fraternal pride at seeing him named champion."

"I'm sure you were ecstatic."

"You were at Mont-Saint-Michel, weren't you? I remember now seeing you on that strange cart. That's where you've been hiding since your escape from Paris."

"Does it matter?"

"I suppose not. But it does explain why Gerard went there."

"If you want me to betray him, you're wasting your breath."

Basquin smiled. "So loyalty is important to you. I'm sure Gerard feels the same way. In fact, I'm counting on it."

With lightning speed, Basquin drew his sword and slashed Henri deeply across the torso in one stroke.

Henri didn't even have a chance to touch his knife. He dropped to his knees as he grabbed his chest, blood gushing through his fingers. He tried to croak out a cry for help, but it came out as a low groan. He collapsed onto the ground.

Basquin stood over him and cleaned his blade on Henri's tunic while watching the life drain from him.

"Now all I have to do is wait for Gerard to be accused of the murder of his own squire."

With his last bit of strength, Henri drew his dagger and launched it at Basquin, who easily batted it away with his sword. Henri's final image was of Basquin's smug amusement.

"Gerard will avenge me," Henri said as his vision faded.

"I sincerely hope he tries."

## 57

The great hall of Château de Tournöel was even more lavishly decorated for the closing celebration than it had been for the opening. Despite the flowers, music, and elaborate food preparations, some of the losing knights were glum, especially Sir Danckaert, who sulked in his seat, ignoring the attention of two young ladies on either side of him. But for most of the attendees, the festivities were raucous and joyful. Even though Fox was eager to pay off his obligations to François and leave first thing in the morning, he could understand why the revelry was so lively. After several years of the Great Mortality ravaging Europe, the gala was a sign that civilization was reviving.

The highlight of the evening was the presentation of the Crusader's Chalice to the champion. Given that he was using the name of an impostor, Fox was uncomfortable accepting his prize directly from His Highness. He kneeled and kissed the king's hand, then passed the chalice to François, whose hands trembled as he took it. Both men then bowed to the king and returned to the table to be greeted by Claire and Willa.

"I believe our transaction is now complete," Fox said, making sure that no one was within earshot.

François nodded. "I didn't think you would do it, but I will make sure the cardinal knows nothing of you or Lady Isabel."

"I wish I could be there when you pay off your debt to Molyneux with this instead of your land."

"And I wish I could write to you and describe the scene, sweet friend," Claire said to Willa.

"Unfortunately, I cannot tell you where we are going," Willa said, making sure François heard.

The two women had decided to keep Catherine's location at La Sacra di San Michele a secret from Claire's husband, and Fox agreed. No sense in tempting him with further information to share with the cardinal.

"You will see that she gets to her destination safely, won't you, Sir Gerard?" Claire asked him.

"I have made a promise, and I intend to keep it."

"I feel much better knowing an accomplished knight like you will be escorting her."

"It seems improper for her to travel without a chaperone," François said. "However, I can't argue with your chivalry in battle, and you did allow me to pay off my debts. You have demonstrated your honor amply. Therefore, I wish that God speed your journey."

The music changed, signaling that the dancing would soon begin.

"François, you promised to present me to the king," Claire said. "Everyone is going to dance so perhaps now is the time."

"My dear, it would be my pleasure." François stood and helped her from her seat.

"Do you enjoy dancing?" Fox asked Willa, even though he didn't feel up to it. His body was covered with bruises from the punishment he'd taken in the tournament, and his muscles ached with every movement.

Willa seemed to pick up on his reluctance to join the dance. "Perhaps we could take a walk back toward the tents instead. I've had enough of these nobles, and we have another long ride to begin tomorrow."

Fox was delighted for the chance to be alone with her. "I would be happy to escort you. I've done my duty here. Let's just hope Henri and Youssef aren't too infirm from their carousing to depart early in the morning."

So that they would not cause a scandal leaving as a couple, they waited until a cluster of men and women were exiting the hall. They accompanied the group out and then slipped away to begin the walk back down the hill to the tents.

Willa looped her arm around Fox's elbow. "How are you feeling?"

"Fatigued, but otherwise fine."

She pursed her lips at him. "You can't fool me. You're as stiff as an oak."

"It's nothing that a little rest won't cure. If it hadn't been for your advice, I'd be in much worse shape right now."

"I'm glad I could be of help. Not many men would have listened. In fact, there aren't many men like you at all."

"And there aren't many women like you."

Now that they were away from the castle, the only sound was the chirping of frogs and crickets. Other than a woman of dubious virtue passing them on the path, they were alone.

After a spell of silence, Willa asked, "Do you think you will ever get your family's land back?"

Fox was surprised by the abrupt question. "I'd like to think it's a possibility, but I don't know how. My hope was that Tonbridge would testify on my behalf to the pope that Molyneux had abducted my mother and therefore unjustly excommunicated me and my father. But I obviously can't count on him to make a truthful statement on my behalf."

"I'm sorry if I'm the cause of that."

"You're not. If I hadn't come across you on that road in England, I likely would have continued on to Tonbridge and been executed by Basquin. No, instead you've given me hope—hope that I can get some small revenge against Molyneux for what he's done to my family."

"I never saw you as someone who would get satisfaction from vengeance," Willa said.

"Perhaps justice is a better word. There isn't much of it in this world, but you've given me a renewed faith that it still exists."

Willa smiled as they approached her tent, out of sight of the two guards posted at François's lodging. "If I can renew the faith of an excommunicated soul, then perhaps the Icon really does bring out the divine in us."

Fox stopped at the entrance and took Willa's hand. He placed the Saint Isabella pendant in her palm.

"I gave that to you as a favor," Willa said.

"To bring me good fortune during the tournament. It did. But I know how much it means to you."

She put it back over his head. "I want you to keep it. Think of it as a memento of our journey together. Besides, you need the luck that it brings more than I do."

"I always thought you were a curious woman," Fox said, "even when I didn't know who you really were."

Willa looked up at him, her eyes glinting in the moonlight. "And now that you *do* know?"

"I think you're remarkable."

Fox felt as if he were mesmerized by her pale beauty. He leaned down and kissed her lightly on the lips. She let out a soft gasp and then kissed him back. Fox pulled her to him, feeling her warm body pressed against his. She caressed his neck as they were locked in a passionate embrace like none he'd ever experienced.

It was some time before the sound of voices intruded. Fox and Willa parted just as a woman came into view followed by one of François's guards.

"Sir Guillaume," the guard said, "I told this woman not to disturb you, but she insisted."

Fox realized it was the same woman they'd passed coming from the castle.

"Sir Guillaume, I have an urgent message for you," she said. "At the castle, they told me you'd already gone, so I was sent here."

"Who has a message for me at this late hour?" Fox asked.

"I don't know his name, but he told me to give you this." She handed him a small piece of folded parchment and ran away as soon as he had it.

The guard shrugged and left to go back to his post.

Fox held it under one of the burning torches. His veins turned to ice as he read.

*We have to talk.*
*Royal box at the lists. Now.*
*Basquin.*

"What's wrong?" Willa asked. "You look as white as a phantom."

"It's Basquin. He wants to meet with me."

She looked as shocked as Fox felt. "Basquin? How did he find us?"

"I don't know. That's what I'm going to find out."

"But he could have you arrested or killed."

"If that's what he wanted, he would have done it already. He wants to make some kind of bargain."

"I'm coming with you," she pronounced, as if there were no debating it. But Fox knew that her presence could imperil any arrangement that Basquin had in mind.

"No. I have to see him alone. Wait here for François and Claire to return. I'll be back as soon as I can."

"And if you don't come back?"

"Then find Youssef and Henri and run."

Despite Willa's continued protests, Fox ushered her into the tent. Then he ran to his own, grabbed Legend, and strapped the sword to his waist as he headed to the stands to face his brother.

 58

Willa was not going to stay in her tent hoping Fox would return from this mysterious meeting. She kept an eye on him from behind the entrance flap, and when he left, she followed him at a discreet distance.

Once they were out of the maze of tents and approaching the tilting field, Willa stayed back farther, only venturing forth when Fox reached the stands. Then she sprinted to catch up, holding her skirts high to keep them from rustling and betraying that she was behind him.

Fox slowed and drew his sword as he moved toward the royal box at the center of the stands. Willa crept along, using the heavy braces in the wooden structure to conceal herself.

Suddenly, Fox stopped, then rushed forward. Just behind the royal box, he dropped to his knees beside something on the ground.

"No," Fox said, his voice strained with torment. "Henri. I'm so sorry, my friend."

Willa edged ahead enough that she could now see that Fox had his hand on a body, feeling the chest for any sign of life. He withdrew it slowly and took a series of ragged breaths to compose himself before he shook his head and stood.

Willa's heart broke when she realized the corpse was Henri's. Liquid glistened on his clothes in the moonlight. It had to be blood. His unseeing eyes stared into the sky.

Before she could gasp in horror at the sight, she froze as someone spoke from the top of the stands.

"I knew you'd come, Gerard."

Fox whirled around and looked up. A man leaned over the railing.

Willa recognized him from Mont-Saint-Michel. Somehow, Basquin had tracked them to the tournament, and now he had slain Henri as some sort of retribution.

"You killed Henri?" Fox asked in disbelief. "For what reason?"

"You'll see."

To Willa's shock, Basquin reared back and shouted at the top of his lungs, "Haro! Guards! Murder! Haro, the royal box! Now! Murder! Hurry!" His voice echoed throughout the quiet valley. Everyone from the castle to the town of Riom must have heard it.

Then he leaned back down and smiled at Fox as if nothing had happened. "You know that if you run now, they'll surely think you killed your squire, *Sir Guillaume.*"

"Come down here so I can kill you, you foul wretch," Fox growled. "Now!"

"You would slay your own brother?"

"You're no brother of mine, bastard," Fox said as he searched for the way up to the balcony. "Your father killed my last relation."

"Your father died of the Pestilence."

"He might not have if Molyneux hadn't taken our land."

"That's going to be my land soon," Basquin said. "And don't bother trying to chase me up here. You'll never catch me before the guards arrive."

Willa could already hear soldiers rushing from both the castle and the tents, roused by the call of murder.

"What is your scheme, Basquin?"

"I wanted to give you a chance. After all, I could have slain you and Lady Isabel in your sleep and taken the manuscript without trouble. But that wouldn't be fair, would it?"

"I know you," Fox said. "You have no interest in fairness."

"True. But I have other interests. Now when the guards arrive, you, of course, will accuse me of murder. I will do the same to you. Quite a conundrum, eh?"

Fox withdrew the parchment from his belt. "But I have this note from you to meet me here. Henri was dead when I arrived."

Basquin waved a similar parchment. "And I have this note from you telling me the exact same thing, so I can make the same claim. One of us will be lying, but they won't know who."

What Basquin didn't know was that Willa was a bystander. She could simply step forward when the guards arrived and declare herself a witness on Fox's behalf that Henri was already dead when he arrived.

"It will be my word against yours," Fox said. "Do you think they'll believe you, the bastard son of a cardinal, or the valiant knight who was just declared tournament champion by the king?"

"Yes, you could do that, but then I would be forced to reveal who you truly are. How do you think the king will feel if he knows he was fooled into giving an Englishman the prize? I'm sure he would take it back."

"I don't care about the chalice."

"But you do care about Lady Isabel. Her identity will be revealed as well. A fugitive from her intended, who is an earl under the protection of Cardinal Molyneux himself, and she has fled to France with the lawful property of her betrothed? That would be quite the scandal, no?"

"France is at war with England."

"But the Church is not, and I do believe the king will favor the cardinal over you and Lady Isabel."

Now Willa understood that she couldn't come forward as a witness. It would be even worse than Basquin foresaw. As soon as she revealed herself, her true identity as a maidservant would be exposed, and her testimony would have no weight. Hers would be the word of a liar and impostor, and she would be executed for theft.

Guards were now rushing onto the field from both directions.

"Do what you must," Basquin said before he leaped down from the stands and drew his sword. "We will blame each other for the crime."

"You planned all of this just so you could be accused of murder?" Fox asked incredulously.

"It's the best way to get what I desire."

"And what is that?"

"To be a knight. And you're going to deliver that honor for me."

A dozen guards raced toward them across the grass, their weapons drawn. Half of them passed close by Willa, who had shrunk farther back into the shadows under the stands. She remained unseen.

The guards surrounded Fox and Basquin.

"Drop your weapons!" one of the guards boomed. "Now!"

Fox and Basquin laid down their swords. Both men were brought to Henri's body.

"Who did this?" the guard demanded.

"He killed him," Fox said. "Henri is my friend. This man is trying to blame me for the murder." He showed them the parchment.

"That's what he wants you to think," Basquin countered, handing over his own message. "Sir Guillaume sent me this note to meet him here, and I arrived to find him standing over the dead body."

"That's a lie!"

The head guard was puzzled by the cross accusations and hesitated. Finally, he said, "Take both of them to the dungeon at Château de Tournöel and lock them in chains. This is a matter for the bailiff to work out. We'll send someone back for the body."

They marched Fox and Basquin toward the castle, leaving two men behind to watch over Henri's corpse as onlookers began to arrive to find out what the trouble was. By the time a sizable crowd had gathered, Willa was able to steal away unnoticed. She knew she had to find Youssef, but she dreaded telling him the terrible news that his best friend was dead and that Fox was imprisoned for the murder.

 59

The morning sun streamed through the bars of the high dungeon window, casting stripes of light on Basquin, who was chained to the wall opposite Fox. At least the guards had done it so both of them could sit. Fox had been up all night, alternating between mourning Henri's death and being outraged about his murder. But Basquin was so relaxed about the situation that he'd been sleeping since they were locked in. The bright light shining on his face finally woke him.

"Not the most refreshing nap I've ever had," Basquin said with a yawn, "but it helped knowing that you're chained up over there out of reach and without whatever tools you used to escape from the manacles at Château de Riquevert."

"Did you think I would strangle you while you slept?"

"Not necessarily. You might have bashed my head in."

"So many choices."

"I know you're angry, and you have cause to be. One of your friends is dead. But he betrayed me, and he had to pay for that."

"He discovered that you were stealing from the Church," Fox said. "He was a loyal and devoted friend to those who deserved it, and I mourn that his good life was cut short by a worm like you."

"The money I took was my rightful fee for all I've done in service to the Church."

"You killed Henri because of me."

"Such conceit. But of course, you're right. The opportunity was ripe for the plucking."

"What opportunity? To be thrown in a dungeon and brought up on charges of murder?"

Basquin shook his head. "That's merely the price of entry."

"I know this must all be part of some devious plan. Are you going to explain it to me?"

"I thought it was obvious. I want to fight you."

"We could have done that last night."

"True. But nobody would have been watching. I want an audience."

"Who's the conceited one now?"

"Not to show off, mind you." Basquin cocked his head. "Although now that you mention it, having the king as a witness to my victory will grant me a renown that will be talked about across Europe. Danckaert could only dream of such fame. You see, a judicial trial would be long, boring, and messy. I want a trial by combat."

"Both sides have to agree to a judicial combat."

"I'm well aware of that. Which is why you and I will both petition the king for one."

"Or you'll reveal my true identity as well as Isabel's?"

Basquin beamed at him. "Now you're understanding."

"What I *don't* understand is why you want to have a trial by combat."

"Because, dear brother, you were born into a nobility that has never been within my grasp," Basquin said, his tone becoming acid. "You have inherited everything. Your status, your land, your title."

"I earned my title," Fox said. "I was knighted before the Battle of Crécy."

Basquin waved that notion away. "You would have been bestowed that title one way or another. I, on the other hand, am entitled to nothing. I'm a bastard, as you've reminded me, under the thumb of my father all of my life. You even knew our mother, but she died during my birth. You had everything that I didn't."

That brought Fox up short. He imagined himself in Basquin's shoes, being raised completely motherless, with only that tyrant Molyneux for an excuse of a father. His brother's accomplishments were admirable, even if his methods were abhorrent. What was tragic was that the two of them weren't so different. In fact, Fox was less like his older brother and more like Basquin. If Fox had been in his place—without the strong and patient guidance of Richard, Emmeline, and James—he might have grown up to be just as cruel and ruthless as Basquin.

"I'm sorry for you," Fox said.

"I don't need your pity. Now I have a chance to earn what you were so easily given."

It suddenly dawned on Fox what he meant. "To fight me in a judicial combat, you have to be knighted as well."

Basquin nodded. "Some of our most revered knights have been bastards, William the Conqueror and Sir Galahad to name just two. The cardinal has dangled that carrot in front of me my entire life. Just one more thing to do for him, and I would be made a noble. But that day never came, and I doubt it ever will. This is the only way. When he finds out that I have been knighted by decree of the king himself before killing you and then I deliver the manuscript to him, he will have no choice but to bequeath Caldecott Mote and the remains of Château de Beaujoie to me. Once the war is over, I plan to split my time between them."

"If you *had* been raised by our mother, you would know how disappointed she'd be in you. She would have wanted us to be allies, not enemies."

For the first time, Basquin's eyes flashed with hate before he regained his composure. "I like to think she'd be proud of what I've achieved all on my own. But you? Landless, excommunicated, reduced to fighting under assumed names? It's pathetic."

Fox leaned forward. "You're the pathetic one. Why don't you straighten your spine and stand up to your father?"

The words cut deeply, and Basquin barked his response. "I'm not telling you all this because I want your advice or your sympathy."

"You would kill your only brother?"

For the first time, Fox saw hesitation in Basquin, who spoke in a solemn tone. "I've always hated you. Maybe I shouldn't have. But you and I are trapped by our circumstances. I need to prove myself. I've always done what I had to, and unfortunately, brother, you're the one in my way. It's too late for anything else."

"I will kill you if you go through with this."

And he would, no matter how wretched the idea of killing his last living relative was. The only alternative was to die in disgrace as Henri's murderer and at the same time fail to protect Willa, who would surely be hanged for her deceptions, with the Hodegetria falling into Molyneux's greedy hands. But victory meant the death of his brother by his own hand and the loss of a piece of his soul.

Basquin recovered his bravado. "Don't worry about the possibility of you winning," he said with a condescending look. "I've already beaten you once."

Basquin was younger, stronger, and more proficient with the blade, so his confidence wasn't misplaced. Fox had guile and experience on his side, but he didn't know if that would be enough. Still, he had no choice but to acquiesce to Basquin's plan.

"Neither of us have motives for Henri's murder," Fox said. "We have to present a convincing case for the trial by combat."

"I've thought of that," Basquin said, obviously pleased that Fox was playing along. "Murder usually comes down to money or women. If I were Lord Tonbridge, Lady Isabel would be the perfect motive. Since he isn't here, both of us will say Henri stole money from the other."

Fox was loath to call his friend a thief. "I will say only that you *thought* he stole from you."

"Very well."

"And why did we send the notes to blame the other for the killing?"

"Because we hate each other with a passion. We don't have to say why."

"I think that will be very believable," Fox said.

Marching footsteps approached.

"They're coming to take us to the king," Basquin said. "Can I conclude you will partake in my game?"

Fox nodded reluctantly, bringing a smile to Basquin's face. The door opened, and a squad of guards entered, unchaining them and rousting them out of the dungeon.

Fox wasn't going along with Basquin's plan in order to get revenge against the cardinal and his son. An entirely different person was at the forefront of his mind, a woman he'd come to admire and love. He was going through with this to protect Willa.

The thought of seeing one more innocent person die because of his failures was unbearable.

## 60

The apocalypse had arrived, and it was worse than Fox could have imagined. As he hurried through the narrow streets piled high with refuse, manure, and dead bodies, the constant wail of the sick and grieving burrowed into his soul. He would remember that sound for the rest of his life.

As he turned a corner, he nearly collided with a man covered with purple welts and coughing uncontrollably. Fox had a linen cloth wrapped around his mouth and nose to ward off the stink of the city, but he was still revolted by the rotten stench of the man's sores.

Fox gave him a wide berth, but there was no abatement to the horrific images he was confronted with as he continued on his way. A delirious woman held the hand of an emaciated child as she aimlessly walked down an alley. A horde of people were cutting strips of meat from a dead donkey, another sign that shipments of food from the farms surrounding London had slowed to a trickle. A carter that was stopped at a house piled a corpse onto the stack of ten he was already carrying.

The Pestilence that had been mere rumors just months before had descended on the city like a fog of doom. Fox had heard that hundreds of Londoners were dying every day, but no one knew the real number. Civilization seemed to be cracking at its core. Order was being maintained only by rough justice or by those few still able to show grace in this time of ultimate suffering.

Fox tried to ignore the dreadful sights and sounds of the disease because he was on a mission. His father had been stricken with this plague two days before, and now he was deathly ill. Fox was desperate to prevent him from dying excommunicant and unshriven. He had tried several physickers with little luck. The only one who would come demanded an exorbitant fee, which Fox had gladly paid, but the leeches he had applied seemingly did nothing to draw the bad blood from Richard.

During his search for medicine this afternoon, Fox had been told of a healer on the other side of London who was having success with an unusual potion. He knew in his heart that it was probably a fortune-hunter's scheme, but he was so desperate for a cure that he was now racing across the city to get it in time. He couldn't stand to sit by his father's pallet doing nothing but watching him slowly die. He would have taken Zephyr, but the congested streets were more easily navigated on foot.

He reached the area of the city where he'd been told to find the healer and ran up and down the alleys looking for the right sign. Finally he saw the image of a green sage leaf and white hemlock flower above a lintel.

Fox burst through the door. A man dressed in the robes of a merchant gawked at his abrupt entrance.

"Matilda!" Fox said. "I need to find Matilda."

A voice came from the next room. "Hold on out there."

"But I have no time to waste."

A woman with a bright shock of white hair emerged from the darkness. She was grinding something with a mortar and a pestle. She looked ancient.

"Everything is urgent these days," she said.

"I was told you have a cure for the Pestilence."

"I'm just mixing my last batch now."

"Wait a moment!" the merchant protested. "I arrived first."

"I can pay," Fox said.

"Do you think I give my services away for free?" Matilda said as she continued to calmly mill her ingredients.

"I can pay as well, and I intend to do so, sire," the merchant said.

"My father is dying."

"And do you think you're the only one with family who are ill?"

Judging by how sick Richard appeared when he left, Fox knew that every moment counted. He ignored the merchant and bored in on Matilda. "How much for the potion?"

"I have already agreed on a price with this woman," the merchant said. He jangled a handful of silver coins in his palm. "I doubt you can pay more than I can."

The woman poured the contents of the pestle into a bottle of liquid and swirled it around. She looked pointedly at Fox and shrugged as if she could do nothing more. She was about to hand it to the merchant when Fox interrupted her.

"Wait. I can pay more."

She drew the bottle back. "What do you have to offer?"

"I object!" the merchant cried.

Fox reached into his purse and withdrew his remaining gold spur bestowed on him during the knighting ceremony on the coast of Normandy. The other one had already gone to pay the physicker who had failed to heal his father. In normal times, it would have had to be pried from his dead hands. Now he was eager to give it up.

"This is gold."

Matilda's eyes gleamed. She snatched it from his hand and bit into it. She smiled, nodded, and gave the bottle over to Fox.

The merchant was apoplectic. "You can't do that! We had a bargain!"

"He has made a better bargain. Take two draughts at each bell until the potion is gone."

"I'm very sorry," Fox said to the merchant as he secured his prize. "I'm sure she will be able to make you more."

Matilda nodded. "As soon as I get more licorice root."

"I should beat you for this," the merchant said to her.

"I wouldn't if I were you," Matilda said with a smile. A gigantic man loomed out of the shadows of the room behind her, his bulging arms crossed and a menacing grimace on his face. "My son wouldn't take kindly to that."

Fox left them to dicker over a replacement. He ran back onto the street and wended his way toward the hovel where he and his father had found refuge. Their excommunication appeal, though now well known in London due to the sensational nature of the crime against a cardinal, had been rejected by the ecclesiastical court. They had been denied the sacraments, ejected from their lands, and made pariahs in Oakhurst. A London landlord badly in need of rent had been the sole person willing to take their rapidly dwindling money. It was only Fox's skills as a freelancing man-at-arms that had kept them from starving and living on the streets.

He was out of breath when he reached the other side of the city and charged into the rowhouse and up the stairs with the bottle in hand. This potion had to work. He didn't know what else to do.

He threw open the door to the room they shared with two other families, but he froze when he saw the empty bed of rushes where his father had lain when he'd left.

Edith, the woman with whom he'd entrusted the care of his father, stood up with tears in her eyes. Fox went cold.

"Where's my father?"

"He took his last breath not long after you left," Edith said. "I tried to keep him here until you returned, but the landlord was here and sent him away on a passing cart."

He gripped Edith by the shoulders.

"Where!"

"They've taken him to No Man's Land."

"Thank you for everything, Edith." He pressed the bottle into her hands. "If you or your family show any signs of the Pestilence, drink this. Two draughts at each bell."

He snatched up his weapons and belongings and ran back down the stairs and around the corner to where Zephyr was being stabled. He was shocked to find three haggard men with knives leading Zephyr away.

"Ho, there!" Fox shouted as he stood in their path. "What are you doing?"

The man with the reins said, "We heard tell that the owner of this horse died. It's ours now."

Fox knew Zephyr would be butchered within the hour.

"It's my horse," he said. "Leave now and I won't kill you for thieving."

"Says you." The men came beside him and brandished their knives.

Fox drew Legend. "Says my sword."

If one of them had so much as twitched in his direction, he would have slayed them all. But after a look between them, the one with the reins dropped them, and they scurried away.

Fox patted Zephyr and led him back to the stable, where he hastily saddled him with shaking hands. Then he took off for No Man's Land, desperate to find his father.

The large field north of the city had been consecrated as the deaths in London mounted and cemeteries overflowed. Word was that thousands had already been buried there, and Fox could see that many more would come. He passed cart after cart of bodies, forcing each one to stop so he could see if Richard was among them, but without success.

When he got to the immense stretch of pastureland turned into a cemetery, he saw dozens of workers unloading bodies, wrapping the adults in linen shrouds and placing children and those of importance in boxes before putting them into the ground. Some of the corpses were accompanied by weeping family members, many of whom looked sick themselves. Two priests walked down the long line of bodies, kneeling and blessing each of the corpses.

Fox's heart seized when he spotted the soiled red and white tunic of his father. He lay with his mouth agape and mud spattered on his face, an undignified end for the towering figure he'd been. He was next in line to be blessed and shrouded.

Fox rode over and leaped from Zephyr, hoping to intervene before the priest reached him. But he was too late.

The priest took one look at Richard and turned to the laborers waiting to wrap him in linen.

"This is Richard Fox of Oakhurst. He is excommunicant and

cannot be interred in consecrated ground. His soul is already writhing in eternal hellfire. His body must be burned."

"I won't allow that," Fox said.

The priest whirled around to see who was so impudent to countermand him. He narrowed his eyes at Fox before a look of recognition and disgust dawned on his face.

"You're the son who attacked Cardinal Molyneux. I attended your trial. You and your father have no place here."

"We are still appealing our case. My father deserves to be buried in holy soil to await the time when he is absolved. He has committed no crime worthy of eternal damnation."

"He deserves to burn for his crime."

"That is not going to happen today."

"Well, he certainly will not be put into blessed ground while I am here." He turned and spoke to all the people who had gathered to watch the argument. "I forbid anyone to bury either of these men in No Man's Land. The Church's judgment must be upheld."

Fox had the urge to knock the priest down and pummel the man until his knuckles were bruised. If it hadn't been for men like him—like Cardinal Molyneux—Fox was convinced that his father would still be alive, safe in their rightful home at Caldecott Mote.

The priest, seeing the fire in his eyes, shrank back, but Fox restrained himself. He grabbed a roll of linen from one worker and threw it over his father before lifting his gaunt body and placing him gently across Zephyr's back. Then Fox took a gravedigger's spade, jumped onto Zephyr, and rode off as the priest called for help.

Fox kept riding east and then turned south to skirt the city's edge. No one followed. There was too much death already for anyone to concern themselves with him.

It was morning by the time he got to his destination. He couldn't go back to Oakhurst, but he knew of an abandoned village not far away with a tiny church. At least his father would have the burial he deserved.

Fox was exhausted from the ride, but he couldn't rest, not until his father was at peace. He dug all day into an empty plot in the church's graveyard, ignoring the ache of his muscles and the pain in his soul.

When he was six feet down, he pulled his father in and laid him out with all the dignity he could muster.

Before he began the backbreaking work of filling in the hole, Fox recited the first psalm of the Office of the Dead in Latin. Even though the Church would consider the thought blasphemous, Fox knew his father was a good and righteous man whose soul would no doubt be welcomed into heaven.

*"Dilexi, quoniam exaudiet Domine vocem orationis meae..."*

*I have loved because the Lord will hear the voice of my prayer...*

When he reached the end of the prayer, Fox sank to his knees and wept, the epic series of losses finally overwhelming him. His father, his mother, his brother, his land, his status, his Church—all taken from him. And he didn't even have a chance to tell his father goodbye. He was truly alone in a world gone mad. It felt as if he couldn't bear it any longer.

Then he heard a voice ringing in his head saying the same phrase he'd uttered on the Crécy battlefield three years before.

*You can't give up.*

It was James.

*But as for you, be strong and do not give up, for your work will be rewarded.*

Fox couldn't remember what verse from the Bible it was, but the timbre of James's tone was reassuring.

*You can't give up.*

Fox stood up on shaky knees, having regained some of his strength. He lifted the spade again and began filling the grave. With every toss of dirt, he vowed anew to clear his family name and make Cardinal Molyneux pay for what he'd done, no matter what Fox had to do or how long it took.

He would never give up.

## 61

*August, 1351*

RIOM

Willa shivered as she entered Château de Tournöel's great hall beside François and Claire, with Youssef following behind them. The stone room looked nothing like it had for the banquet the night before. All of the decorations had been taken down, and the only furniture that remained was a chair that had been fashioned as a throne for the king and writing tables for the clerks who would be recording what transpired.

The mood of the crowd that had gathered for the hearing was equally changed. Instead of the frivolity and cheer of the previous days, a mixture of curiosity and somberness permeated the attendees. Since word of Henri's killing went out, all who had come for the tournament were even more intrigued by the crime committed in their midst. It was a rare event to witness the king confront accused murderers, and no one wanted to miss the occasion.

Willa had wrestled all night with the decision whether to come forward. Despite Youssef's aching grief for his friend and his desire for Basquin to be held responsible, he had agreed that if she did announce herself as a witness, her identity as an impostor would be unveiled and no one would listen to her testimony.

François stopped them at the back of the room, far from the rest of the attendees, and turned to Willa, lowering his voice. He'd been agitated by the revelation of Fox's arrest ever since the news had reached him.

"Do you know what a terrible position this puts me in? If Sir

Gerard is discovered for who he truly is, not only will I be forced to give up the chalice, but I could also be held as an accomplice to the murder and for deceiving the king by pretending he is Sir Guillaume."

Willa was shocked at his self-centered words while Henri lay dead. "You could say that he was the one who deceived you," she replied.

"That would be even worse. I would look like a fool for having been taken in. And they will discover that you are Claire's cousin."

"Then blame me," Claire interjected. "I was the one who talked you into this venture."

François grimaced. "And be thought of as a weakling who takes orders from his wife? I'd rather give up my estate."

"The estate that was deeded to you in my dowry."

"No matter. It will be Molyneux's soon enough."

"Have faith, Sir François," Willa said. "I believe that your involvement in this charade may yet be secure."

"And why would you say that?"

"Because I think Basquin will keep his mouth quiet about Sir Gerard's true identity."

François scoffed at her. "Why would he do such a thing? How could you possibly know that?"

Willa shrugged. "It's just a feeling I have."

"Your feelings are worthless. Come, Claire. As the bearers of the champion's arms, we are expected to be standing close to the throne." He shook his head in disdain at Willa. "Stay here beside the attendant."

He limped off. Claire took Willa's hands.

"Stay strong," she said. "You may not be my cousin, but I am proud of how well you've carried on with Isabel's mission to keep the Hodegetria out of Cardinal Molyneux's hands."

"Thank you," Willa replied. "Though your husband may not have faith, I do. I believe that the Icon will not become the tool of a tyrant."

Claire gave her a wan smile and left to join her husband.

"I can't believe it has come to this," Youssef said, shaking his head in sadness. "Knowing that I'll never see Henri again pierces me to my core. I should never have let him go off without me."

"There is nothing you could have done," Willa said. "Basquin would have killed you as well. He must be doing this because of me and the manuscript."

"You can still run. If we leave now, we could retrieve the manuscript and you could ride south. I would stay behind to distract from your escape."

"With François's guards watching the chest where the manuscript is stored, we wouldn't get near it."

"I can find a way."

Willa shook her head. "I won't leave Sir Gerard, and I wouldn't get far by myself even if I did. Besides, Lady Claire might reveal my destination if she thought I had betrayed her."

"She wouldn't," Youssef said. "But I understand your decision."

"You should leave. Nothing good can come from your staying."

"Henri was my best friend. I will not go until either Basquin is punished for what he has done or I die trying to avenge him."

Then it was settled. Neither of them would leave. Their fate was now tied up in what would occur in this hearing.

The crowd hushed as a herald entered the room and called out, "His Highness, the king!"

All of them dropped to their knees and bowed as the king came in, blue robes flowing behind him as he went to his throne and sat. The attendees got back to their feet.

"The hearing will be conducted on behalf of the king by Marshal Thibault," the herald announced.

A grizzled man wearing the king's livery stepped forward and cleared his throat to speak.

"In the matter of the murder of Squire Henri de Carcassonne," he said, "we are gathered to hear testimony from two accused of the crime. Bring them in."

Six guards escorted Fox and Basquin into the room. They were positioned directly in front of the king and kneeled before him to kiss his hand before rising. Basquin seemed well rested while Fox looked drawn and exhausted.

"Your Highness," the marshal said, presenting them, "Monsieur Basquin d'Avranches, who serves Cardinal Molyneux, and Sir Guillaume d'Amboise, whom you already know as champion of the tournament. Both of them were found last night in the vicinity of Squire Henri de Carcassonne, who was slashed by a sword. Both of these men were armed with swords at the time."

He nodded to one of the guards, who held up the weapons.

"Neither sword was found to have blood on it," Thibault continued. "Nevertheless, these were the only men near the body. Each of them accuses the other of the murder. They both say that they were lured to that spot by way of a message written on parchment. Both claim that the motive for the crime was a mistaken belief that the victim stole money from the other claimant."

He held the parchment pieces up for the crowd to see, although many in attendance wouldn't be able to read the words even if they were legible from that distance. Both were written in the same script that every learned person was taught.

"I will now read them. Sir Guillaume was found with a note that reads, 'We have to talk. Royal Box at the lists. Now. Basquin.' Likewise, Basquin produced a note that reads, 'We have to talk. Royal Box at the lists. Now. Guillaume.'"

He handed the parchments to the king, who read the messages carefully before returning them.

"Given these facts, one of these men is lying. A trial will be set to ascertain the truth. Each of you will have an opportunity to retain a lawyer to make your defense. Before the king renders a ruling on the trial provisions, you will now have a chance to make a statement. Sir Guillaume, as a knight and tournament champion, you are allowed to speak first."

Fox stood tall and spoke clearly. "Your Highness, this man has wrongfully accused me of a crime I did not commit. I do not believe that a trial by jury will effectively be able to prove my innocence because of the false evidence that he has concocted. Therefore, I respectfully request a trial by combat. The Lord knows that I am innocent, and He will favor me in battle."

A murmur rippled through the great hall before it was hushed by the marshal. Willa could sense Youssef tensing next to her.

The king raised his eyebrows at the extraordinary request.

"That is a matter for the courts to consider..." Thibault began before the king cut him off with a raised hand.

"Sir Guillaume, are you certain this is what you desire?" the king asked.

"I am, Your Highness. And I request that the judicial combat commence without undue delay."

Willa had heard of trials by combat, but they had grown increasingly uncommon. In complicated cases, they could take months to adjudicate and prepare as the two sides gave their motions and negotiated the terms of the battle.

"You are still weary from the tournament, are you not?" the king said.

"I will be ready whenever Your Highness wishes me to be."

"Very well. Monsieur Basquin, how do you respond to Sir Guillaume's request?"

"Your Highness, I agree that my accuser's baseless and dishonorable claim leaves me little choice for clearing my good name," Basquin said. "I, too, request a trial by combat to decide the matter, as soon as Your Highness deems it acceptable."

"You are not a knight. It would not be proper for Sir Guillaume to fight someone who is not his peer."

"You are wise to note that, Your Highness. Of course, if you believe it is right for me to be knighted as a prerequisite for the trial by combat, I will humbly accept your ruling."

There was silence as the king peered at the two of them. He stood and said, "I will withdraw to consult with my advisers and judges as to the proper course of action. I will consider your pleas and render my judgment. Remain here until I return with my verdict."

Thibault and a gaggle of courtiers followed the king out of the room. The chamber immediately buzzed with conversation.

"I must talk to him," Willa said. She pressed forward, leaving Youssef protesting behind her.

She rushed past the guards and embraced Fox. She spied Basquin looking at them with amusement. The guards simply watched, as they were there only to keep Fox and Basquin from fleeing.

"I'm so sorry about Henri," she said quietly, looking up at Fox.

"I can honor him now by avenging his death," he whispered, "but I told you to go if I didn't come back."

"I can't leave. Not after what I saw and heard last night."

"What do you mean?"

"I followed you to the royal box. I heard you and Basquin talking."

"Then you know why you need to leave. If the king grants our trial by combat and I lose, you will be turned over to Tonbridge by François."

"You know I wouldn't get far without you," Willa said. "Not with the Icon. Once Basquin revealed who you and I were, the king would send an entire regiment after me."

There was no doubt they were stronger together than apart. During the past weeks, she had dared to dream that maybe there was more in her future than the life of a maidservant, and Fox seemed entirely undeterred by their differences in rank, as she had been with his excommunication. If they were to complete their quest, it would only be as a team.

When Fox said nothing, Willa added, "We both know this is the only way."

She stared at him until he relented. "You make your point. The king may return at any moment. If he orders the judicial combat, I will need to prepare quickly. Go and tell Youssef that I will need his assistance. And if you have any more observations for me, I will gladly take them."

Willa glanced at Basquin, who returned her gaze intently. "I have no jousting advice since I've never seen him in battle, but I understood him from the instant I met him at Mont-Saint-Michel. His confidence oozes out of his skin, and he is not easily tricked."

"That's your advice?"

"Men like him are sometimes overconfident, which can make them vulnerable, if only for a moment. It's in that one grain of sand falling in the hourglass in which you have to act."

Fox gave her a curious look. "How did you become so astute?"

Willa smiled back at him. "I read books."

A commotion arose, and it was clear the king was returning. Willa was pulled away from Fox, and she made her way back to Youssef.

"What did he say?" Youssef asked.

"That you should be ready to help him prepare for battle," Willa said nervously.

"Don't worry," Youssef said. "I will do everything in my power on the day of the duel to ensure that he is ready. I have faith that he will win the battle."

The king re-entered the great hall and took his seat on the throne. The crowd waited breathlessly for his judgment.

"I have made my decision," the king said. "Since both litigants make the same request without reservation, I hereby order that a trial by combat take place tomorrow on the tilting field under my watch. It will be a battle to the death. There will be no quarter or mercy. The man who is victorious will have been chosen by God as the truthful witness. The man who falls will be pronounced a murderer, his head placed on a pike as a warning to others."

The king nodded to Thibault, who said, "The combatants will be restricted to the castle as they prepare for the judicial combat. If a combatant disgraces himself and attempts to flee, the duel will be forfeited, and the king will order him summarily executed. Are these terms clear?"

Both Fox and Basquin nodded.

Willa swallowed hard. If Fox were killed tomorrow, the truth about her identity would surely come out, and her life would also be forfeit.

## 62

Most men would be apprehensive the morning of a duel. Basquin felt nothing but excitement. This day would be a new beginning for him, and the only thing that stood in the way was a brother he envied who was spent from three days of fighting in the tournament. Nevertheless, Basquin couldn't end the battle quickly. He needed to put on a show for the king and the crowd so that his name would be spread far and wide.

As the one who had called the guards to the site of the murder, Basquin was designated as the appellant in the case, so he was the first to arrive on the field. The barricades of the enclosure had been reinforced during the previous day so that neither of the combatants would be able to leave during the duel and no one would be able to wander onto the lists. Word of the duel had gone out quickly, and it seemed as if every person within a day's ride was gathered around the perimeter.

Gates were set up at either end, and Basquin rode through the one on the king's right-hand side. As was the custom, he was mounted on a palfrey for the pre-duel ceremony, dressed in a padded *bascinet* helmet, an attached mail *aventail* draped over his neck and shoulders, a mail *haubergeon* tunic under a leather-covered coat of plates to protect his chest and back, gauntlets for his hands, and *chausses*, *poleyns*, and greaves to guard the front of his legs. A broadsword and a dagger the length of his forearm hung from his belt. A squire who had been assigned to him led his armored warhorse behind him, with an axe fixed to the saddle. Other attendants carried his shield, lance, and great helm.

The sound of the spectators was nothing like it had been for the tournament. Instead of boisterous laughs and cheers from the stands, the crowd talked to each other in hushed murmurs. King John was already atop his throne. To his left were Sir François, Lady Claire, and Lady Isabel, who wore a somber expression and a simple dark blue kirtle, though it might as well have been black, the color of the condemned. As soon as the duel was over, Basquin intended to reveal her for the thief she was, and her fate would be sealed. Basquin smiled and nodded at her, and she stared back with undisguised loathing.

The tone of the crowd shifted at the sight of Fox arriving at the opposite end of the lists, also on a palfrey and equipped in the same manner. As the defendant, he would complete every part of the introductory ritual after Basquin. The armored Zephyr trailed behind, led by Youssef and other attendants carrying his gear. Both Fox and Youssef looked at Basquin stoically, likely not wanting to betray their nerves.

Basquin had no illusions about the task ahead of him. Though Fox was a skilled fighter and a wily opponent, it would be easy for Basquin to conclude that his brother was no match for him. After all, he had the advantage of youth, vigor, and training from the best knights in Paris, arranged by his father, along with being completely fresh. Still, Fox was a dangerous foe who had survived this long on his wits and tenacity. Basquin would not make the mistake of letting his guard down.

Thibault, as the marshal for the occasion, rode out to meet Basquin with the herald and two knights who would be guarding the gate once it was closed. Two more knights went to the opposite gate, one of them the vanquished Danckaert. He stopped to say something to Fox that Basquin could not hear.

For the crowd, the marshal asked Basquin to declare who he was and why he was there.

In a loud voice, he announced, "My very honored Lord Marshal of the Field, I am Monsieur Basquin d'Avranches, who appears here as ordained by our lord the king, to present himself armed and mounted as a gentleman who must enter in battle against Sir Guillaume d'Amboise, concerning the wrong and evil quarrel he has brought, to prove him the traitor and murderer that he is. I thereby swear before Our Lord, Our Lady, and the good knight Saint George to complete my quest this day."

The marshal rode to the other end and had Fox make a nearly identical statement, all of which had been rehearsed by them the day before in the castle. The only tension Basquin felt was that Fox would slip up and use his real name, thereby threatening the duel going forward, but he likewise referred to himself as Sir Guillaume.

Once the formalities were complete, both of them rode forward to the center of the lists holding aloft parchment scrolls containing their written grievances. The scrolls were presented to the marshal, who then asked the king to open the field for battle.

The king commanded them to dismount, and Basquin and Fox took seats on raised chairs facing each other, never averting their eyes from their opponent as they sat.

The next step was the inspection of their weaponry by the king of arms. Though the weapons had been supplied to them for the duel, they nevertheless had to be checked for charms or magic spells, and the horses were searched for any scrolls of enchantment that might deliver an unfair advantage to one of the combatants. Ranged weapons were forbidden, as were any weapons seemingly forged by magical means, so Fox would be without his horseman's bow and his Damascus-steel sword with the fantastical swirled pattern in its blade.

While the inspection was carried out, the herald spoke.

"Oyez, oyez, oyez, lords, knights, squires, and all other manner of people, our lord the King of France commands that it is strictly prohibited, on threat of death and the loss of property, for anyone here to be armed, to carry a sword or dagger or any other weapon whatsoever, unless he be one of the guards of the field or one who has been given permission by our lord the king."

The herald went on to list other prohibitions for the spectators, including entering the field of battle, being mounted on a horse, or rising from one's seat during the combat. There was one final deed that would exact a death penalty.

"Furthermore," the herald added, "our lord the king commands that each person, whosoever he may be, during the battle, may not speak, nor gesture, nor cough, nor spit, nor cry out, nor do any such thing, whatever it may be; and this under pain of losing his life and goods."

The duel would be conducted in complete silence. None of the spectators would dare risk even an involuntary gasp or whispered aside.

"Monsieur Basquin," Thibault said, drawing his sword. "Step forward."

It was finally the moment Basquin had been waiting for all his life. Under the watchful eye of the king, he walked to the marshal.

"Kneel," Thibault said.

Basquin went to one knee and lowered his head.

Thibault tapped Basquin on the shoulder three times with the flat of his sword. "Arise, Sir Basquin d'Avranches, in the name of God. Be brave, bold, and loyal."

Though his armor weighed more than fifty pounds, Basquin felt as light as a hummingbird's feather as he bounded to his feet. He strode back to his chair as a noble.

When he was again seated, the marshal recited the rules of combat. Although illegal arms and those created with enchantments were forbidden, the combatants were allowed to carry food and wine because the battle might last all day. But nothing other than what they carried on horseback would be permitted into the lists. The marshal also noted that they could fight on horseback or on foot with whatever arms they pleased and in whatever manner they wanted. There would be no expectation of chivalry. Nothing was illegal or ungentlemanly in a duel. This was mortal combat.

The lone rule was that the fight would end only upon the death of one of the combatants or if one of them shouted "Craven!" to confess their guilt, which would then lead to them being hanged without delay.

At the end of his pronouncements, the marshal gave way to the presiding priest. Since the winner of a duel was deemed to be favored by God for their innocence in the matter, the Church had a crucial role by sanctifying the proceedings. The priest and his companions placed an altar draped with a stark white cloth in the field and set a prayer book and a large silver crucifix on it.

The priest motioned for Basquin and Fox to come and kneel before the altar on opposite sides facing each other. Basquin could almost feel the animosity radiating from Fox.

After a blessing from the priest, they touched the crucifix with their right hands and removed their gauntlets, grasping each other by the bare left hand. The right hand was used for friendly agreements such as marriages and loyalty oaths, but as this was a belligerent affair, joining of *la main sinistre* was called for. Basquin gripped Fox by the palm. His brother's skin was hot and drenched with sweat.

The gravity of what he was about to do hit Basquin. *His brother.* That's who he was about to kill. The thought preyed on his mind for an instant, but he forcefully dispelled those doubts. He wouldn't allow himself to become sentimental now. This was what he had to do.

As the appellant, Basquin was first to swear his oath. "O thou, Sir Guillaume d'Amboise, whom I hold by the hand, I swear that my cause is true, and I have good and loyal cause to call you to combat. And you have bad cause and no quarrel to fight and defend yourself against me."

As they continued clasping each other by the left hand, Fox replied: "O thou, Sir Basquin, whom I hold by the hand, I swear that the cause for which you have called me is false and evil, and I have good and loyal cause to defend myself and battle against you this day."

They released hands and took turns kissing the crucifix.

"Sir Basquin and Sir Guillaume d'Amboise," the priest intoned, "perdition awaits the one who is in the wrong, in both body and immortal soul, because of the great oaths ye have sworn. Ye will be judged by the sentence of God, which will uphold the good and the right."

They stood, and with a last look at Fox, Basquin turned and

walked back to his pavilion as the altar and chairs were taken away.

He inhaled a full breath of air, which smelled even sweeter with his new noble status, and he savored the thought of the surprised look that would be etched on his father's face upon hearing the news. He would finally be the son his father had wanted.

Then Basquin quickly dispelled that image as the priest's final words rang in his ears. He needed to focus fully on the upcoming battle because the stakes couldn't be higher.

The winner of this duel would be pronounced innocent of all charges and enjoy the benefits and comforts of victory.

The loser was promised not only death, but eternity in Hell.

## 63

Fox stood inside his preparation pavilion as Youssef did one last check of his equipment.

"Are you sure you don't want me to pack extra wine and bread on Zephyr?" Youssef asked.

Fox shook his head. "I know Basquin. We won't be out there that long."

"At least you've had two days of jousting for practice." Youssef cinched the belt. "Is that too tight?"

"No, it's good."

Youssef continued to babble. "I made sure the sword and dagger are sharp and strong. Your axe is already hanging from your saddle ring. Be careful, the spike on the end is as pointed as a needle. When you—"

Fox grasped him by the shoulders. "Youssef, my friend, you have been loyal and kind to join me on this venture. Now you can do nothing more. I thank you."

"God is with you, Gerard. I know Henri would be honored by your actions here today."

Fox reached into his purse and removed the book his mother gave him, the *Secretum philosophorum*. He handed it to Youssef.

"Take care of this while I'm out there."

Youssef took it and placed it carefully in his own purse. "It will be waiting for your safe return." They understood it would become Youssef's if Fox fell in battle.

The herald called from the field, "Do your duty!" three times. The moment of the duel had arrived.

Youssef took a retention chain attached to Fox's *haubergeon* at the chest and locked the other end into a slot in the great helm, designed that way so a knight could recover it easily if it were knocked off. Youssef placed the helm on Fox's head, and they exited the pavilion into the bright morning sun.

Zephyr was waiting outside along with attendants holding the shield and lance. Thanks to Youssef, the horse's wound was covered and healing nicely. Fox rubbed Zephyr's muzzle, virtually the only part other than his legs not covered in armor. Zephyr responded with a whinny and chewed on Fox's fingers with his lips.

Fox put on his gauntlets as he strode toward the lists with his entourage in tow. The weakest parts of his armor were the mail over the back of his legs and on his forearms, made thin enough to give him mobility while still providing protection from slashing weapons.

Danckaert stood with another knight at the opening to the lists with lances crossed to prevent anyone from entering. Once Fox went through, they would close the gates behind him and guard it until the duel was finished. Along with the knights at Basquin's end, they would also serve as official witnesses to the proceedings.

When Fox reached the mounting platform, he crossed himself and couldn't help but think of his brother James. What would he say at this moment? Fox thought he knew. Another Bible quote, this one from Ephesians about preparing to fight against evil.

*Be strong in the Lord and in the strength of His might. Put on the whole armor of God, that you may be able to stand against the schemes of the devil. For we do not wrestle against flesh and blood, but against the rulers, against the authorities, against the cosmic powers over this present darkness.*

Fox felt his true brother with him as he prepared to fight a brother with whom he shared nothing but a lost mother.

Danckaert looked at Fox and nodded his good wishes. Fox bowed his head in response. They may have been adversaries in the tournament, but they were respected peers to each other now.

Basquin stood beside his own mounting platform on the other end, his head already encased in his cylindrical great helm.

Marshal Thibault walked into the field through a small gate by the royal box, a white glove in his hand. He raised it high over his head. When he was sure that both Fox and Basquin were in position, he threw it forward, shouting, "Let them go! Let them go! Let them go!" Then he hurried back to the safety of the stands, closing the gate behind him.

Fox was already on Zephyr's saddle by the third repetition of the call to fight. He took his shield, and then lastly Youssef handed him the lance. As soon as it was securely upright in his grip, he spurred Zephyr forward and trotted toward the lists. Danckaert and his companion dropped their lances to the ground to let him pass and slammed the gates closed when he was through.

Except for his breath in the closed helm and the stamping of Zephyr's hooves, the field was eerily quiet. Fox took a quick glance at the stands, and every spectator watched with rapt anticipation. From this distance, Willa's face was difficult to read, but he knew she must be sick with concern.

Basquin paced back and forth on his horse, appearing to size up his opponent. Since he was the appellant, it was his duty to make the first move, so Fox watched and waited.

It wasn't long. Basquin lowered his lance and kicked his horse with a battle cry, racing forward into a full gallop.

Fox lowered his own lance and yelled, "Zephyr, *oppugna!*" while squeezing his legs. Zephyr understood the call to fight and charged ahead.

Fox was already sweating from the sun heating up the steel surrounding him. He gripped the lance tightly, aiming for the center of Basquin's shield. If he could unhorse his brother on the first pass, he would have a distinct advantage as a mounted horseman against a single knight fighting on foot.

Zephyr snorted from the effort of running at top velocity carrying both his own armor and Fox's weight as well. Though Basquin's horse was bigger, it didn't have Zephyr's speed.

They met at the center of the field, exactly in front of the royal box. Their war lances, stouter than the hollow ones used in the joust, slammed into each other's shields simultaneously. The impact rocked Fox back in the saddle, but he was able to remain in the seat, and his lance was still intact.

He whirled around to see what damage he'd caused, but was disappointed to see Basquin on his horse with an unbroken lance.

They retreated to the sides opposite from the ones they'd entered to regain their breath and prepare for another charge. On this pass, Fox planned to aim for a different target. Although more difficult to hit, a strike to Basquin's head with the lance might produce a fatal blow, especially if the steel tip penetrated the eye slit. It was a challenge to hit a smaller moving target like that, but Fox's aim had improved markedly since the beginning of the tournament.

They raced at each other once again. Fox held the lance higher as he focused on Basquin's helm.

At the moment of impact, Fox's lance struck the helm, the steel tip causing sparks to fly, but it slid off without effect.

Basquin's lance, on the other hand, embedded itself in Fox's shield and splintered as it hoisted Fox out of the saddle. As he flew through the air, Fox braced himself for the familiar sensation of smacking into the ground. The impact caused the wind to be knocked from his lungs, and his head slammed against the turf.

Normally, this action would elicit an enormous cheer from the crowd during the joust, but there was no sound to mask his groans as he caught his breath.

Fox couldn't take time to recover. If a knight on his feet against a horse was a disadvantage, a knight lying flat was a death sentence.

Luckily, Fox had flipped over while falling and landed face down, so he pushed himself to his knees and staggered to his feet. Zephyr had circled around to come back to him, and he briefly entertained the idea of trying to get back on until he saw Basquin.

He was halfway across the field and still on his horse, but the lance had been splintered down to the hilt. Basquin tossed it aside and lifted the battle axe from the ring. It was a fiendish weapon, with the flat curved blade of the axe head on one side, a wicked dagger-like projection on the other, and a notched spear point extending from the top. He twirled it in his hand as if testing its weight, then spurred his horse into a gallop in Fox's direction. One swing of that heavy blade from a charging horse could decapitate Fox, mail or no.

He was already exhausted from the fall and from getting to his feet. Mounting the saddle would take time and strength he didn't have to spare, especially without a mounting platform. He could still be trying to haul himself into his seat by the time Basquin rode by to finish him.

Instead, Fox plucked his identical axe from Zephyr's saddle and smacked his rump to shoo him out of the way.

Fox took a fighting stance, holding the battle axe with two hands, as Basquin raced toward him. The odds of this scenario were not in Fox's favor.

Seeing Basquin and the horse fill the eyehole slits in his helm, Fox knew that he had to take a huge risk to have a fighting chance at keeping this duel from ending barely after it began.

He needed to even the odds.

## 64

Willa could scarcely breathe as Basquin barreled toward Fox, his battle axe held in one hand and shield in the other. If a blow from the axe didn't cleave Fox's head from his neck, the massive warhorse running over him could be deadly.

She had to stifle the urge to shout encouragement to him. All she could do was grasp Claire's hand tightly and pray for a miracle.

When Basquin was only a few horse lengths away, Fox did something that completely shocked her. Holding his own axe with both hands, he raised it high above his head and with a mighty heave sent it spinning toward Basquin.

Willa put her hand to her breast at the daring move. As the axe hurtled end over end through the air, she was sure it would slice through Basquin's mail and sink into his chest. She squelched the gasp that threatened to escape her lips.

But Basquin reacted faster than she could have imagined. In a lightning maneuver, he swung his shield around to his right side so that it covered him behind the axe he held with his right hand. Fox's hurtling axe struck between Basquin's hand and the axe head, slicing through the handle and embedding itself deeply in the shield. The process of protecting himself unbalanced Basquin, and the powerful impact of Fox's axe caused him to twist off his horse and tumble to the ground. Basquin's horse ran away as he shrugged off the conjoined axe and shield.

Willa allowed herself some hope now that both of them were on their feet and their weapons matched. As Fox advanced and drew his sword, the nimble Basquin sprang to his feet on fresh legs. He unsheathed his sword barely in time to parry Fox's first blow.

When the initial attack was unsuccessful, Fox retreated, his chest heaving from exertion. The two of them circled each other, gathering strength for the next assault.

Willa didn't know much about the strategy and tactics of battle, so Youssef had given her some lessons the day before in preparation for the duel.

The battle axe was the more useful weapon against armored soldiers. In strong hands, a swing of the axe head was able to exert enough force to scythe through the mail links like they were ripe wheat. Connecting with the great helm likely wouldn't split it, but it could knock a man unconscious or worse. And the dagger-like projection on the opposite side of the axe head had the ability to penetrate the mail if the tip hit just right, as could the spear point on top.

The swords, however, did not have nearly as much power. Mail was specifically designed to resist any damage from an edged weapon, and the broadsword's tip was too wide to squeeze apart the mail links. A sword was more useful if one could find a space between armored areas. Or the wielder could aim for the relatively unprotected back of the leg. Also, according to Youssef, the mail did not fully absorb the force of the impact, so a strong blow from the heavy steel blade could break ribs or arms.

Their daggers were relatively useless. The weapon had no purpose unless a weak spot in the armor could be found, and the wielder had to be very close to his opponent to make it effective.

Given how devastating an axe could be, they would surely try to get to the remaining intact one currently lodged in the shield, which their maneuvering had now put at an equal distance from both of them. Willa noticed Fox edging toward it, but it would take effort and time to free it from the shield.

"If you want your axe back," Basquin taunted, "be my guest."

"My sword will do," Fox answered.

"Are you sure about that?"

Basquin ran at him, two hands on the hilt. Fox countered his attack, and the sound of clashing steel rang across the lists as they fought furiously.

Fox was the first to make a hit. His sword slammed into Basquin's side, causing him to groan from the impact. But it wasn't enough to disable him. He whirled around and connected with Fox's helm, sending him reeling.

Each of them regrouped, and they charged again, exchanging a flurry of slashing strikes that sent a shiver down Willa's spine.

They continued like that, neither making any progress, but Willa could tell Fox was fatigued. The effects of the tournament were catching up with him.

With a series of savage hits, Basquin was able to drive Fox backward. Fox stumbled on the torn-up ground, and Basquin used the opportunity to kick Fox in the stomach.

Willa's breath caught. The impact sent Fox sprawling onto his back. With a triumphant laugh, Basquin leaped beside Fox and rained down blows that were barely parried. Fox was in an awful position to fight back, as helpless as an overturned turtle.

The problem for Basquin was that there was no place on Fox's body that made for a clear killing blow. He attempted to go for Fox's legs, but the plates protected him, and Fox nearly kicked the sword out of Basquin's hands.

Basquin changed tactics and seemed to be trying to force his sword under the *aventail*, the mail piece draping over Fox's neck and shoulders. If he could get the sword beneath it, he could slit Fox's throat.

Unable to protect himself with his sword, Fox dropped it and put the fingers of his mailed gauntlet around the tip of Basquin's sword to keep it from flipping up the end of the *aventail*.

Seeing the futility of his effort, Basquin let go of his own sword and went to his knees, pummeling Fox with his armored fists. As they wrestled, Basquin fumbled with something on Fox's helm, and Willa went cold when she realized what he was doing.

Basquin was trying to unlock the mechanism lashing Fox's great helm to his mail. Fox had his hands around Basquin's wrists, but he couldn't stop him. Basquin twisted, and the chain came free.

Basquin yanked Fox's great helm from his head and tossed it

away. For the first time since the opening rites, Willa could see Fox's face. It was contorted in a desperate grimace, ruddy and slick with perspiration.

Basquin put a knee onto Fox's midsection, plucked his dagger from its scabbard, and stabbed down onto Fox's face.

Fox threw his gauntlets up and grabbed Basquin's wrists, stopping the gleaming point of the dagger inches from his cheek. As both men's arms were locked together, they shuddered from the effort, but the knife inched closer and closer to Fox's skin. His life would be over in a matter of moments.

Basquin yelled with a strained voice so all could hear. "Confess! Confess the truth! Confess that I am the better man!"

Fox grunted something in response, but Willa couldn't make out the words. She clenched her teeth to keep them from chattering.

Basquin cried out, "Louder!"

Fox freed one hand and slugged Basquin in the neck with his mailed glove, pushing Basquin back momentarily and giving Fox a slight reprieve.

At the top of his lungs, he shouted one word.

"*Oppugna!*"

 65

Fox didn't have a chance to yell twice. The dagger came down again, and Fox blocked it, but he felt its needle-sharp tip prick against the skin of his cheek. Basquin used every ounce of his strength to push the knife into Fox's face. Sweat dripped through the eye slits of his great helm. He was so intent on killing Fox that he didn't notice the galloping hooves coming toward them.

His head finally tilted up, and he dived aside as Zephyr charged directly at him, a hoof smacking into his helm as he rolled away. The helm flew off and dangled from the chain attached to Basquin's chest.

Fox was nearing exhaustion and struggled to his elbows. He could only watch as Zephyr turned and reared onto his hind legs, throwing his front hooves at Basquin again, catching him in the torso. Rather than attempt to replace his dented helm, Basquin snapped its chain loose and let it fall to the ground. He scrambled over to the axe that was embedded in the shield, put a foot on the ruined shield, and wrenched the axe free.

When Zephyr attacked once more, Basquin swung at him with the axe, slicing a gash in his leg. The horse let out an angry squeal.

"Zephyr, *veni!*"

Upon hearing Fox call for him to come, Zephyr trotted over, blood oozing out of the wound. Now on his hands and knees, Fox checked the injury. Fortunately, it didn't seem serious, nothing that a dressing couldn't stanch.

Fox grabbed a stirrup and pulled himself to his feet with enormous effort. With the great helm tossed aside, Fox could tell that the fight was beginning to take a toll on Basquin as well. Sweat poured from his brow, and he was straining to catch his breath.

"If you do that again," Basquin thundered, his chest heaving, "I will put this axe into your beloved horse's neck."

Fox put up a hand to indicate he understood. He patted Zephyr's nose and said, "Zephyr, *exi*."

Zephyr trotted off with a snort.

"Do you feel like taking a rest?" Fox asked. "You look tired."

"I won't rest until you are dead."

Fox plucked a sword from the ground. "Then let's end this."

Basquin strode toward him holding the axe. He took a mighty swing, and Fox met it with the sword, but it was no match for the heavier weapon. The broadsword slowed the swing but didn't prevent the flat of the axe blade from hitting his shoulder. The glancing impact caused Fox to wince and back up.

Basquin continued coming at him, driving him closer and closer to the stands. Fox deflected each chop until one caught the flat of his blade. The sword snapped in two. Fox threw the useless hilt to his feet.

Basquin stepped back and smiled at Fox's dire predicament.

"Would you care to confess your sins now, Sir Guillaume?"

Fox drew the only weapon he had left, his dagger.

"I have nothing to confess."

"What about being a liar?" Basquin waved at the crowd. "Don't you think you should tell them who you really are?"

"I am the son of a stolen mother and an unjustly dishonored father. That is all I or anyone else need know. You will pay for those crimes."

Basquin looked amused. "Is that so? Am I not the one with the battle axe and you with the dagger?"

Fox's eyes caught Willa in the stands staring at him. He remembered what she had said when they last spoke. Basquin's arrogance would undo him, even if it were for only a brief instant, and that was when Fox would have to act without hesitation.

"I am practically defenseless," Fox said. "Now that you are a brave and noble knight, defeating me should be a simple challenge. Or are you not up to the expectations of your newly bestowed title?"

Basquin looked disappointed. "An insult? Do you really think that will cause me to act rashly?"

"No, I don't. Your *father* might. But then, he wouldn't expect you to win at all, would he?"

Basquin's lip curled and his nostrils flared at the mention of Molyneux. He lunged forward and hacked at Fox with a huge swing that was meant to slice through his neck.

Fox ducked under the axe and thrust the dagger forward, aiming for the only vulnerable spot on Basquin's body, his face.

But his timing was off. Basquin's head turned, and the dagger glanced off the side of the *bascinet*.

Basquin jumped back when he realized he'd almost made a fatal mistake.

"Clever," he said admiringly. "But you've played out your scheme and it failed." He twisted the axe so that its spear tip pointed at Fox. "I don't have to use this as an axe. I can just as easily run you through."

The other sword was behind Basquin, who kept himself between Fox and the last potent weapon left on the battlefield.

Basquin moved forward, jabbing at Fox and pushing him back toward the railing of the stands. It might take several attempts, but eventually the spear point would either hit him in the face or penetrate his mail.

Fox briefly considered flinging his knife at Basquin's head, but Basquin wouldn't be surprised by the same trick twice, and then Fox would be left with just his fists.

He had to get Basquin closer, within arm's reach of his exposed face.

If Fox could trap the head of the axe between his arm and body, he might be able to twist it free or pull Basquin close enough to use the dagger.

He had one chance. If it didn't work, Basquin would figure out what he was attempting and change his tactics yet again.

Fox crouched lower as he backed toward the timber wall of the stands, the knife in his right hand.

When Fox had no more room to move, Basquin made his lunge. He thrust the axe tip at the center of Fox's face.

Instead of trying to avoid the strike, Fox stood and opened his left arm to allow the axe to pass harmlessly under his armpit.

But with the reflexes of a striking viper, Basquin adjusted his aim. The spear point plunged through the lighter mail on Fox's left forearm.

Fox screamed in agony. Basquin openly reveled as he twisted the blade. Fox nearly passed out from the pain before it was partially numbed by the shock.

Basquin tried to yank the axe back for the killing blow, but his grin disappeared when he realized the spear tip was stuck. Fox could feel it grinding between the bones of his forearm, locked in place by the notch on each side of the spear tip.

Fox understood that this was the moment he'd been waiting for. Willa was right. His chance was the duration of only one grain of sand in the hourglass. With Basquin's grip on the axe handle firm, Fox yanked his impaled arm backward, pulling Basquin so close that he could feel his breath.

Basquin's eyes widened in fear, but he was too late to react. Fox drove the dagger into Basquin's right eye all the way to the hilt.

Basquin's mouth opened in a voiceless cry. He released the axe and sank to the ground, his one unblinking eye staring straight up into the blue sky.

Relief and remorse coursed through Fox in equal measure at causing the death of his last living blood relative. Basquin was his mother's son, too, and she would have been distraught that they had pitted themselves against each other. But she would have understood his need to protect the woman he loved.

He gritted his teeth, rotated the axe, and pulled it out of his arm. He dropped the weapon and clamped his hand over the wound to stem the blood pouring out.

He turned to the king, who sat only a few steps away, and softly said, "Your Highness, I have done my duty."

The king stood and said, "I congratulate you, Sir Guillaume." He raised his arms and loudly proclaimed to the spectators, "God has smiled on our champion!"

The crowd went wild, the stands shaking as the entire audience leaped to their feet and gleefully cheered their victor.

Fox stumbled over to Willa, who ran to the railing, pulled the mail sleeve up to his elbow, and tightly tied her kerchief around his bleeding arm. Her relief was palpable.

"You're a mess," she said as the king's guards kept Fox's admirers at bay. "We need to have this looked after."

"We can't spend long on it," Fox said, grimacing in pain as she tended to his wound. "We need to leave as soon as possible for La Sacra di San Michele to find Catherine."

"I know."

"You do? Have you heard something?"

"Just that the king plans to reward you with five hundred gold *livres* in honor of the spectacle."

"Then what do you fear? That Cardinal Molyneux will find us? Because I agree. If Basquin knew we were here, it won't be long until Molyneux does as well. But without Basquin as his strong arm, he'll have to find another ally to do his dirty work."

Willa shook her head. "He already has. It's Lord Tonbridge."

Fox was taken aback. "Tonbridge? He can't be as formidable as Basquin was."

"You don't know the earl's unrelenting focus the way I do," she replied with a dark cast to her eyes. "He won't stop hunting for me and the Icon. Ever. Basquin may have been deadly, but he was a lone man. I assure you, with the resources and soldiers at his disposal, Tonbridge will not rest until he destroys us."

# 66

*Two months ago*
*June, 1351*

### TONBRIDGE, ENGLAND

"I should never have been so careless," Isabel said as she paced the solar of Tonbridge Castle. With just a week before the wedding, she'd been brought to his estate to prepare for the nuptials.

"It's not your fault," replied Willa, who stood at the window. "He would have found out about the Hodegetria eventually."

"But I thought by that time, we'd be long married, and I'd have more influence over him. How could I have been so stupid to be looking at it while he was at my home?"

Tonbridge had walked into her chambers uninvited and caught sight of the golden manuscript during Isabel's evening prayers before the Icon. The moment he understood what it was, he immediately began to think of how he could use it for his own gain.

"Are you sure he intends to sell it?" Willa asked.

Isabel nodded. "That's where he is returning from today. A meeting with his patron to make a bargain."

Since the day she'd laid eyes on Lord Tonbridge, Willa had disliked the man, but she didn't speak up. She knew Isabel had no choice in the marriage, and the earl promised to provide her lady with an opulent life. But for Isabel, safeguarding the Icon was a sacred duty, one she was unwilling to compromise, and Willa felt united with her in her mission to protect it.

"What will you say to him?" Willa asked.

Isabel shook her head. "I can try persuading him, but he was adamant about using it to improve his position."

"Did he tell you any details?"

"Just that it involved an important man in Paris. He's expecting to hand it over the day of our wedding."

"And if His Lordship refuses to change his mind?"

Willa held her breath as Isabel considered the question.

Finally, she said, "Then we must flee with the Hodegetria before the wedding ceremony."

Willa's heart raced with both elation and trepidation at the thought. She would follow her lady to the ends of the earth.

"Where would we take it?"

"To my cousin Claire in Paris. You remember her, don't you?"

"Forget my only journey away from England? I remember every moment of it. Do you think Lady Claire would provide you asylum?"

"I do," Isabel said. "It's her husband I worry about since I don't know him. Our only other choice would be to find Catherine and ask her for refuge."

"We don't even know where she is or if she still survives." Isabel's regular letters from her sister that had been routed through Claire had been interrupted shortly after the Great Mortality, and she hadn't heard anything from her in more than six months.

"If I can find her, I'm sure Catherine would carry on the responsibility handed down to us. The bigger problem is how to escape."

Willa raised her eyebrows. "Actually, I've given that some thought."

Isabel stopped pacing and stared at her. "You have? And you said nothing?"

"I know this marriage has been weighing heavily on you, and I didn't want to burden you with ideas that might upset you. I was just trying to think ahead in case it became necessary."

"My dear Willa, you could never burden me. What is your idea?"

"Lord Tonbridge's mother lives on one of the estate's manors, correct?"

Isabel nodded.

"Then we will volunteer to take your carriage to retrieve her the day before the wedding. I believe Reginald is loyal to you, so he will go along with the scheme. He can sneak a trunk with our belongings into it the night before. When we are far from the castle, we can make our escape."

"But what about the men-at-arms the earl is sure to send with us?"

"I will feign that the motion of the carriage has made me ill. When we stop, you will send them into the forest to search for some nightshade to treat me. Once they are away from their horses, we will take them with us and canter off. By the time they are able to return to the castle with the news of our flight, we will be long gone."

Isabel shook her head in wonder and then broke into a huge smile. "You are delightfully brilliant, my friend. What would I do without you?" She came over and pulled Willa into a tight embrace.

"You would be lost, my lady. Utterly lost."

A commotion in the courtyard below broke the spell. They looked out the window and saw Tonbridge dismount from his horse. He was fairly beaming and strode into the castle.

"Whatever happens, my lady," Willa said, "I am always your faithful servant."

"I know, Willa. I am proud to know you."

Tonbridge marched into the room, his arms wide.

"My beloved, I have some truly astounding news to share."

"I think we should talk first, Your Lordship. I want—"

"You will have time to speak after I am done. I have just come from meeting that important man from Paris I told you of." He clapped his hands together. "He has agreed to my terms. You will someday be a queen! My son will be heir to a kingdom!"

Isabel nodded. "May I speak now, Your Lordship?"

"Certainly, although I thought a measure of gratitude would be your first response."

"I do appreciate what you do for me. But I cannot allow you to sell what is not yours."

Tonbridge's smile faltered. "Did I just hear you correctly? You will not *allow* me, your husband-to-be, to do something? Since our betrothal, there is no yours and mine. I make the decisions about what is good for the family."

"The Icon has been entrusted to the women of my family for generations. Eudocia herself saw a vision of the Virgin Mary appear in front of her, bestowing responsibility for the Hodegetria on her and the women who would come after her."

"And I have had a new vision, one that showed me how the Hodegetria is a gift to our family legacy. You may object now, my dear, but someday you will see the value in this transaction."

Willa felt her blood roiling at Tonbridge's casual dismissal of the Virgin's miraculous apparition, but as a mere handmaid she could not inject herself into the conversation.

"The Icon should not be involved in a transaction at all," Isabel said.

"You continue to argue with me?" Tonbridge said in disbelief. "I expect to have a loyal wife, and that is what you shall be. Once I have made a decision, there will be no further discussion."

"I need you to understand the meaning of your actions. Disobeying the Virgin could bring grave consequences for—"

Tonbridge stalked over to her and slapped her hard, sending Isabel to the floor. Willa could see the red welt rising on her cheek as she stood petrified in shock.

"That is the consequence of *your* action. I told you that I will take care of you, but you owe me unwavering support in return."

"When it comes to the Icon, I will not waver."

The earl reared his leg back to kick her, but Willa threw herself in front of Isabel to block it. The blow landed on her instead, and she went tumbling across the floor.

Tonbridge stabbed his finger at Willa. "Do that again, and it will be my blade that strikes you instead of my boot."

He straightened his surcoat to compose himself and shook his head at Isabel. "I can't have two unruly women in my charge. On the day of our wedding, I will assign you a new maidservant, one who will be a proper influence on you."

Isabel gasped. "And what about Willa?"

Tonbridge shrugged. "Don't worry, my dear. I'll find her a place as a scullery maid at another of my estates." He gave her a humorless smile. "A distant one."

Willa took the words like a dagger to her heart.

They were interrupted when a guard tentatively entered.

"Your Lordship, the steward has arrived. Shall I take him to the dungeon?"

Tonbridge appraised Isabel before saying, "No. Bring him here. I think my betrothed needs to see this."

Willa got up and helped Isabel to her feet, caressing around the redness on her face.

"I'll be all right," Isabel said quietly. "Are you hurt?"

"No, my lady," Willa said, although she could feel the bruise that was already forming on her side.

A man was roughly pulled into the room by two guards and shoved to the floor. His face was bloody and beaten.

Tonbridge looked down at him dispassionately. "You didn't think I'd ever find you, did you, Bancroft?"

Tears streamed down Bancroft's face. "Mercy, Your Lordship! I beg of you, mercy!"

That only made Tonbridge give him a derisive laugh. "You relinquished your chance for mercy two years ago during the Pestilence when you stole from me."

"I shouldn't have done it, Your Lordship. Mercy!"

"No, you shouldn't have. And then to make matters worse, you fled. You didn't face the toll of your traitorous behavior like a man."

Tonbridge faced Isabel as he spoke. "There is nothing—*nothing*—I treasure more than the loyalty of those in my charge. Loyalty of servants, loyalty of men-at-arms, loyalty of family. If you are devoted to me, I will ensure your well-being and happiness in turn."

Then he turned back to Bancroft. "But if you are a traitorous blackguard who knows nothing of loyalty, I will track you down no matter how long it takes. Two years ago after your thievery was discovered, you slunk away to London, where you thought you would be out of my reach. But I never stopped hunting for you, did I? And I am an excellent hunter. If you are my intended prey, I *will* find you, and the punishment will be as severe as the betrayal."

He casually flicked his hand at the guards. "Now you may take him to the dungeon. Send word to the sheriff that he has been found so that his hanging can be arranged."

The sobbing Bancroft was hauled away. Tonbridge walked over to Isabel and took her hands in his, smiling at her as if nothing had happened. "I know you will be faithful to me to your dying day. Now let us forget this ugly moment and continue planning our nuptials."

Willa felt sick and might have been ill then and there if she hadn't noted the steely glint in Isabel's eye. There was no doubt in Willa's mind that they would make their escape attempt, whatever the outcome.

## 67

*August, 1351*

### MONTLUÇON, FRANCE

Despite setting an arduous pace traveling from Paris, Cardinal Molyneux's entourage didn't arrive at the Duke of Bourbon's castle in Montluçon until four days after the tournament was over. They were still a full day's ride away from Château de Tournöel, but there was hope of information about the games. The king's banner was flying over the castle, which meant he was staying there on his way back home.

Molyneux sent Tonbridge to see if Basquin, François, and Claire were also staying at the castle while he took an audience with the king.

He was escorted to the great hall where the monarch was meeting with his advisers. Molyneux approached the king, who was seated. He stood, and they exchanged the traditional kiss on the lips to greet each other.

"Cardinal Molyneux," the king said, "what a pleasant surprise to see you here. Although my news will bring you sadness if you have not heard it already."

Molyneux was perplexed. "I have heard no news, Your Highness. I was not expecting to find you here. I was simply on my way to Avignon." He wasn't about to share the real reason he'd come so far. The king would be just as happy to take possession of the Icon of the Virgin and Child if he were aware of it.

The king nodded solemnly. "Yes, you surely look down on entertainments such as tournaments. Then have you not heard about the judicial combat that followed?"

Molyneux shook his head. "Why would I concern myself about a duel?"

"Because you are well acquainted with the loser. It was your man Basquin."

The cardinal inhaled sharply at the revelation. He knew well the fate of a duel's loser. His son was dead, his head on a pike somewhere. He swallowed hard and gathered himself.

"May I ask of what crime he was accused?"

"Murder. Both participants blamed each other for the killing. I'm sorry to say God's judgment was that Sir Basquin was the murderer."

"*Sir* Basquin?"

"Of course. He had to be knighted to fight a fellow peer. His combatant was Sir Guillaume d'Amboise. My condolences. I know Basquin has been with you for many years as a faithful... servant."

As soon as the king mentioned that Basquin had been knighted, he knew why his son had come alone. Sir Guillaume had to be Gerard Fox in disguise.

"Your Highness's sympathy is very kind," Molyneux said smoothly as he controlled his reaction to the shocking revelation. "My servant will surely be missed."

His emotions took him by surprise, the news of his son's death hitting him harder than he ever would have expected. Basquin had always chafed at his position, hounding Molyneux to deliver the knighthood he so desperately craved but wasn't ready for. Now his impatience had been his downfall, just as the cardinal feared it would be someday.

But Molyneux felt a surge of pride at the ingenuity Basquin had displayed by getting himself knighted. That inventiveness reminded Molyneux of Emmeline, and he realized that perhaps he resisted bestowing the Fox lands to him over all these years not because Basquin was a useful tool, but simply because he wanted his only son to be in his life.

And now Gerard Fox had taken that from him.

"Perhaps Your Highness can tell me where—"

"Ah, there he is!" the king said, beckoning to someone at the back of the hall. "Come and deliver your surprise to the cardinal."

Molyneux turned and saw François striding toward him wearing a wide smile and carrying the Crusader's Chalice.

"I know you have coveted the chalice given to the saintly King Louis, Cardinal Molyneux," the king said. "When my men saw your entourage approaching, Sir François asked for the honor of delivering it to you in my presence. He told me that you agreed to take it in payment of his debts, which seems a more-than-reasonable arrangement for you."

François bowed and handed the magnificent chalice to Molyneux, who quietly seethed at François's cunning machinations. The knight knew that giving it to him in front of the king would mean that there was no way for the cardinal to back out of his agreement.

Molyneux nodded and passed it on to one of his attendants.

"I will make sure to get a writ from your clerk eliminating my debt," François said.

"I know this doesn't make up for the loss of Sir Basquin," the king said, "but I'm pleased that you have nevertheless gained something of value."

"Thank you, Your Highness. I must excuse myself so that Sir François and I may conclude our business."

The king nodded and waved his hand to dismiss them.

Molyneux exited the hall with François and went into the courtyard to find Tonbridge haranguing Claire, with François's Frenchmen and Tonbridge's Englishmen staring each other down. Luckily for both sides, on the king's orders, they had all surrendered their weapons upon entering the castle, otherwise a bloody battle might already be in motion.

"Where is Lady Isabel?" Tonbridge shouted in Claire's face.

François stalked up to Tonbridge and yanked him backward. "How dare you treat my wife like this!"

"She knows where my betrothed is," Tonbridge said, shrugging off François. "And she'll tell me if she understands what's good for her."

He advanced on Claire again, but François shielded his wife.

Molyneux put a hand on Tonbridge to stop him. "You will not fight in the presence of the king. Besides, there are better ways to get what we need." He looked at the men around them. "Give us this space."

Nobody moved until François and Tonbridge both nodded at their men-at-arms. All of them retreated into the castle.

"Now we can talk like civilized people," Molyneux said.

"I gave you what you wanted," François said.

"The chalice, yes. Your debt is wiped clean, as you so neatly arranged. I can't very well go back on my word with the king as our witness."

"Then what do you want?" Claire demanded.

Molyneux tilted his head at her. "You are an impertinent lady, aren't you?"

"I know you hold no more power over us."

"Is that so? We know that your husband procured the services of Gerard Fox to fight for him under an assumed name and that Lady Isabel was with him. Do you deny it?"

She said nothing and fixed him with an icy stare. His accusation was verified by her silence.

"I knew it," Tonbridge said to Molyneux. "Lady Isabel scurried away to take refuge with her cousin."

Claire's eyes flared curiously at his words, but Molyneux couldn't understand why.

"She's gone now," François said.

"Where did she and Fox go?" Molyneux asked.

"Why should we tell you?" Claire said defiantly.

"Because I will reveal to the king that you won the tournament with an impostor as your champion."

"Then I shall tell the king why you really want to catch her. I've seen it with my own eyes."

François looked at her, puzzled. "Seen what?"

"The Hodegetria. The Icon of the Virgin and Child painted by Saint Luke himself. It's the most beautiful object I've ever seen."

François gaped at her. "Lady Isabel had that treasure with her the entire time?"

"I didn't want to burden you with the knowledge, my dear."

Tonbridge took a step forward. "By rights it's mine. Isabel is my betrothed."

"Tonbridge, stop threatening them," Molyneux said. "They've rolled their dice, and the result is in their favor." Tonbridge reluctantly stepped back.

Molyneux peered at Claire and continued, "It's clear where she has gone. To the bosom of her sister, Prioress Catherine."

Claire's expression faltered briefly. She regained her composure and jutted out her chin. "They have a three-day head start on you. You'll never catch up to them."

"You're wrong," Tonbridge said. "We will capture them soon enough because we know where they're going."

"And where is that?"

"You may think you're sly, Lady Claire," Molyneux said. "But we discovered that Prioress Catherine was sent to Avignon, in the shadow of the Papal Palace."

"Is that true?" François said to Claire.

Claire hesitated for a long moment, her face unreadable, as if she were trying not to betray her emotions further, but Molyneux thought he'd struck a nerve. She then said, "Why bother denying it? You would not believe me anyway."

Molyneux shook his head. "You are correct, Lady Claire. I would not."

# Avignon

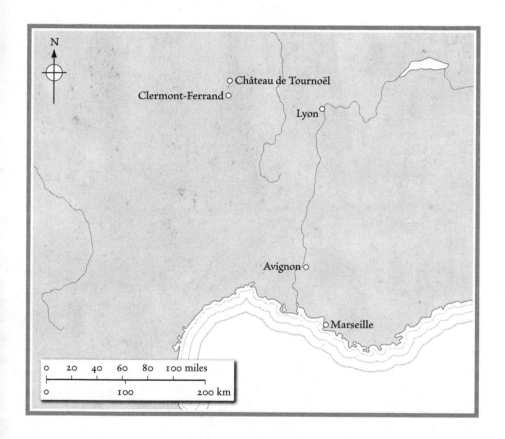

N

Château de Tournoël
Clermont-Ferrand
Lyon

Avignon

Marseille

0   20   40   60   80   100 miles

0            100           200 km

 68

AVIGNON, FRANCE

During their ride south from Château de Tournöel, Fox's condition had worsened steadily. Despite the bandages and sling, the wound where Basquin had impaled his left arm became tainted, with angry lines of red stretching up his arm. By the fourth day he was fevered and going in and out of delirium. Willa and Youssef finally convinced him that they had to seek medical attention or they'd never reach the coast.

The plan was to avoid a perilous crossing of the Alps to get to La Sacra di San Michele, the monastery where Isabel's sister Catherine was now abbess. Instead, they would head south through the Papal State of Avignon toward Marseille, where they could board a ship to Savona and ride north to Turin. According to the information in Catherine's letter, the abbey was located in the mountains west of the city.

The Saint-Bénézet Bridge at Avignon was the only one across the wide Rhône River within several days' journey. As they approached the bridge through the town of Villeneuve-lès-Avignon, Willa was worried about Fox staying on his horse. He was pale and sweaty and could barely hold on to the reins. She looked at Youssef with concern.

"Don't worry," Youssef said, not altogether convincingly, "Gerard will make it to Mordecai's. I just hope my old friend survived the Great Mortality."

"Why do you think Gerard should not go to a Christian physicker?" she asked.

"Leeching the blood out of him won't fix what ails him. He needs a Jewish surgeon. I met Mordecai when I spent time in the city long ago. He can heal most any wound with balms that his people swear by."

"Gerard?" She waved at Fox until she had his attention. "Gerard, are you willing to visit a Jewish surgeon?"

He nodded in a daze. "That physicker is doing nothing for my father. I know where we can get a potion that might work."

"I'll take that as a 'yes'," Youssef said.

The entrance to the bridge was through the Philippe-le-Bel tower, which guarded the crossing on the French side of the river opposite the land of the Papal States. They were stopped by two guards and a clerk collecting tolls. All three were leery of Fox and his drawn complexion.

"Stop there!" one of the guards said before they could get too close.

"We want to cross," Youssef said. "We have money for the toll."

More than enough. They had the five hundred *livres* given to Fox by the king for his victory in the duel.

"What's wrong with him?" the clerk asked.

"He was injured and his wound has festered," Youssef said. "We are taking him to a healer in the city."

"Are you sure it isn't the Pestilence?"

Youssef pulled up Fox's sleeve to show them the bloody bandages. He had none of the distinctive purple splotches or lumpy skin of a Pestilence victim.

The clerk nodded. "Fine. We can't be too careful these days given the resurgence of the illness here and there. We got a reminder two weeks ago after a flood marooned a boat on a shoal near the Saint Nicholas Chapel at the other end of the bridge. Full of dead Pestilence victims. No one has gone near it since it arrived." He crossed himself. "God save us from another Great Mortality."

They paid the toll and started across the thousand-yard-long bridge. It was so narrow that they could only ride two abreast. Unlike most bridges, it didn't go straight across the water, but curved over a series of small islands that sat in the middle of the river. The structure was built out of stone arches spanning the water between large, diamond-shaped footings that jutted out on both sides.

Halfway across, at the largest bend in the bridge, they came to a section that was made of wood, with timber braces and a platform made of rickety boards. A windlass crane twenty feet taller than the bridge was hauling new stones up from a barge on the river for the masons to install.

"Why is it under construction?" Willa asked Youssef. "You told us this bridge was old."

"It is. Over a hundred years old. Remember the flood the clerk mentioned? Happens all the time, undermining and washing out the bridge supports. This thing is always under construction, just like the Papal Palace."

He pointed toward Avignon. The grand edifice rising above the city loomed over the walls surrounding it. Stones the color of sand were shaped into an impressive array of parapets, arches, crenellations, and towers that made Château de Tournöel look like a shack. The palace's imposing size and style exuded the power that lay within. Willa felt a thrill at the thought of how close she must be to the pope himself at the moment.

"Saint Nicholas Chapel," Youssef said, startling her. He nodded at a petite stone chapel mounted right on the bridge a short distance from the city gates on the far side.

Willa recalled what the clerk had said and steered Comis over to the stone parapet so she could see out over the river. There was the Pestilence boat, stranded on a rocky islet in the middle of the Rhône. Its deck was littered with bodies that had been picked over by crows, and the stink of death was noticeable even at this distance. The sight sent a shiver down her spine.

When they had crossed the rest of the bridge and reached the gates of the city, they went through the same questioning about Fox's sickly appearance before being let in. As they rode through the city streets, Willa was astounded by the multitude of different languages spoken by the passing crowds. They were dressed in a wide variety of garments that she had never seen before.

Youssef must have noticed her gawking. "Now that Avignon is the seat of the papacy, people from every corner of Christendom come here," he said as a brilliantly robed emissary who must have been from an African kingdom walked by. "I'll stick out much less here."

The entire city was made from stone, and none was more impressive than the giant structure that rose in front of them as they entered the main square. The Papal Palace looked even grander up close, with a wide staircase leading up to its entrance. Willa could imagine the pope blessing the masses from the balcony above. As with the bridge, large parts of the building were still under construction, and workers scuttled over its face like ants.

They rode on until they reached the walled Jewish quarter, which was located in the center of the city. When Youssef told the gatekeeper that they were looking for Mordecai, Willa was relieved to hear he could still be found in a house near the synagogue.

After a bit of searching, they found the house and were greeted by a jovial man with a long gray beard. Youssef jumped down from his horse, and the two men hugged each other tightly.

"So good to welcome you, my friend," Mordecai said, beaming. "I thought I'd never see you again."

"And I feared that the Pestilence might have taken you," Youssef replied.

Mordecai waved the thought off as if it were nothing to worry about. "We did have a bad year when it descended on Avignon, but my family got through it. We sadly lost a nephew and a cousin. Others had it much worse."

"I didn't know if you would be blamed for it. I've heard about Jews who were killed in other places."

"The pope has been good to us. He issued an edict saying we weren't at fault."

A woman came out of the house wiping her hands on an apron. Her curly hair was tucked in a kerchief, and she strode toward them with purpose.

"Mordecai, what is this…" She spotted Youssef and regarded him fondly. "Well, if it isn't our old Egyptian friend."

"Hail and God save you, Esther."

"And who are these people with you? Oh, that one doesn't look so good. Mordecai, have you been ignoring a patient in need?"

"This is Gerard and Willa," Youssef said.

"What happened to him?" Mordecai asked.

"A wounded arm," Willa said. "He has a fever."

"This horse is falling over," Fox said as he clumsily attempted to dismount. Youssef and Mordecai rushed to help him down.

"Let's get him inside," Mordecai said as he took a quick look under the bandage. "Esther, prepare the skin salve."

They carried him in by the shoulders, ushering him up the stairs to a small room with an open cot where they laid him down. Mordecai stripped the bandage to inspect the wound's crude stitching more carefully. He clucked his tongue and shook his head, murmuring to himself in Hebrew.

Willa held Fox's hand while his eyes fluttered.

"Father, I want Mother," he muttered. "Where is she?"

"I'm right here, dear one," Willa said. "You're going to be all right."

Willa looked up at the surgeon with a silent question asking if her statement was correct.

"I'll do what I can," Mordecai said. "He's far along with the fever, but our salve has saved others in a similar condition."

"Not as bad as this," Esther said as she entered with a ceramic pot. "Don't give them false hope, Mordecai."

He took the pot and plucked a brush from it. The hairs dripped with a thick liquid.

"What is that?" Youssef asked.

Mordecai spread it on the wound as he spoke. "It's a recipe Esther and I have developed over the years, a concoction of honey, garlic, cow's bile, and a few secret herbs. If this doesn't heal him, nothing will."

"How long will it take to work?" Willa asked.

"We might not know for a day or two," Esther said. "We can't move your friend, so he'll stay here. You're welcome to hold vigil during the day, but you'll have to find a stable for your horses and a place of your own to sleep."

Fox was shivering with chills now and his pallor had turned gray. He was close to death's door. Esther didn't have to tell her that he might not survive the night.

They'd come so far and been through so much that Willa didn't want to believe that God would take Fox now. She wasn't sure she'd have the strength to finish her journey without him.

Esther looked at her with a sorrowful gaze. "This is a Jewish household, but we worship the same God. Go ahead, my dear."

Willa bowed her head and prayed.

## 69

Cardinal Molyneux's expansive office inside Avignon's Papal Palace was designed to be majestic, a symbol of his stature and power. Lord Tonbridge used the wide space to pace between the oak table where the cardinal was sitting and the hearth at the opposite end of the room.

It was now a week after they'd talked with François and Claire, and Tonbridge was still stewing about Molyneux's decision not to force the *chevalier* and his wife to come with them as insurance. Now that they knew she'd been sent to Avignon, the cardinal had assured him that the records here would tell them Catherine's whereabouts, but nothing had been found since they arrived the day before.

"I thought we'd know the location of Lady Isabel's sister by now," Tonbridge said. "You said the papacy kept meticulous books."

"Calm down, Tonbridge," Molyneux said as he casually leafed through parchments that had been waiting for his perusal. "Normally, our records are well-kept. However, the archives are a mess after so much chaos over the past few years. The Great Mortality caused a huge disruption as clerks fell to the disease in droves. There is a backlog of unmarked documents that will take time to sift through."

"How long?"

"I have a dozen clerks checking every piece of administration they can find. Catherine is a common name, but I have faith that they will eventually discover her current posting."

"And if Fox and Lady Isabel flee with Sister Catherine once they find her? We may then have lost them for good."

Molyneux sighed and sat back. "What are you proposing?"

"Sister Catherine could still be in the surrounding area. I'll search every nunnery and abbey for her within a day's ride. If she's still here, Fox and Lady Isabel will be with her."

"An Englishman rampaging through the city and countryside right within view of the Papal Palace? I can only protect you so much from the French."

"Then give me a number of your soldiers equal to mine and a new clerk to come with me. That will give me the authority to search wherever I deem necessary."

Molyneux tented his fingers as he thought. "You will take care to conduct your search as inconspicuously as possible? I still answer to the pope. If he finds out that you're ransacking religious institutions in his realm, he will put a stop to it, and my position will be compromised."

Tonbridge approached the table and used his most reassuring voice. "I will take the utmost care while I seek out my treasonable betrothed and her blasphemous accomplice. They can't evade us forever."

Molyneux held up a finger. "While your most likely success will be with the abbeys and convents, take particular care to look in the hospitals as well. According to what we heard about the duel, Fox was grievously injured. He might have sought medical attention. If not, then we will simply have to wait for the results of the archival investigation."

"How can you be so blasé about all this?" Tonbridge asked. "You seem completely unconcerned about our predicament. Those two are an affront to us, from their theft and betrayal of me to their heresy at defying you."

Molyneux's eyes bored into him. "Do not mistake my relaxed demeanor for a lack of concern or righteous anger. Your betrothed stole what was rightfully yours, and therefore what is rightfully mine. Gerard Fox murdered my son. Both of them will be judged for their actions and pay with their lives in the most painful manner at my disposal."

Tonbridge broke into a huge smile. He was thrilled to hear

that Molyneux shared his resolve. He would not cease until he had overturned every wretched stone under which they might be hiding.

Although Tonbridge had begun his search in good spirits, they evaporated little by little with each failure to find his quarry. After an entire day of searching, he had come up empty, and his hopes were flagging. He and his cadre of twelve men had searched virtually every place a nun would be posted in the city's outskirts. No one had ever seen or met an English nun named Catherine from Saint-Quentin.

On his way back across the Avignon Bridge, he remembered Molyneux's point about Fox's injured arm. He stopped at the Philippe-le-Bel tower gate to speak to the clerk.

"I represent Cardinal Molyneux on a matter of great importance," Tonbridge said. "We are looking for criminals who may have entered the city. A man and woman traveling alone. The woman is blonde and the man is on a mottled silver horse."

The clerk shook his head. "No one like that was traveling alone."

Tonbridge grimaced at the news. He was about to ride into Avignon when the clerk spoke up.

"But I did see two people who fit those descriptions. They weren't by themselves. A dark-skinned man was riding with them."

Tonbridge hadn't heard anything about a manservant accompanying Fox and Isabel.

"Was the man on the silver horse injured?" Tonbridge asked.

The clerk nodded. "He looked sickly. I thought he might have the Pestilence. But he showed me his arm. It was wrapped in a bloody bandage."

"Isabel's here," Tonbridge muttered under his breath. To the clerk, he said, "Where did they go?"

"The dark-skinned man said they were going to seek out a healer."

"Did he say which hospital?"

The clerk shook his head. "There are several Christian ones."

Tonbridge gave him a puzzled look. "Christian ones? Are there other kinds of healers in Avignon?"

"Yes," the clerk said. "In the Jewish quarter."

 70

For the past three days, Youssef and Willa had been taking turns watching over Fox during the day. Willa would read to him from his book, which lay on a small table beside him. This afternoon, it was Youssef's turn to sit with him while Esther nursed him. Willa had gone to the apothecary to acquire more herbs for Mordecai's salve.

Despite the medicine, Fox's condition had worsened for more than a day after they'd arrived, and his chances for recovery looked grim. But at the end of the second day, his fever broke, and the bright red lines on his arm began to recede. Since then, they'd been spoon-feeding him broth and allowing him to rest as he recovered his strength.

Mordecai entered and lathered another layer of the balm on the wound as Fox napped.

"How long until we can travel again?" Youssef asked in a whisper.

Mordecai tilted his head back and forth as he considered. "He's still very weak. Fever saps your muscles. But I'd say if he continues to get better at the rate he has been, he could ride on horseback in another day or so if it were absolutely necessary."

Youssef was startled when Fox's eyes batted open.

"I'm not dead yet?" he said in a hoarse voice as he took in his strange surroundings. Then his gaze settled on Youssef. "Where am I?"

"You're under the care of a healer." He nodded to Mordecai. "This man saved your life."

"It's lucky you came to someone who knows what he's doing," Mordecai said.

"Then my thanks are in order," Fox said.

He tried to raise himself onto his elbows, but Mordecai gently pressed him back down. Fox resisted for a moment and then collapsed back onto the cot.

"Your will is strong," Mordecai said, "I'll give you that. I've never seen anyone recover as quickly as you. But if you push yourself too hard, the fever may come back more viciously than before."

"Don't worry," Youssef said. "I'll make sure he follows all of your advice."

"Once Willa returns from the apothecary, she will have everything she needs to make more of my salve should he require it while you travel."

"I remember small portions of the last few days," Fox said to Mordecai. "Your wife is Esther. You both have been very kind to me. I know it's a hardship having me here in your home."

"Not at all," Mordecai said. "Any friend of Youssef is a friend of ours."

"Still, we will pay you handsomely for your care."

"I've already taken care of that," Youssef said. The monetary award from the king also meant they'd been able to buy everything that Mordecai required to cure Fox, as well as lodging for them and the horses.

"Where's Zephyr?" Fox asked.

"At a stable nearby. We—"

A commotion outside interrupted Youssef. He went to the window and saw a dozen men on horses trotting toward Mordecai's house. The squat man in the lead had the bearing of a noble and shouted for the crowds of pedestrians to make way.

Mordecai had joined Youssef at the window and said, "What's all this about?"

"I'm sorry, Mordecai," Youssef said as he rushed over to Fox to try to help him out of bed. "They're here for us. I think it's Lord Tonbridge." Youssef snatched up Fox's book and tucked it in his waistband, then put his arm under Fox's shoulders to help him stand. "Is there a way out the back?"

"There's the window in our bedroom that overlooks the garden and privy," Mordecai said. "You'll have to jump. I'll go downstairs and keep them there as long as I can." He headed for the stairs.

"Don't resist them," Fox called after Mordecai as he staggered to his feet. His legs wobbled from the effort to stay upright. "Youssef, if something happens to me, take Willa and flee."

Youssef ignored the statement. "Come on, Gerard. You can make it."

The horses outside came to a stop, and boots tramped on the paving stones of the street. Someone banged on the door downstairs and demanded that it be opened.

Youssef dragged Fox to the other room and flung the shutters open as he listened to the ruckus downstairs. Esther opened the home's front door and tried protesting to slow down Tonbridge and his men, but nobles could do whatever they wished to commoners—particularly Jews. If Tonbridge wanted to tear the house apart looking for Fox, he had that right. Anybody who tried to stop him could be justifiably killed.

The shadowed courtyard below the window was paved with rough stones in front of the garden. In his condition, Fox could break a leg jumping down that far, so Youssef went first to catch his friend. As he leaped, footsteps pounded up the stairs.

He landed hard and rolled, which would certainly result in a mass of bruises later. He got to his feet and turned with his arms wide. Fox leaned forward to jump, but rough hands yanked him backward out of sight.

"We have him!" a man shouted.

Youssef retreated to the shadows behind the privy and saw two soldiers peering out of the window. They withdrew when they didn't spot him.

"He's the only one here," one of the soldiers said.

"Two men will wait here until Lady Isabel and the Moor return," someone answered. It had to be Tonbridge, who obviously knew that Youssef was with them, even if they mistook Youssef for an infidel.

Youssef could do nothing more for Fox now. He had to warn Willa or she might run right into Tonbridge.

He pulled up his hood and hopped over the garden wall, repeating the process in the adjacent yards until he found an alley that led back to the main street. The soldiers at Mordecai's house were no more than sixty paces away from where he stood at the intersection.

He knew where the apothecary was but he didn't have to go that far to find Willa. She was humming gaily as she walked toward him carrying a small pouch. The satchel carrying the manuscript was slung across her back as always. She insisted on taking it everywhere with her.

When she recognized Youssef, she raised her hand and was about to call out to him. He rushed out of the alley and put his hand over his own mouth hoping she would understand his warning. She looked at him strangely but stayed quiet, her smile vanishing. She stopped, a stricken look on her face.

When he reached her, she said, "Has Gerard taken a turn?"

"In a way," Youssef said, taking her hand. "Hurry."

He pulled her back toward the alley.

"Tell me what is going on this instant," Willa said.

He beckoned her with a finger so that they could both look around the corner down the street to Mordecai's home.

Willa gasped when she saw Fox being dragged out of the house in his hastily thrown-on tunic, hose, and boots. Youssef was relieved to see Mordecai and Esther unharmed, warily watching from the doorway.

Fox's hands were bound and a rope leading from his wrists was lashed to the saddle of Tonbridge's horse. The English earl climbed on with a self-congratulatory smirk. All but two of the men mounted their horses.

"Cardinal Molyneux will be very pleased to see you, Sir Gerard."

"It's been too long," Fox retorted. "I've missed him."

"Then we mustn't make you wait. You look tired, but it's only a short walk to the Papal Palace." He turned to the soldiers standing beside Mordecai and Esther. "Keep them in the house. We'll take your horses so Lady Isabel and her companion won't be alerted to your presence when they return."

Tonbridge tapped his spurs for a hasty departure, nearly pulling Fox over. Fighting to stay on his feet, he trotted to keep up.

Youssef and Willa pressed themselves against the alley wall so they wouldn't be seen as the horses rode by.

When they were past, Youssef said, "Gerard told me to take you and leave the city if something happened to him." He understood the need to get the manuscript far from Molyneux, but the idea of abandoning his friend nearly made him retch.

"Gerard is not in his right mind at the moment," Willa said, refusing to be undone by the sudden turn of events. "We're not going anywhere."

## 71

When Fox arrived at the Papal Palace, Tonbridge and a phalanx of armed guards took him on a labyrinthine route through the compound, passing through several reception halls decorated with brightly painted walls and lavish sets of tapestries, as well as some more intimate secular chambers featuring forested hunting scenes along the walls. When they dragged him up the stairs to the top floor, Fox caught a glimpse through a window of the buildings sprawling out to the city walls. He hoped Willa and Youssef were already on the other side and riding toward La Sacra di San Michele.

Molyneux was waiting in his private suite, lounging on a cushioned chair. Flanking him were two palace guards standing at attention and holding vicious-looking halberds taller than they were.

Tonbridge shoved Fox into the room, leaving the other guards outside. Fox was exhausted from his march to the palace, but he was determined to stay on his feet, planting them shoulder-width apart so he wouldn't sway.

Molyneux eyed Fox from head to toe. "Where did you find him?"

"In the house of a surgeon in the Jewish quarter, exactly what could be expected of an excommunicant," Tonbridge said. "I told you I would prevail."

"You also told me you would find the manuscript, and yet I do not see it before me."

"It will soon be ours. I have left two men at the surgeon's to capture Lady Isabel and their friend when they return."

Fox felt a surge of relief. At least Willa and Youssef hadn't been captured.

"And if they don't return?"

Tonbridge nodded at Fox. "We have him. He will tell us where they are."

"I won't," Fox said. "In fact, I don't know where they are."

"Then I must go and warn the guards at every gate to be on watch for them." Tonbridge turned to Molyneux.

Molyneux nodded. "Take my clerk so that he can show them my seal."

"And make sure that the gate guards know you're there because your betrothed ran out on you," Fox said. "I think it's important they understand that inspiring loyalty is not your strong point."

"I hope you refuse to talk," Tonbridge said with a snarl. "I would like to watch as the truth is extracted from you." He stormed out.

"Your hunting dog needs some training," Fox said. "He only caught one of us."

"It's true that I must depend on him now that you have killed Basquin."

"A tragic loss to you, I am sure," Fox taunted.

He could see that he'd hit a soft spot. The cardinal's cheek twitched at the jape.

"It is," Molyneux said, "but not as great a loss as Emmeline's death. Her youngest son's birth was very difficult for her."

Fox took a step forward, causing the guards to snap their halberds down, the needle-sharp points only a finger's length from Fox's chest.

"You and your filthy mouth have no right to utter my mother's name."

The cardinal tsked at him. "So disrespectful. Normally I would have you run through simply because you failed to address me as Your Eminence, but you are obviously not well."

Fox would have strangled Molyneux with his shackles, but in his condition he had no chance against two armed guards.

He stepped back, and the guards resumed their positions at the cardinal's side.

Molyneux called out, "Guard!"

The commander of the guards who'd brought him in entered.

"Your Eminence?"

Molyneux looked around until his eyes settled on a heavy chest. "Shackle the prisoner to one of those iron handles. Make quite sure it is secure. I would like to have some privacy with him."

"Yes, Your Eminence."

While the guards with the halberds watched them with weapons at the ready, the commander sat Fox on the chest and looped the manacles through the iron ring, locking them again tightly.

"Now leave us," Molyneux said. "All of you."

The three guards left.

"You can't stand for them to hear the truth?" Fox asked. He tested the manacles, but they were firmly shackled to the chest. "Perhaps you're afraid they would be sickened by the details and empty their stomachs in your private quarters."

"The truth is that I loved your mother," Molyneux said. "She was a remarkable woman."

"'Obsessed with her' is likely more accurate. She never would have been with a man of your low character, no matter the circumstances."

"I will admit that Emmeline attempted to escape many times, one of the reasons I admired her. Of course, once she learned of her pregnancy, she was too ashamed to return to your father, and she stopped trying to flee." Molyneux looked wistful as he pictured her in his mind. "From the moment I saw her, I knew she had no equal. Beautiful, vibrant, intelligent, resourceful. A perfect mother to bear a son." He leaned forward in his seat, his eyes flaring with rage. "And you took that son from me."

"It was Basquin's idea to duel, not mine."

Molyneux nodded and sat back. "He always was cocksure. I've always wondered how different he would be if Emmeline had lived through his birth. Such a waste."

"Are you expecting my sympathy?"

"I am trying to explain that I have nothing more to lose and everything to gain. You can do no harm to my position, but I can cause whatever pain I like to you."

"I know about your desire to use the Icon to ensure your claim to the papacy. But if you want me to tell you how to find the manuscript, save your breath. Your threats are empty."

Molyneux nodded in agreement. "I realize you might say anything to stop whatever torture I could inflict on you, and that's the problem. I wouldn't know whether to believe you."

"Then you'll have to become pope like anyone else, by convincing the other cardinals to select you."

"I would not have risen to this status if God had not ordained it, and I know He has greater plans for me. The papacy is my divine right, and when that opportunity presents itself, I will be prepared to seize it."

"You will go to Hell for what you have done."

"I am trying to recover a priceless relic and guarantee the Church's victory over the infidels. You cannot even obtain forgiveness for your sins. It is you who will be damned."

"At least I will go there knowing you did not acquire the Hodegetria."

"What if I could offer something to you instead of threatening you?"

"You have nothing I want."

"Not even your ancestral land?"

Fox narrowed his eyes at Molyneux. "A bribe?"

Molyneux dismissed the word with a wave of his hand. "Consider it a reward. Tell me where the manuscript is, or at least where it's being taken, and I will reinstate not only your land but also your good graces with the Church."

"You would help absolve my excommunication?" It was the goal Fox had been pursuing for four long and difficult years, and now Molyneux was offering it to him in exchange for a few simple words.

"Your father's as well. And you can be sure that there will be no other chance. Only the pope can absolve you, and since I was the one to instate it, it would take my testament to convince him. You have no witnesses on your behalf. This is a one-time-only offer, and it expires the moment we find the manuscript on our own. Decline it, and you will never get your land and title back."

Fox was tempted, if only for a brief moment. He'd been fighting so hard to restore the good name of the Fox family and to guarantee that he and his father would not suffer hellfire, and now the chance was being handed to him on a golden platter. But then he was just as quickly ashamed for considering the proposition. He had already rejected the idea that his father's immortal soul was in danger, no matter what the Church said. As painful as his own excommunication had been at first, Fox now realized that he had never really lost his faith. It was just that he no longer believed the Church was the arbiter of his eternal fate.

Molyneux mistook his silence for dithering and continued, "I repeat, Caldecott Mote and Château de Beaujoie will belong to me and the Church forever. You will never again be a knight."

And it suddenly became clear to Fox what James had been trying to impress upon him. If he accepted Molyneux's offer, he would be a knight in name only. Yes, he would have his lands and status back, but by betraying Willa and Youssef, he would also be betraying the sacred oaths he took in front of his brother. Only by declining Molyneux's offer would he be a true knight.

Fox nodded. "My choice is made."

"Do you know the current whereabouts of Lady Isabel?" Molyneux probed.

He merely shrugged.

"We know she intends to take the manuscript to her sister Catherine," Molyneux said. "Where is she?"

Fox was happy to hear that they didn't know. He shrugged again.

"You don't intend to cooperate? Do your good name and land mean nothing to you? Your relationship with the Church? Your father's reputation?"

"They mean more to me than you could ever understand," Fox

replied, letting his anger harden into steely determination. "But my father would never want me to help you after what you did to us, no matter the cost. You took everything from me but my honor. I will not surrender that."

Molyneux sighed. "Very well. You may regret that decision when your soul is writhing in Hell."

"The only thing I will regret is not being there when God's judgment is delivered upon you."

"And such a glorious judgment in my favor you will miss. But think on this while you are in your dungeon cell. The two people you think you are protecting will suffer the same fate as you, and I will still have the manuscript. Then what good will your honor do you?"

The cardinal called out, and the guards outside the door came in to haul Fox away.

Molyneux stood and mockingly reassured Fox as he was unshackled from the chest.

"Don't fret about your friends, Sir Gerard. The moment we have them in custody, you will certainly be the first to know."

 72

Willa soon realized that her statement to Youssef about not going anywhere wasn't entirely correct. They had to go *somewhere*, otherwise they'd be trapped in Avignon. But they wouldn't be going far. She and Youssef got the horses immediately and left the city before Molyneux and Tonbridge could instruct the guards at every city gate to apprehend them on sight. It was Youssef who found a place for them to stay in Villeneuve-lès-Avignon, the town on the opposite end of the Saint-Bénézet Bridge.

At an isolated stone building far from the center of the village, smoke rose from a makeshift chimney set into the far wall. Willa watched as Youssef dismounted and knocked on the door. Someone on the other side cracked it ajar.

"What do you want?" said a gruff voice.

"Olivier, is that you, you odd duck?" Youssef replied.

"Who are you calling a duck?"

"Olivier, it's me, Youssef. Remember?"

The door swung wide, and a small man waddled out on bowed legs. A straggly beard streaked with gray sprouted haphazardly from his face, and on his head he wore a frayed chaperon that flopped over one ear. The left half of his face was disfigured from a horrible burn.

Olivier squinted at Youssef, then nodded without changing expression. "It *is* you. What are you doing back here? I thought you were gone forever."

"It is a long story, and we are in trouble. We need your help."

"We?" For the first time, Olivier noticed Willa. "Who is she?"

"As I said, long story. May we tell it to you inside?"

He grimaced at both of them, then nodded at the open door and went back in.

Willa dismounted and helped Youssef tie the horses' reins to a ring on the wall.

"Are you sure he's going to aid us?" she asked.

"He may not have a gracious demeanor, but Olivier is a generous man. And he's no friend of authority."

They went inside, and Youssef closed the door behind them. Willa nearly gagged from the overpowering smell of burning wood, sour grain, and something else that seemed familiar, but she couldn't place it. When her eyes adjusted to the darkened interior, she recalled where she'd encountered the odor before.

Under the large chimney was an elaborate collection of iron pots and vessels connected by tubes and pipes. Ceramic containers held barley mash and other ingredients for Olivier's concoction.

"Remember at Mont-Saint-Michel when I told you I learned how to make spirits from a friend in Avignon?" Youssef said to her. "Olivier is the master brewer who taught me."

Olivier grunted as he tended to his equipment. "And what does my apprentice do but leave just as he was getting good at his craft."

The expansive interior was filled with small kegs on one side of the room and a fully loaded wagon on the other side. A mule stood beside it busily munching on hay. A wide door was set into the opposite end.

Youssef pointed at the door. "This was intended to be the stable of a palace for one of the cardinals who planned to spend his leisure time on this side of the Rhône, but the cardinal died and his manor was never completed. Olivier added the chimney after he bought it for a very cheap price." He motioned to the stacks of kegs. "It looks like business is going well for you."

Olivier shrugged. "Between the pilgrims who come through and the members of the Church who consume my product in private, I have a never-ending demand for my curative tonic. Although it does not have official approval, a few coins to the toll clerks get my kegs going back and forth to Avignon under a pile of straw without trouble."

"Then it sounds like you will have the knowledge and connections we need."

"So you're here to collect on what I owe you?" Olivier asked. He noticed Willa's quizzical look. "He didn't tell you, my lady?"

"Tell me what?"

Olivier drew his hand across the scar. "This could have been over my whole body if Youssef hadn't rolled me in the dirt when I caught fire. Kept my building from burning up, too."

"It was a near thing, too," Youssef said.

"What has brought you to my place?"

"Willa and I have a friend who has been taken captive at the Papal Palace. His captors will be searching for us, so we need discreet lodging."

"We can sleep here in your workshop," Willa said.

"You'd have to," Olivier said. "My quarters are a small room on the backside of this building."

"You'll let us stay?"

Olivier walked over to the mule and kept talking as he hitched the animal to the wagon. "You saved my life, didn't you? I can accommodate you as long as you want. I'll hear the rest of your story when I get back in the afternoon. Tend the fire. You still know what to do, yes?"

Youssef nodded and opened the big door for Olivier, who lashed the mule and rode out. Youssef and Willa brought their horses inside and closed the door behind them.

"At least we won't get caught now," Youssef said. "But that doesn't change Gerard's situation."

"I'm not leaving him in Molyneux's hands."

"A bold statement, but what can we possibly do against a cardinal and an earl?"

"We have something they want."

Youssef shook his head when he understood what she meant. "The manuscript? Gerard would rather die than let Molyneux get hold of it."

"It's not his choice. It's mine. And I have a thought for how to save Gerard while preventing Molyneux from getting what he wants. Your addition to the *Secretum philosophorum* gave me the idea. We will make an exchange on the bridge. The manuscript for Gerard. All we need is a long length of thin twine."

Youssef looked at her, puzzled for a moment, then his face dawned with recollection at the passage. He nodded as he considered her plan.

"I suppose that could work. We'd have to get a message to the cardinal somehow about what we're proposing."

"I bet your friend knows someone who could deliver it."

"But we don't want to tell them the place and time too early," Youssef said. "Tonbridge would be waiting for us long before we got there."

"Then we send one message with the time, noting that a second message will arrive with the meeting place only a short interval before the rendezvous. The first note will say vespers tomorrow, then the second note will get to them just beforehand instructing them to come to the bridge near the Saint Nicholas Chapel."

"Well done," Youssef said. "There is only one problem I foresee with that plan."

Willa nodded. "Our escape. Once we have Gerard, we will need to ride fast to get away, but Tonbridge and his men will give chase. I doubt we could elude them for long. We need a good head start."

Youssef looked around the interior as they considered the problem. His gaze settled on the fire heating the spirits, and his dour expression slowly transformed into a smile.

"What is it?" Willa asked.

"I have a way to keep Tonbridge and his men from following us."

Molyneux stood at the window of his chambers as he watched the sun go down over the city. Behind him Tonbridge idly tapped his fingers on the table as they waited for his men to return with Lady

Isabel. Molyneux had long since given up hope that she would make an appearance.

"Where is she?" Tonbridge complained.

"Perhaps she was warned away by your attack on the surgeon's home."

"She is too stupid to expect my men to be waiting inside."

"Her escape from your clutches before your wedding belies that statement. Besides, she would have returned to Gerard's side by now if she intended to, don't you think?"

"Then she must be hiding in the city. With the guards on watch at the city gates, she can't get out. We'll find her eventually."

"Hmm," was all Molyneux uttered. He wasn't so sure.

There was a knock at his door.

"Come!"

An attendant entered holding a folded parchment with a seal at the bottom.

"Your Eminence, this was delivered for you at the palace gates."

Molyneux turned from the window. "By whom?"

"A boy. He said it was regarding someone called Gerard Fox."

Tonbridge bolted out of his seat and snatched the letter from his hand.

"This is Lady Isabel's seal."

Molyneux waved his hand. "Go." The clerk left, and Molyneux looked at Tonbridge. "Well, read it."

Tonbridge unfolded the parchment. His eyes grew dark as he scanned it.

"That disloyal harlot—" he muttered.

"Aloud!" Molyneux yelled.

Tonbridge cleared his throat. "To Cardinal Molyneux and Lord Tonbridge, from Isabel, Lady of Kentworth. I know you have captured Gerard Fox. I offer an exchange. You give me Gerard, I give you the manuscript. Tomorrow before Vespers, I will have another letter delivered to you. You will then have until sundown to arrive at the place I indicate. If you do not appear, I will destroy the treasure. And no harm should come to the Jewish surgeon and his wife who helped us. If they are hurt, I will know."

Tonbridge handed the parchment to Molyneux in disgust. "Now what do we do?"

Molyneux read the note again and sighed. "What do you suppose we do? We get every man we have and meet her at the designated place with Gerard Fox in hand. She may dictate the terms now, but once I have the Icon you will have free rein to dispose of them both."

 73

Although she had created a pocket of air over her face, Willa still felt like she was suffocating under the pile of straw. Little of the day's waning light filtered through the stalks, and she could barely make out Youssef's face next to her. Their feet touched one of the four kegs of spirits loaded onto the wagon. The satchel holding the manuscript was cradled in her arms. The wheels creaked on the dirt road as the mule pulled it through the town toward the Saint-Bénézet Bridge, and the three horses of Willa, Youssef, and Fox clopped behind them.

Willa thought their plan was sound, but she was worried that Molyneux hadn't received their instructions. They didn't leave any way for him to contact them in return, lest he follow the messenger back to them.

"Are you sure Olivier's friend will deliver our note in time?" she asked Youssef.

"Olivier said he is reliable," Youssef replied.

"What should we do if they don't come?"

"Then we ride back to Villeneuve-lès-Avignon and think of a new plan."

"Be quiet, will you?" Olivier scolded from his seat on the driver's bench. "This will end before it begins if the guards know you're under there. We're nearing the bridge's tower gate."

A short time later, the wagon came to a stop.

"You're a little late for your crossing today, aren't you, Olivier?" the toll collector said.

"I make my deliveries when they're needed," Olivier said.

"And the horses? Where did they come from?"

"A cardinal whom I am not allowed to name wanted them

brought back from his villa. I expect this will cover their transport across to the city."

Coins clinked as they were passed to the toll collector. According to Olivier, the bribe would be shared with the two guards who were watching.

"That will do nicely," he said. "I hope you have more business like this in the future. Continue."

The wagon started up again, and soon the wheels were rolling over the bridge's smooth stones.

Several times Olivier warned them to stay silent as they passed a few pedestrians going in the opposite direction, but the traffic was sparse this late in the afternoon. It wouldn't be long before sundown.

Finally, the sound changed as the wagon rolled onto the wooden part of the bridge. It stopped, and Olivier said, "There is no one near us. You can get out."

Willa and Youssef sat up, pulling the straw from their hair. Youssef got out first, shaking the rest of the stalks from his clothes. Then he helped Willa out, brushing the dust from her gown.

"Pardon me, my lady."

"Not at all," Willa said. "Thank you."

They were standing on the wooden section in the middle of the bridge. She looked both directions and saw only a few stragglers at each end four hundred yards away. The guards were mere pinpricks from this distance and would have no idea what they were seeing near the wagon even if they could distinguish Willa and Youssef in the shadow cast by the giant construction crane that sat idle beside them.

Olivier unhooked the mule from his harness and led him by the reins back the way they'd come. He stopped to grip Youssef's hand.

"Although this is likely the last I will see of you," Olivier said, "I hope this is not the last day for you, my friend."

"I appreciate all you've done," Youssef said. "I hope we left you with enough to buy a fine new wagon." Another use for the king's gold.

"More than enough to cover that and the spirits." Olivier moved on and bowed his head to Willa. "My lady, may God be with you on your journey."

"He will be, in part because of you."

Olivier nodded and kept walking. When he arrived at the Tour Philippe-le-Bel, he would tell them that the wagon had a broken wheel and that guards at the Avignon end would have men sent from the palace to recover the horses. He would be back at first light with a wheelwright to repair his wagon.

While Willa unhitched the horses, Youssef climbed back into the wagon and pulled the stoppers on two of the kegs. The spirits began to flow out, soaking the straw.

He hopped out carrying an unlit torch whose tip was now wet from the spirits. Careful to keep it away from the wagon tinderbox, Youssef used a piece of flint to set it aflame. Then he stuck it in a pile of chiseled blocks next to the wagon so that it would keep burning.

Storm clouds to the north were approaching fast, and the river was already swollen from the rain upstream. They got on their horses, with Willa still holding her satchel and Youssef grasping Zephyr's reins.

"Are you ready?" he asked.

She nodded. "Let's get Gerard."

Fox once again trailed Tonbridge's horse on foot as they approached the city gate onto the Saint-Bénézet Bridge, his hands bound by rope and tied to the saddle. At least the two days' rest since being captured had given back some of his strength, though his meals had consisted of little more than runny gruel. Thankfully, his fever had not returned. Molyneux rode next to the earl and a dozen men-at-arms, both English and French, followed behind armed with swords and loaded crossbows.

Nobody had told Fox why he was making this walk through

Avignon. He assumed the journey was for one of two reasons. Either it had something to do with the search for Willa and Youssef or they were leading him to his execution. Neither required comment from him, and he certainly wasn't going to volunteer any information or give them any indication that he feared death. If this was his time, he believed God's judgment would be fair. Although he'd been embittered by his excommunication from the Church, it now no longer held the power over him that it once did. The faith Willa had shown in her quest had restored his own. At the very least, Fox would die knowing that Cardinal Molyneux had been denied what he valued most.

As they passed the tollman, the riders went two-by-two onto the bridge. A hundred yards in the distance, not far past the Saint Nicholas Chapel, Fox saw three horses standing still. He squinted and recognized Zephyr's coloring. His heart started racing when he realized why Molyneux and Tonbridge had brought him here.

Youssef stood beside the horses, which had been turned to face the other direction. Willa was thirty paces in front of him, standing beside the stone parapet on the edge of the bridge. He saw her fiddling with something and then her hand came to rest on the manuscript, which was balanced on the parapet with the sunset glinting off its gilded cover. He had no idea what Willa and Youssef were doing, but they were playing a dangerous game.

Molyneux looked at Tonbridge, and they exchanged smiles. When they were within thirty yards, Willa shouted, "Stop!"

When Tonbridge was slow to halt his horse, Willa nudged the manuscript closer to the edge.

"Stop, you fool!" Molyneux hissed at Tonbridge. "If she throws it into the river, it would be ruined even if we could find it."

Tonbridge pulled on his reins and came to a stop, tossing a look of disgust at Molyneux. He turned back and said in a taunting voice, "Lady Isabel, my lovely betrothed, why don't you come here and…"

He ceased speaking as if suddenly strangled and leaned forward in his saddle. Even in the fading light, Fox could see his face turn crimson with rage.

"Why, you infamous witch!" Tonbridge yelled.

Molyneux regarded Tonbridge with confusion. "What's wrong?"

"That's not Isabel," Tonbridge said, pointing at her. "It's her maid, Willa."

"Her maid? But you said your men killed her maid and her coachman."

Tonbridge's eyes widened with the emerging realization. "Both of them are blonde. My man-at-arms must have thought they had killed Willa instead of Isabel."

"*You* killed her, just as if you'd done it with your own hands," Willa said. "She was far too kind and good for the likes of you."

"Enough!" Molyneux shouted. "I don't care who she is. She has the manuscript, and that's all that matters."

"If you want the manuscript," Willa said, "tell your men to throw their crossbows in the river."

Tonbridge shook with anger. "You don't order us what to do!"

"Yes, she does," Molyneux said. He looked back and nodded. Every man-at-arms threw his crossbow over the side, where they splashed into the water below. "Now bring us the manuscript."

"Send Gerard this way," Willa said.

Tonbridge drew his sword and held the tip to Fox's neck. "Give it to us now, you little strumpet, or I slit his throat!"

"Do that and the manuscript goes into the water. It will sink to the muddy bottom before anyone can get to it."

"Put that sword away!" Molyneux cried out.

Tonbridge momentarily looked as if he'd defy the cardinal, but he followed the command and sheathed the weapon.

"When Gerard reaches me," Willa said, "I will leave the manuscript on the parapet and we will back away together. When we reach the horses, you may have the manuscript. I have your promise we will be free to go?"

"Of course," Molyneux said.

Fox shook his head at her. This was sheer madness. There was no reason to think Molyneux would keep his word. Not only would he get the manuscript, but the three of them would be slaughtered before they could get to the other end of the bridge.

Willa smiled back at Fox and nodded, throwing a quick glance at Youssef, who pulled the *Secretum philosophorum* halfway out of a pouch. They were signaling him that they had a plan.

Tonbridge motioned for Fox to come closer and drew his dagger. Fox smiled up at him as Tonbridge sliced through the rope that bound his wrists.

"Go on, Sir Gerard," Molyneux said. "She has purchased your freedom."

"If she tosses the manuscript over the parapet before she starts to back off," Tonbridge warned, "I will run you both down before you can reach those horses."

Fox said nothing and started walking. He kept a steady pace, not wanting to spook the jumpy Tonbridge from rushing at them and spoiling whatever Willa and Youssef had in mind.

When he got to Willa, she said quietly, "Are you all right?"

"Never better. But I was hoping you were halfway to your destination by now. You should have left me."

She smiled at him. "And have you miss what's about to happen?"

"Can't wait to see."

Willa balanced the manuscript carefully on the parapet, then let go of it but kept one hand on the stone. She took Fox by her other hand and began to back away from the manuscript slowly, edging alongside the parapet.

Molyneux and Tonbridge watched with rapt attention. They were like wolves licking their chops at the sight of a deer.

Out of the corner of his eye, Fox noticed a thin coil of twine unspooling from Willa's palm, which gave him a sense of what she planned to do. In the low light of the coming dusk, he didn't think the string would be visible from a distance, but he nevertheless kept his eyes straight ahead so that he wouldn't draw attention to it.

When they were twenty paces from the manuscript and only ten from the horses, Tonbridge couldn't contain himself any longer. Despite Molyneux's protestations, Tonbridge drew his sword, pointed it at Fox and Willa, and cried, "Charge!"

Willa yanked on the twine, pulling it taut. Molyneux screamed, "No!" as the manuscript tumbled over the side into the Rhône.

 74

As he raced forward and saw the manuscript disappear from view, Tonbridge couldn't believe he'd been outsmarted by a simple maid. He would make her pay for her insolence and treachery.

By the time he reached the point where he could have snatched the manuscript into his hands had it not fallen, Fox, Willa, and their friend were already on their horses and galloping along the bridge. They were only a few dozen yards ahead. It wouldn't take long to catch them. All but two of the men-at-arms had joined him and left Cardinal Molyneux behind.

The slick stones caused the shoes on his horse to slide as he reached the section where the bridge began to curve over the islets below. He had to decrease his speed to keep from pitching over the parapet like the manuscript had, which made the men behind him slow to a trot as well. Still, once they were off the bridge, it would be easy to run down his quarry.

Ahead of them, he noticed the dark-skinned man who was bringing up the rear slow down as the three fugitives approached the wooden construction zone where a wagon was blocking most of the width, leaving only a narrow path for them to squeeze through. Perhaps Tonbridge would be able to catch them on the bridge after all.

His confidence vanished when he saw the dark-skinned man pluck a burning torch from a pile of chiseled blocks. As he rode past the wagon, he tossed it into a heap of straw. By the time he was onto the stones again, the wagon had erupted into an inferno, the flames reaching as tall as the crane next to it.

Tonbridge pulled up his horse as the blaze seared his skin even this far away. He turned to the men behind him.

"Push that wagon off the bridge!"

The men looked at each other but didn't budge.

Tonbridge pointed his sword at them. "Your earl commands you!"

They lashed their horses forward, but the animals reared back when they got within ten yards. The men dismounted and tentatively moved forward.

Before they could get any closer, the wagon exploded in a fireball, sending the men diving to the ground. Pieces of wood went flying in all directions, and the force of the blast split several of the crane's support beams. The heavy crane groaned as it toppled over, plunging through the wooden section of the bridge. The entire segment collapsed into the river below, leaving only a few flaming remnants standing on either side of the forty-foot gap.

Willa turned to look, and when she saw Tonbridge flailing impotently on the other side of the gap, she gave a breezy wave. All he could do was watch as the trio reached the opposite end of the bridge and trotted out of sight through the Tour Philippe-le-Bel. By the time Tonbridge could backtrack to Avignon and figure out a way to ferry himself and his men across, Willa, Fox, and their accomplice would be long gone.

Molyneux was less concerned about the fire that raged in the distance than he was about the manuscript.

He rode with his men to where it had disappeared and dismounted. He leaned over the side and saw what the maid had done. A nail was hammered into the mortar between the stones in the parapet. The string she had been holding must have been hooked around it to pull the manuscript over the edge.

Molyneux didn't think there would be much point to searching for the manuscript now. The heavy gold and jewel-encrusted cover would surely pull it down to the bottom of the river. Even if it floated, the water would ruin the painted image of Mary and Jesus.

But he was astonished and crossed himself in thanks to God when he saw a miracle below him. He was able to see it only because he was looking straight down over the parapet. The boat holding the bodies of the Pestilence victims that had been stuck in the middle of the river had come loose from the island because of the flood waters. A rope stuck on something under the surface had caused it to come to a stop directly below the bridge.

In the dim light, Molyneux could spot the glint of gold where the manuscript lay on the deck between two of the corpses.

He turned to his men. "Find a boat right now and row out into the river to retrieve the manuscript."

The two men peered over the side of the bridge. Both of them went ashen at what they saw. Neither of them looked willing to venture onto the boat of lost souls.

To the north, Molyneux could see a sheet of rain approaching. It wouldn't be long before the downpour reached them.

"Fifty *livres* to each of you if you bring it to me," Molyneux said. "The noose for you both if you don't. Hurry!"

The men gulped and nodded. They jumped on their horses and galloped back to the gates of Avignon to find a boat. It was then that Tonbridge returned.

"They got away," he said. "And the manuscript is lost."

"Don't be so sure," Molyneux said, pointing over the side of the bridge.

Tonbridge leaped from his horse and leaned over the parapet. When he looked up, the joy on his face was evident.

"So Willa's devious plan was for naught," he said.

Molyneux nodded. "God has smiled on us. I will be the pope and you will be a king."

"How do we get it?"

"I have sent men to find a boat and bring the manuscript back to shore. When they do, kill them and throw them in the river. I don't want them near me after they've been so close to the Pestilence." Molyneux gestured at the coming tempest. "Now I'm returning to the palace before I get soaking wet and catch my death of cold."

 75

Warmed by the large fire in his chamber's hearth, Molyneux sipped wine from the Crusader's Chalice to celebrate his victory while he waited for Tonbridge to return with the manuscript. Rain lashed against the shutters, making him very glad he'd returned before the worst of the storm. With every taste of the exquisite vintage, he plotted how he would unveil the Icon of the Virgin. It had to be a gala ceremony, one where there would be no doubt about who was responsible for revealing the true Hodegetria to the world.

He thought about revealing it in Avignon, but that was far too close to the papacy itself. He would take it back to Paris for the Feast of the Nativity of Mary, displaying it in Notre Dame, where pilgrims from all over Christendom would make the journey to the greatest cathedral devoted to the Virgin to see what Molyneux had delivered to them. The Icon would cement his power in the north of France and bring enough cardinals to his side to secure the vote at the next papal conclave. Given the pope's recent condition, he didn't think he would have long to wait.

There was a stiff rapping on the door.

"Come."

Tonbridge entered dripping wet, his hair matted to his skull. He laid a leather satchel on the table and strode over to the hearth, removing his soaked outer garments and gloves before warming his hands in the fire.

"The manuscript is in there," Tonbridge said. "I ran your guards through the moment they put in to shore. They're now floating down the Rhône with that cursed boat."

Molyneux got up and went to the table. He pointed to the jug of wine next to the chalice on the sideboard. There was a more mundane cup beside it.

"You may help yourself. It'll ward off the chill."

As Tonbridge poured his drink, Molyneux carefully put his hand on the satchel. He could almost feel the holy power from what lay within.

He pulled the flap open and reached inside. But instead of the hard gold of the cover, he felt a wet cloth. He removed the object from the bag and saw that it was a woolen blanket.

When he looked at it in confusion, Tonbridge said, "Your men wrapped it in that when they removed it from the Pestilence boat. It started raining hard just as they reached the boat, and they didn't want the manuscript to get wet."

Molyneux's sense of triumph evaporated at that news. He yanked the blanket off, concerned that the Icon might have been damaged by the pouring rain.

Thankfully, the bejeweled cover was intact, and the edges of parchment seemed only slightly damp. He unbuckled the clasps and opened it to the first page. The parchment was bone-dry, the ink of the text and the surface of the illumination undamaged. The cardinal heaved a sigh of relief.

With trembling fingers, he began to turn the pages, slowly at first to savor the moment when he reached the Icon. However, his impatience soon became too much, and he flipped through the leaves with increasing speed.

When he got to the final page, he was dumbfounded. The Icon wasn't there, and neither was the letter from Eudocia proving its authenticity. Did he miss them?

He went back to the beginning and turned the pages again, inspecting each one with care. It wasn't until he reached the beginning of the Book of Luke that he noticed something he'd overlooked the first time.

One of the pages had been cut out, the parchment stub just visible near the center of the binding. He checked through the rest of the book and found another place at the end where a leaf had been removed.

"No," he whispered. His voice grew more furious as he realized Willa's deception. "No. No! NO!"

Tonbridge looked at him with alarm. "What's the matter? Isn't that the manuscript? I recognized it when she held it up on the bridge."

"It's the manuscript, all right," Molyneux said, slamming the book closed. "But it's useless. The simple maid of your dead betrothed tricked us. She cut out the Hodegetria." He threw the infernal book at Tonbridge. It bounced against the wall and landed at his feet, its cover dented.

Tonbridge picked it up and paged through it. "It can't be. Are you sure?"

"Do you think I'm daft?"

Tonbridge stared at the spot where it had been removed in disbelief. "What has she done?"

"Isn't it obvious?" Molyneux said, exasperated by Tonbridge's stupidity. "She wanted us to think the Icon had been destroyed in the river when she dropped the manuscript into the water as they fled. If we thought it was gone, we would have no further need to pursue them. It's a different version of the same trick they tried before."

"But she didn't know the boat would catch the manuscript."

"And now *we* know she still has the Icon. We still have a chance to recover it."

"How?" Tonbridge asked. "She won't go back to Lady Claire."

"That leaves only Lady Isabel's sister—the nun."

"But we don't know where she's been sent."

"We will soon. If my men don't find a record of it in our archives here, we will return to Paris and make Lady Claire tell us. Fox and Willa must have gotten Sister Catherine's location from her."

"That Jewish surgeon might know," Tonbridge said. "I can return there and question him."

"Don't be a fool. They wouldn't divulge something like that to the surgeon, and I don't want you causing any more trouble in the Jewish quarter."

"I am only a fool, Your Eminence, if I stand around doing

nothing." Tonbridge dropped the manuscript onto the sideboard next to the jug of wine and stomped to the door. "I will not wait in Avignon long. If we don't have an answer in three days, I insist that we return to Paris and force Lady Claire to confess her sins."

Molyneux nodded. "You will have my blessing."

Tonbridge exited and slammed the door behind him.

Tomorrow Molyneux would add every available clerk in the palace to the search of the archives. He wasn't giving up the pursuit of the Icon, not while he still breathed.

He took the disgusting blanket from the table over to the hearth and tossed it into the flames. Steam and smoke hissed as it burned.

Molyneux flinched from a sudden bite on his forearm. He looked down to see a flea on his skin. It must have come from the blanket that those guards used to wrap the manuscript.

He pinched the pest between his fingers and squeezed before flicking it into the fire.

## 76

Fox, Willa, and Youssef found an abandoned hut south of Avignon in which to dry out and spend the night, the Icon and letter from Eudocia tucked safely into a flat leather scrip beneath Willa's heavy traveling cloak. Willa had explained to Fox the heart-wrenching choice to separate the Icon from the manuscript during their ride away from the city. Because of her deception, Molyneux no longer had a reason to support and protect Tonbridge in his pursuit now that the manuscript was destroyed, but Fox was eager to get going the next morning anyway. The farther from the papal seat they got, the better he would feel.

After they prepared their horses for the day's ride toward the Mediterranean coast, Youssef cleared his throat and gave them a half-hearted smile.

"I'm glad you are safe, my friends. And now that you are, it is time for me to leave you."

Fox frowned at him. "What do you mean?"

"You're not coming with us the rest of the way?" Willa said.

Youssef shook his head. "My purpose at your side has come to an end. I have a new task. I must return Henri's family seal and silver cross to his brother and mother and inform them of his death."

"Where do they live?"

"In Carcassonne. It's in the opposite direction from your destination. Last night we passed a road leading west, and that's where I'm headed. I wish I could accompany you, but I feel that I owe it to Henri to tell his family his heroic and tragic tale. Don't worry, you will both feature prominently in the story of how he was avenged."

"I'm not sure they will believe such an improbable tale," Fox said. "But tell them of our grief."

Youssef smiled at him. "With my skill at spinning a yarn, you will both become legends."

"Then what will you do?" Willa asked.

"I don't know exactly. Perhaps I'll become a wandering trader. Settling down in one place doesn't seem to suit me."

"I will miss you, old friend," Fox said.

"We were brought together for a reunion once," Youssef said. "Maybe my trading will take me to England and I will see you when you return."

"I hope we meet again, but I have no home in England to return to," Fox said. He told them that it was unlikely that he would ever regain his ancestral lands.

"I'm sorry for your family's honor," Youssef said. "But there is always need for a man with your skills. You should have no problem finding work."

Fox hadn't thought that far yet. "I appreciate your confidence in me."

"I owe you a debt of gratitude for what you've done," Willa said. "Without you, I would have died several times over, and the Hodegetria would now be in Cardinal Molyneux's possession."

Youssef walked over to her and kissed both of her cheeks. "It has been my pleasure, Lady Willa. You are a true inspiration." He nodded to the scrip that held the sacred relic. "The Icon of the Virgin and Child could not be in safer hands."

"I appreciate you using that title, but you know that I am no lady."

"On the contrary," Youssef said with a gleam in his eye and a courtly bow. "You are more of a lady than any noblewoman I have ever known."

He embraced Fox and said, "I hope *she* continues to keep *you* safe."

Though Fox chuckled at that, he knew how right Youssef was to put it that way. "I won't let her out of my sight. God be with you and speed you on your journey."

"You as well."

Youssef climbed on his horse and rode north. He turned in his saddle to wave and took off at a trot, soon disappearing over a hill.

Fox and Willa got onto Zephyr and Comis. Fox flexed his left hand. The salve that Mordecai had applied in Avignon was still doing its job healing the wound on his arm, but it would be a long time before he got his full grip strength back.

"It's just the two of us again," he said.

"Married or eunuch?" Willa asked as they headed south.

"What do you think?" Fox replied.

"Eunuch it is, then," she said with a smile. "But this time, before we get on the ship in Marseille, let's make sure we find some ginger for that tender stomach of yours."

 77

After three days of being stuck in the Papal Palace while he waited for news of the archive search, Tonbridge was getting sick of the glances he was getting for being so out of place. Because he was a secular English nobleman, the clerics looked askance at him and his six remaining men.

He chafed at Molyneux's resistance to returning to Paris and squeezing Catherine's current location out of Claire. He considered going by himself, but traveling through the heart of France would be suicidal without the cardinal accompanying him. He hadn't even seen Molyneux since they'd acquired the manuscript. Tomorrow morning he would insist that they depart from Avignon and head for Paris.

Tonbridge was leaving his room for vespers when one of Molyneux's young clerks stopped him in the corridor.

"Lord Tonbridge, I have been sent to bring you to Cardinal Molyneux's chambers immediately."

*At last,* Tonbridge thought. *Catherine's location has been discovered.*

The clerk held out a posy composed of lavender, thyme, and rosemary and thrust it at Tonbridge.

"You will need this," the clerk said.

Tonbridge was suddenly struck by fear. "Why?"

The clerk cleared his throat, as if he didn't want to discuss it. "The cardinal has fallen ill. You will need the herbs to ward off the evil humors he is emitting."

"Then I don't need to see him in person," Tonbridge said, desperate to avoid the cardinal's presence. "Relay the message he has given you."

The clerk shook his head. "I have no message. I was merely sent to retrieve you."

Tonbridge swallowed his dread and snatched the posy out of his hand. "I know the way."

He marched to Molyneux's chambers. Outside in the corridor, a group of priests and monks were chanting softly, their faces etched with fear. The door was ajar, and soft murmurs came from inside. Tonbridge knocked, and a weak voice said, "Come."

Tonbridge held the posy in front of his face and tentatively pushed the door open. The murmurs ceased as Tonbridge entered.

At the opposite end of the room, a priest holding his own posy stood far back from a man beside the bed who was placing a corked jar with a dirty-looking liquid back into a box. He closed it and tucked it under his arm.

"I will return when they have had their fill of blood," the man said to the priest. He scuttled out without glancing at Tonbridge.

The priest walked toward Tonbridge, who instinctively took a step back.

"I'm glad you came quickly," the priest said in a low voice. "The cardinal fell ill last night. It has only gotten worse throughout the day. I do not think he will live to see another sunrise. The Pestilence has reared its ugly face again."

Tonbridge blanched at the name of the disease that had wiped out his family and decimated his estates. It was only by a miracle that he had survived when it tore through England. Simply being in the same room as a victim of the Pestilence was terrifying, and he forced himself not to run screaming.

"Why does he want to see me?"

"I don't know. All he would say is that he had information to share with you. I will leave you alone."

Tonbridge watched him leave and flinched at the sound of the door closing behind him.

"Tonbridge, is that you?" Molyneux said in a hoarse croak.

The earl slowly turned, careful to keep the posy in front of his face. Through the stems, he could make out the cardinal's bedridden form in the flickering light behind a gauzy curtain.

"I am here, Your Eminence. Do you have news for me?"

"Closer. I can't see you."

Tonbridge briefly wondered whether the information was worth the risk, but he couldn't give up now. He gulped and edged forward until the curtains were no longer blocking his view. He came to an abrupt stop, repulsed by the vision before him.

Molyneux lay on his back, his face a mask of pain. The linen sheet was soaked with perspiration, as was his brow. His nose and fingers were blackened, and hideous swollen nodules protruded from his neck. The smell of vomit and waste penetrated the fragrance of the posy. A dozen black leeches glistened as they suckled from his arms. The man with the jar must have been the physicker, who would return when the creatures were filled with blood.

"The physicker tells me I will be better soon, once the leeches have done their work," Molyneux said in a halting cadence.

For a moment, Tonbridge could only stare in disbelief at the man's fantasy of regained health. He knew enough of the Pestilence to know that once the blackened spots appeared, there was no chance for recovery. He finally said, "God be praised."

"We have good news. I was informed this evening that my clerks' search has borne fruit. The archives have yielded what we have been looking for."

Tonbridge's heart pounded at the revelation.

"Where is she? Tell me where Sister Catherine is so that I can hunt Willa down and take back what she has stolen."

The cardinal raised his hand as if he were holding something. "She is at a monastery in Piedmont, high on a mountain. I have been there once before, long ago when I was a lowly priest myself. If you hurry and take the shortest route across the Alps, you may yet beat them there."

"But where exactly? There must be many mountaintop abbeys in that region."

Molyneux ignored the request for a more specific location. "And then you'll bring the Icon back to me. My priest outside has a writ of safe passage with my personal seal so that you may journey safely throughout France."

He really was getting delirious, Tonbridge thought. "Bring it back to you?"

"Yes, once I have recovered."

Tonbridge couldn't believe his ears. Molyneux must have known there was no recovery once the Pestilence had progressed this far.

"But Your Eminence, surely you understand that is unlikely."

Molyneux coughed in a spastic jolt that racked his body. "Unlikely?"

"You are stricken with worst form of the Pestilence. I've never…"

It suddenly occurred to Tonbridge that if Molyneux died, so would their arrangement to crown the earl as a king.

"What other cardinals would want the Icon?" he asked. "Who would honor the bargain we've struck?"

Molyneux shook his head. "No one but me. They know nothing of ambition and sacrifice."

"Then what am I to do with the Hodegetria?"

"We have a bargain. You will give it to me, and I will make you a king."

Tonbridge had had enough of Molyneux's delusions. "You will be dead long before I return, if not by the end of this night."

Molyneux struggled to sit up. "I am going to be pope, blast you!" Molyneux exploded into another coughing fit, doubling over with his head nearly between his knees.

"Look at you," Tonbridge said. "You will never be pope!"

The cardinal looked up at him with rheumy eyes. "Are you backing out of our bargain, Tonbridge?"

"A bargain with a dead man? What good are you to me now? I already have wealth. You promised me something I cannot otherwise acquire myself. I was going to be King of Jerusalem. My son would be born a prince. The Icon is worthless to me if it can't deliver that."

"No! The Icon is fated to be mine!"

"The Icon is no longer your concern. I will track Willa to the ends of the earth. Then I will burn the Hodegetria in front of her.

All she cares about is protecting the Icon, and I will make sure she understands how utterly she has failed in that task before my men and I slaughter her and Gerard Fox. Now tell me where they are, you fool!"

"How dare you speak to a cardinal like that!"

"Where!"

Tonbridge was shocked to see Molyneux swing his feet over the side of the bed and struggle to stand. He finally was able to get all the way upright.

"Even if you now swore to bring the Icon back to me, I would never tell you where she is."

The effort to get out of bed must have completely drained the cardinal, for he suddenly went limp and crumpled to the floor.

Tonbridge stared down at him, but he didn't rush to Molyneux's aid. "How can you not see it? Face your fate. You're dying."

Molyneux, who lay on his side in a most undignified position, shook his head in disbelief. Drool dripped from the side of his mouth as he spoke.

"This isn't right. It is surely just a test of my will. To be the pope is my destiny."

"Tell me where Fox and Willa are. At least we can both exact our vengeance upon them."

"It's not enough," Molyneux whimpered. "I want what is due to me."

"It will have to do. All I need is their location, and I will make them pay for how they've wronged us."

"Why!" Molyneux cried out as he raised his head and seemed to gather his strength for one last paroxysm of fury. "Why have you forsaken me, Lord? Damn you! Damn everything to Hell!" Then he slumped to the floor, his energy spent.

Tonbridge gasped at his blasphemous wail. Even in this moment, an eminent cardinal cursing God shook him to his marrow.

Molyneux seemed to have a sudden awful vision. His voice came out in a whisper. "He is coming."

The cardinal's hand fell open and a creased piece of parchment dropped onto the floor. Tonbridge raced forward to scoop it up and quickly retreated. While keeping the posy in place, he thumbed the parchment apart until he could read the two lines of scrawled lettering.

*Prioress Catherine from Saint-Quentin.*
*Assigned as abbess of La Sacra di San Michele. Piedmont near Turin.*

Despite the circumstances, Tonbridge found himself inadvertently smiling. Fox and Willa were as good as dead.

A rasping sound erased his smile and brought his attention back to Molyneux, who suddenly turned onto his back and went into an even more violent bout of coughing, spittle and blood spraying the air above him. Tonbridge stepped back in fear as the cardinal went into convulsions, as if his body were possessed by a demon. Then he became rigid, his eyes focused in terror on something Tonbridge couldn't see. Molyneux let out a ragged breath and went still. His final expression was a haunting stare into the abyss.

Tonbridge stumbled backward, shaking as he fled the room in horror.

# LA SACRA DI SAN MICHELE

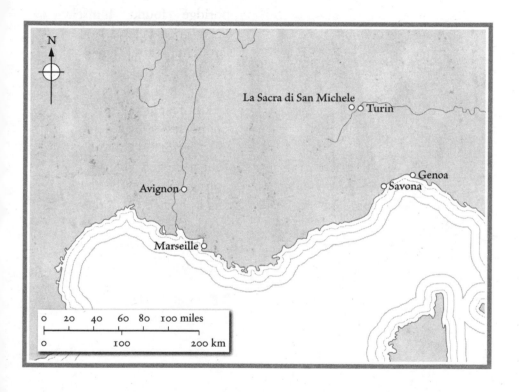

## 78

PIEDMONT

Upon arriving in Marseilles, Fox and Willa had to wait two days before they could board a ship bound for Savona. Willa was pleased that she found some ginger in that time, but Fox still felt mildly queasy for much of the sail. He seemed quite happy to get off the ship when they arrived.

At the port, they came upon a group of tradesmen traveling to Turin, the city closest to La Sacra di San Michele. They all decided that safety in numbers was mutually beneficial, especially now that Fox's wounds had finished healing during the journey at sea. The traders liked the idea of having a skilled knight to protect them.

Three days later, Fox and Willa parted ways with them, and they were now riding up a misty trail through the forest that they were assured was the way to La Sacra di San Michele. They'd seen it briefly from below, clinging to a wooded peak commanding the entire valley. For a moment it looked like the fortress of Paradise itself before it was lost again in the clouds.

Willa felt a mix of anxiety and thrill as they neared their final destination. This was the last chance to find safety for the Icon, and she clung to her faith that their odyssey had been worth it.

"It must be an omen," Willa said as Comis chuffed from the strenuous climb.

"What is?" Fox asked.

"That Saint Michael is looking out for us. First at Mont-Saint-Michel, now here at La Sacra di San Michele."

"We haven't arrived yet."

"We've been ascending for a long time already. We must be nearly there."

"I'll be more at ease when you lay eyes on Sister Catherine. You *will* recognize her, won't you?"

"I think so. It's been many years, but she can't have changed so much, can she? I just worry that she won't remember me. I was a child when she left."

"I sincerely doubt that outcome," Fox said. "You're quite memorable."

"I will take that as a compliment. But I am more worried that she isn't at the abbey."

"I thought *I* was the doubting Thomas."

Willa sighed. "I suppose you're right. She has to be there."

As if the skies answered her, the mists parted. Willa was awed by the sight of the monastery that suddenly appeared through a gap in the trees.

The gray stone edifice of La Sacra di San Michele was built over, around, and among the craggy rocks atop the mountain. It was constructed in multiple tiers. The bottom level formed the base of the structure, and within the enclosing walls there were several smaller buildings.

The next tier was a slab-sided face dotted with windows and capped with a tile roof. Based on her experience with Mont-Saint-Michel, Willa assumed those were the dormitories and other rooms making up the residence for those who had devoted themselves to the religious life.

Topping the whole assembly was the church itself, made of green stone and red brick. A semicircle of delicate arches adorned the front of the church, which faced the valley.

Given their long ride up the mountain, Willa couldn't imagine the effort it took to haul all of those building materials to this great height.

"You were right," Fox said. "We have arrived."

Now it was Willa's stomach that was queasy.

"What if Sister Catherine doesn't believe our story?" she said. "What if she rejects me from the moment she sees me? After all,

I've come to tell her that Lady Isabel is dead, and the manuscript I swore to protect is gone."

"I promise she will be grateful for all you've done, just as Lady Claire was."

Willa didn't know if he was right, but the time for second-guessing was gone.

They passed a time-worn octagonal church at the base of the hill leading to the monastery.

"I can see the stable," Fox said. He pointed to a wooden building below the entrance to the monastery, whose stairs were too steep for horses.

Once inside the stable, they found a boy who helped find a place for Zephyr and Comis. Two carthorses were the only other occupants.

Without a place to store their belongings, Fox carried his scrip, the pouch with his book, and his weapons, while Willa's possessions had been reduced to a small bag for her few remaining clothes and the flat leather scrip containing the Icon. They crossed a small drawbridge, and Willa took a deep breath as Fox knocked on the heavy door coated with iron plate to protect the monastery from intruders.

From his hiding place in the forest overlooking the path, Tonbridge watched Willa and Fox approach the monastery entrance. He'd been there for two long days already devising his plan to take back what was his, and the wait had finally paid off.

Molyneux had been right that the trek through the Alps was the most direct, but Tonbridge had lost one of his men along the way when his horse took a bad step on a narrow mountain pass and fell down a cliff. That left him with only five men to attack Fox, who Tonbridge knew all too well was highly skilled as a mounted archer.

He would have preferred that his soldiers kill Fox with

crossbows from hiding spots in the forest, but his men had been forced to toss theirs into the Rhône by Willa. As an English earl deep in French territory and no longer protected by Molyneux except for the writ of safe conduct, he couldn't possibly acquire such weapons of war. His best option now was to take Fox when his guard was down and he was without his weapons, after he was inside the abbey.

When he'd first arrived, Tonbridge had gone up himself, dressed as a pilgrim and without his horse, to scout the location. He'd searched the stable for Fox's distinctive horse and didn't find it, but he'd familiarized himself with the layout of the sprawling monastery so that he and his men would be ready once their prey was defenseless. When Tonbridge returned, he and his men had set up camp deep in the woods to wait and watch, lighting a fire only at night so that their smoke wouldn't be spotted.

If they rode up to the monastery on horses, armed and in full battle dress, not only would Fox be alerted to their arrival, but they also wouldn't get past the barricaded iron door. Tonbridge didn't have the time or resources to lay siege to the fortress-like abbey.

Once he saw Fox and Willa at the monastery door, Tonbridge said, "This is the time, men. Prepare yourselves." The six of them took off their bulky, noisy mail and changed their attire so that they looked like poor pilgrims who'd made the long journey on foot. They hid their swords under the tattered cloaks wrapped around their bodies. The monk at the entrance would not see the weapons until he opened the door.

When Tonbridge was convinced that they could pass as commoners who had come to pay their respects to Saint Michael, he led them out onto the path and up toward the monastery.

If he had timed this right, there would be no battle. It would be an execution.

 79

The iron-bound door blocking the entrance to the monastery was mounted in a small tower that served as the sole gate. Fox had to knock several times before he heard someone shuffling inside. A piece of metal slid aside to reveal a square door viewer. A man with the tonsure and hooded robes of a monk rubbed his eyes as if he'd just woken from a nap.

"*Salve filiorum Dei,*" he said.

In Latin, Fox said, "I am Sir Gerard of Oakhurst and this is Lady Willa of Kentworth."

When the monk heard that they were English nobles, he raised an eyebrow. "*Parlez-vous français?*"

Fox nodded and switched to French, the language of the court. "We are here to call on Abbess Catherine on a matter of great importance. Is she here?"

"Of course, she is here. Where else would she be?"

Fox shared a glance of relief with Willa.

"Then may we see her?"

The monk inspected both of them carefully. Willa was dressed in a beautiful kirtle and surcoat given to her by Claire, and Fox's tunic and sword indicated he was a man of means.

The monk nodded at Fox's sword and bow. "No weapons allowed in the monastery. You will have to leave those here. Your dagger, too. You'll get them back when you depart, of course. They will be safer with me than in the stable."

A bar clanged, and the door swung open. The stooped monk who greeted them looked as if he'd been at the monastery for decades.

"I am Brother Alfano." He waved them in and closed the door

behind them. Alfano took Fox into a small warming room with a stool where the monk had likely been napping and indicated a large lockbox where Fox was to place his weapons. Under the watchful eye of the porter, he divested himself of Legend, the unstrung recurved bow, the arrow bag, which also held the bowstring, and finally his dagger.

The monk closed the box and locked it with the key hanging from his neck. When he replaced it, Alfano beckoned. "Come this way."

They exited the gate tower, and he led them up a set of steep switchback stairs that ended beside the corner of the monastery that loomed over them, seeming to pierce the sky itself. At the bottom of the south-facing, slab-sided residence of the abbey was a small stairway leading inside. Across from it was a crenellated stone building equal in length to the monastery.

"That is the pilgrims' hall," Alfano said. "It's not crowded today. We only have three people staying there." He regarded their dress again. "I imagine you will be staying at the guesthouse."

He turned and pointed at a smaller two-story structure on the east periphery of the abbey. A pathway circumnavigating the main building separated the guesthouse from an outdoor staircase leading up to the front entrance of the monastery. It was so long that it was divided into two sections by a landing and ended on a small terrace in front of the door.

As he walked up the outdoor stairs, Alfano said, "You better get used to climbing steps here."

At the terrace, they paused to take in the expansive view of the valley laid out below them. A river split the plains in two, with fields and orchards on either side. Smoke rose from the tiny buildings of several towns, but they were too far away to make out any people.

"It seems as if we can see to the end of the world from here," Willa said.

"You can spy fires blazing in Turin on a clear night. That's a long day's walk from here."

He ushered them through the front door of the abbey, and they entered a high vaulted space with a steep staircase going up to the right and then back to the left around a massive pillar in the center. Sunlight shone through several large windows.

The design was magnificent. The stairwell was built into the mountain, with areas of exposed rock visible among the building stones. The expanse of steps led up through a vaulted passage four stories tall. Thick stone columns rose high to support the ceiling. One side of the stairway was open to the huge chamber, the other was bordered by a wall with inset arches, ledges, and alcoves.

Apparently Brother Alfano's guided tour was second nature to him because he continued narrating.

"This is called the Stairway of the Dead. If you look into the alcoves carved into the surrounding rock, you can see why."

Fox peered into one of the darkened niches. Willa must have recognized what was in there at the same time he saw the contents because she startled at the sight. It was an entire human skeleton.

"This serves as an ossarium," Alfano said as they continued up past a two-tiered ledge under an arched window at the turn in the stairs. The remaining steep flight of twenty-foot-wide steps led up to the doorway high above them. "But the abbots and high-ranking Benedictine officials are in tombs above." Alfano pointed to a series of alcoves halfway up the stairs that held stone sarcophagi. A construction platform in front of the alcoves stretched from the window to a point halfway up the stairs.

"Please pardon the scaffolding. We are in the midst of doing some much-needed repair work on the tombs."

Alfano was breathing hard by the time they got all the way to the top, which was another small landing beyond the doorway. From this point, there was a final short flight of stairs leading up to a terrace, with the church entrance on the right and the abbey residence on the left. Before they went further, he held up a finger to catch his breath, then he ran his hand along the doorjamb.

"This is the Zodiac Doorway. Notice the intricate carvings of the different signs."

Fox and Willa looked more closely and read the Latin lettering. *Sagittarivs, Scorpivs, Libra*. Next to each name was its symbol carved into the stone. A centaur with a bow, a scorpion, and a scale.

"This is all fascinating, Brother Alfano," Fox said, "but we must speak to Abbess Catherine as soon as possible."

"And who is hoping to see her?" a voice asked from above.

They turned to see a nun in full habit standing on the terrace. Fox recognized the angular jaw and dimpled chin she had in common with the deceased Lady Isabel.

"Ah, Abbess Catherine," Alfano said. "This is Sir Gerard and Lady Willa. They have come to see you with some important business."

Catherine's brows knitted together as she peered at Willa, then her eyes went wide with shock.

"Wilhelmina, is that really you?"

Willa rushed up the short flight of stairs and into Catherine's arms, seeming to forget that the woman was an abbess instead of merely her lady's older sister. Her chest heaved with sobs. Catherine fully returned the embrace.

Alfano shrugged and said to Fox, "I suppose my task is done. I will return to my post." He went through the Zodiac Doorway and started the long trek down the Stairway of the Dead back to the monastery's entrance.

Fox climbed up to the top of the short stairway and stood quietly away from them. At last, they released the embrace and held each other by the hands.

"My dear Wilhelmina," Catherine said, "you're still as lovely as ever, but you've grown so much since I last saw you. Why have you traveled so far from England and why are you presenting yourself as Lady Willa?"

Before Willa could speak, several other nuns emerged from the church and stopped to look at the odd sight of the stranger holding hands with their mother superior.

To avoid Catherine's inevitable questions about Isabel in front of others, Fox interjected. "Perhaps the three of us should speak together in private, Abbess. Willa and I have much to tell you."

## 80

Catherine suggested they go to the welcome room that the monastery used for visiting dignitaries. Willa trembled as they walked, wondering how she would break the news that Isabel had been killed. She glanced at Fox, who nodded encouragement.

As they walked, Catherine explained that the Pestilence had run its course through the monastery, leaving it with only a handful of monks to maintain it. The monastery was then converted to a nunnery in thanks to the services of the selfless nuns who had cared for the sick in the region. Because of her great administrative abilities, Catherine was brought in from the seat of the papacy to run it. Except for Brother Alfano, along with a resident priest-confessor who was in Turin at the moment and a few young lay brothers, the abbey was populated entirely by nuns. She had taken advantage of San Michele's extensive library for the education of the sisters, who spent a good portion of their time reading and copying the ancient texts.

They entered the top floor of the residence across from the church, went down a set of stairs to the third story, and turned into a long corridor that angled out of sight at the other end. On their left were the cloisters, an outdoor courtyard for quiet contemplation that could be seen through the hallway windows. A nun was just entering from it, and Catherine asked her to bring some mulled wine to the welcome room to warm the visitors after their long ride. On the right they passed the lavatorium, the kitchen, the refectory where the nuns ate, and finally they went around the corner and into an elegant room with six chairs and a large oak table in the middle of the room. There was a second door that must have led into the refectory.

Catherine gestured to the chairs. All of them took seats around the table.

Catherine looked at Willa and said, "I can see on your face that you do not come bearing good tidings. Where is Isabel?"

Willa cleared her throat. "I am very sorry to deliver the sad news that she is dead. It happened in England two days before the Feast of the Translation of Saint Thomas."

Catherine's lip quivered. She made the sign of the cross and clasped her hands together as she whispered a prayer.

"May I ask how she passed?"

"Her betrothed, Sir Conrad Harrington, Earl of Tonbridge, had her killed."

It took a moment for Catherine to digest the information. "I didn't even know she was engaged to be married. We had lost touch since the Pestilence and I was reassigned to La Sacra di San Michele. I wrote a letter to her through my cousin Claire only a few months ago."

"I know," Willa said. "Lady Claire shared it with us."

"You saw her?"

"We met her in Paris," Fox said.

"I beg your pardon," Catherine said to him, "but who are you and how are you involved in this? Did you accompany Willa all this way just to tell me the sorrowful news?"

Willa put her leather scrip on the table and opened it. "We came to give you this."

She carefully removed two large pieces of parchment from inside the flat protective case and placed them gently on the table. The image of the Virgin and Child was still as vibrant as the day she'd first seen it, the gold of the halos catching the sunlight coming through the window. The letter from Eudocia beside it still had its wax seal intact.

Catherine rose from her chair and gazed at the glorious illumination.

"It can't be. Where is the manuscript?"

"We had to destroy it," Willa said. "It was the only way to make

Cardinal Molyneux and Lord Tonbridge think the Icon was lost as well."

At the look of confusion and dismay on Catherine's face, Fox and Willa took turns recounting their story. At first, Catherine seemed skeptical, but the further it went, the more she seemed convinced of its truth.

"I have heard rumors about Cardinal Molyneux, of course," she said at one point, "but I am astonished that he would be involved in such a nefarious scheme."

"You would not be if you saw his face that evening I met him in Avignon," Willa said. "I do not know how such evil came to wear the robes of a cardinal."

The nun entered bearing a tray of pewter wine goblets, bread, and cheese. She set them on the table, glancing curiously at Fox and Willa.

"Mother Abbess," she said, "I am about to go down and prepare bedding in the hall for the new pilgrims who are arriving. While I am there, shall I ready the small guesthouse for your visitors?"

"Thank you, Sister Maria," Catherine replied. "Yes, two separate rooms, I imagine?"

Willa blushed and nodded.

Maria was about to leave when Fox said, "Did you say pilgrims are about to arrive?"

Maria nodded. "I saw them from the upper terrace. They were walking up the road a little while ago. They should be coming in at any moment."

"How many are there?"

Maria was bewildered by the odd question. "I counted six men."

Fox stood and went to the window, but the clouded glass was merely translucent enough to let light in. "I can't see down there." He turned back and walked straight to Maria. "You say they were on foot, not on horseback?"

"Yes. Horses are beyond the means of the poor pilgrims who come to pray here."

"Thank you, Maria," Catherine said. "That will be all."

Maria gave a last puzzled glance at Fox and exited.

He looked at Catherine. "Can I continue down the stairs inside the residence to get outside instead of going all the way back up and around to the Stairway of the Dead?"

Catherine nodded. "Yes, they let out on the south side of the residence just across from the pilgrims' hall."

Willa stood, alarmed by the intensity of Fox's eyes.

"Gerard, what's wrong?"

"It may be nothing," he said. "Stay here while I see who they are."

He was gone.

"What is going on?" Catherine asked. "Why does he care about a group of pilgrims and whether they are walking instead of riding horses?"

Willa's heart started racing when she understood his concern.

"We spent most of the morning at a good pace riding up the mountain trail to get here," Willa said. "Not once did we pass any pilgrims on foot."

 81

Inside the monastery's gate tower, Tonbridge stood over the dead body of the monk who let them in, his sword wet with blood. He felt oddly invigorated. After slaying a holy member of the church, there was no going back.

"We're going to do this quietly," he said to the five men gathered around him. "No warnings. Fox may not be armed, but he's still dangerous. Kill him the moment you see him. In fact, kill anyone you see except Willa. She will give me the Icon and then I will do with her as I please." He had already lied to them that the sins they committed in the abbey would be pardoned once he had the Icon.

Thankfully, since he had scouted the monastery a few days ago, he knew exactly how to proceed and where to look. He pointed at three of the men. "You will check for them in the guesthouse first and then the pilgrims' hall. Go into the abbey up the south entrance." He looked at the two remaining men. "You will come with me through the main entrance."

They all nodded, and Tonbridge raced up the switchback stairs as silently as he could. At the base of the abbey, three of the men peeled away to search the little guesthouse on the right. Tonbridge didn't stop, taking the outdoor staircase to the front door two steps at a time.

He pushed the door open and stepped inside the Stairway of the Dead.

Fox hurried out the south entrance and down the path leading to the gate tower. The fact that they hadn't passed any pilgrims on the trail up the mountain might not have meant anything. They could have simply been camping in the forest, but he didn't remember seeing any smoke from a fire. His innards were telling him something was wrong.

He peered over the wall, but he didn't see anyone waiting to get in or coming up the switchback. Perhaps he had gotten down in time to have Alfano give him a look at the visitors before they were admitted to the grounds.

He went down the path to the gate tower and came to an abrupt stop ten feet away when he saw the feet of a figure lying on the ground through the open doorway. Fox didn't hear anyone inside, but he crept down quietly just in case.

He was filled with sadness and guilt at seeing Alfano staring sightlessly at the ceiling of the entryway, his robes soaked with blood. Then his regret transformed into rage at the violation of this holy sanctuary. Fox may have had his problems with the Church, but he would never take out his anger on its innocent representatives.

Clearly, Molyneux and Tonbridge had discovered where they were and planned to finish the job they couldn't complete in Avignon, revenge for the loss of the Icon and manuscript. That meant Willa was in mortal danger.

Fox checked under Alfano's robe and found the key to the weapons trunk on a leather cord around his neck. He pulled it free and went into the warming room to unlock the trunk. He was relieved to see Legend and his bow and arrows still inside.

He snatched them up, not bothering to strap on his sword belt or string his bow. He had to get to Willa before they found her.

He raced up the switchback stairs and turned the corner to come face to face with a man he remembered from his capture at Mordecai's house. It was one of Tonbridge's men-at-arms. That had to mean Tonbridge was here himself.

Fox dropped the bow and arrows. Before the soldier could

react, Fox slashed him from shoulder to hip. The man opened his mouth, but no words came out. He fell over backward as if he were a plank of wood.

Two more men who were ten yards away walking toward the pilgrims' hall turned at the noise. It took them a moment to register that their comrade had just been killed, but their hesitation was brief.

Since the two of them were standing by the south entrance Fox had come out of, he could go that way only by fighting through them. He didn't have that kind of time. Tonbridge could already be making his way to Willa, and Fox knew her life would be forfeit once the earl found her.

Instead of fighting them, Fox turned and ran up the outdoor staircase to the front door of the abbey. Footsteps pounded behind him, but with his head start they wouldn't be able to catch him before he reached the residence. Then he could set an ambush in the narrow halls where he could deal with them one at a time.

Fox burst through the abbey's front door and climbed the first steps of the Stairway of the Dead. He rounded the turn and began the steep climb but stopped nearly halfway up when he saw three shadows in the Zodiac Doorway above him.

"Sir Gerard," a familiar voice said, echoing through the vaulted tomb. Fox could make out Tonbridge's face. "Are you surprised to see us?"

The two soldiers who were following Fox came to a stop below. Fox was now on the stairway equidistant between the two sets of swordsmen.

"Willa said that you were relentless," Fox said.

"Molyneux might have left you alone if he thought the Hodegetria had been destroyed, but I wouldn't have."

"But it *was* destroyed. It's at the bottom of the river."

Tonbridge smiled. "I would be delighted to stay here all day and explain the bounty of mistakes that you and Willa made in trying to deceive and elude me, but I have to go fetch my rightful property, which includes that impudent maid." He turned to the two men-at-arms beside him. "Be quick about it."

Then he ran through the doorway and out of sight. The men at the top of the stairs and the two at the bottom began to edge toward their target, careful not to act rashly even when they had him outnumbered four to one.

While he had his hands full, a warning was all Fox could give. At the top of his lungs, he shouted repeatedly, "Willa, run!"

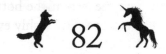 82

Willa was still in the welcome room when she heard Fox's muted yell. She couldn't tell where it came from, but she did get the message. Her stomach lurched as she realized that Tonbridge must have somehow tracked them down. Molyneux must have helped him by determining Catherine's location, though he wouldn't be here himself and risk his position as cardinal.

"What is going on?" asked Catherine, confused. "Was that Sir Gerard?"

"We must go now," Willa said. She quickly placed the Icon and letter from Eudocia back in the scrip and secured the leather pouch around her shoulder.

"Go where?"

"To the church. Perhaps if we lock ourselves in, he won't violate the sanctity of its walls."

"Who won't?"

"Lord Tonbridge, the man who had your sister killed."

Willa took Catherine by the hand and pulled her out of the room.

She abruptly stopped when she saw Tonbridge on the stairs at the other end of the hall.

"You!" he cried, that single word dripping with savagery.

Willa pushed Catherine back into the welcome room and slammed the door shut.

She started to push the heavy table toward the door. "Help me!"

Catherine didn't hesitate and shoved with all her might. The table slid across the floor until it jammed against the door handle just as Tonbridge crashed against it on the other side.

"Open this door now!" he shouted.

"I am the abbess here," Catherine said. "La Sacra di San Michele is a temple to God. You have no right to attack us in this holy place."

"You are harboring a minion of the Devil. I will have her!"

The door creaked under another pounding. It wouldn't take long for Tonbridge to break it down.

With the four men-at-arms only steps away in both directions, Fox couldn't wait any longer to act. Fighting all of them at once would lead to the quick death that Tonbridge had ordered.

So he charged the two above him.

The Stairway of the Dead was so steep that the two men's knees were level with Fox's eyes when they were only four steps above him, which made it awkward for them to reach down to fight him.

The closer man didn't realize his disadvantage and tried to attack Fox from straight above. Fox easily parried his sword and slashed him across both thighs. Legend's razor-like edge cut to the bone. The man emitted an ear-shattering scream and went tumbling down the stairs, fountains of crimson arcing into the air. The men below had to dodge him so they wouldn't be bowled over. If the fall didn't finish him off, the blood loss would.

The fallen man's comrade above didn't make the same mistake. He took an angled path on the wide staircase and attacked Fox from the side. Fox would have been able to defeat him rapidly as well, but he slipped on a patch of blood from the wounded man and missed his killing thrust. The swordsman pushed Fox back with a series of vicious strikes that drove him onto the construction scaffold built along the tomb alcoves.

The narrow confines meant there was little room to maneuver as he backed his way along the scaffolding, watching the two men rushing up the steps to aid their comrade. The farther Fox moved along its length, the higher he got above the stairs sloping down below and the more likely that he'd snap a leg by jumping off the platform.

The swordsman countered Fox's strikes and finally rushed him, pinning him against one of the tombs, his blade only inches from Fox's throat. Fox's hip was grinding on the stone edge, and he couldn't move to either side. The soldier leaned down with all his weight, his breath hot on Fox's face.

Fox could feel his balance tipping backward, and he took advantage of it. He pitched all the way onto the top of the flat tomb, taking the swordsman with him. He kicked upward with his knee, catching the man in the stomach. The air went out of him, and he fell back.

Fox took advantage of the opening and planted both feet against the swordsman's chest. Using the tomb for leverage, Fox thrust him backward, and the man went flying off the scaffold.

Fox didn't watch the impact, but he heard the skull crack as the soldier's head hit the stairs far below.

Two more men to go. Fox launched himself off the tomb and back onto his feet, ready to fight them one at a time. But these two had learned from their vanquished brethren. They had squeezed themselves side by side onto the scaffold, their swords held straight out.

The intent was clear. They would force Fox to retreat until his back was against the wall and then use that favorable position to finish him off.

Willa wasn't going to wait for Tonbridge to come bursting into the room. She pulled Catherine through the welcome room's other door and into the refectory, but the long trestle tables there were too big for the two of them to move.

Willa spoke to Catherine in a hushed voice. "Forgive my orders, Mother Abbess, but you must warn everyone to take sanctuary in the safest part of the church. Even better if you can have someone ring the bell to alert everyone to the danger."

"And where will you be?"

"Tonbridge wants me and the Icon. If I can get to the stable, I can lure him away and San Michele and its nuns will be safe."

Catherine didn't argue. She simply nodded.

Willa peeked out of the door and saw Tonbridge's back as he continued to hack at the welcome room door with his sword. He wasn't aware there was a second door in that room, but he would soon find out.

She and Catherine ran out of the refectory and around the corner where they couldn't be seen anymore.

Willa left Catherine quietly ushering confused nuns out of the cloisters and kitchen while she ran downstairs.

Behind her, she heard the welcome room door finally burst open and the table pushed aside.

"No!" Tonbridge screamed in a rage. "I will find you, Willa!"

Tonbridge rushed through the welcome room's second door and saw no one hiding in the refectory.

"You think you can steal from me!" he shrieked, spit flying from his mouth.

He launched himself into the hall and caught a nun as she was leaving the kitchen.

"Where did they go?"

The terrified nun didn't say anything, but her eyes glanced in the direction of the stairs leading down to the next floor.

Tonbridge released her and ran to the stairway. There was a figure in the shadows near the bottom landing hurrying down the steps.

Tonbridge raced down the stairs, his sword clanging against the stone walls as he balanced himself.

She was already gone when he reached the second floor.

Tonbridge sprinted down the corridor and spotted someone ducking into a side room. He snatched at her arm and yanked her out.

It wasn't Willa. It was Catherine, the abbess.

Tonbridge recognized the sisterly resemblance in her face immediately. She might have been even more lovely than Isabel. A shame he couldn't have married her instead.

"Where is Willa?"

"God will forgive your sins if you leave now," Catherine said without a shred of fear.

"Your sister broke her vow to marry me," Tonbridge said. "It is your family who betrayed me."

"I cannot answer for what Isabel has done to you, but it does not justify your actions now."

"My actions are about to get much worse if Willa doesn't do what I want."

Tonbridge wrapped his hand around Catherine's arm and dragged her toward the stairs.

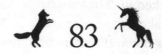 83

Tonbridge's two remaining men-at-arms must have been the ugliest he could find, and judging by their gnarled faces, both had obviously been in many fights before. One had a crooked nose and the other was missing his front teeth, so maybe they'd lost those fights, which Fox took as a good sign.

Still, his current situation wasn't encouraging. They advanced by taking turns jabbing at Fox with their swords, neither of them opening themselves for a retaliatory strike. With his back nearly to the wall, Fox passed the final alcove. He didn't dare look behind him, but if he remembered correctly, there might be a possibility for escape down onto the two-tiered ledge under the window at the turn in the stairs. Judge his leap wrong, and he'd break his legs or worse. Hesitate when he was on the scaffold, and he'd be skewered.

Fox thrust forward with Legend, sending the men onto their heels for a moment. He used the distraction to launch himself from the scaffold. Just as he recalled, ten feet below him was the higher platform of the two-tiered ledge holding several skeletons. On the landing below the ledges was the moaning man whose legs had been slashed, as well as the one whom Fox had tossed onto the stairway, his head twisted at an inhuman angle.

Fox landed on the first higher ledge, but his feet tangled with the bones of some ancient corpse, and he twisted his ankle. Unable to arrest his fall, Fox tumbled onto the next ledge and cracked his head against the unyielding stone wall.

Before he could recover, Crooked Nose followed him down. He landed even less gracefully, but he had Fox's body to cushion himself. Both of them went over the ledge onto the stairs, landing on the two men Fox had already disabled. The soldier with the wounded legs shrieked in pain.

No Teeth had taken the easier route back along the scaffold and was now racing down the stairs. Fox punched Crooked Nose in the jaw and rolled onto his feet.

He got out of the way barely in time to avoid the sword of No Teeth, which instead went into the chest of the injured man, finishing him off.

Hobbling on only one good foot, his head pounding, Fox traded blows with No Teeth as he retreated down the vaulted space's lower staircase. Crooked Nose, now with a bloody lip, joined in the fight.

Fox limped backward down the stairs, his ankle in agony with every step. But if he made it through the door and out into the open, perhaps he could maneuver better. If he tripped on these stairs, he wouldn't be getting up again.

On the fifth step from the bottom, he steeled himself for the impact to come and jumped down to the floor, grimacing in pain as he landed. He went out the abbey's front door and leaped onto the terrace as Crooked Nose and No Teeth pursued him.

By now Fox's lower leg was screaming at him and he was slow to turn and dodge a strike from No Teeth's sword. The miss carried him into a clinch with Fox, and the two of them went down on the top step of the outdoor stairway.

Both of them rolled down the stairs, losing their swords in the scuffle. The stone steps battered Fox's back and arms as they tumbled all the way down to the mid-landing and came to a stop.

Fox was pinned underneath No Teeth, who had his hands around Fox's neck. Fox could barely breathe as he pounded No Teeth with his fists, but the man wouldn't release his grip. Fox could feel his strength ebbing and his vision blurring.

Worse, Fox could make out Crooked Nose from the corner of his eye as the soldier picked up Legend and sauntered down the stairs with a sword in each hand, sure that he and his comrade had already won the fight. To him, killing Fox was now nothing more than a formality. Fox feared he was right.

On the first floor inside the residence, Willa was frantically trying to get three young pilgrims to safety, but they spoke a language she couldn't understand. She didn't want them to go up the stairs she had just come down and risk running into the murderous Tonbridge, so she was pointing at the pilgrims' hall in an attempt at getting them to take refuge there.

They spoke rapidly as she waved for them to go outside, but they didn't budge.

"God's fingernails!" She pointed above her and said, "*Diabolus venit! Vadite!*"

She hoped telling them in Latin to go because the devil was coming would work, and her entreaty seemed to make sense to them. They hastened out the door and down the short set of stairs to the pilgrims' hall entrance across the way.

Willa followed them out and dashed toward the switchback stairs that would lead down to the stable. There was a dead body at the top of those stairs, and her heart stopped for a moment when she saw a bow and arrow bag next to it. It took her an instant to realize the body wasn't Fox's, and she kept going toward it.

But when she reached the body and was at the corner of the monastery, she came to a halt. There were two men wrestling on the stairway above and to her left.

This time, it *was* Fox, and he was on his back on the mid-landing fifteen yards away. A man-at-arms lying atop him was strangling him. Another soldier was coming down the stairs with two swords in his hands, a bloody lip, and a feral glint in his eyes.

It was clear that Fox was in dire straits. If she kept going to the stable, Fox would be dead in a matter of moments. She knew he would want her to get to safety with the Icon, but Willa couldn't let him die for her without even trying to help him.

And there *was* something she could do. She snatched the bow and arrow bag from the ground. She quickly took out the string, unfurled it, looped it around the notch at one end of the bow, which she had bent around her leg, and snapped it on to the other end.

She withdrew an arrow and nocked it against the string as the man on his feet reached the mid-landing by Fox's head. Willa pulled back on the string as far as she could. The man with the bloody lip raised the swirled metal blade of Legend, ready to kill Fox with his own sword. Willa loosed the arrow.

She was aiming for the center of the man's chest but misjudged the upward angle. Instead, the arrow sank into his nether regions. He screamed in pain and dropped both swords as his hands went to his injured privates. The soldier sank to his knees with a high-pitched wail.

Willa withdrew another arrow from the bag, which was still lying on the ground. She was about to go up the stairs for a cleaner shot at the man atop Fox when she was startled by the unexpected sound of a voice to her left.

"Willa!" Tonbridge shouted as he came out the residence door where she had exited. "Lady Isabel would want you to see this!" He yanked Catherine outside and pushed her in front of him as they walked down the short stairway, his sword at her back.

 84

Tonbridge was taller than Catherine so he could easily see Willa standing there twenty yards away, her body facing the abbey's main entrance but her head toward him. She was armed with a bow and arrow. It wasn't pointed at Tonbridge but rather at something on the east side of the abbey that he couldn't see. His men had probably slain Fox and were now advancing on her, and she was putting up a token resistance.

"Do you want Lady Isabel's sister to die just like she did?" Tonbridge asked as he forced Catherine forward. Willa turned to face him, lowering the bow.

"If you kill an abbess, Cardinal Molyneux won't be able to save you," Willa said. Though her tone was defiant, Tonbridge could sense the underlying fear.

"Cardinal Molyneux is dead. The Pestilence took him. I know you still have the Hodegetria. The manuscript fell into a boat full of Pestilence victims floating in the river and we found that the Icon was missing. Your deception failed."

Willa looked stunned by the news of the cardinal's death, but she was more focused on saving Catherine.

"If he's dead, what good is the Icon to you?"

Tonbridge stopped ten yards from her. "You are a mouthy girl, aren't you? I'll do with it what I please. Now put down that bow and bring the Icon to me. I will kill her if you don't."

He could tell that Willa was thinking of using the bow, but he was shielded by Catherine's body. He almost wished the slight maid would send an arrow in their direction. She would undoubtedly miss, and he could be on her before she had a chance to nock another one.

"What will it be, Willa?" Tonbridge asked, raising the point of his sword to Catherine's neck. "It's time to make your choice."

Fox could hear Tonbridge's ultimatum, but he could do nothing to help Willa. With the distraction of Crooked Nose's pitiful screams, Fox was able to loosen No Teeth's hands and elbow him in the head. They rolled over, and now Fox was on top as he strained to catch his breath, pinning No Teeth below him.

Crooked Nose was beside them, cradling the arrow sticking out of his ruined nethers. He drew his dagger with a groan and bellowed in rage as he slashed Fox's arm.

Fox recoiled and saw that Legend was only a few feet away where it had been dropped. He kneed No Teeth in the stomach and lunged forward, somersaulting over the man's head. He wrapped his fingers around Legend's grip and whipped it around, cutting Crooked Nose's throat and putting him out of his misery.

As No Teeth scrambled to his feet, he picked up the other sword. Momentarily forgetting the pain in his ankle, Fox launched himself at the man, knocking aside the swipe of No Teeth's blade and plunging Legend into his chest.

The man-at-arms coughed up blood and slumped to the ground as soon as Fox withdrew the sword.

Fox wheeled around to see Willa fifteen yards below. She turned her head briefly and looked up at him with a pained expression.

She knew there was no way Fox was going to get all the way down those stairs before Tonbridge killed Catherine and then her.

Willa didn't know how many men Tonbridge had left. Maybe it was just Tonbridge himself. But she understood him. He would kill Catherine no matter what to keep his crimes there secret.

Fox was too far away to help her, and judging by his visible condition—bleeding head, slashed arm, pronounced limp—he was worse for the fighting he'd already done. At the very least, Tonbridge would kill Catherine and take Willa hostage before Fox could get down to their level.

"Willa," Tonbridge said with a teasing voice, "I won't wait much—"

Willa didn't let him finish. She raised the bow and drew in one smooth motion, hoping Catherine wouldn't flinch and somehow get in the way. Without thinking about it any longer than it took to aim, Willa loosed the arrow.

It flew true and straight, hitting Tonbridge in the shoulder of the arm holding the sword, just to the side of Catherine's head.

He cried out and dropped the sword. Catherine screamed and darted toward the pilgrims' hall.

Without his human shield, Tonbridge was now even more vulnerable, but Willa had to act quickly, for Tonbridge bent to pick up the sword with his left hand.

Willa went to one knee and reached into the bag to select another arrow.

Tonbridge raised the sword, his eyes white-hot with ferocity, and charged toward Willa with a barbaric screech.

Willa fumbled the arrow, then was able to grasp the fletches and pull it out.

Tonbridge was only five yards away, the sword brandished like an axe ready to cleave her in two.

With no time to stand and aim properly, she nocked the arrow, pulled back, and let it go at the figure looming toward her.

Tonbridge lurched as the arrow went through his neck. The sword fell behind him and his eyes bulged in surprise, but his legs kept churning. He collapsed as he reached Willa, falling upon her and smacking her into the ground.

His face was lying next to Willa's, and she stared at him for an instant as the life faded from his eyes.

"That was for Lady Isabel," she said.

Tonbridge gurgled something in response, but no words formed. He finally hissed out a last fetid breath and went still.

Willa pushed him aside far enough to wriggle out from under him just as Fox staggered down the last step toward her. She dropped the bow and rushed into his arms. But her embrace wasn't to find reassurance over what had just happened. Fox looked like he was about to keel over from his injuries and exhaustion.

"Are they all dead?" she asked him.

He nodded. "Are you all right?"

"I am, now that Lord Tonbridge and Cardinal Molyneux are gone forever."

"I heard Tonbridge's declaration that the cardinal was struck down by the Pestilence," Fox said. "It couldn't have been an easy death, but I can't think of anyone more deserving of misery. I only wish I had been there to see it. How is the mother abbess?"

Willa, who could feel her temporary spike of vigor draining after the ordeal, pointed at the pilgrims' hall, where Catherine was standing with the three foreign pilgrims. All of them gazed in horror at the carnage in front of them.

Fox looked down at Tonbridge's dead body. "I thought it was the knight who was supposed to save the damsel in distress."

She patted the leather scrip with the intact Hodegetria. "You did."

"Still, I thank you for your sharp aim." He turned toward the two dead men-at-arms who had almost killed him and nodded as he considered his words. "The damsel who saved the knight in distress. I like the way that sounds."

Willa shook her head at his uncommon view of life and smiled up at him. "You are a curious man, Sir Gerard."

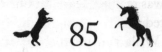 85

This time Fox's injuries mended much faster. After a week, his headache was gone, he was able to walk normally if a bit stiffly, and the knife wound on his arm was healing nicely thanks to some of Mordecai's salve that Willa had concocted. The recipe was listed at the back of his *Secretum philosophorum* courtesy of Youssef, who had carefully detailed the key ingredients and how to mix them while Fox was ill.

Once the bodies were buried and the abbey cleaned of blood, Fox spent much of his recovery time on the upper terrace taking in the spectacular view. He even prayed in the grand church at the pinnacle of the monastery, his first time in years. No lightning bolt came from the sky to indicate God's displeasure, so Fox had hope that Molyneux's unjust sentence hadn't doomed him after all. However, he and Willa kept his excommunicated status hidden from Catherine. There was no sense burdening her with that knowledge.

He thought the news of the cardinal's death would leave him with a sense of relief, and it did, but there was also an emptiness to go along with it. At first he believed it was because his best chance for recovering his family's lands and good name was now gone. But the longer he pondered on it, the more he came to realize that the hollow feeling was there because he no longer had the weight of vengeance pressing on his shoulders. Without the burden of regaining his family's honor driving his every waking moment, he was aimless. It was time to find a new purpose.

Although Catherine was happy to let Fox stay as long as he'd like, he felt out of place in the abbey. He'd been moving around for so long since losing his land that remaining in a single location for days on end doing nothing seemed strange. Now that he was back on his feet, he was ready to leave. But he had one question to ask before he departed.

He searched for Willa and found her with Catherine in the welcome room. The Icon was on the table along with a number of books. The painting of the Virgin and Child was luminous in the morning sunlight streaming through the window.

"I am glad you are here, Sir Gerard," Catherine said. "Willa and I have been discussing how to safeguard the Hodegetria and Eudocia's letter. I plan to commission a new manuscript to hold the Icon, but until then in what book do you think it would be appropriate to store them?"

"You won't be displaying the Icon?" he asked.

Willa shook her head. "Abbess Catherine and I have agreed that its existence can't stay a secret forever, but we must wait until the time is right to reveal it to the world. After all of the fighting and bloodshed over it, we think it should remain hidden until it can be unveiled and protected as a beacon of glory and salvation, not treated as a bid for power."

Catherine nodded. "The uncertainty of these times makes it important to keep such a holy object out of the hands of those who would do evil with it. For now, it will have to stay in our archives as a hidden relic, safeguarded by my convent's order as it was by the women in my family for generations."

"Then it sounds like the Icon is in good hands," Fox said, "and I will leave it to your wise judgment to know where its rightful place is. By the by, I haven't yet formally apologized for bringing such mayhem to this sanctuary. I hope you will forgive me."

"There is nothing to forgive," Catherine said. "You protected Willa and the Hodegetria and brought them both to me. I am grateful for what you have done. Thank you."

"You're welcome. If anything, I should thank Willa for giving me something I never thought that I would get."

"Which is?"

"Justice." Fox glanced at Willa. "Abbess, would you mind giving us a few moments alone?"

"Not at all."

She placed the Icon and letter in its protective scrip, collected the books, and exited the room.

Fox could feel his heart pounding as he and Willa stared at each other in silence.

Finally, she broke the tension. "You look well."

"I'm almost fully recovered, thanks to you," he replied. "In fact, it's time for me to go. I don't belong here."

A melancholy smile creased Willa's lips. "I understand. But what did you mean when you told the abbess you'd found justice? I prevented you from redeeming your family's honor."

"You showed me what it truly means to be a knight. I was too impulsive and impatient back when my brother James tried to teach me the importance of my vows—to act with honor and kindness, to protect the innocent and the weak, to serve those in need. I never really understood those words until I met you. Being a knight has nothing to do with owning land or having a title. And it's not something anyone else, even the Church, can take away. It's who I am. And if I can find some small measure of justice in a lawless land, perhaps I can help others do the same."

Willa grinned at him. "And all it took was a grand and dangerous journey across the continent for you to realize that?"

Fox smiled. "I'm a slow learner."

"Maybe I'm just a bad teacher." She gazed up at him softly. "I wish I could see what you are going to learn next."

Fox paused before he finally built up the courage to speak. "I thought perhaps we could go together. I may not have land anymore, and I doubt I ever will now that Molyneux is dead, but I can promise a life of adventure and excitement. We can travel the world together, as man and wife."

"You're asking me to marry you?"

Fox nodded. "I've loved you almost as long as I've known you."

Willa stepped forward and caressed his face with both hands. He could see conflict within her.

"Oh, sweet man. I love you, too. I am so honored that you

would want me to go with you. And I am sorely tempted. But how can that possibly work?"

"I know it might be difficult on the road, but we could manage. We've done it before."

Willa shook her head. "In this world, the way it is, a woman is not supposed to be a wanderer. We barely made it from England to this abbey together with our lives."

"But we *did* make it. You are a capable woman. You can do so much."

She took a deep breath that caught in her chest. "The mother abbess was so thankful for my bringing her the Icon that she offered to let me join her convent as a nun. It's an opportunity that would otherwise never have been available to me as a handmaiden. I have to take it."

Fox couldn't conceal his surprise. "I can't imagine you staying here in the confines of the abbey."

"Remember that I was born into service." Her voice was halting. "Isn't it right to continue that mission, just in a different manner? Here I will be able to have the intellectual life that I always thought was out of reach, indulging my passions of reading and writing to my heart's content. That will be an adventure for my mind as important as this journey has been with you." Although the explanation was meant for him, it sounded as if she were trying to convince herself of her decision.

"Perhaps you don't have to join the convent. I can remain instead and find local work." But even as he said it, the words felt wrong.

"No, you cannot. I see it in your eyes. You have a restless soul. For a short time, being together would feel magical, but you would quickly come to resent me. I can't bear that thought. Your calling is to travel the land and serve justice as a knight. I can make my place here with Abbess Catherine, helping to minister to the needy who come seeking guidance and redemption. You and I will be doing the same thing, but in our own ways."

"But I—"

"Please don't make this harder than it already is. I must stay."

Fox was gutted by Willa's answer. He didn't agree with her reasoning, but he respected her decision.

"How do you come to be so sensible at such a young age?"

"By having experiences that would otherwise be out of bounds for the simple maid I was. I have you to thank for that."

Fox smiled at her. "Then I will take credit where it is due." He patted the pendant she had given him, which lay against his chest. "You shall remain close to my heart. I will love you always, Lady Willa."

"And I, you, Sir Gerard."

She stood on her toes and kissed him on the cheek. Tears welled up in her eyes. "Give Zephyr a pat for me." After taking one last look at Fox, she left the room.

Fox watched her go, savoring the memory of their journey and wistful at what might have been. But she was right. He needed to roam, fighting against all odds, sometimes at great cost. That seemed to be the Fox family legacy, and it would continue to be his cross to bear.

Fox walked slowly down to the gate tower to collect his weapons, strapping on Legend and taking his bow and arrow bag from the lay brother who was now manning the entrance.

The rest of his things were already packed, including fresh food and supplies, care of the nuns in the abbey. Zephyr was saddled and ready to go. Fox stowed his bow and arrows and stroked his horse's muzzle.

"That's from Willa."

Zephyr whinnied in reply.

Fox eased himself onto the saddle and gave Zephyr a nudge to steer him out of the stable.

Once he was a good way down the path, he paused to look up at La Sacra di San Michele, but he saw no sign of Willa on the terrace. They'd had their goodbyes, but Fox would have been glad to see her one last time, her blonde hair shining in the sunlight like spun gold. He rode into the trees and out of sight of the abbey.

Fox sighed and turned back to the trail ahead. "It looks like it's just you and me again."

Zephyr chuffed at that and started walking.

They continued on in silence and were halfway down the mountain path when Zephyr's ears pricked up. A moment later, Fox heard it, too. There were hooves pounding toward them from behind.

A single horse.

He pulled to a stop and turned to see Willa canter around a bend atop Comis. She was dressed for travel and flanked by stuffed saddlebags.

Fox's chest felt like it would burst as he was reminded of Willa's first charge into his view on that English road so long ago. She was even more breathtaking now than she had been then.

She came to a stop beside them, her chest heaving and her eyes locked on his. The complex range of emotions that played across her face told him volumes about her change of mind.

Fox opened his mouth to speak, but his heart was too full for words to form. Willa seemed similarly tongue-tied and said nothing. Instead, she held out her hand. Fox took it in his. She nodded, and he gave her hand a squeeze. Everything that needed to be conveyed between them was carried in that instant.

Together, they continued riding down the path.

Zephyr liked to hear something as they traveled, so Fox broke into an old English drinking ballad. After the first line, he was pleasantly surprised that Willa joined the singing in a hearty voice.

The forest that had seemed so lonely just moments before now swelled with a lively duet about loyal friends, passionate loves, and adventures yet to come.

# AFTERWORD

*By Beth Morrison*

When my brother Boyd first approached me with the idea of collaborating on a novel set in the Middle Ages, I could hardly believe my luck. Work with one of my favorite people on a creative project involving a subject that was my passion as well as my profession? What a dream come true! I had been an avid reader of my brother's books for years and was excited to partner with him on this project.

When I was fifteen, I saw my first medieval manuscript, and I was sold—I just knew exploring these treasures was what I wanted to do for the rest of my life. For the past twenty-five years I have been a curator in the Department of Manuscripts at the J. Paul Getty Museum. I regularly study spectacular illuminations meticulously painted on parchment, which bring to life stories of gallant knights, heroic damsels, and the common people from the Middle Ages.

But despite my decades of research, some aspects of daily life in the Middle Ages—what a city entrance toll would cost, how people cursed, what all the different types of horses would be called—were well beyond my previous training and required additional investigation. In fact, there are certain details about the fourteenth century that no one knows, including me. We just had to take our best educated guess. So although the medieval elements of the novel are based on my knowledge, the book is nonetheless fiction. We took creative license when it suited the story, while keeping it period-appropriate as far as possible by incorporating real facts that we thought would fascinate readers.

It is difficult for us in the twenty-first century to understand what the fourteenth century was like. Many of the aspects that dominated daily life in the period are key elements that appear in this book. The drawn-out series of conflicts between England and France later known as the Hundred Years' War (1337–1453) resulted in a breakdown in law and order, particularly in France. Throughout the era, Christianity was not simply the dominant form of religion in western Europe, but it permeated nearly every aspect of life, from telling time (according to the canonical hours of prayer celebrated by monks and nuns) to communal society (which revolved around the local church). One of the worst punishments that could be inflicted was excommunication. Not only were you cut off from the life of the Church and faced everlasting damnation, but you were treated as a pariah by your friends and neighbors and could have all your possessions seized. And then, of course, there was the Plague.

The novel is set just after one of the most cataclysmic events in human history, the terrible pandemic that killed anywhere from 75 to 200 million people in Eurasia and North Africa. It's almost impossible to imagine losing a third of all the people you have ever known in a matter of weeks or months. Today we know this event as the Black Death, but in the European Middle Ages it was known as the Pestilence or the Great Mortality. At the time, no one realized the disease was spread by rat fleas. Instead theories about its cause abounded, including unfavorable astronomical planetary conjunctions or evil airs. But many people understood that simply being in its presence was dangerous. Out of desperation, they carried posies comprised of herbs and flowers to ward off the illness.

By sheer coincidence, COVID-19 broke out as Boyd and I were writing this book. Despite the passage of over half a millennium, with all our technical and scientific advancements, we found ourselves just as scared as our medieval counterparts, and without significantly different abilities to fight the disease in the short term. After all, the word "quarantine" comes from quaranta, "forty" in Italian, which was the number of days infected ships had to stay at harbor before being able to offload people during the time of the Black Death. Like those living around 1350, we in the present huddled in our homes, tried to avoid any contact with others, and traced the progress of the disease with dread. Our personal knowledge of the fear of pandemic infused the medieval story with an eerie parallel reality.

Long before the pandemic of 2020, Boyd and I traveled the same route through Europe that Willa and Fox took in the story, although not on horseback. Most of the locations in the book are real places that we visited and researched in person to help the reader see what life would have been like over 600 years ago.

Our first stop was Canterbury, where we toured the cathedral before attending Mass, then stood on the exact spot where Thomas Becket was murdered in 1170. We then walked the streets of Canterbury, picturing them filled with timber-framed houses and medieval vendors. Although there was no actual abandoned plague town of Ravenswood for us to visit, as many as 3000 ghost villages dating from that time period dot the English countryside. The depopulation had dire effects on the available workforce, which led to the ability of laborers to demand higher wages. In the story, we allude to the Statute of Laborers, issued in February 1351 by King Edward III to enact harsh penalties on workers who tried to demand higher wages than before the Black Death struck.

For the second section of the book, Boyd and I trekked out to Mont-Saint-Michel and back to Paris by high-speed train in one long day, a round trip that would have taken Willa and Fox over two weeks. We saw the spectacular abbey from the same aspect as anyone approaching in the fourteenth century, rising from the mudflats like a Disney castle. Upon seeing the human-operated windlass used to raise and lower supplies from the monastery, we knew we had to write a scene with the mechanism as the critical element. We came to learn later that it was installed in the eighteenth century when the island was used as a prison during the French Revolution, but such windlasses were used extensively during the Middle Ages. Boyd came up with the idea to make Youssef an early distiller, as distillation had made its way to Europe in the fourteenth century via Spain thanks to Arabic influence.

In Paris, it was providential that we visited Notre Dame in person, as the terrible fire that devastated the cathedral occurred just a month later. In the medieval version of the church, Fox and Willa encounter his namesake, Reynard, depicted on a column capital. Although no such sculpture was found at Notre Dame, medieval cathedrals were full of such secular imagery, intended to entertain and edify the masses as the incomprehensible Latin services were recited. Under the southern part of Paris, now part of the city proper but originally outside the fourteenth-century walls, you can still find a complex of abandoned subterranean passages created by the mining of limestone and gypsum.

Unfortunately, we couldn't visit Château de Tournoël, which is private property now, but the impressive castle still holds a commanding view of the plains below. The trial by combat that takes place there in the book was a component of medieval judiciary practice, although such an event was rarely seen by the mid-fourteenth century. In reality, the combat would have taken place only after years of court battles, but for the sake of the narrative, we sped up the process considerably. Likewise, the melee and joust were popular aspects of medieval tournaments, but usually the melee was featured as the finale to the multiday entertainment, rather than its beginning. No such tournament took place in 1351 at Château de Tournoël, but they were certainly popular across France in the fourteenth century.

From 1309 to 1376, the papacy was relocated from Rome to Avignon, where the great Papal Palace was built. We explored the imposing building and were delighted to discover a high-tech tablet system that allows visitors to see what each room in the palace would have looked like at the height of its magnificence in the fourteenth century. Across the Rhône River in Villeneuve-lès-Avignon, the lavish weekend homes built by high-ranking Church members of the time have largely disappeared. When we visited the stub that is the only portion of the famed Avignon bridge still standing, Boyd and I watched a video of the time-consuming and sophisticated process used to build that technological marvel in the twelfth century. Floods did periodically wash away portions that were temporarily replaced by wooden spans in the Middle Ages, until the entire bridge was abandoned to the river's power by the end of the seventeenth century.

Our last stop was La Sacra di San Michele in Italy. Like Mont-Saint-Michel, its otherworldly beauty at first seems like a made-up medieval fantasy rather than the real edifice it is. The monastery fell into ruin in the late fourteenth century after the Black Death and was forsaken by the sixteenth, though it was never used as a nunnery. The final battle in the story, however, is structured around the real layout of the monastery, which has been restored and can be visited today.

Although most of the places mentioned in the book are real, almost all of the characters are fictitious. Besides brief appearances by King John II (r. 1350–1364) and King Edward III (r. 1327–1377), all of the other individuals who play a role in the story, such as Cardinal Molyneux and Lord Tonbridge, were invented by us. A similar authorial decision led us to update the dialogue of the novel. Anyone who has ever tried to read Chaucer in the original will testify to the fact that fourteenth-century English only somewhat resembles modern English. We did, however, try to avoid current slang and specialized words developed in recent centuries that might have jarred the reader out of the medieval ambiance we were trying to create.

It will probably come as no surprise that the idea to have the narrative involve manuscripts was my idea. The Hodegetria was thought to be a portrait of the Virgin and Child created by Saint Luke himself (it didn't bother those in the Middle Ages that Saint Luke in the introduction to his own Gospel makes clear that he never met Jesus). According to medieval accounts, the portrait was painted on wood, although in our story, we imagined it painted on parchment. In the fifth century it was supposedly brought by Eudocia, Empress of the Byzantine Empire, from the Holy Land to Constantinople. Various legends about the whereabouts of the Hodegetria since then were in simultaneous circulation during the Middle Ages. Some believed that it stayed in Constantinople where it could be seen at the Hodegetria monastery until the fall of that city in 1453. Others thought that it was taken to Italy in 1261, where it was displayed at the church of Montevergine. A third theory claimed that the Icon made its way to Russia to the Assumption Cathedral in Smolensk. To this day, no one knows if it really existed.

The authenticity of individual relics was sometimes a matter of debate in the Middle Ages, but for most people, symbolic value was far more important than historical truth. As long as you believed the relic had power, then it did. That is true for our story as well. Molyneux and Willa fervently believed this version, an illumination in the possession of English aristocracy, to be the true Hodegetria, and many others of the era no doubt would have followed suit.

The idea of a treasured manuscript being handed down through generations of women via a handmaiden isn't far removed from reality. Just months after Boyd and I finished *The Lawless Land*, a news article swept the internet about the personal prayer book of Anne Boleyn, King Henry VIII's second wife. It seems that as she kneeled before her executioner in 1536, she handed her cherished book to one of her ladies-in-waiting, Elizabeth Hill. Recent scientific analysis of that book revealed secret messages written by Hill and her descendants in the book's margins. For fear of retribution by the king if it were discovered that they were keeping a relic from a known traitor to the Crown, they kept the manuscript hidden, similar to what Willa did for Lady Isabel.

The second manuscript featured in the book is Fox's copy of the *Secretum philosophorum*, a real text written in England sometime shortly before or after 1300. Just under thirty medieval copies of the text survive today, which sounds ludicrously small to us, but indicates that it was a popular read in its day. The poor quality of the existing manuscripts suggest that it was used as a hands-on manual by laymen. It contains diverse information, ranging from recipes for glue and invisible ink to sections devoted to ciphers and practical jokes, just the kind of handy material a knight errant might need.

We are indebted in the story to many publications that helped us set the scene, listed at the end of this afterword. We also relied on the input of experts and friends who are discussed in the acknowledgments. But many of the details found in the book were inspired directly by medieval illuminations or literary writings of the period. All mistakes regarding the Middle Ages are my own, as Boyd would write out things like "they go to a drug store" and it was my job to translate it into the proper terminology from that era. If I didn't, I apologize to my discerning medieval colleagues, but I hope you enjoyed the adventure anyway. I certainly did!

Andrew Ayton and Philip Preston, *The Battle of Crécy, 1346.* The Boydell Press, 2005.

*Cérémonies des gages de bataille selon les constitutions du bon roi Philippe de France*, ed. by G. A. Crapelet. Impr. de Crapelet, 1830.

Nicole Crossley-Holland, *Living and Dining in Medieval Paris: The Household of a Fourteenth Century Knight.* University of Wales Press, 1996.

Jeffrey Forgeng, *Daily Life in Chaucer's England.* Greenwood Press, 2009.

Eric Jager, *The Last Duel: A True Story of Crime, Scandal, and Trial by Combat in Medieval France.* Broadway, 2004.

John Kelly, *The Great Mortality: An Intimate History of the Black Death, the Most Devastating Plague of All Time.* Harper Perennial, 2005.

Helen Matthews, *The Legitimacy of Bastards: The Place of Illegitimate Children in Later Medieval England.* Pen and Sword History, 2019.

Ian Mortimer, *The Time Traveler's Guide to Medieval England: A Handbook for Visitors to the Fourteenth Century.* Touchstone, 2011.

Steven Muhlberger and Will McLean, *Murder, Rape, and Treason: Judicial Combats in the Late Middle Ages*. Freelance Academy Press, 2019.

Paul B. Newman, *Travel and Trade in the Middle Ages*. McFarland and Company, Inc., 2011.

Eva Oledzka, *Medieval and Renaissance Interiors*. The British Library, 2016.

Michael Prestwich, *Knight: The Medieval Warrior's Unofficial Manual*. Thames and Hudson, 2010.

Barbara Tuchman, *A Distant Mirror: The Calamitous 14th Century*. Random House, 1978.

Elisabeth Vodola, *Excommunication in the Middle Ages*. University of California Press, 1986.

# ACKNOWLEDGMENTS

We wholeheartedly thank our agent John Talbot for believing in this book, and our foreign rights agents Danny Baror and Heather Baror-Shapiro for putting us together with our wonderful publisher, Head of Zeus. We are grateful to the supportive and enthusiastic team at Head of Zeus, including Nic Cheetham, Holly Domney, and Greg Rees. Our two content editors, Richenda Todd and Lydia Mason, provided invaluable feedback that encouraged us to add depth to the storyline. We also thank Helena Newton, our diligent copy editor. Nat Ambrosey supplied the lively graphic designs for the novel, and Jeff Edwards created the instructive maps. Scott Barer offered instrumental legal advice at the beginning of the project.

We thank the medieval scholars who helped with research questions, including Anne D. Hedeman and Cathleen Fleck. We especially thank Eric Jager for his insights and advice along the way.

We relied on specialists during our travels to the European sites where the novel is set, including Dean Robert Willis and Fletcher Banner in Canterbury, Father Reji at La Sacra di San Michele, and walking tours with Stephanie in Paris and Philippe in Avignon.

Acting coach Howard Fine has provided valuable insights into character building, and web designer Maddee James supported this project in many ways.

We appreciate the time our first readers took to provide constructive feedback after we finished the initial draft, including Barbara Peters, Graham Brown, Janet Cussler, Wendy Enden, Kim Yates, and Bill Huls. We particularly recognize JT Ellison and Jeff Ayers for urging us to make a key change to the ending that will greatly impact the continuing series.

Lastly, we thank our family. Kyrie Robinson helped us talk through vital aspects of the characters' motivations. Kailin Clarke and Frank Moretti were eager and welcome readers of various drafts. Our numerous siblings, nieces, and nephews (and pets) kept our spirits up with their boundless enthusiasm along the way. Beth's partner John Espinoza offered unwavering and essential support while she balanced contributing to this book with the demands of her job. Boyd's wife Randi Morrison was there from start to finish on this adventure, acting as chief sounding board, ingenious plot problem-solver, and official documentarian. Lastly, we thank each other for being not only a great brother-sister team, but also really good friends.

Any errors in matters medieval are Beth's; any errors in science or engineering are Boyd's; blame for anything else we'd be happy to equally share. Any resemblance of the main characters to real persons, living or dead (or in the case of the Middle Ages, very, very dead) is purely coincidental.